EXPLORE THE UNKNOWN
AT YOUR OWN RISK

Religion and science fiction long have had an unspoken relationship, for both involve the future, the unknown, and have a focus in "the heavens." PERPETUAL LIGHT makes this bond explicit with twenty-three stories that offer twenty-three ways of understanding the word "religion." Here angels and fools alike tread the paths of speculation through landscapes ranging from next door to the far galaxies. It is dangerous speculation, but endlessly intriguing.

As Alan Ryan says in his introduction: "I'm perfectly certain in my own mind that God is alive. I'm less certain that He's well. I think, in fact, that He may be fighting for His life in the pages of this book."

Edited by Alan Ryan

Perpetual Light

WARNER BOOKS

A Warner Communications Company

Cover art by Jill Bauman

Warner Books, Inc., 75 Rockefeller Plaza, New York, N.Y. 10019

 A Warner Communications Company

Printed in the United States of America

First Printing: October, 1982

10 9 8 7 6 5 4 3 2 1

This book is dedicated to

ELLEN LEVINE

for never losing faith

and to

CHARLES L. GRANT
MARILYN HOLLERAN
CHELSEA QUINN YARBRO

for an afternoon's laughter

Table of Contents

Perpetual Light

Introduction

I'm perfectly certain in my own mind that God is alive. I'm less certain that He's well. I think, in fact, that He may be fighting for His life in the pages of this book.

Speculative fiction—including everything from "hard" science fiction at one end of the spectrum to dark fantasy and horror at the other—seems to me eminently well suited to examine the questions raised by thoughtful people about God and religion. When we first began corresponding about *Perpetual Light*, Brian Aldiss suggested in a letter that it is impossible to write science fiction without at least acknowledging the religious considerations. "Religion," he wrote, "is an integral part of the sf vision. Directly we look to the future or to mankind in the mass, we have a pararational situation on our hands." I think he's right. And I think that the broad range of both matter and method available to the writer of speculative fiction offers a unique opportunity to explore ideas unmanageable in other ways.

Certainly religion has provided the subject matter for some of the best writing the field of science fiction has ever produced. James Blish's *A Case of Conscience,* Walter M. Miller, Jr.'s *A Canticle for Leibowitz,* Roger Zelazny's *Lord of Light,* and Michael Moorcock's *Behold the Man* come immediately to mind, as do novels by authors as inventive and distinguished as Robert Silverberg, Philip K. Dick, and Philip José Farmer.

There have been anthologies of short science fiction dealing with religion before this one. In general, they have not been all one might have hoped or expected. The best of them, Mayo Mohs's *Other Worlds, Other Gods,* was a reprint anthology, published in 1971. The worst of them, Roger Elwood's *Flame Tree Planet,* had an introduction by Roger Lovin that smoothly assured the reader: "As many stories as you read, so many praises to God will you find."

I can't make any such promise.

The stories that follow vary from the serious to the zany. All of them raise questions about some aspect of the religious experience. Not all of them provide answers. I like it that way. I also like the good story-telling, the exciting ideas, and the cast of characters that live in these pages. They include, among others, a nervous angel named Herschel, a priest whose vocation is murder, a genie who lives in a bottle and happens to be a professional wrestler, an alien spiritual leader who dotes on Ella Fitzgerald, a saintly Chicago gangster, a chimpanzee named Leo, and half a dozen Jesuits. If the Mad Hatter were alive today, he'd have them all over for tea. I think he'd probably invite the writers too; they're his kind of folks.

It is now two and a half years, endless hours and a fortune in postage and phone bills since I first conceived this book. I worked on it, in one way or another, at home in New York City, in Los Angeles, Santa Ana, San Francisco, Seattle, Bristol, R.I., Washington, D.C., Philadelphia, Boston, Nashville, and a handful of other cities. I wrote the headnotes for the stories in the subway, in a hospital room, and in McGowan's Bar on Greenwich Avenue. Despite the fact that I wanted very much to do this book, the year in which I actively worked on it was, personally, a very difficult one. Many people, in a variety of ways, played a part in keeping me at it—people who share my interest in good writing and in work worth doing, and whose support and help made this a better book than it would have been without them. They have my appreciation and my thanks:

Josephine Flavin, my mother, for knowing when not to ask a question and for doing a lot of my worrying for me.

Virginia Kidd, for her long interest in the project.

David G. Hartwell, for the warning and for the good advice I didn't have time to take.

Ellen Levine, my agent, for the overseas phone calls, the questions and answers, and the hand-holding.

Jill Bauman, for talking when I only wanted to listen.

Merrilee Heifetz, for listening when I only wanted to talk.

Marie Marino, for recalling all the details.

Brian Aldiss, for a telephone call very early one Monday morning.

Robert Silverberg, for a conversation begun in Los Angeles and continued two months later in Boston.

Philip K. Dick, for an afternoon of margaritas and philosophy in Santa Ana.

Charles L. Grant, for all the answers to all the questions, both technical and aesthetic, for all the good advice, even when I didn't take it, and for telling me the precise moment to panic.

Howard Kaminsky, president of Warner Books, for the phone call from the airport.

Nansey Neiman, my editor at Warner Books, for her ideas and suggestions.

Alan Ryan

New York City
June 1982

The Pope of the Chimps

Robert Silverberg

For a quarter of a century, Robert Silverberg's stories and novels have set a standard for other writers of speculative fiction to match, a level of achievement attested by numerous awards and by both popular and critical acclaim. He tells, in clean and graceful prose, stories that are exciting as much for their ideas as for their action. His work ranges from the moving psychological novel, Dying Inside, *to his recent epic fantasy,* Lord Valentine's Castle.*

Silverberg has frequently explored religious ideas in novels such as Downward to the Earth, Tower of Glass, *and* The Book of Skulls, *and such widely read stories as "Good News from the Vatican," "The Feast of St. Dionysus," and "Born With the Dead." In "The Pope of the Chimps," he uses a contemporary topic and setting to raise some universal and thought-provoking questions.*

Early last month Vendelmans and I were alone with the chimps in the compound when suddenly he said, "I'm going to faint." It was a sizzling May morning, but Vendelmans had never shown any sign of noticing unusual heat, let alone suffering from it. I was busy talking to Leo and Mimsy and Mimsy's daughter Muffin and I registered Vendelmans's remark without doing anything about it. When you're intensely into talking by sign language, as we are in the project, you sometimes tend not to pay a lot of attention to spoken words.

But then Leo began to sign the trouble sign at me and I turned around and saw Vendelmans down on his knees in the grass, white-faced, gasping, covered with sweat. A few of the chimpanzees who aren't as sensitive to humans as Leo is thought it was a game and began to pantomime him, knuckles to the ground and bodies going limp. "Sick—" Vendelmans said. "Feel—terrible—"

I called for help and Gonzo took his left arm and Kong took his right and somehow, big as he was, we managed to get him out of the compound and up the hill to headquarters. By then he was complaining about sharp pains in his back and under his arms, and I realized that it wasn't just heat prostration. Within a week the diagnosis was in.

Leukemia.

They put him on chemotherapy and hormones and after ten days he was back with the project, looking cocky. "They've stabilized it," he told everyone. "It's in remission and I might have ten or twenty years left, or even more. I'm going to carry on with my work."

But he was gaunt and pale, with a tremor in his hands, and it was a frightful thing to have him among us. He might have been fooling himself, though I doubted it, but he wasn't fooling any of us: to us he was a *memento mori*, a walking death's-head-and-crossbones. That laymen think scientists are any more casual about such things than anyone else is something I blame Hollywood for. It is not easy to go about your daily work with a dying man at your side—or a dying man's wife, for Judy Vendelmans showed in her frightened eyes all the grief that Hal Vendelmans himself was repressing. She was going to lose a beloved husband unexpectedly soon and she hadn't had time to adjust to it, and her pain was impossible to ignore. Besides, the nature of Vendelmans's dyingness was particularly unsettling, because he had been so big and robust and outgoing, a true Rabelaisian figure, and somehow between one moment and the next he was transformed into a wraith. "The finger of God," Dave Yost said. "A quick flick of Zeus's pinkie and Hal shrivels like cellophane in a fireplace." Vendelmans was not yet forty.

The chimps suspected something too.

Some of them, such as Leo and Ramona, are fifth-generation signers, bred for alpha intelligence, and they pick up subtleties and nuances very well. "Almost human," visitors like to say of them. We dislike that tag, because the important thing about chimpanzees is that they *aren't* human, that they are an alien intelligent species; but yet I know what people mean. The brightest of the chimps saw right away that something was amiss with Vendelmans, and started making odd remarks. "Big one rotten banana," said Ramona to Mimsy while I was nearby. "He getting empty," Leo said to me as Vendelmans stumbled past us. Chimp metaphors never cease to amaze me. And Gonzo asked him outright: "You go away soon?"

"Go away" is not the chimp euphemism for death. So far as our animals know, no human being has ever died. Chimps die. Human beings "go away." We have kept things on that basis from the beginning, not intentionally at first, but such arrangements have a way of institutionalizing themselves. The first member of the group to die was Roger Nixon, in an automobile accident in the early years of the project, long before my time here, and apparently no one wanted to confuse or disturb the animals by explaining what had happened to him, so no explanations were offered. My second or third year here Tim Lippinger was killed in a ski-lift failure, and again it seemed easier not to go into details with them. And by the time of Will Bechstein's death in that helicopter crackup four years ago the policy was explicit: we chose not to regard his disappearance from the group as death, but mere "going away," as if he had only retired. The chimps do understand death, of course. They may even equate it with "going away," as Gonzo's question suggests. But if they do, they surely see human death as something quite different from chimpanzee death—a translation to another state of being, an ascent on a chariot of fire. Yost believes that they have no comprehension of human death at all, that they think we are immortal, that they think we are gods.

Vendelmans now no longer pretends that he isn't dying. The leukemia is plainly acute and he deteriorates physically from day to day. His original this-isn't-actually-happening attitude has been replaced by a kind of sullen angry acceptance. It is only the fourth week since the onset of the ailment and soon he'll have to enter the hospital.

And he wants to tell the chimps that he's going to die.

"They don't know that human beings can die," Yost said.

"Then it's time they found out," Vendelmans snapped. "Why perpetuate a load of mythological bullshit about us? Why let them think we're gods? Tell them outright that I'm going to die, the way old Egbert died and Salami and Mortimer."

"But they all died naturally," Jan Morton said.

"And I'm not dying naturally?"

She became terribly flustered. "Of old age, I mean. Their life-cycles clearly and understandably came to an end, and they died, and the chimps understood it. Whereas you—" She faltered.

"—am dying a monstrous and terrible death midway through my life," Vendelmans said, and started to break down, and recovered with a fierce effort, and Jan began to cry, and it was generally a bad scene, from which Vendelmans saved us by going on, "It should be of philosophical importance to the project to discover how the chimps react to a revaluation of the human metaphysic. We've ducked every chance we've had to help them understand the nature of mortality. Now I propose we use me to teach them that humans are subject to the same laws they are. That we are not gods.''

"And that gods exist,'' said Yost, "who are capricious and unfathomable, and to whom we ourselves are as less than chimps.''

Vendelmans shrugged. "They don't need to hear all that now. But it's time they understood what we are. Or rather, it's time that we learned how much they already understand. Use my death as a way of finding out. It's the first time they've been in the presence of a human who's actually in the process of dying. The other times one of us has died, it's always been in some sort of accident.''

Burt Christensen said, "Hal, have you already told them anything about—''

"No,'' Vendelmans said. "Of course not. Not a word. But I see them talking to each other. They know.''

We discussed it far into the night. The question needed careful examination because of the far-reaching consequences of any change we might make in the metaphysical givens of our animals. These chimps have lived in a closed environment here for decades, and the culture they have evolved is a product of what we have chosen to teach them, compounded by their own innate chimpness plus whatever we have unknowingly transmitted to them about ourselves or them. Any radical conceptual material we offer them must be weighed thoughtfully, because its effects will be irreversible, and those who succeed us in this community will be unforgiving if we do anything stupidly premature. If the plan is to observe a community of intelligent primates over a period of many human generations, studying the changes in their intellectual capacity as their linguistic skills increase, then we must at all times take care to let them find things out for themselves, rather than skewing our data by giving the chimps more than their current concept-processing abilities may be able to handle.

On the other hand, Vendelmans was dying right now, allowing us a dramatic opportunity to convey the concept of human mortality. We had at best a week or two to make use of that opportunity; then it might be years before the next chance.

"What are you worried about?'' Vendelmans demanded.

Yost said, "Do you fear dying, Hal?"

"Dying makes me angry. I don't fear it; but I still have things to do, and I won't be able to do them. Why do you ask?"

"Because so far as we know the chimps see death—chimp death—as simply part of the great cycle of events, like the darkness that comes after the daylight. But human death is going to come as a revelation to them, a shock. And if they pick up from you any sense of fear or even anger over your dying, who knows what impact that will have on their way of thought?"

"Exactly. *Who knows?* I offer you a chance to find out!"

By a narrow margin, finally, we voted to let Hal Vendelmans share his death with the chimpanzees. Nearly all of us had reservations about that. But plainly Vendelmans was determined to have a useful death, a meaningful death; the only way he could face his fate at all was by contributing it like this to the project. And in the end I think most of us cast our votes his way purely out of our love for him.

We rearranged the schedules to give Vendelmans more contact with the animals. There are ten of us, fifty of them; each of us has a special field of inquiry—number theory, syntactical innovation, metaphysical exploration, semiotics, tool use, and so on—and we work with chimps of our own choice, subject, naturally, to the shifting patterns of subtribal bonding within the chimp community. But we agreed that Vendelmans would have to offer his revelations to the alpha intelligences—Leo, Ramona, Grimsky, Alice, and Attila— regardless of the current structure of the chimp/human dialogues. Leo, for instance, was involved in an on-going interchange with Beth Rankin on the notion of the change of seasons. Beth more or less willingly gave up her time with Leo to Vendelmans, for Leo was essential in this. We learned long ago that anything important had to be imparted to the alphas first, and they will impart it to the others. A bright chimp knows more about teaching things to his duller cousins than the brightest human being.

The next morning Hal and Judy Vendelmans took Leo, Ramona, and Attila aside and held a long conversation with them. I was busy in a different part of the compound with Gonzo, Mimsy, Muffin, and Chump, but I glanced over occasionally to see what was going on. Hal looked radiant—like Moses just down from the mountain after talking with God. Judy was trying to look radiant too, working at it, but her grief kept breaking through: once I saw her turn away from the chimps and press her knuckles to her teeth to hold it back.

Afterward Leo and Grimsky had a conference out by the oak grove. Yost and Charley Damiano watched it with binoculars, but they couldn't make much sense out of it. The chimps, when they sign to each other, use modified gestures much less precise than the ones they use with us; whether this marks the evolution of a special chimp-to-chimp argot designed not to be understood by us, or is simply a factor of chimp reliance on supplementary non-verbal ways of communicating, is something we still don't know, but the fact remains that we have trouble comprehending the sign language they use with each other, particularly the form the alphas use. Then, too, Leo and Grimsky kept wandering in and out of the trees, as if perhaps they knew we were watching them and didn't want us to eavesdrop. A little later in the day Ramona and Alice had the same sort of meeting. Now all five of our alphas must have been in on the revelation.

Somehow the news began to filter down to the rest of them.

We weren't able to observe actual concept transmission. We did notice that Vendelmans, the next day, began to get rather more attention than normal. Little troops of chimpanzees formed about him as he moved—slowly, and with obvious difficulty—about the compound. Gonzo and Chump, who had been bickering for months, suddenly were standing side by side staring intently at Vendelmans. Chicory, normally shy, went out of her way to engage him in a conversation—about the ripeness of the apples on the tree, Vendelmans reported. Anna Livia's young twins Shem and Shaun climbed up and sat on Vendelman's shoulders.

"They want to find out what a dying god is really like," Yost said quietly.

"But look there," Jan Morton said.

Judy Vendelmans had an entourage too: Mimsy, Muffin, Claudius,

Buster, and Kong. Staring in fascination, eyes wide, lips extended, some of them blowing little bubbles of saliva.

"Do they think she's dying too?" Beth wondered.

Yost shook his head. "Probably not. They can see there's nothing physically wrong with her. But they're picking up the sorrow-vibes, the death-vibes."

"Is there any reason to think they're aware that Hal is Judy's mate?" Christensen asked.

"It doesn't matter," Yost said. "They can see that she's upset. That interests them, even if they have no way of knowing why Judy would be more upset than any of the rest of us."

"More mysteries out yonder," I said, pointing into the meadow.

Grimsky was standing by himself out there, contemplating something. He is the oldest of the chimps, gray-haired, going bald, a deep thinker. He has been here almost from the beginning, more than thirty years, and very little has escaped his attention in that time.

Far off to the left, in the shade of the big beech tree, Leo stood similarly in solitary meditation. He is twenty, the alpha male of the community, the strongest and by far the most intelligent. It was eerie to see the two of them in their individual zones of isolation, like distant sentinels, like Easter Island statues, lost in private reveries.

"Philosophers," Yost murmured.

Yesterday Vendelmans returned to the hospital for good. Before he went, he made his farewells to each of the fifty chimpanzees, even the infants. In the past week he has altered markedly: he is only a shadow of himself, feeble, wasted. Judy says he'll live only another few weeks.

She has gone on leave and probably won't come back until after Hal's death. I wonder what the chimps will make of her "going away," and of her eventual return.

She said that Leo had asked her if she was dying too.

Perhaps things will get back to normal here now.

*   *   *

Christensen asked me this morning, "Have you noticed the way they seem to drag the notion of death into whatever conversation you're having with them these days?"

I nodded. "Mimsy asked me the other day if the moon dies when the sun comes up and the sun dies when the moon is out. It seemed like such a standard primitive metaphor that I didn't pick up on it at first. But Mimsy's too young for using metaphor that easily and she isn't particularly clever. The older ones must be talking about dying a lot, and it's filtering down."

"Chicory was doing subtraction with me," Christensen said. "She signed, *'You take five, two die, you have three.'* Later she turned it into a verb: *'Three die one equals two.'*"

Others reported similar things. Yet none of the animals were talking about Vendelmans and what was about to happen to him, nor were they asking any overt questions about death or dying. So far as we were able to perceive, they had displaced the whole thing into metaphorical diversions. That in itself indicated a powerful obsession. Like most obsessives, they were trying to hide the thing that most concerned them, and they probably thought they were doing a good job of it. It isn't their fault that we're able to guess what's going on in their minds. They are, after all—and we sometimes have to keep reminding ourselves of this—only chimpanzees.

They are holding meetings on the far side of the oak grove, where the little stream runs. Leo and Grimsky seem to do most of the talking, and the others gather around and sit very quietly as the speeches are made. The groups run from ten to thirty chimps at a time. We are unable to discover what they're discussing, though of course we have an idea. Whenever one of us approaches such a gathering, the chimps very casually drift off into three or four separate groups and look exceedingly innocent—"We just out for some fresh air, boss."

Charley Damiano wants to plant a bug in the grove. But how do you spy on a group that converses only in sign language? Cameras aren't as easily hidden as microphones.

We do our best with binoculars. But what little we've been able to observe has been mystifying. The chimp-to-chimp signs they use at these meetings are even more oblique and confusing than the ones we had seen earlier. It's as if they're holding their meetings in pig-latin, or doubletalk, or in some entirely new and private language.

Two technicians will come tomorrow to help us mount cameras in the grove.

Hal Vendelmans died last night. According to Judy, who phoned Dave Yost, it was very peaceful right at the end, an easy release. Yost and I broke the news to the alpha chimps just after breakfast. No euphemisms, just the straight news. Ramona made a few hooting sounds and looked as if she might cry, but she was the only one who seemed emotionally upset. Leo gave me a long deep look of what was almost certainly compassion, and then he hugged me very hard. Grimsky wandered away and seemed to be signing to himself in the new system. Now a meeting seems to be assembling in the oak grove, the first one in more than a week.

The cameras are in place. Even if we can't decipher the new signs, we can at least tape them and subject them to computer analysis until we begin to understand.

Now we've watched the first tapes of a grove meeting, but I can't say we know a lot more than we did before.

For one thing, they disabled two of the cameras right at the outset. Attila spotted them and sent Gonzo and Claudius up into the trees to yank them out. I suppose the remaining cameras went unnoticed; but by accident or deliberate diabolical craftiness, the chimps positioned themselves in such a way that none of the cameras had a clear angle. We did record a few statements from Leo and some give-and-take between Alice and Anna Livia. They spoke in a mixture of standard signs and the new ones, but, without a sense of the context, we've found it impossible to generate any sequence of meanings. Stray signs such as "shirt," "hat," "human," "change," and "banana fly," interspersed with undecipherable stuff, *seem* to be adding up to something, but no one is sure what. We observed no mention of Hal Vendelmans nor any direct references to death. We may be misleading ourselves entirely about the significance of all this.

Or perhaps not. We codified some of the new signs and this afternoon I asked Ramona what one of them meant. She fidgeted and hooted and looked uncomfortable—and not simply because I was asking her to do a tough abstract thing like giving a definition. She was worried. She looked around for Leo, and when she saw him she made that sign at him. He came bounding over and shoved Ramona away. Then he began to tell me how wise and good and gentle I am. He may be a genius, but even a genius chimp is still a chimp, and I told him I wasn't fooled by all his flattery. Then I asked *him* what the new sign meant.

"Jump high come again," Leo signed.

A simple chimpy phrase referring to fun and frolic? So I thought at first, and so did many of my colleagues. But Dave Yost said, "Then why was Ramona so evasive about defining it?"

"Defining isn't easy for them," Beth Rankin said.

"Ramona's one of the five brightest. She's capable of it. Especially since the sign can be defined by use of four other established signs, as Leo proceeded to do."

"What are you getting at, Dave?" I asked.

Yost said, " *'Jump high come again'* might be about a game they like to play, but it could also be an eschatological reference, sacred talk, a concise metaphorical way to speak of death and resurrection, no?"

Mick Falkenburg snorted. "Jesus, Dave, of all the nutty Jesuitical bullshit—"

"Is it?"

"It's possible sometimes to be too subtle in your analysis," Falkenburg said. "You're suggesting that these chimpanzees have a theology?"

"I'm suggesting that they may be in the process of evolving a religion," Yost replied.

Can it be?

Sometimes we lose our perspective with these animals, as Mick indicated, and we overestimate their intelligence; but just as often, I think, we underestimate them.

Jump high come again.

I wonder. Secret sacred talk? A chimpanzee theology? Belief in life after death? A religion?

They know that human beings have a body of ritual and belief that they call religion, though how much they really comprehend about it is hard to tell. Dave Yost, in his metaphysical discussions with Leo and some of the other alphas, introduced the concept long ago. He drew a hierarchy that began with God and ran downward through human beings and chimpanzees to dogs and cats and onward to insects and frogs, by way of giving the chimps some sense of the great chain of life. They had seen bugs and frogs and cats and dogs, but they wanted Dave to show them God, and he was forced to tell them that God is not actually tangible and accessible, but lives high overhead although His essence penetrates all things. I doubt that they grasped much of that. Leo, whose nimble and probing intelligence is a constant illumination to us, wanted Yost to explain how we talked to God and how God talked to us, if He wasn't around to make signs, and Yost said that we had a thing called religion, which was a system of communicating with God. And that was where he left it, a long while back.

Now we are on guard for any indications of a developing religious consciousness among our troop. Even the scoffers—Mick Falkenburg, Beth, to some degree, Charley Damiano—are paying close heed. After all, one of the underlying purposes of this project is to reach an understanding of how the first hominids managed to cross the intellectual boundary that we like to think separates the animals from humanity. We can't reconstruct a bunch of Australopithecines and study them; but we *can* watch chimpanzees who have been given the gift of language build a quasi-protohuman society, and it is the closest thing to traveling back in time that we are apt to achieve. Yost thinks, I think, Burt Christensen is beginning to think, that we have inadvertently kindled an awareness of the divine, of the numinous force that must be worshipped, by allowing them to see that their gods—us—can be struck down and slain by an even higher power.

The evidence so far is slim. The attention given Vendelmans and Judy; the solitary meditations of Leo and Grimsky; the large gatherings in the grove; the greatly accelerated use of modified sign language in chimp-to-chimp talk at those gatherings; the potentially eschatological reference we think we see in the sign that Leo translated as *jump high come again*. That's it. To those of us who want to interpret that as the foundations of religion, it seems indicative of what we want to see; to the rest, it all looks like coincidence and fantasy. The problem is that we are dealing with non-human intelligence and we must take care not to impose our own thought-constructs. We can never be certain if we are operating from a value system anything like that of the chimps. The built-in ambiguities of the sign-language grammar we must use with them complicate the issue. Consider the phrase "banana fly" that Leo used in a speech—a sermon?—in the oak grove, and remember Ramona's reference to the sick Vendelmans as "rotten banana." If we take *fly* to be a verb, "banana fly" might be considered a metaphorical description of Vendelmans's ascent to heaven. If we take it to be a noun, Leo might have been talking about the Drosophila flies that feed on decaying fruit, a metaphor for the corruption of the flesh after death. On the other hand, he may simply have been making a comment about the current state of our garbage dump.

We have agreed for the moment not to engage the chimpanzees in any direct interrogation about any of this. The Heisenberg principle is eternally our rule here: the observer can too easily perturb the thing observed, so we must make only the most delicate of measurements. Even so, of course, our presence among the chimps is bound to have its impact, but we do what we can to minimize it by avoiding leading questions and watching in silence.

Two unusual things today. Taken each by each, they would be interesting without being significant; but if we use each to illuminate the other, we begin to see things in a strange new light, perhaps.

One thing is an increase in vocalizing, noticed by nearly everyone, among the chimps. We know that chimpanzees in the wild have a kind of rudimentary spoken language—a greeting-call, a defiance-call, the grunts that mean "I like the taste of this," the male chimp's territorial hoot, and such: nothing very complex, really not qualitatively much beyond the language of birds or dogs. They also have a fairly rich non-verbal language, a vocabulary of gestures and facial expressions; but it was not until the first experiments decades ago in teaching chimpanzees human sign language that any important linguistic capacity became apparent in them. Here at the research station the chimps communicate almost wholly in signs, as they have been trained to do for generations and as they have taught their young ones to do; they revert to hoots and grunts only in the most elemental situations. We ourselves communicate mainly in signs when we are talking to each other while working with the chimps, and even in our humans-only conferences we use signs as much as speech, from long habit. But suddenly the chimps are making sounds at each other. Odd sounds, unfamiliar sounds, weird clumsy imitations, one might say, of human speech. Nothing that we can understand, naturally: the chimpanzee larynx is simply incapable of duplicating the phonemes humans use. But these new grunts, these tortured blurts of sound, seem intended to mimic our speech. It was Damiano who showed us, as we were watching a tape of a grove session, how Attila was twisting his lips with his hands in what appeared unmistakably to be an attempt to make human sounds come out.

Why?

The second thing is that Leo has started wearing a shirt and a hat. There is nothing remarkable about a chimp in clothing; although we have never encouraged such anthropomorphization here, various animals have taken a fancy from time to time to some item of clothing, have begged it from its owner, and have worn it for a few days or even weeks. The novelty here is that the shirt and the hat belonged to Hal Vendelmans, and that Leo wears them only when the chimps are gathered in the oak grove, which Dave Yost has lately begun calling the "holy grove." Leo found them in the toolshed beyond the vegetable garden. The shirt is ten sizes too big, Vendelmans having been so brawny, but Leo ties the sleeves across his chest and lets the rest dangle down over his back almost like a cloak.

What shall we make of this?

Jan is the specialist in chimp verbal processes. At the meeting tonight she said, "It sounds to me as if they're trying to duplicate the rhythms of human speech even though they can't reproduce the actual sounds. They're playing at being human."

"Talking the god-talk," said Dave Yost.

"What do you mean?" Jan asked.

"Chimps talk with their hands. Humans do too, when speaking with chimps, but when humans talk to humans they use their voices. Humans are gods to chimps, remember. Talking in the way the gods talk is one way of remaking yourself in the image of the gods, of putting on divine attributes."

"But that's nonsense," Jan said. "I can't possibly—"

"Wearing human clothing," I broke in excitedly, "would also be a kind of putting on divine attributes, in the most literal sense of the phrase. Especially if the clothes—"

"—had belonged to Hal Vendelmans," said Christensen.

"The dead god," Yost said.

We looked at each other in amazement.

Charley Damiano said, not in his usual skeptical way but in a kind of wonder, "Dave, are you hypothesizing that Leo functions as some sort of priest, that those are his sacred garments?"

"More than just a priest," Yost said. "A high priest, I think. A pope. The pope of the chimps."

Grimsky is suddenly looking very feeble. Yesterday we saw him moving slowly through the meadow by himself, making a long circuit of the grounds as far out as the pond and the little waterfall, then solemnly and ponderously staggering back to the meeting-place at the far side of the grove. Today he has been sitting quietly by the stream, occasionally rocking slowly back and forth, now and then dipping his feet in. I checked the records: he is 43 years old, well along for a chimp, although some have been known to live fifty years and more. Mick wanted to take him to the infirmary but we decided against it; if he is dying, and by all appearances he is, we ought to let him do it with dignity in his own way. Jan went down to the grove to visit him and reported that he shows no apparent signs of disease. His eyes are clear, his face feels cool. Age has withered him and his time is at hand. I feel an enormous sense of loss, for he has a keen intelligence, a long memory, a shrewd and thoughtful nature. He was the alpha male of the troop for many years, but a decade ago, when Leo came of age, Grimsky abdicated in his favor with no sign of a struggle. Behind Grimsky's grizzled forehead there must lie a wealth of subtle and mysterious perceptions, concepts, and insights about which we know practically nothing, and very soon all that will be lost. Let us hope he's managed to teach his wisdom to Leo and Attila and Alice and Ramona.

Today's oddity: a ritual distribution of meat.

Meat is not very important in the diet of chimps, but they do like to have some, and as far back as I can remember Wednesday has been meat day here, when we give them a side of beef or some slabs of mutton or something of that sort. The procedure for dividing up the meat betrays the chimps' wild heritage, for the alpha males eat their fill first, while the others watch, and then the weaker males beg for a share and are allowed to move in to grab, and finally the females and young ones get the scraps. Today was meat day. Leo, as usual, helped himself first, but what happened after that was astounding. He let Attila feed, and then told Attila to offer some meat to Grimsky, who is even weaker today and brushed it aside. *Then Leo put on Vendelmans's hat* and began to parcel out scraps of meat to the others. One by one they came up to him in the current order of ranking and went through the standard begging maneuver, hand beneath chin, palm upward, and Leo gave each one a strip of meat.

"Like taking communion," Charley Damiano muttered. "With Leo the celebrant at the Mass."

Unless our assumptions are totally off base, there is a real religion going on here, perhaps created by Grimsky and under Leo's governance. And Hal Vendelmans's faded old blue work-hat is the tiara of the pope.

Beth Rankin woke me at dawn and said, "Come fast. They're doing something strange with old Grimsky."

I was up and dressed and awake in a hurry. We have a closed-circuit system now that pipes the events in the grove back to us, and we paused at the screen so that I could see what was going on. Grimsky sat on his knees at the edge of the stream, eyes closed, barely moving. Leo, wearing the hat, was beside him, elaborately tying Vendelmans's shirt over Grimsky's shoulders. A dozen or more of the other adult chimps were squatting in a semicircle in front of them.

Burt Christensen said, "What's going on? Is Leo making Grimsky the assistant pope?"

"I think Leo is giving Grimsky the last rites," I said.

What else could it have been? Leo wore the sacred headdress. He spoke at length using the new signs—the ecclesiastical language, the chimpanzee equivalent of Latin or Hebrew or Sanskrit—and as his oration went on and on, the congregation replied periodically with outbursts of—I suppose—response and approval, some in signs, some with the grunting garbled pseudo-human sounds that Dave Yost thought was their version of god-talk. Throughout it all Grimsky was silent and remote, though occasionally he nodded or murmured or tapped both his shoulders in a gesture whose meaning was unknown to us. The ceremony went on for more than an hour. Then Grimsky leaned forward, and Kong and Chump took him by the arms and eased him down until he was lying with his cheek against the ground.

For two, three, five minutes all the chimpanzees were still. At last Leo came forward and removed his hat, setting it on the ground beside Grimsky, and with great delicacy he untied the shirt Grimsky wore. Grimsky did not move. Leo draped the shirt over his own shoulders and donned the hat again.

He turned to the watching chimps and signed, using the old signs that were completely intelligible to us, "Grimsky now be human being."

We stared at each other in awe and astonishment. A couple of us were sobbing. No one could speak.

The funeral ceremony seemed to be over. The chimps were dispersing. We saw Leo sauntering away, hat casually dangling from one hand, the shirt, in the other, trailing over the ground. Grimsky alone remained by the stream. We waited ten minutes and went down to the grove. Grimsky seemed to be sleeping very peacefully, but he was dead, and we gathered him up—Burt and I carried him; he seemed to weigh almost nothing—and took him back to the lab for the autopsy.

In mid-morning the sky darkened and lightning leaped across the hills to the north. There was a tremendous crack of thunder almost instantly and sudden tempestuous rain. Jan pointed to the meadow. The male chimps were doing a bizarre dance, roaring, swaying, slapping their feet against the ground, hammering their hands against the trunks of the trees, ripping off branches and flailing the earth with them. Grief? Terror? Joy at the translation of Grimsky to a divine state? Who could tell? I had never been frightened by our animals before—I knew them too well, I regarded them as little hairy cousins—but now they were terrifying creatures and this was a scene out of time's dawn, as Gonzo and Kong and Attila and Chump and Buster and Claudius and even Pope Leo himself went thrashing about in that horrendous rain, pounding out the steps of some unfathomable rite.

The lightning ceased and the rain moved southward as quickly as it had come, and the dancers went slinking away, each to his favorite tree. By noon the day was bright and warm and it was as though nothing out of the ordinary had happened.

Two days after Grimsky's death I was awakened again at dawn, this time by Mick Falkenburg. He shook my shoulder and yelled at me to wake up, and as I sat there blinking he said, "Chicory's dead! I was out for an early walk and I found her near the place where Grimsky died."

"Chicory? But she's only—"

"Eleven, twelve, something like that. I know."

I put my clothes on while Mick woke the others, and we went down to the stream. Chicory was sprawled out, but not peacefully—there was a dribble of blood at the corner of her mouth, her eyes were wide and horrified, her hands were curled into frozen talons. All about her in the moist soil of the streambank were footprints. I searched my memory for an instance of murder in the chimp community and could find nothing remotely like it—quarrels, yes, and lengthy feuds, and some ugly ambushes and battles, fairly violent, serious injuries now and then. But this had no precedent.

"Ritual murder," Yost murmured.

"Or a sacrifice, perhaps?" suggested Beth Rankin.

"Whatever it is," I said, "they're learning too fast. Recapitulating the whole evolution of religion, including the worst parts of it. We'll have to talk to Leo."

"Is that wise?" Yost asked.

"Why not?"

"We've kept hands off so far. If we want to see how this thing unfolds—"

"During the night," I said, "the Pope and the College of Cardinals ganged up on a gentle young female chimp and killed her. Right now they may be off somewhere sending Alice or Ramona or Anna Livia's twins to chimp heaven. I think we have to weigh the value of observing the evolution of chimp religion against the cost of losing irreplaceable members of a unique community. I say we call in Leo and tell him that it's wrong to kill."

"He knows that," said Yost. "He must. Chimps aren't murderous animals."

"Chicory's dead."

"And if they see it as a holy deed?" Yost demanded.

"Then one by one we'll lose our animals, and at the end we'll just have a couple of very saintly survivors. Do you want that?"

We spoke with Leo. Chimps can be sly and they can be manipulative, but even the best of them, and Leo is the Einstein of chimpanzees, does not seem to know how to lie. We asked him where

Chicory was and Leo told us that Chicory was now a human being. I felt a chill at that. Grimsky was also a human being, said Leo. We asked him how he knew that they had become human and he said, "They go where Vendelmans go. When human go away, he become god. When chimpanzee go away, he become human. Right?"

"No," we said.

The logic of the ape is not easy to refute. We told him that death comes to all living creatures, that it is natural and holy, but that only God could decide when it was going to happen. God, we said, calls His creatures to Himself one at a time. God had called Hal Vendelmans, God had called Grimsky, God would someday call Leo and all the rest here. But God had not yet called Chicory. Leo wanted to know what was wrong with sending Chicory to Him ahead of time. Did that not improve Chicory's condition? No, we replied. No, it only did harm to Chicory. Chicory would have been much happier living here with us than going to God so soon. Leo did not seem convinced. Chicory, he said, now could talk words with her mouth and wore shoes on her feet. He envied Chicory very much.

We told him that God would be angry if any more chimpanzees died. We told him that *we* would be angry. Killing chimpanzees was wrong, we said. It was not what God wanted Leo to be doing.

"Me talk to God, find out what God wants," Leo said.

We found Buster dead by the edge of the pond this morning, with indications of another ritual murder. Leo coolly stared us down and explained that God had given orders that all chimpanzees were to become human beings as quickly as possible, and this could only be achieved by the means employed on Chicory and Buster.

Leo is confined now in the punishment tank and we have suspended this week's meat distribution. Yost voted against both of those decisions, saying we ran the risk of giving Leo the aura of a religious martyr, which would enhance his already considerable power. But these killings have to stop. Leo knows, of course, that we are upset about them. But if he believes his path is the path of righteousness, nothing we say or do is going to change his mind.

* * *

Judy Vendelmans called today. She has put Hal's death fairly well behind her, misses the project, misses the chimps. As gently as I could, I told her what has been going on here. She was silent a very long time—Chicory was one of her favorites, and Judy has had enough grief already to handle for one summer—but finally she said, "I think I know what can be done. I'll be on the noon flight tomorrow."

We found Mimsy dead in the usual way late this afternoon. Leo is still in the punishment tank—the third day. The congregation has found a way to carry out its rites without its leader. Mimsy's death has left me stunned, but we are all deeply affected, virtually unable to proceed with our work. It may be necessary to break up the community entirely to save the animals. Perhaps we can send them to other research centers for a few months, three of them here, five there, until this thing subsides. But what if it doesn't subside? What if the dispersed animals convert others elsewhere to the creed of Leo?

The first thing Judy said when she arrived was, "Let Leo out. I want to talk with him."

We opened the tank. Leo stepped forth, uneasy, abashed, shading his eyes against the strong light. He glanced at me, at Yost, at Jan, as if wondering which one of us was going to scold him; and then he saw Judy and it was as though he had seen a ghost. He made a hollow rasping sound deep in his throat and backed away. Judy signed hello and stretched out her arms to him. Leo trembled. He was terrified. There was nothing unusual about one of us going on leave and returning after a month or two, but Leo must not have expected Judy ever to return, must in fact have imagined her gone to the same place her husband had gone, and the sight of her shook him. Judy understood all that, obviously, for she quickly made powerful use of it, signing to Leo, "I bring you message from Vendelmans."

"Tell tell tell!"

"Come walk with me," said Judy.

She took him by the hand and led him gently out of the

punishment area and into the compound, and down the hill toward the meadow. I watched from the top of the hill, the tall slender woman and the compact, muscular chimpanzee close together, side by side, hand in hand, pausing now to talk, Judy signing and Leo replying in a flurry of gestures, then Judy again for a long time, a brief response from Leo, another cascade of signs from Judy, then Leo squatting, tugging at blades of grass, shaking his head, clapping hand to elbow in his expression of confusion, then to his chin, then taking Judy's hand. They were gone for nearly an hour. The other chimps did not dare approach them. Finally Judy and Leo, hand in hand, came quietly up the hill to headquarters again. Leo's eyes were shining and so were Judy's.

She said, "Everything will be all right now. That's so, isn't it, Leo?"

Leo said, "God is always right."

She made a dismissal sign and Leo went slowly down the hill. The moment he was out of sight, Judy turned away from us and cried a little, just a little; then she asked for a drink; and then she said, "It isn't easy, being God's messenger."

"What did you tell him?" I asked.

"That I had been in heaven visiting Hal. That Hal was looking down all the time and he was very proud of Leo, except for one thing: that Leo was sending too many chimpanzees to God too soon. I told him that God was not yet ready to receive Chicory and Buster and Mimsy, that they would have to be kept in storage cells for a long time, until their true time came, and that that was not good for them. I told him that Hal wanted Leo to know that God hoped he would stop sending him chimpanzees. Then I gave Leo Hal's old wristwatch to wear when he conducts services, and Leo promised he would obey Hal's wishes. That was all. I suspect I've added a whole new layer of mythology to what's developing here, and I trust you won't be angry with me for doing it. I don't believe any more chimps will be killed. And I think I'd like another drink."

Later in the day we saw the chimps assembled by the stream. Leo held his arm aloft and sunlight blazed from the band of gold on his slim hairy wrist, and a great outcry of grunts in god-talk went up from the congregation and they danced before him, and then he donned the sacred hat and the sacred shirt and moved his arms eloquently in the secret sacred gestures of the holy sign language.

There have been no more killings. I think no more will occur. Perhaps after a time our chimps will lose interest in being religious, and go on to other pastimes. But not yet, not yet. The ceremonies continue, and grow ever more elaborate, and we are compiling volumes of extraordinary observations, and God looks down and is pleased. And Leo proudly wears the emblems of his papacy as he bestows his blessing on the worshippers in the holy grove.

Written in Water

Tanith Lee

Since The Birthgrave *was published in 1975, Tanith Lee has deservedly enjoyed a reputation as one of the most gifted new writers of recent years. Her novels—*Drinking Sapphire Wine, Night's Master, Sabella, Kill the Dead *and* Lycanthia *among them—have ranged from science fiction through sword-and-sorcery to dark fantasy and horror. Her writing also includes books for children and radio dramas for the BBC, and she seems quite capable of writing successfully anything she wants. The hallmarks of her work are a seemingly endless invention and a rich, allusive, and evocative prose that, like all the best writing, suggests even more than it says.*

It is no accident that the title of "Written in Water" is borrowed from Catullus; everything else in it, however, is uniquely Tanith Lee.

It was a still summer night, coloured through by darkness. A snow-white star fell out of the sky and into the black field half a mile from the house. Ten minutes later, Jaina had walked from the house, through the fenced garden patch, the creaking gate, toward the place where the star had fallen. Presently, she was standing over a young man, lying tangled in a silver web, on the burned lap of the earth.

"Who are you?" said Jaina. "What's happened to you? Can you talk? Can you tell me?"

The young man, who was very young, about twenty-two or -three, moved his slim young body, turning his face. He was wonderful to look at, so wonderful, Jaina needed to take a deep breath before she spoke to him again.

"I want to help you. Can you say anything?"

He opened a pair of eyes, like two windows opening on sunlight in the dark. His eyes were beautiful, and very golden. He said nothing, not even anything she could not understand. She looked at him, drinking in, intuitively, his beauty; knowing, also intuitively, that he had nothing to do either with her world, or her time.

"Where did you come from?" she said.

He looked back at her. He seemed to guess, and then to consider. Gravely, gracefully, he lifted one arm from the tangle of the web, and pointed at the sky.

He sat in her kitchen, at her table. She offered him medication, food, alcohol, and caffeine from a tall bronzed coffee pot. He shook his head, slowly. Semantically, some gestures were the same. Yet not the same. Even in the shaking of his head, she perceived he was alien. His hair was the colour of the coffee he refused. Coffee, with a few drops of milk in it, and a burnish like satin. His skin was pale. So pale, it too was barely humanly associable. She had an inspiration, and filled a glass with water. The water was pure, filtered through the faucet from the well in the courtyard, without chemicals or additives. Even so, it might poison him. He had not seemed hurt after all, merely stunned, shaken. He had walked to her house quietly, at her side, responding to her swift angular little gestures of beckoning and reception. Now she wanted to give him something.

She placed the glass before him. He looked at it, and took it up in two finely made, strong, articulate hands. They were the hands of a dancer, a musician. They had each only four fingers, one thumb, quite normal. He carried the glass to his mouth. She held her breath, wondering, waiting. He put the glass down carefully, and moved it, as carefully, away from him. He laid his arms across the table and his head upon his arms, and he wept.

Jaina stood staring at him. A single strand of silver, left adhering when he stripped himself of the web, lay across his arm, glittering as his shoulders shook. She listened to him crying, a young man's sobs, painful, tearing him. She approached him, and muttered: "What is it? What is it?" helplessly.

Of course, it was only grief. She put her hand on his shoulder, anxious, for he might flinch from her touch, or some inimical thing in their separate chemistries might damage both of them. But he did not flinch, and no flame burst out between her palm and the dark, apparently seamless clothing which he wore.

"Don't cry," she said. But she did not mean it. His distress afforded her an exquisite agony of empathic pain. She had not felt anything for a very long time. She stroked his hair gently. Perhaps some subtle radiation clung to him, some killer dust from a faraway star. She did not care. "Oh, don't cry, don't cry," she murmured, swimming in his tears.

She drove into the morning town in her ramshackle car, as usual not paying much attention to anything about her. Nor was her programme much changed. First, petrol from the self-service station, then a tour of the shops, going in and out of their uninviting facades: a tour of duty. In the large hypermarket at the edge of town, she made her way through the plastic and the cans, vaguely irritated, as always, by the soft mush of music, which came and went on a time switch, regardless of who wanted it, or no longer did. Once, she had seen a rat scuttle over the floor behind the frozen meat section. Jaina had done her best to ignore such evidence of neglect. She had walked out of the shop stiffly.

She had never liked people very much. They had always hurt her, or degraded her, always imposed on her in some way. Finally she had retreated into the old house, wanting to be alone, a hermitess. Her ultimate loneliness, deeper than any state she had actually imagined for herself, was almost like a judgment. She was thirty-five and, to herself, resembled a burned-out lamp. The dry leaf-brownness of her skin, the tindery quality of her hair, gave her but further evidence of this consuming. Alone, alone. She had been alone so long. And burned, a charred stick, incapable of moistures, fluidities. And yet, streams and oceans had moved in her, when the young man from outer space had sobbed with his arms on her table.

She supposed, wryly, that the normal human reaction to what had happened would be a desire to contact someone, inform someone of her miraculous find, her 'Encounter.' She only played with this idea, comparing it to her present circumstances. She felt, of course, no onus on her to act in a rational way. Besides, who should she approach with her story, who would be likely to credit her? While she herself had no doubts.

But as she was turning on to the dirt road that led to the house, she became the prey of sudden insecurities. Perhaps the ultimate loneliness had told, she had gone insane, fantasizing the falling star of the parachute, imagining the young man with eyes like golden sovereigns. Or, if it were true. . . . Possibly, virulent Terran germs, carried by herself, her touch, had already killed him. She pictured, irresistibly, Wells' Martians lying dead and decaying in their great machines, slain by the microbes of Earth.

Last night, when he had grown calm, or only tired, she had led him to her bedroom and shown him her bed. It was a narrow bed, what else, fit only for one. Past lovers had taught her that the single bed was to be hers, in spite of them, forever. But he had lain down there without a word. She had slept in the room below, in a straight-backed chair between the bureau and the TV set which did not work anymore. Waking at sunrise, with a shamed awareness of a new feeling, which was that of a child on Christmas morning, she had slunk to look at him asleep. And she was reminded of some poem she had read, long, long ago:

> *How beautiful you look when sleeping; so beautiful*
> *It seems that you have gone away....*

She had left him there, afraid to disturb such completion, afraid to stand and feed parasitically on him. She had driven instead into town for extra supplies. She wanted to bring him things; food he might not eat, drink he might not drink. Even music, even books he could not assimilate.

But now—he might be gone, never have existed. Or he might be dead.

She spun the car to a complaining halt in the summer dust. She ran between the tall carboniferous trees, around the fence. Her heart was in her throat, congesting and blinding her.

The whole day lay out over the country in a white-hot film. She turned her head, trying to see through this film, as if underwater. The house looked silent, mummified. Empty. The land was the same, an erased tape. She glanced at the blackened field.

As she stumbled toward the house, her breathing harsh, he came out through the open door.

He carried the spade which she had used to turn the pitiful garden. He had been cleaning the spade, it looked bright and shiny. He leaned it on the porch and walked toward her. As she stared at him, taking oxygen in great gulps, he went by her, and began to lift things out of the car and carry them to the house.

"I thought you were dead," she said stupidly. She stood stupidly, her head stupidly hanging, feeling suddenly very sick and drained.

After a while she too walked slowly into the house. While he continued to fetch the boxes and tins into her kitchen like an errand boy, she sat at the table, where he had sat the night before. It occurred to her she could have brought him fresh clothing from the stores in the town, but it would have embarrassed her slightly to choose things for him, even randomly off the peg in the hypermarket.

His intention had presumably been to work on her garden, some sort of repayment for her haphazard, inadequate hospitality. And for this work he had stripped bare to the waist. She was afraid to look at him. The torso, what was revealed of it, was also like a dancer's— supple, the musculature developed and flawless. She debated, in a dim terror of herself, if his human maleness extended to all regions of his body.

After a long time, he stopped bringing in the supplies, and took up the spade once more.

"Are you hungry?" she said to him. She showed him one of the cans. As previously, slow and quiet, he shook his head.

Perhaps he did not need to eat. Perhaps he would drink her blood. Her veins filled with fire, and she left the table, and went quickly upstairs. She should tell someone about him. If only she were able to. But she could not.

He was hers.

She lay in the bath, in the cool water, letting her washed wet hair float round her. She was Ophelia. Not swimming; drowning. A slender glass of greenish gin on five rocks of milky ice pulsed in her fingers to the rhythm of her heart.

Below, she heard the spade ring tirelessly on stone. She had struggled with the plot, raising a few beans, tomatoes, potatoes which blackened and a vine which died. But he would make her garden grow. Oh, yes.

She rested her head on the bath's porcelain rim, and laughed, trembling, the tips of her breasts breaking the water like buds.

She visualised a silver bud in the sky, blossoming into a huge and fiery ship. The ship came down on the black field. It had come for him, come to take him home. She held his hand and pleaded, in a language he did not comprehend, and a voice spoke to him out of the ship, in a language which he knew well. She clung to his ankle, and he pulled her through the scorched grass, not noticing her, as he ran toward the blazing port.

Why else had he wept? Somehow and somewhere, out beyond the moon, his inexplicable craft had foundered. Everything was lost to him. His vessel, his home, his world, his kind. Instead there was a bony house, a bony, dried-out hag, food he could not eat. A living death.

Jaina felt anger. She felt anger as she had not felt it for several months, hearing that spade ring on the indomitable rock under the soil. Still alone.

When the clock chimed six times that meant it was one quarter past five, and Jaina came down the stairs of the house. She wore a dress like white tissue, and a marvellous scent out of a crystal bottle. She had seen herself in a mirror, brushing her face with delicate pastel dusts, and her eyes with cinnamon and charcoal.

She stood on the porch, feeling a butterfly lightness. She stretched up her hand to shield her eyes, the gesture of a heroine upon the veranda of a dream. He rested on the spade, watching her.

See how I am, she thought. *Please, please, see me, see me.*

She walked off the porch, across the garden. She went straight up to him. The sun in his eyes blinded her. She could not smile at him. She pointed to her breast.

"Jaina," she said. "I am *Jaina."* She pointed to him. She did not touch him. "You?"

She had seen it done so frequently. In films. She had read it in books. Now he himself would smile slightly, uneasily touch his own chest and say, in some foreign otherworld tongue: *I am. . . .*

But he did not. He gazed at her, and once more he slowly shook his head. Suddenly, all the glorious pity and complementary grief she had felt through him before flooded back, overwhelming her. Could it be he did not know, could not remember, who he was? His name, his race, his planet? He had fallen out of the stars. He was amnesiac. Truly defenceless, then. Truly hers.

"Don't work any more," she said. She took the spade from his hand, and let it drop on the upturned soil.

Again, she led him back to the house, still not touching him.

In the kitchen, she said to him, "You must try and tell me what food you need to eat. You really must."

He continued to watch her, if he actually saw her at all. She imagined him biting off her arm, and shivered. Perhaps he did not eat—she had considered that before. Not eat, not sleep—the illusion of sleep only a suspended state, induced to please her, or pacify her. She did not think he had used the bathroom. He did not seem to sweat. How odd he should have been able to shed tears.

She dismissed the idea of eating for herself, too. She poured herself another deep swamp of ice and gin. She sat on the porch and he sat beside her.

His eyes looked out across the country. Looking for escape? She could smell the strange sweatless, poreless, yet indefinably masculine scent of him. His extraordinary skin had taken on a water-couler glaze of sunburn.

The day flickered along the varied tops of the reddening horizon. Birds swirled over like a flight of miniature planes. When the first star appeared, she knew she would catch her breath in fear.

The valves of the sky loosened and blueness poured into it. The sun had gone. He could not understand her, so she said to him: "I love you."

"I love you," she said. "I'm the last woman on Earth, and you're not even local talent. And I love you. I'm lonely," she said. And, unlike him, she cried quietly.

After a while, just as she would have wished him to if this had been a film, and she directing it, he put his arm about her, gently, gently. She lay against him and he stroked her hair. She thought, with a strange ghostly sorrow: *He has learned such gestures from me*.

Of course, she did not love him, and of course she did. She was the last survivor, and he was also a survivor. Inevitably they must come together, find each other, love. She wished she was younger. She began to feel younger as his arm supported her, and his articulate fingers silked through and through her hair. In a low voice, although he could not understand, she began to tell him about the plague. How it had come, a whisper, the fall of a leaf far away. How it had swept over the world, its continents, its cities, like a sea. A sea of leaves, burning. A fire. They had not called it plague. The official name for it had been 'Pandemic.' At first, the radios had chattered with it, the glowing pools of the TVs had crackled with it. She had seen hospitals packed like great antiseptic trays with racks of the dying. She had heard how silence came. At length, more than silence came. They burned the dead, or cremated them with burning chemicals. They evacuated the towns. Then 'they' too ceased to organise anything. It was a selective disease. It killed men and women and children. It could not destroy the animals, the insects, the birds. Or Jaina.

At first, the first falling of the leaf, she had not believed. It was hard to believe that such an unstoppable engine had been started. The radio and the television set spoke of decaying cylinders in the sea, or satellites which corroded, letting go their cargoes of viruses, mistimed, on the earth. Governments denied responsibility, and died denying it.

Jaina heard the tread of death draw near, and nearer. From disbelief, she came to fear. She stocked her hermitage, as she had always done, and crouched in new terror behind her door. As the radio turned dumb, and the TV spluttered and choked to blindness, Jaina stared from her porch, looking for a huge black shadow to descend across the land.

They burned a pile of the dead on a giant bonfire in the field, half a mile from the house. The ashes blew across the sunset. The sky was burning its dead, too.

A day later, Jaina found little fiery mottles over her skin. Her head throbbed, just as the walls were doing. She lay down with her terror, afraid to die. Then she did not care if she died. She wanted to die. Then she did not die at all.

A month later, she drove into the town. She found the emptiness of the evacuation and, two miles away, the marks of another enormous bonfire. And a mile beyond that, dead people lying out in the sun, turning to pillars of salt and white sticks of candy, and the fearless birds, immune, dropping like black rain on the place.

Jaina drove home, and became the last woman on earth.

Her life was not so very different, she had been quite solitary for many years before the plague came.

She had sometimes mused as to why she had lived, but only in the silly, falsely modest way of any survivor. Everyone knew they could not die, hang the rest, they alone must come through. They had all been wrong, all but Jaina.

And then, one night, a snow-white star, the silver web of the alien parachute, a young man more beautiful than truth.

She told him everything as she lay against his shoulder. He might still be capable of dying, a Martian, susceptible to the plague virus. Or he might go away.

It was dark now. She lifted her mouth to his in the darkness. As she kissed him, she was unsure what he would do. He did not seem to react in any way. Would he make love to her, or want to, or was he able to? She slid her hands over his skin, like warm smooth stone. She loved him. But perhaps he was only a robot.

After a little while, she drew away, and left him seated on the porch. She went into the kitchen and threw the melted ice in her glass into the sink.

She climbed the stairs; she lay down on the narrow bed. Alone. Alone. But somehow even then, she sensed the irony was incomplete. And when he came into the room, she was not surprised. He leaned over her, silently, and his eyes shone in the darkness, like the eyes of a cat. She attempted to be afraid of him.

"Go away," she said.

But he stretched out beside her, very near, the bed so narrow. . . . As if he had learned now the etiquette of human love-making, reading its symbols from her mind.

"You're a robot, an android," she said. "Leave me alone."

He put his mouth over hers. She closed her eyes and saw a star, a nova. He was not a robot, he was a man, a beautiful man, and she loved him. . . .

Twenty million miles away, the clock chimed eight times. It was one quarter past seven, on the first night of the world.

*   *   *

In the morning, she baked bread, and brought him some, still warm. He held the bread cupped in his hands like a paralysed bird. She pointed to herself. "Please. Call me by my name. *Jaina*."

She was sure she could make him grasp the meaning. She knew he had a voice. She had heard his tears, and, during their love-making, heard him groan. She would teach him to eat and drink, too. She would teach him everything.

He tilled the garden; he had found seedlings in the leaning shed and was planting them, until she came to him and led him to the ramshackle car. She drove him into town, then took him into clothing stores, directing him, diffidently. In accordance with her instructions, he loaded the car. She had never seen him smile. She pondered if she ever would. He carried piled jeans with the same eternally dispassionate disinterest: still the errand boy.

During the afternoon she watched him in the garden. Her pulses raced, and she could think of nothing else but the play of muscles under his swiftly and mellifluously tanning skin. He hypnotised her. She fell asleep and dreamed of him.

She roused at a sound of light blows on metal. Alarmed, she walked out into the last gasps of the day, to find him behind the courtyard, hammering dents out of the battered car. She perceived he had changed a tyre she had not bothered with, though it was worn. She relaxed against the wall, brooding on him. He was going to be almost ludicrously useful. For some reason, the archaic word *help-meet* stole into her mind.

Over it all hung the smoke of premonition. He would be going away. Stranded, marooned, shipwrecked, the great liner would move out of the firmament, cruel as God, to rescue him.

She woke somewhere in the centre of the night, her lips against his spine, with a dreadful knowledge.

For a long while she lay immobile, then lifted herself onto one elbow. She stayed that way, looking at him, his feigned sleep, or the real unconsciousness which appeared to have claimed him. *It seems that you have gone away.* No. He would not be going anywhere.

His hair gleamed, his lashes lay in long brush strokes on his cheeks. He was quiescent, limpid, as if poured from a jar. She touched his flank, coldly.

After a minute, she rose and went to the window, and looked out and upward into the vault of the night sky. A low blaring of hatred and contempt ran through her. *Where are you?* She thought. *Do you see? Are you laughing?*

She walked down the stairs and into the room where the dead TV sat in the dark. She opened a drawer in the bureau and took out a revolver. She loaded it carefully from the clip. She held it pointed before her as she went back up into the bedroom.

He did not wake up—or whatever simulation he contrived that passed for waking—until the hour before the dawn. She had sat there all the time, waiting for him, wanting him to open his eyes and see her, seated facing him, her hand resting on her knee, the revolver in her hand. Pointing now at him.

There was a chance he might not know what the gun was. Yet weapons, like certain semantic signs, would surely be instantly, instinctively recognisable. So she thought. As his eyes opened and fixed on the gun, she believed he knew perfectly well what it was, and that she had brought it there to kill him with.

His eyes grew very wide, but he did not move. He did not appear afraid, yet she considered he must be afraid. As afraid of her as she might have been expected to be of him, and yet had never been: the natural fear of an alien, xenophobia. She thought he could, after all, understand her words, had understood her from the beginning, her language, her loneliness. It would have been part of his instruction. Along with the lessons which had taught him how to work the land, change a tyre, make love, pretend to sleep . . . . About the same time, they must have inoculated him against the deadly plague virus, indeed all the viruses of Earth.

"Yes," she said. "I *am* going to kill you."

He only looked at her. She remembered how he had wept, out of dread of her, loathing and despair. Because he had known there would be no rescue for him. Neither rescue from her planet nor from herself. He had not fallen from a burning spacecraft into the world. The craft had been whole, and he had been dropped neatly out of it, at a designated hour, at a calculated altitude, his parachute unfolding, a preprogrammed cloud. Not shipwrecked, but dispatched. Air mail. A present.

The great silent ship would not come seeking him. It had already come, and gone.

Why did they care so much? She could not fathom that. An interfering streak—was this the prerogative of gods? Altruistic bene-factors, or simply playing with toys. Or it might be an experiment of some sort. They had not been able to prevent the plague, or had not wanted to—recall the Flood, Gomorrah—but when the plague had drawn away down its tidal drain, washing humanity with it, they had looked and seen Jaina wandering alone on the earth, mistress of it, the last of her kind. So they had made for her a helpmate and companion. Presumably not made him in *their* extraterrestrial image, whoever, whatever they omnipotently were, but in the image of a man.

She was uncertain what had triggered her final deduction. His acquiescence, the unlikely aptness of it all, the foolish coincidence of survivor flung down beside survivor, pat. Or was it the theatricality which had itself suggested puppet masters to her subconscious: the last man and the last woman left to propagate continuance of a species. Or was it only her mistrust? All the wrongs she had, or imagined she had suffered, clamouring that this was no different from any other time. Someone still manipulated, still *imposed* on her.

"Well," she said softly, looking at him, it appeared to her, through the eye of the gun, "I seem to be missing a rib. Do I call you Adam? Or would it be *Eve?*" She clicked off the safety catch. She trembled violently, though her voice was steady. "What about contraception, Adameve? Did they think I'd never heard of it, or used it? Did they think I'd risk having babies, with no hospitals, not even a vet in sight? At thirty-five years of age? When I dressed up for you, I dressed thoroughly, *all* of me. Just in case. Seems I was wise. I don't think even your specially designed seed is so potent it can negate my precautions. In the tank where they grew you, or the machine shop where they built you, did they think of *that?* I don't want you," she whispered. "You cried like a child because they condemned you to live on my world, with me. Do you think I can forgive you that? Do you think I want you after that, now I *know?*"

She raised the gun and fired. She watched the sun go out in the windows of his eyes. His blood was red, quite normal.

Jaina walked across the burn scar of the field. She pictured a huge wheel hanging over her, beyond and above the sky, pictured it no longer watching, already drawing inexorably away and away. She dragged the spade along the ground, as she had dragged his body. Now the spade had turned potatoes, and beans, and alien flesh.

She stood in the kitchen of the old house, and the darkness like space came and coloured the sky through. Jaina held her breath, held it and held it, as if the air had filled with water, closing over her head. For she knew. Long before it happened, she knew. She only let out her breath in a slow sigh, horribly flattered, as the second snow-white star fell out of the summer night.

The Meat Box

Daniel Gilbert

Daniel Gilbert, at this writing, is a doctoral candidate in experimental psychology at Princeton. He has been writing since 1979 and several of his stories have appeared in the smaller magazines in the science fiction field. His lady and his son, he tells me, are both "unashamedly blond-haired and blue-eyed and beautiful, in telling contrast to my own swarthy Semitic appearance. I am a bearded Jew living with two people who could be Hitler Youth."

"The Meat Box" is written in a powerful voice that rings absolutely true on the ear. And be forewarned. Gilbert himself says of the story: "There is certain to be something in it to offend anyone."

Yes, I love to tend the Meat Box.

It is like a little grinning city, this one is, with dials and buttons set in all its towers and electricity moving up and down its streets. Sometimes I imagine that it is a real city, like the ones Out Down, on Earth, and I pretend that I'm looking on it and all the people look up at my big face and are afraid. At first. Then they are real happy because they know that I won't hurt them.

Real and true.

My job is just to make sure the meat comes out all right, and to make sure there's enough K-Tol running from the vat to the nutrient bath. But I really do more than that; more than smooth a flank and make sure it doesn't get hooked on a platen-roller, more than fill the feed tray with K-Tol when the dial goes down near 2 or 3, more than fold the marbled sheets of meat when they come churning red-brown from the Meat Box.

The whole hospital depends on me. This is my job and the whole hospital knows I do it. Chuckie from H-Ward told me this once: he said, "Neil, you sure do make the meat good."

I do. I make it the best it *can* be made.

I say prayers over the Meat Box, when Dick isn't around to razz me about it, and that's what makes it so good. The meat from a Meat Box doesn't taste at all like killed meat, because the K-Tol solution swishes up near the starter-cells and makes it taste real chem. But I say over it like the Galilean Rabbi, I say, *"Baruch atah adoni, elohanu melach ha'olam,"* which is old talk of the Jews that means *Blessed art thou, O Lord Our God, King of the Universe.* I learned it from an article called *Judaism and the Jewish People* in the encyclopedia at Yorb-9. Volume J.

You could look it up there yourself, but I know I got it right.

The tat on my arm says YORBITON-5 HOSPITAL WARD H, which is what almost everything here says or has stamped on it. The smocks, the 'forms, the bowls, the crap-paper rollers. When I went to see Dr. Pash up on B-Ward for a skin infection, I had to wait in the commute-way for about twenty minutes and I got to see the skips coming in and unloading more patients. On the sides of the skips it says YORBITON-5 HOSPITAL FOR THE MENTALLY AFFECTED, right below the fuel tanks.

I don't know what kind of skip they brought me in.

But the tat on my arm is special because it says YORBITON-5 HOSPITAL, but it also says WARD-H. And when I take the first letter from each word (and you don't count the 5 because it's not a letter, but a number) it spells Y H W H, which is the unpronounceable word, which is the holiest of holies, which is my father's name.

When I figured this out, I told Chuckie from H-Ward about it, and he scrunched up his face and looked at his own tat. He said, "Yahweh?" Then he grinned and yelled right out, "Yahoo! Yahoo!"

Yorb-9 is one of the thirteen orbital colonies that link up in a circle to make the Lesser Catena, and the Greater Catena links up twenty-nine and makes a loop around that. It's like two big strings of hollow sausages, one inside the other, orbiting the sun.

I would have been a New Apostles priest on Yorb-9—almost was—except that I took a skip and headed for the Out Down, and the Church thought I was crazy to want to go in the sixteenth year of the war Out Down, so they got on a comm and waved the Military Technologists—the Empties—who grounded me before I even made the outside loop. I had dreams.

Go forth unto the wastelands and tarry not, for you are of both Me and the Flesh. Bring forth a dove in the Time of the Raven and you shall be named as the Blessed One, for my Kingdom is Mighty and soon at hand.

I was afraid.

When the Empties grounded me I was afraid; not for me, but afraid I'd never get to Earth, afraid for you and you and you, afraid for all those little grinning cities—those that might still be standing— for they are filled with hedonists and barbs and nobody's told them that the Kingdom of God is at hand.

I was afraid so I took a tangle with the Empties and they broke my arm real quick.

I was delivered here at Yorb-5. I sat in the detention hold, my right arm in a healer and my eyes still burning from the sleep they sprayed on me in the tangle. Chuckie was a trustee then, just made, and he came in and handed me some forms to sign.

I signed with my left.

"Real and true," said Chuckie, "I'd give my right arm to be ambidextrous," and I looked up, and there was the sloppiest of Chuckie-grins you could ever imagine; all crooked teeth spread out under that big pelican nose.

Things would be all right, and I knew it right then.

And sometimes at night now, when I'm bunked and thinking about the war Out Down, I still see that Chuckie-grin like stained glass with the stars coming through it, and I smash my head into my pillow so that I don't scream out his name and wake the ward.

I signed and played with the pen and looked around the room, but there was nothing to look at except for Chuckie. He was a real and true roly-poly, you don't see many on the Yorbs; there hasn't been much import for sixteen years, and you don't get pudged on Meat Box meat.

"What do you like to do, Neil?" said Chuckie.

"I have to go Out Down," I said.

Chuckie let out a long whistle and nodded.

"Earth," I said again.

"Yeah," said Chuckie.

We looked around some more and then he took me to H-Ward and signed me a bunk and some toothstrippers and some chocolate. He said that not everybody got chocolate, but that sometimes it made the sleep wear off quicker.

"Why do you want to go Out Down?" he said when I was in the headroom, scrubbing at my eyes with my left hand. He sat on the crapper like it was a chair, and watched me.

I didn't say about the dreams. "Now when the Queen of Sheba heard of the fame of Solomon concerning the name of the Lord, she came to test him with hard questions."

"Real and true," said Chuckie, nodding. I looked at him, and he at me, and we were real serious for a second both, sizing each other up, and then we broke out—broke out laughing with soap all over my face and him on the crapper, and there was something real and true between us and we didn't even have to ask what it was.

I met some of the other guys on H-Ward, and Chuckie met me to Old Crane, who Chuckie said was a *special* friend. Old Crane could have been over a hundred years, and he'd been at Yorb-5 longer than anybody remembered.

He scared me.

Old Crane seemed to look right through you—not like you weren't there, he didn't pretend that—but like you were standing in the way of something, something real max that was happening just behind your back, but if you turned to see what Old Crane saw, you knew you'd be dead or sorry.

"Neil wants to go Out Down," Chuckie said to Old Crane.

Old Crane studied me like all my dreams were in his notebook and that lying to him would only make me look like a real stoop.

"Which Catena?" said Old Crane.

I waited a minute. I didn't know if I was supposed to answer right away or not. I looked over to Chuckie.

"Neil's from the Lesser. Nine. Right, Neil?"

"Nine." I nodded a whole bunch of times.

"Neil was going to be a priest on Nine. He borrowed a skip and got grounded, so now he's here. Right, Neil?"

I noticed that Chuckie said *borrowed,* not *stole.* He understood. "Now I'm here," I said.

"Why?" said Old Crane, and I knew he meant the same thing that Chuckie had asked me, that the Empties had asked me, that I had asked myself—but I also knew I couldn't say the thing about Solomon.

"The Kingdom of God is at hand," I said. "I want to tell them that, that it's at hand." It didn't sound right.

"You gonna stop the war?" said Old Crane.

"I—"

"God gonna stop the war?"

"I just want to tell them—"

"Nobody goes Out Down," said Old Crane.

I swallowed real hard. "Traders go sometimes." Chuckie shifted around and looked away. I said the wrong thing.

"You a trader?"

"No." I looked at my feet.

"Nobody goes Out Down," said Old Crane. "Nobody."

At mess the first night we got fed meat.

It tasted so bad. Meat Box meat always tastes chem and is real mealy and grainy, but this was worse. Probably old Boxes; the starter-cells have to be real bovy, but if you don't change them every thousand cycles or so, you can taste it.

"Mind?" said Chuckie, looking at my meat. I nodded and he forked at it, over to his own tray. He gobbled on it. "New Apostles eat meat. Real and true?"

"I just don't like it is all."

"Yeah. Tastes pretty bad." Chuckie crosshatched his pud and gar with his fork, but left it sitting all yellow in his tray. He lit up a ciggy. "Smoke? Greater Twenty-one."

"Uh-uh."

"What's wrong with the meat," said Chuckie, a big cloud of blue ciggy smoke drifting out over the table, "is that it has no soul. It's born without a soul. Do you think?"

I told him I'd never really thought about it.

"Real and true. No soul. Cow's got a soul. You think?"

"Sure," I said.

"So there. No soul in a Meat Box. I'm a trustee, Neil."

"You told me that."

"And, Neil, I could get you a job at the Meat Box."

"I don't think I'd like that."

"You're a priest, Neil. Give the meat some soul. You know, you could do that. Whatever you do to your congregation, you know, whatever gives them their souls, you could do that to the meat."

"I'm not a priest," I told Chuckie. I saw Old Crane sitting at a table back three and across the aisle, watching us.

"If you're not a priest, Neil, what are you?" Chuckie looked at me like the question made sense. "Now I'm a mechanic, but just because I don't get to mechanic *here* doesn't change that I'm still a mechanic. I can fix anything."

"I guess . . ."

"I could swing you that job. It's not very max if you do like the other tenders do. But now, if you could give it . . . *soul* . . . ." Chuckie leaned back and stared off into space—not real space; there isn't a clear-panel or egress-hatch below E-Ward—but into the drifting layers of blue smoke.

Old Crane kept watching us.

"Could we go now?" I said.

"Soul, Neil." Chuckie winked at me.

The next day I started working at the Meat Box.

The Meat Room doesn't smell bad, like some of the wards or the mess; it just smells like K-Tol. Everything on J-Ward smells like K-Tol. The K-Tol fills from the vat and swims around the starter-cells. The starter-cells are real bovy protein, from the Out Down, so I have to add a lump of fat every cycle so that the meat comes out marbled.

I marble the meat and hang it up and add the K-Tol if it gets too low and say the prayers.

Nobody else says the prayers. I do.

When Dick came around and told me to go off shift early, I thought maybe I did something wrong. Dick is real max, but he wouldn't look right at me, just told me to wash and go back to my ward.

I got an Empty to tube me to H-Ward, but Chuckie wasn't there. Two orderlies were waiting for me in the day room.

"I went to see Dr. Pash," I said, "about a skin infection. This afternoon, but I didn't do anything wrong."

One orderly put his hand around my arm, not squeezing, but I knew he could. I followed them without a tangle.

We took a tube up to C-Ward. The tube runs the length of the Yorb, a little capsule riding on hot air pumped from the machines. All the machines in a Yorb vent through the tube, even the Meat

Box. At C-Ward we took a roller, and I noticed that all along the commute-way there were no clear-panels or egress-hatches. Just like the patient wards, which was strange, because all the wards above E-Ward are supposed to have them.

The room they took me to was pretty nice; it had softies on the floor and some real plants hanging under UV-lights. There was a guy sitting at a big L-bent desk. He didn't have a regular 'form, just a jumper and a head-scarf, like they wear on 12 and 13.

"Welcome. I'm Dr. Dennis." He smiled and showed me lots of nice teeth. "You've been assigned to me for therapy. Sit down." He nodded at the orderlies, and they left. I looked around the room.

"What happened to Dr. Sheldon?" I said.

"Dr. Sheldon thought that perhaps you and I could have a talk." Dr. Dennis tapped some papers on his desk. "He didn't feel as though you and he were making much progress."

"Who's behind the mirror?"

Dr. Dennis glanced over his shoulder at the big wall mirror, then turned back and smiled. "You're not new to therapy then. No one's behind the mirror today, Neil. Sometimes we use this room for observation. Ciggy?"

"Why didn't Dr. Sheldon tell me?"

"Neil, let's get to know each other a bit better, shall we? These reports tell me something of you, but a man is more than a bundle of reports, do you think?"

If anyone else had said it, I would think. But his voice was so warm I shuddered; warm like a tube vent, not real and true.

"It says here you were a . . . No, I'm sorry, that you were *studying* for the priesthood on Yorbiton-9, that you didn't seem to be having any particular problems there, you got along well, and then, inexplicably, you stole a skip to—"

"Thou shalt not steal," I said. "I borrowed the skip."

"Borrowed, yes. I'm sorry. You *borrowed* this skip and were intercepted near the Greater Catena. You told the Military Technologists you were going to Earth."

I never heard anyone but an Empty call them *Military Technologists*. I looked over at the mirror again.

"I want to go Out Down. Have to, I mean."

"Yes, I see that here. Neil, do you think you would be able to pilot a skip to Earth?"

I moved around in my chair. "Suppose."

"Entering a gravity well, computing complex trajectories for rotating objects—this is all a great deal different than skipping about in free space. It requires technical training which my notes don't indicate you've received."

"Oh."

"The Military Technologists saved your life, Neil. Is it possible that you didn't *want* to make it Out Down?"

"I wanted to."

"Were you happy, Neil? In the priesthood, I mean?"

"I was happy," I said. "I was okay."

"And you had dreams. Revelations?"

"Dreams is okay."

"Dreams then. God told you to st . . . *borrow* a skip and go to Earth. Is that right?"

It sounded so stoop. "I guess."

"Why would God want you to go Out Down, Neil?"

"I don't know."

"You don't know?"

"Why would He want me to stay here?" I said. My stop was coming un. "In mysterious ways doth He move, yet the left hand doth question the right." I was getting confused; that wasn't correct.

"Indeed." Dr. Dennis made a note on the report. "Neil, I'd like to work with these dreams. I'd like you to dream for me. Would that be okay?"

"Max," I said.

Dr. Dennis chuckled and got up to get the orderlies. I stood up and glanced over at my report. He'd written *SUICIDAL* on about the third line. The orderlies came in with a cart.

They lifted me up on the cart and Dr. Dennis gave me a little spray of sleep, not enough to konk me, but I drowsed. We went rolling down the commute-way, into another room; the orderlies were rubbing my forehead and neck with plasty, and strapping my arms to the cart. They put needles into my forehead and neck, but the plasty wouldn't let me bleed. I saw wires connected to the needles, but they ran back behind me—too far, too far away.

Suicidal. But why. . . .

"Neil, can you hear me?" Then softly: "Am I hooked in? Can he hear me?" Some voices.

The room had a clear-panel on the wall to my right. I could see the Out Down, see . . . but it was April. Orion. You can't see Orion in April from the Lesser . . . but. . . .

A holo. I breathed quietly.

"Neil, I'm going to ask you a question and I want you to think about it for me. Can you do that?"

I didn't answer him.

"Neil, why do you *really* want to go Out Down?"

"Because . . ." and a shock hit me so hard that my head felt like it was ripped open, my neck twisted backward. I began to dream.

"Because . . ." *I was Out Down. I was standing in a city on Earth; tall towers all around me and the sky a surreal blue—no stars. People were running by me, knocking and shoving me, with sticks in their hands. They were chanting something, then yelling and screaming, and then—the sky blazed white!*

"Because . . ." *The city was in ruins. A hot rain began to fall and patter on the bodies lying at my feet. Little particles of ash and soot floated in the air, falling driftly, and I couldn't breathe. Fire smoldered in the slag heaps of broken towers, and my skin felt tingly.*

"Because . . ." *Hordes of soldiers came flying over the hill, skipping over the bodies. They looked like giant insects in their radiation suits. They were pointing at me, calling . . .*

"Because . . ." *I cried to the soldiers for help. I said, "I am the Son, please do not forsake me!" but they didn't understand. They pointed with their weapons and shook their heads. I tried it in Click, in English, in Esperanto . . . they didn't know my name, they didn't remember!*

"Because . . ." *They bound me to a charred, twisted tree, and the bindings cut into my hands. They retreated a few meters, then aimed*

*their weapons. The sky was thick with swirling particles, clogging
my eyes and nose.* "My God," I screamed, "why have you for—"

"Because . . ." *I was alone.*

"Because . . ." *I was alone.*

"Because . . ." *Beneath the grey sky, I was alone. Nothing moved
about me. No surge of life, no trickle. I put my hands to my eyes and
cried, "No!" but the answer was "Yes" and the Earth was dead.*

"No!"

"Because . . ."

"Shhh." Chuckie was in my bunk with me. I opened my eyes.
The ward was dark, a single light in the headroom.

"Neil?"

In the dream I had been Out Down. It must have been . . . there
were blue skies. No place on Yorb. I wanted to vomit.

"Neil?"

Chuckie was rubbing my stomach. I could feel that he didn't have
a 'form on, his hairy belly up against my side. I was naked.

"Neil, are you okay? You're okay. They said you went out during
therapy and that you were screaming stuff. They brought you in.
I've been with you all night. Are you okay?"

"Yes," I whispered to Chuckie. My voice, even in a whisper,
sounded so old, so withered and dried.

Chuckie began to rub my legs, twisting on his side to reach them.
"Neil, I've been thinking about something. I think we could get Out
Down."

"No," I said. *I put my hands to my eyes and cried, "No!" but
the answer was "Yes" and the Earth was dead.*

"How come? You always said, and we could go together."

"Chuckie," I whispered.

"You could be a priest, and me a carpenter or engineer or
something. You could be a real priest, Neil, I wouldn't tell anyone
that you're not."

"Chuckie."

"It's a war, but there's got to be some safe. Isn't New York a safe? Did you hear that? You wouldn't have to be scared because we'd be together."

"Chuckie," I said, my voice so flat, so old, "Earth is dead."

"What, Neil?"

"I feel sick."

"But about Out Down?"

"I dreamed it."

Chuckie relaxed beside me. He rubbed his face against my arms and kissed me on the shoulder. I felt warm, real and true, lying there. I began to cry.

He let me cry with my face in his hair, his chin in the crook of my neck, me whimpering like a floppy-eared pupper, hoping that nobody else on the ward could hear me.

Beneath the grey sky, I was alone. Nothing moved about me.

I hugged him so tight.

"Are you okay?" he asked me afterward.

"I'm okay," I said.

The next day I was tending at the Meat Box and Chuckie came down to see me. I had seven sheets hanging in back of the Box, ready for the cryo. I had a cycle down to six days—lowest anybody's ever done—and everyone said my meat tasted best.

Chuckie glanced around the Meat Room.

"Dick gone?"

I nodded. Chuckie came over and stood by the Meat Box, ran his fingers over the metal edges, studied his tat. I kept my eyes fixed on the K-Tol dial.

"How do you feel after last night?" Chuckie said finally.

"About going Out Down?"

"Well, yeah." He didn't mean that. He meant about sexing with him.

"I feel better, Chuckie. I hurt a lot last night and you made me feel better." Chuckie looked up and grinned.

"Did you ever sex before?"

"No," I said. I wished he'd shut up about it now.

"I used to," said Chuckie. "Old Crane."

I wanted him to go away, and I wanted him to hold me. I wanted to be back on Yorb-9, reading from *The Book Of His Many Faces* or lighting a Sabbath candle. I wanted to be dreaming of a free-space carnival, acrobats and zg-jugglers, not about the Out Down—I didn't want to think.

Beneath a grey sky, I was alone. Nothing moved about me ...

"We could go, Neil. Old Crane's got a keycard."

"To open egress-hatches?"

"And call a tube and flight a skip. He's been here a long time. Says he could have done it himself a million times, except. . . ."

"Except what?"

"If you get grounded . . . well, but they wouldn't do much to you, Neil, since you just came and they figure you're sick anyhow. They'd probably just take your job away and put you on T-Ward. Need a new tat." He grinned.

"You? What would they do to you, you think?"

Chuckie looked up, his eyelashes blinking and he bit his lip. "I'd get hatched. I'm a trustee so I'd get hatched. That's why old Crane's never done it, he doesn't want to chance getting hatched."

I thought of Chuckie's old roly-poly body going *wooshoot!* out a hatch, one tenth of a second of horror in his eyes before they squirted out of the sockets like foam-jelly and his lungs collapsed, his body a drifting prune with a million crystals all over it.

"Just for trying to get out they'd hatch you?"

"We'd have to steal a skip," he said.

"Borrow. It's not so bad."

"And maybe kill someone."

I hesitated. "Thou shalt not kill." I shook my head. "Who?"

"Well, I mean if someone got in our way, we'd have to do *something*. Like an Empty or someone."

"I couldn't do that, Chuckie." I checked the K-Tol dial.

"I would take care of it, Neil. It's just, do you want to go? With me?"

"No."

"How come?" Chuckie was pleading.

"I can't let someone get killed," I said.

He wiped his forehead; the Meat Room gets pretty hot in mid-cycle. "We wouldn't have to. I just thought about it and we wouldn't. We could spray sleep at them maybe."

"Where will you get sleep?"

"I don't know. I can. Just, *do you want to go with me?*"

I looked at the man I had sexed with. He had listened to me, even when I didn't know what I was saying. He took care of me when I hurt so bad from the dreams. He let me cry in his hair.

"I would go," I said. "If you go."

"Okay." Chuckie breathed a big sigh. I began to turn away, but he reached over the Meat Box and held my chin, gently.

"Yahoo," he said softly. "Yahoo, yahoo."

"I dreamed that Earth was dead. That the war was over."

Dr. Dennis stood, studying a holo-panel, his face turned away from me. The panel hadn't been there before. Still, the Out Down, Orion. April.

"And how did that make you feel, Earth dead?"

"What kind of question is that?" I said.

"A direct question, a simple question. How did you *feel?*"

I thought about it. "Awful, I guess. Dreggy."

"Nothing else?"

"How would *you* feel?" I said. Hold the stop, I thought.

He whirled around and stared at me. "Goddamnit, Neil! I'm not asking how *I'd* feel. Don't ask me how *I'd* feel." He sat down and fiddled with some papers on his desk. "Okay?"

"Okay."

He looked so haggard. Whatever was keeping him up nights was all right with me. I didn't mind.

"Now, in the dream, Neil, you saw soldiers."

"Yeah."

"In radiation suits, you said. What color were the suits?"

"White. Kind of."

"And they spoke to you?"

"Maybe. I didn't understand. They had helmets."

"What kind of helmets?"

"Big ones."

"And they said?"

"I didn't understand."

"What did it sound like?"

"I don't know."

"Which city were you in?"

"I don't know."

"Tokyo? New York?"

"Could have been."

"Which?"

"Either."

"And there was nothing around you?"

"There was something."

"What?"

"Ruins."

"Of what?"

"Of the city."

"Which city?"

"I don't know."

"And the Earth was dead?"

"The Earth was dead."

"Nothing alive?"

"Nothing alive."

"How did you know?"

"I just knew."

"How far did you walk?"

"I didn't walk."

"Then *how* can you tell?"

"I could tell."

"Why did you think there was nothing alive?"

"Why did you write *suicidal* on my report?"

"Because we—" He stopped, looked confused, then glared at
me. There was a bump from behind the mirror. The sound hung
there in the air between us.

"Because we what?"

"Neil, I—"

"Why are you doing this to me? All these questions about the dream? It was a dream, a *dream!*" I took a deep breath, held my stop. "Or was it?"

When they talk about seconds that last all eternity, this is what they mean: I stared at Dr. Dennis and he stared at me, and we were suspended there, motionless, in time and space, staring.

Without taking his eyes from me, he stabbed a button on his comm.

The orderlies came running in and he told them, "Neil will be staying on C-Ward tonight."

I didn't scream when he put his hand over my mouth. I knew it was Chuckie's hand.

The little cell they put me in on C-Ward didn't even have a light in the headroom, but I could smell him, feel him, leaning over me in my bunk. He put his mouth so close to my ear that I could feel his tongue, hear his teeth touch as he whispered, "Quiet. In the commute."

I nodded.

As I rose from my bunk and followed him into the commute-way I noticed that he was naked, a sloppy fat silhouette against the dim lights. As soon as I stepped out he pulled me to the wall.

"Take off your clothes," he whispered.

"Why?"

"They maybe can sensor them."

I was only wearing tie-bottoms, so I slipped the string and left them at the doorstop.

"Maybe auds in your room," said Chuckie. "What did you do, Neil?"

"How did you find me?"

"Old Crane's got ears all over. What have they got you here for?"

"Dreaming," I said. Chuckie shrugged.

"Don't step on a roller. Start one up and they'll track it. You got to walk right along the edge here, hug the wall. Watch me."

Chuckie began to move down the commute-way, belly to the wall.

He carefully avoided stepping onto the wide row of rollers, which were now silent and still, waiting only for the pressure of a footstep to start moving again. He slid real well, considering his size, and I watched until I realized he was about six meters down and not looking back.

I caught up to him by the tube.

"Chuckie, we have to talk."

"Not here."

"Here."

"About what? You said you wanted to go." He reached between his legs and pulled a keycard from between his butt-cheeks. "I got it here, Neil."

"I know, but—"

"All we've got to do is tube up to A-Ward, flight a skip and hatch it. We're going Out Down."

"Chuckie, I dreamed Earth was dead. Real and true. I mean *everything* gone."

"Yeah, but, Neil—"

"But they're really interested. There's something about the dream that they keep asking questions. Chuckie, I'm up on C-Ward! They've got me on *C-Ward!* They watch me through mirrors, wrote suicidal on my report! If they kill me the records'll show that—"

"Don't get so excited." He looked around the commute. "So?"

"Chuckie, think on this thing. What if Earth *is* dead?"

"Neil, I saw a news—"

"They can *fake the goddamned news!*" Thou shalt not take the name of the Lord thy God in vain. Never mind. "Chuckie, what if Earth's been dead for sixteen years? What if the war *ended* already? How would we know?"

"Traders go," said Chuckie.

"Govy traders. It would look real and true. Why did they get jumpish when I wanted to go? Why not just let me go?"

Chuckie looked kind of worried, hugging to the metal wall, his giant butt hanging right out over the rollers.

"Okay, Neil. Maybe. *Maybe.* But why wouldn't they tell us? Why keep it all mummed?"

I stared out into the commute-way.

I'd spent the whole night figuring out *how*. It's like lying in a dark room, but still you know where everything is. Or you *think* you know. And after a million times of sleeping in that room and waking up and finding everything where you thought it was, you start to believe it's all there—real and true—even in the dark.

But one night it could change.

The Yorbiton orbit isn't synched at all with the Out Down. Sometimes it looks close enough to spit, other times like a little bright star, and getting waves back and forth is expensive and sometimes impossible. There's never been such a thing as a private comm; you used to be able to patch through the govy's system when these circles were first settled, but even that ended sixteen years ago. Most traders went out of business with the Out Down War; the govy took on a few.

We get *told* about the Out Down, but who do you know that's ever *heard*?

That's a max reason why my dream bothered them so much. I was waking up and noticing that the bunk had been moved.

But Chuckie was right. I never figured *why*.

"I don't know," I said.

"I do," said Chuckie. "The govy's been nose-clean for sixteen years, Neil. It wouldn't take much to get the Yorbs involved in the war Out Down. Govy lets a screw-head preacher go Out Down to yap up his God and Salvation and Kingdom-at-Hand and next you know they say the Yorbs are interfering or taking up sides or sending these no-wits to spy on this flag or that. The Yorbs are sitting scared and just out of sight and damn if we need a screw-head Out Down to bring the attention back here! They find something new to laze at, you think that would be max?"

I stared at Chuckie in the silence.

A screw-head preacher. He called me that.

There in the commute-way.

"I'm sorry, Neil." He reached for me, but I pulled away. He looked so scared, turning his head every minute looking down the commute. "Look, it's just that of all the times for you to start talking this stuff, it had to be now? I've got a *keycard*. I could get *hatched* if an Empty comes rolling down this commute. We can talk about this all later, okay?''

A screw-head preacher. He called me that. There in the commute-way.

I guess he was right.

"Okay," I said.

Chuckie and me edged a few meters to the tube. He slipped the keycard into the call-slot and we waited there, hanging on the wall.

"Can't track the tube?"

"I don't think," said Chuckie. "I used to build them."

The tube arrived and the door opened. We clambered and strapped in. Chuckie carded for A-Ward.

We slowed and unstrapped. The display said A-WARD, and the door opened.

I didn't even have to think. You wonder sometimes how much the genies are right, how much a man is nothing but an instinctive killing machine, and all these thoughts and feelings are just to keep the mind busy when it's got nothing to kill.

When I saw Dr. Dennis, I jumped him.

He was standing in front of the tube door, looking a little preoccupied, obviously waiting for the tube to arrive. Chuckie just froze when he saw him. So did Dr. Dennis.

I leapt at his throat.

I put my hands to my eyes and cried, "No!" but the answer was "Yes" and the Earth was dead.

I jammed my hand into his mouth, I felt teeth give. He bit down hard as we rolled over and over, I could feel blood running down my wrist, but he wasn't making noise. I hooked my left arm around his neck and squeezed.

The bite loosened.

Beneath the grey sky, I was alone. Nothing moved about me, no surge of life, no trickle.

So slow. I could see Chuckie still standing in the tube, his face just blanked, just staring. I could see Dr. Dennis's foot come up, and smash down on my knee. I could feel something shatter. I heard the gurgle and saw his spit spray as I squeezed tighter, the tops of his ears purple.

. . .but the answer was "Yes" and the Earth was dead.

I hugged him so tight.

I felt it go . . . felt it go.

I think I kept hugging him, even long when he was dead, just squeezing at his neck from in back, his body spread out on top of me, so still. Chuckie was pulling at my arm, trying to unclamp it.

"Neil for Godsakes, *let go!"*

I think it was the hardest thing I ever did: letting go.

Chuckie rolled the body off me and helped me to my feet. I leaned on him. Dr. Dennis's eyes were bulged out of their sockets, his throat bright red and wrinkled like an old 'form where I'd held him.

"Your hand is bleeding," said Chuckie.

I killed a man. I killed a man. I killed a man. Write one thousand times: *I killed a man.* Not enough. Write again.

"I killed a man," I said.

"An Empty. Okay. We've got to go quick, Neil. Grab my waist, there. The skip-port is down the end of the commute. C'mon."

I leaned on Chuckie and we wobbled, naked, blood-smeared, like a broken machine, down the commute. There was no way to hug the walls; the rollers whirred beneath us, jetting us forward.

"Damn," said Chuckie. He fiddled with the keycard in the skip-port slot. I leaned against the wall, looked back, could still see Dr. Dennis lying by the tube door, arms twisted backwards at strange angles.

I killed a man. Write ten thousand times. Not enough. Again!

"Won't open. We're tracked."

I closed my eyes and thought of the time I'd spent here on Yorb-5. I'd murdered a man; not with a removed consent, or through negligence, but with my fingers, my muscles—I couldn't let go. I'd met Chuckie here. I'd never had a friend like Chuckie before, no one ever held me . . . or touched me like that. And I had a job, I made the meat. Got the cycle down to six days once, lower than anybody, and I could've done five if they'd have replaced. . . .

—ing moved about me. No surge of life, no trickle.

—the starter-cells. The—

—*lone. Nothing moved about me, no sur*—

—starter-cells, replaced the—

"Chuckie."

"Listen, we'll get the tube and go up to above A-Ward, where the main gyros are. I've worked on them before. We can break down over the skip-port, if we suit up, break down and flight one, if you—"

"It's the starter-cells."

"C'mon, Neil." He half-dragged, half-carried me down the commuteway, my leg a limp stick trailing behind me. The rollers whined.

"The starter-cells. They have to be replaced."

"Don't worry about the fucking starter-cells!" He pulled at my waist.

"Real bovy. Dick told me. Nothing else works. The meat tastes so bad because the starters are old, over a thousand cycles. Another two hundred—maybe four years—and they'll be gone!"

"We'll be Out Down, if you hurry."

"No," I said. "We won't."

He stopped and leaned me up against the wall by the tube-door. Dr. Dennis still lay on the floor, looking up on forever. Chuckie carded the tube. I heard sirens, maybe two wards down, screaming.

"C'mon, you damned tube." Chuckie was sweating heavy.

"It's the why," I said.

"Get straight, Neil!"

"The cells. No cows, no bovy starters. The boxes will die." I was shouting—so strange, I felt *gleeful!* The pieces falling together, like little letters come tumbling down on the page, arranging themselves into words—*and the Word was Death. And I felt joy!*

Chuckie wasn't listening. My leg was hanging there, like a wet rag, but I didn't feel it—not a thing.

"The Meat Boxes, the Kelp Boxes, they'll die. No starters and you can't clone a clone—mutation over generations, two cycles and it wouldn't be meat. In four years there won't be any food on the Yorbs. We don't grow, we *generate*, but no cows Out Down, no—"

"Neil, help me pull this door. The tube's stuck."

"That's why they're mumming it, Chuckie, we're all going to die because the Out Down's dead."

A blast of hot, fetid air almost hurled me to the ground. I clutched the wall. Chuckie had opened the tube-shaft, but there wasn't any car.

He braced himself against the sides of the open door and peered down the shaft, his hair blowing straight up. His face began to blister and peel. "It's stopped down maybe ten wards. They've jammed it."

An orbiting crypt, a spinning tomb, a mausoleum of rotting bodies turning tricks around the sun, skip-ports ravaged, skips fleeing to nowhere.

"C'mon, Neil, we have to jump."

"Jump," I said. Not like a question.

"Into the shaft. The air'll take us up—hot, it'll burn, but we only need to go one ward. We come out near the gyros and break down. If the tube's jammed they can't get to us too quick."

Chuckie pulled me toward the shaft. I felt the heat; from a half meter I could smell my hair singeing, my face baking, brutal heat.

"Just ride it up."

I remember those words: *Just ride it up. Write one trillion times, Just ride it up. Never enough! Again!*

Chuckie edged to the open shaft, looked over at me—just once—and jumped. He floated there for one horrible second, like crap-paper caught in the draft-vent of a head, his chub legs kicking at air.

Then he began to fall.

Down. Throughout the known universe, the word *down* means a number of things. It can mean *away from heaven* or *feeling sorta dreggy, toward the center* or *nearer to thy feet*. On a Yorb, it means whatever the gyros want it to mean. Gravity is the whim of a machine.

In Chuckie's case, it meant *toward J-Ward*.

I stumbled into the shaft, grabbing at him as he hung.

The look in his eyes as he fell: he'd do a spin, his huge body smacking against the sides of the hot shaft, stare up at me—not angry, almost frightened, mostly perplexed—buoy for a second, clutch at the blistering sides of the shaft, scramble, tumble, sink, blister.

Aerodynamics. I looked it up later. Volume A.

The car seals the shaft, builds pressure under the floor plate and rides. Water-skips in the Out Down do it. Scrambling people in the water bob, up, one second, down. Mostly down.

I didn't thrash; flew straight, pretty much. I felt a peculiar calm, shooting through the air-sea. When my hand touched the side of the shaft, my skin bubbled, but I did not cry. I'd get lifted by a draft, but I wouldn't tumble.

Chuckie tumbled. Over and over, smashing the sides of the shaft, leaving little splotches of crisp skin and fluid, which I saw as I fell past them. After a while in that endless fall, he didn't even have his eyes open anymore.

I came back with a cart.

I'd left him lying on the roof of the jammed car, stalled about a meter above J-Ward. I half-crutched on the cart, my knee was shattered; my blisters had started to pus, but where Chuckie was lying on the hot ceiling of the car his skin was carbon black.

His chest was caved. I'd fallen on him.

I hauled him out of the shaft, leaving most of the skin from his back stuck to the car. It felt like his arms would any minute pull from the sockets, easy like well-cooked flesh. I could only load him halfway on the cart, his chest down on the platform, his butt and legs jutting over the sides.

I wheeled. I let the rollers wheel, too.

I wheeled him into the Meat Room.

The sirens were loud now, like the shrieks of condemned men waiting to be hatched. The Meat Room was dark—but even in the dark you know where things are, you come to believe.

"*Baruch atah adoni, elohanu melach ha'olam.*"

I lifted the lid on the K-Tol vat, wheeled the cart real close.

It was the easiest thing I'd ever done.

Chuckie fell in with a *plop*, sank quietly, quickly, without bubbles. It would be days before the K-Tol ate him up, before it returned him to ashes or quarks or whatever, before it swished him up near the starter-cells, before it played him out as a sheet of marbled meat.

It would be days. Three days. Eons.

And a funny thought occurred to me then. Funny thoughts. Volume F.

The Yorbs would never starve.

Days? Eons? Before they used their own cells as starters, before the Meat Boxes were churning out sheets of white, pale meat?

I heard footsteps down the commute-way, the rollers turning at high speed, carrying the footsteps toward the Meat Room. I sank down and leaned with my back against the Meat Box. It felt cool, good to my skin.

And I laughed.

Laughed—as I was grabbed, battered, beaten, thrown against the Meat Room floor.

I laughed.

"Yahoo!" I said as I swallowed my teeth. "Yahoo! Yahoo!"

Ifrit

R.A. Lafferty

If any modern writer is imbued with the true spirit of Hamlet's "antic disposition," that writer is R.A. Lafferty. His stories are light, bright, inventive, shaped with cunning and written with panache. But always lurking behind the wit and the charming grace is a new perception, a new angle of vision, a way of seeing something old through eyes that are new.

In "Ifrit," Lafferty takes us to a place we've never been before and presents us with a unique angle on questions of life, liberty, and the pursuit of happiness. But don't trust him; the strangest things can seem to make sense in Lafferty's world.

I am Henry Inkling, newspaper reporter and feature story writer. I am the best around here, but I never seemed to have anything to show for it until quite recently, within the last several days. It was always the expenses of keeping up my life style that swallowed up everything I could make.

But now I've whipped that. Now I have a beautiful home on a beautiful lake. I have stunning mountains rising right out of my own back yard. I have food and drink beyond anything I ever imagined before. And my friends and visitors are absolutely astonished by my setup. I have elan, I have style, I have class. I have become the hottest host in the newsy fraternity in town, and I never knew that adulation could be heaped so high. My evenings-at-home are probably the most cultural in town and likely the most boozy, and they are certainly the most In-Groupy. And the whole business doesn't cost me anything at all. Everything I earn goes straight into the bank now. I don't need it, but it seems like a good idea to put it somewhere. Not only do I have no new expenses at my new and luxurious setup, but I have no expenses at all. All is free. I have it made.

This change of life and change of circumstance began about two weeks ago when editor Sandow X. McGoshla gave me a story to do.

"Wrestling," he said. "I'm sorry, Henry, but the wrestling shows advertise pretty big in the papers, and we try to do a wrestling special once a year. Do this, and I'll give you a really good assignment the day after tomorrow. Ugh, wrestling, ugh!"

"Ugh," I said. "Well, at least there can't be anything new in wrestling. We've had the Wild Man of Borneo who was wheeled up to the ring in a cage. We've had Number 131313 arriving with his handcuffs and his ball-and-chain and his prison-striped trunks. We've had Le Canonnier with his brass cannon that he was always wheeling around and pointing at his opponent while he almost got it torched off with a burning fuse. We've had Hayfield Hooligan with the giant bale of hay in his corner which he always cut open and scattered around the ring. He was the only one who could keep his footing when the ring was knee-deep in hay. We've had the Hangman with that little gallows on wheels, and the rope with its noose that he was always trying to put around his opponent's neck to hang him right there in the ring. Is there anything new this year?''

"There's the Weeping Genii, Henry. He arrives as the Genii in the bottle. His manager carries him into the ring in a half-gallon bottle. Then he takes the cork out of it, and the Genii pours out. He's about as big as a squirrel at first, but then he expands till he's six-foot-nine and three hundred and eighty pounds. He can't wrestle much, but he's good show. I'm sorry, Henry, but he's about the only new thing in wrestling this year.''

"How could he do that?" I asked. It hit me a little odd. "How could his manager carry him into the ring in a half-gallon bottle and then have him expand to such a size as that?''

"Oh, it's all a fake, Henry. You know that everything in professional wrestling is a fake.''

So that night I went out to the Junior Pavilion at the Fairgrounds to see the wrestling matches. Sure they were all fakes, but they were good show and they drew the crowd along with them.

Lord Stamford Heather-Rose had his valet spray the ring out of a commercial-sized crop sprayer that had the words "Attar of Roses" lettered on it. Then his opponent Josh Pole-Cat had *his* valet spray the ring with an even larger sprayer that had the words "Essence of Skunk" stenciled on it. Josh Pole-Cat was the good guy for that evening, however, and Lord Stamford Heather-Rose was the villain. And Josh won it all in a bout that degenerated into something very near to straight wrestling.

Horseshoe Jones was matched with Rexford "The Lawyer" Pettifogger in the next bout. Horseshoe always seemed to have a horseshoe in his hand, and he brandished it as a weapon. As many horseshoes as the referee took away from him, Horseshoe always seemed to come up with one more. Rexford "The Lawyer" Pettifogger had an equally never-failing supply of large writs with the words "Legal Writ. Cease and Desist!" written on them so big that everybody in the Pavilion could read them easily. The Lawyer would hand one of these big writs to his opponent, Horseshoe Jones. Horseshoe was a slow reader. He read letter by letter rather than word by word, and about the time that his finger finally came to the last letter, "The Lawyer" would knock him down with a whanging blow right on the button. But Horseshoe would always come up off the mat with another horseshoe in his hand, and they would go at it again.

The Weeping Genii was in the semi-final match against Battering Ram Bently, and I felt a curious excitement as they got ready for that bout. Battering Ram came into the ring with his manager. And then the other manager seemed to come into the ring alone. He carried several towels and a half-gallon bottle. Then, when the referee motioned the wrestlers to come to the center of the ring, the Genii's manager pulled the cork out of that bottle, and the Genii poured out of it. Sure enough, he was only about as big as a squirrel at first, and then he expanded to six-foot-nine-inches and three hundred and eighty pounds. The two wrestlers joined battle. And nobody seemed at all amazed by the unbottling trick. Well, it amazed me.

"How did they do that?" I asked a lady next to me.

"Oh, it's all a fake," the lady said. "You know that everything in professional wrestling is a fake. Yi, yi, yi, kill him, kill him, kill him, Genii!"

"How in the world did that huge creature come out of that little bottle?" I asked the lady on the other side of me.

"Oh, they borrowed that from the Arabian Nights that we read when we were little," the lady said. "It's all a trick, of course. You know that everything in professional wrestling is a trick. Wow, wow, wow, gouge his eyes out, Weeper! Break him in two, Battering Ram!"

The Weeping Genii wept when the Battering Ram battered him around, and it was good show to see that great hulk crying like that. And yet the Genii had the better of it, and he won the bout. He was popular. The Battering Ram was the good guy and the Genii was the villain. But he was a villain that everybody liked. And after his hand had been raised in victory, he diminished and entered into the half-gallon bottle again. And his manager corked the bottle and carried it away with him. And still nobody seemed to regard it as an extraordinary trick.

I didn't stay to see the main event. I followed the manager with his bottled Genii. I had to get an interview with them. I caught up with them in the dining room of the Fairmont Mayo downtown. The manager had a fine meal already spread out before him. And the Genii in the bottle also seemed to have a fine meal spread out before him, on a banquet table not even an inch long. The Genii had a lot of room to move about in that bottle.

"I want an interview with either or both of you," I said. "Nobody else seemed to pay much attention to it, but yours is the slickest trick that I ever saw in my life."

"It's a little too sophisticated for the common people," the manager said, "but it's a good trick and I have my livelihood from it." He took the cork out of the bottle. "I'll answer any question you want to ask, as will my associate, Ifrit the Genii. But he's a little hard to hear in his smaller state. You'd just about have to get down on his mensural level to hold conversation with him. You may as well ask me what you have on your mind first."

"How does the Genii grow small, or how do you make him grow small?"

"It only works for persons of honest heart," the manager said. "Persons of good heart, whether of the Genie or the human sort, have only to say four words in Arabian, 'El-hadd el-itnein el-talat el-arba,' and they will grow small quickly, but not so quickly as to bewilder them."

"You said the words and you did not grow small," I charged.

"No, I'm a black-hearted and dishonest-hearted person. I don't know what you are. But, so that you will not find yourself marooned, let me tell you that to grow large again you must say three other Arabian words 'El-khamis el-goma el-sabt.' "

"That's the damnedest spoof I ever heard of," I said.

"Try it," the manager told me. "If you are of brave heart as well as honest heart, try it. You have nothing to lose except your own orientation and perhaps your life. And you stand to gain a whole new way of looking at things.''

''*El-hadd el-itnein el-talat el-arba.*'' I spoke the words bravely. No. I didn't begin to grow smaller. Everything else in the world began to grow larger. I climbed onto the enlarging table. I hooked my fingers over the rim of the mouth of the bottle, and soon I was dangling there. I pulled myself up and over, and then I climbed down a ladder that was inside the bottle. And when I was in the bottle and had become stabilized in my smaller size, I conducted an interview with Ifrit the Genii. In this I use the form Genii for the singular and Genie for the plural. I know that's incorrect, but that's Ifrit's usage and that of the other Genie.

MYSELF: Just what is a Genii?

IFRIT: We are a species a little lower than the Angels. To put it bluntly, we're a species a little bit lower than almost everything. There are three races of the Genii, the Gul who are always male, the Ifrit who may be either male or female, and the Sila who are always female. I am a male Ifrit. Ifrit is not my personal name. We do not have personal names. But that is what my manager calls me for want of something better, and that is what you may call me for convenience.

MYSELF: How in the world do the Gul who are all male or the Sila who are all female have offspring?

IFRIT: Mostly by the natural method. Some of them have their births by section, though. And some of them give birth under hypnosis or anesthesia, much as do humans. But in the beginning it was always by the natural method.

MYSELF: This is quite luxurious here, Ifrit. This seems to be a larger place by the moment. It's a real manor house you have here. This veranda is as big as a castle by itself. How does it all come about?

IFRIT: I carve some of the things out of little pieces of wood when I'm in my larger form. Rough carving is all that's needed. And my manager buys some of the little things in toy stores and drops them into the bottle. Then, when I come into the bottle, the things are no longer little, and they're no longer rough. They become perfectly arranged and perfectly formed. And they become incredibly detailed. New details add themselves from only shadowy hints or from none at all.

MYSELF: But that's beyond all reason and nature. That's magic.

IFRIT: Oh sure. Magic on a small scale is always freely given, and we make use of it by going on a small scale ourselves. That grand piano there, it's of concert quality. And yet the original of it was only a penny piece of plastic out of a crackerjack box. But, as we say, there's really nothing magic about magic. It is the natural ambient of us Genie.

MYSELF: Are you the slave of your manager? Is he your master?

IFRIT: Oh, I suppose so. The arrangement is a pretty good one. A Genii can only have one manager at a time, and if he has a good master he's safe from falling under the dominion of a bad one. Mine is a pretty good master, and I have a good life. In two-thirds of the towns on the circuit I'm visited by others of my kind. We have our own methods of getting together. And I have my books and my records here, more than ten thousand of each. I have my flute and my violin and my piano. I have all the best to eat and drink. I have my correspondence. We have our own bottle-to-bottle instant mail service. The phrase 'A message found in a bottle' has more meanings than you'd believe. And I have several hundred human friends who have mastered their fear and who visit me on my estate here. Even my gladiatorial combats are rather fun. It is to play the 'Giant of the First Kind' in a miming form of comic drama when I do the wrestling. There are also times when I become a 'Giant of the Second Kind,' a giant who is more than a mile tall. Oh, we're a prodigious people! And when I look up from my estate here, it is the humans who are the giants. Sometimes a bunch of them look like a skyful of giants to me. We Genie must always have masters because we belong to an inferior race.

MYSELF: But what about the Genie who are slaves to bad masters?

IFRIT: Oh, they have a bad time of it. There's a breaking point, but it's so final a breaking point that it's never been used yet. If you ever get a Genii completely in your power, Henry, don't push him to the limit. Every Genii knows a word he can say that will bring the world to its end. It's a dangerous and fearful situation.

MYSELF: What is the word, Ifrit?

IFRIT: It's *El-jhokholimfhorad*—Oh, no, no, no. I almost said the direful word. If I'd gone on and said the last eleven syllables of it, the world *would* have come to its end. Never again ask me what that word is. I might forget myself and say it. I'm surprised that the world hasn't already been destroyed by some Genii saying the word. Lots of Genie are even goofier than I am.

MYSELF: Why are you billed as the 'Weeping Genii'? Why do you weep?

IFRIT: I've always been a very emotional person, and tears come easy to me. And it's a miming role that I enjoy. I used to be billed as the 'Weeping Axe-Man' when I was a gladiator at Rome.

MYSELF: How old *are* you, Ifrit?

IFRIT: I'm a little over eleven thousand years old. My master, that giant in the sky above us, above this bottle, has fallen asleep over his wine. You had better lam now or he may decide to hold you for ransom. All he has to do is put the cork in the bottle and you're trapped. He does tricks like that. Up the ladder quickly now! That's fine. Now the three words!

MYSELF: *El-khamis el-goma el-sabt*.

Then I was out of the bottle and was my own size again. I found myself rather awkwardly standing on a table in the dining room of the Fairmont Mayo, but I jumped down quietly and left the room as nonchalantly as I could.

Ifrit and his manager left town quite early the next morning. Ifrit had a wrestling date that night in Muskogee, and then he had them on successive nights in Fort Smith, Little Rock, Texarkana, Shreveport, Baton Rouge, Port Arthur, and Beaumont. I followed along after them and had further interviews with Ifrit in each of those eight towns. In five of them, he was also visited by friends, either human or Genie, in his estate-in-the-bottle. Ifrit and I became the best friends in the world. He was a person of deep-rooted culture; and he also had a strong and endearing streak of goofiness in him. He may even have been a tall-story teller. He told me that he had a wife, that she was currently living in a three-liter gin bottle in the Netherlands, that she was carrying a child of his, but that the birth would be not at all soon. The gestation period of Genie, Ifrit said, was a hundred and eighty-seven years, and only half of that time had passed with his wife. But another Genii, also of the Ifrit race, told me that my friend Ifrit had been spoofing me, that the gestation period of Genie is only ninety-four years, and that the wife of Ifrit would come to her time within thirty years. Which one to believe?

All things that are worn or carried by a person when he enters a bottle are miniaturized along with him. But it is not really the case of the person or his things being miniaturized at all, but of his being put into a different juxtaposition with all things else in the world so that there is greater variance of apparent size. And for this reason also, the space inside a bottle may sometimes seem much more vast than at other times. And it is generally the case that as a person develops his estate-in-a-bottle he is given more space in which to develop it.

All in all, my friendship with Ifrit was among the most rewarding of my life. When I left the wrestling circuit after eight days with it on the road, I felt a terrible loss.

"But after all, I will be wrestling through this part of the country again in three months' time," Ifrit reassured me.

He had heard through their own networks that about a thousand humans in the United States alone had now set up plush estates-in-bottles. This had become the most exclusive of all the *in* movements. You had to be pretty well *in* even to have heard of it. But some of those thousand humans, Ifrit gave the opinion, didn't really have the temperament to handle bottled estates.

This was on the night that Ifrit had defeated the Alligator Man in a bout in Beaumont, and had then fulfilled his vaunt to cut enough out of the Alligator Man's hide to have made for himself a pair of alligator shoes. And Ifrit *did* cut the pieces out of the hide of his defeated opponent right there in the ring with a big knife. It was all a hoax, though. That was not the real hide of the Alligator Man. He actually had an ordinary skin like that of yourself or myself, and the alligator hide was only part of his costume.

And the Shoemaker from the "Great Colossal Imperial Alligator Shoe Factory of Tampa Florida" was faking it all when he went for the world's record (nineteen seconds) for making a pair of alligator shoes right there in the ring. Nevertheless the Shoemaker seemed to be making the shoes, while drum rolls marked off the seconds, and while the Alligator Man still lay on his belly and writhed and screamed at the holes that were cut in his hide. And the shoes, size eighteen very wide, did fit Ifrit's big bare feet perfectly, though really they had been bought previously and only seemed to be made by the Shoemaker in the ring. The loudspeakers announced though that the new world's record for making a pair of alligator shoes had been set, and that it was eighteen-point-nine-nine-two seconds.

This was all fun. It was part of the folk fakery of professional wrestling. Yet I realized at my heart-wrenching leave-taking that night that there was one thing in professional wrestling that was not a fake. Ifrit the Genii was not a fake. He was the most genuine person I had ever met.

The last words he said to me that night at our parting were, "Why don't you get a bottle of your own, Henry?" And then he added, "Beware of the Pride of Lions in the Sky. That is the only threat to you that I see."

I smiled. We have very few lions in the skies in my part of the country.

No, there is not any twist to this account, no flashy ending. I will not hoke it up in any way. There is nothing here except the plain observed facts about a patient creature who was born into slavery, a valiant member of a vanishing species that is something of an anomaly in the modern world, a good person, an admirable person, a friendly person. No great deeds attach to him, no exciting actions, and none will be invented for him.

I write only, "He is a good person," and if that is not exciting, then we will do without excitement this day.

*   *   *

I did, as Ifrit had suggested, get a bottle of my own, an empty gallon bottle that had once held Red Rosa wine. I put it in a fence corner off an alley behind St. Louis Street, about four feet above the concrete, where two of the fence braces joined. No one would notice it there or bother it there. I put just enough water in it to make a large lake, and enough dirt and pebbles to supply spacious and rolling meadows and sudden mountains. I seeded other things in there with microscopic tokens of themselves. I came and went into my bottle, into my own estate or universe there. I felt like Superman entering that little bottle that contained a great estate and world. And my estate thrived quickly, as I explained at the beginning of this account. In my estate-in-the-bottle I had beautiful friends, a beautiful manor house, a beautiful lake, and beautiful mountains. Listen, did you ever course and race fine horses for mile after mile on the inside of a gallon bottle that had once contained Red Rosa wine? Were your evenings-at-home ever the most cultural in town, the most boozy, the most In-Groupy? Did you ever feel that your bottle was so full that it was running over?

Then disaster struck! Oh, it struck only five minutes ago. It was so sudden that I am not yet able to appreciate the magnitude of it. My seven best friends, including my fiancée, went up the ladder to the mouth of the bottle just at dawn after the happiest night we had ever experienced together. Then I looked up to watch them going, and I saw the *Lions in the Sky*, and I froze with fear and horror. And my friends, as they emerged from the throat of the bottle and began to say the three enlarging words, were slapped to their deaths. It was a mother cat there, and she slapped each of my friends (including my fiancée) to one of her seven kittens to eat like bugs.

This, since the striking of that disaster, has been the longest five minutes of my life.

Oh, I see too late that I am one of those humans who lacks the temperament to run an estate-in-a-bottle. And I failed to heed the warning of Ifrit about the dreaded Lions in the Sky. And now I fear that there is no way that I can escape gory death.

Still and all, I was the hottest host in town for a while, and to the Innest Group. And it may have been worth it.

The biggest of the Lions in the Sky, the mother cat, has her paw over the mouth of the bottle, and she is wobbling the bottle. By the flick of her giant tail in the sky I can tell that she is calculating everything minutely. She will tip the bottle. It will fall four feet to the concrete below, and it will shatter.

How fast can I say the three enlarging words after I stand free from the shattered bottle? How fast can the mother cat and those seven kittens pounce on what they believe is a tasty bug?

I'll race you for it, Lions in the Sky!

Contamination

Richard Bowker

*Richard Bowker lives in Massachusetts, where he belongs to
the same Cambridge writers workshop as Craig Shaw Gardner.
A couple of years ago Gardner introduced us, telling me that
Bowker, who at that point had sold only one story, to Antioch
Review, was a very fine writer indeed. And so he is. "Contamination" was his second short story sale, but other stories
have already appeared elsewhere and his first novel, Forbidden Sanctuary, was recently published by Del Rey.*

*In "Contamination," a very ordinary priest is sent on a
typical priestly mission, only to find that some very extraordinary circumstances prevail... circumstances for which, like
most of us, he is not quite prepared.*

You will recall, Your Eminence, that I never asked to be sent 7,000 light-years away from Rome. I admit to a certain amount of bad judgment, but after all—no, no, too whiny. *Erase all. Restart*.

Cardinal Todesco, I am preparing this report so that you will be apprised of the facts immediately upon my arrival. A more formal presentation will be prepared if you so desire. I do not wish to hide anything; rather, I trust that you will understand the complexities of the case, and make allowances accordingly.

As you recall, the Catholics in the Anthor colony had requested a priest to minister to their spiritual needs. The United Nations Commission on Extraterrestrial Exploration, after considerable delay, approved the request and sent it along to the Vatican. I was chosen to go (I am quoting from your letter of appointment) because of my pastoral experience, linguistic facility, diplomatic acumen, and my youth.

(Never mind that my pastoral experience consisted of six dismal months in a rundown inner-city parish in Hoboken before getting to Rome and wheedling my way into your Secretariat, and never mind that the best example of my diplomatic acumen has been to refrain from attacking you with the letter opener when you make some particularly asinine comment about, say, women priests.) *Erase paragraph*. Oh, never mind. I'll revise the printout.

Having received my orders, I departed for Anthor, with my Vatican career in limbo (or, more probably, consigned to a warmer region of the afterlife), and little idea what to expect. I knew that Anthor was the first planet with intelligent life on which a human colony had been set up. I knew that I was the first "person of the cloth" to go there. But beyond that, nothing.

I was intrigued, of course, by the prospect of seeing an alien: those "mild hirsute herbivores," *Time* called them in the one article I managed to read about the place. But what contact was I likely to have with them? UNCEE was, to put it mildly, paranoid about what it referred to as "cultural contamination." Economic realities had forced it to go along with the initial colonization agreement. The natives readily agreed to let us plunder their planet (what did they need with tungsten?) in return for simple advice on crop rotation, medical supplies, and as many jazz cassettes as we cared to give them (UNCEE was a little late on that one). It couldn't keep out *le jazz hot*, but it could prevent the Anthorians from swilling Coca-Cola and taking up touch football, at least until our exoethnologists and what-not got through studying them. No one talked to a native without permission, or without UNCEE personnel there to monitor the conversation. What reason could a priest have to talk to an Anthorian? So I endured the ennui of hyperspace (as I am enduring it now), and then settled into the ennui of colonial life.

For a while, of course, there is a tremendous sense of novelty: it is always raining, but it is not *Earth* rain; that creature which looks vaguely like a squirrel has a third eye in the back of its head and can hop two meters straight up; that smallish, loping animal with long dark hair runs a large farm near the human compound and likes Dizzy Gillespie.

But I am not a biologist, and the mysteries of that "squirrel" were only of passing interest to me. I'm not a metallurgist, to be concerned with the quality of the tungsten. I am a priest; a priest is interested in souls. And the souls on Anthor were no different from those in Hoboken, or Rome. There were the same sins, the same doubts, the same inchoate yearnings for God. I did my best to forgive the sins, ease the doubts, foster the yearnings.

The novelty, then, yielded to routine. Up at dawn (although we rarely saw the sun); a brisk walk through the drizzle to the Administration Building; celebrating Mass in the lounge area that UNCEE had grudgingly turned into a chapel. I was continually surprised by the attendance: engineers, technicians, programmers, laborers, day after day. Perhaps God's presence becomes important when "home" is an invisible speck in the night sky, or a videocassette delivered by the latest transport, played and replayed until one's lips move along with the message it repeats. I digress.

The mornings I usually spent with Tony Gammali, the zoologist, lending an inexperienced hand in turning the teeming planet into phyla and subphyla. The afternoons I spent in sick bay, giving comfort to the people with broken arms and appendicitis and (hardest of all) alien diseases that were far more frightening than they were dangerous. The evenings were my own, unless some troubled soul came by to confess his trifling offenses or to argue about free will. It was a quiet life.

The only excitement in it was provided by a certain Henry Farthing of the UNCEE command. Farthing is one of those people who was probably told by some senile priest that he would rot in hell for masturbating at the age of fifteen, and has had it in for the Church ever since. He is a thin, purse-lipped Englishman with shifty eyes and a dripping nose (the Anthorian climate doesn't agree with him). He was sure my presence on the planet was part of some obscure Jesuitical plot.

"The exploration of space must be a cooperative multinational effort for the benefit of all mankind. Religion and ideology have no place in this effort," he told me haughtily at our first, rigidly formal meeting.

"I entirely agree. However, the psychological and spiritual health of those who explore—"

"Such people should not have come into space, if they had need of this business"—waving at my lounge-chapel. "There are more than enough volunteers."

"But wouldn't exclusion of such people be a form of religious discrimination, which UNCEE professes to abhor?"

"They can believe whatever they like, so long as they don't ask for cargo space to bring an official representative of their religion."

Not a friend of the Church, Eminence.

I stayed out of his way in the months that followed, and I imagine he avoided me as well. I was a trifle surprised, then, when I found him standing at the door of my little cubicle one morning. "Ansus Hver has conveyed to me a desire to meet you," he said stiffly, not deigning to come into the room.

"Oh? Who is Ansus Hver?"

I don't think I have ever actually seen a man grit his teeth before. "Ansus Hver is the native chieftain in this region."

"Oh," I replied, suddenly quite interested. "Well of course I would be delighted to meet him."

"Her."

"Of course."

Farthing then went into what was evidently a carefully prepared speech about what would and would not happen. I would be allowed to meet Hver—Anthorian requests were granted whenever possible. A representative of UNCEE would be present at the meeting—in fact, he himself would go. I would answer Hver's questions fully, but would not volunteer information beyond what was requested. I would remember that, as a member of the colony, I was subject to all UNCEE regulations. I would report to his office in the Ad Building at 0900 tomorrow morning, and we would proceed from there to Hver's residence.

Very good, sir. Now what did this chieftain want with me? Farthing wasn't about to tell me, so I talked it over with a couple of the ethnologists in the rec room that night.

"She wants to chat, I'd guess," Dave Aronson said. "The Anthorian chieftain is the religious as well as civil ruler. Word probably got back to her what your position was here—these things do slip out—and she decided she'd like to talk religion with you."

"Has anyone 'talked religion' with her before?"

"After a fashion," Julie Fraser said. "But, what with UNCEE there, and none of us being, er, believers, I never got the feeling she was entirely satisfied."

"What's their religion like?" I had asked the question when I first arrived on the planet, and received nothing but bemused shrugs for an answer. I'd made a mental note to follow it up when I was a little more familiar with my surroundings. *Later* had become *now*, but the answer was no more enlightening.

Fraser and Aronson exchanged glances. "It'll probably be more interesting if you find out from her," Aronson said. "Wouldn't want to spoil it."

So at 0900 I presented myself at Farthing's office, ready for my

adventure—almost. "You will need a gift for the chieftain," Farthing said accusingly, as if I should have known.

"What do you suggest?"

He looked at me with disgust, wiped his nose, then consulted a
typed sheet. "Miles Davis. 'Bitch's Brew.' She likes Miles Davis."
He extracted a cassette from a desk drawer and slid it over to me.
"We shall bill you for it," he said.

And off we went. For once it wasn't raining, and we bumped
merrily along the rutted path in Farthing's two-seater, top down. I
listened to the strange cawings and cluckings from the alien forest,
and took quick, satisfied glimpses of the slightly-too-large sun.

Our compound had been built close, but not too close, to the
chieftain's residence. We wanted to be friendly, but we did not want
to contaminate. In fifteen minutes we came to a stop in front of a
large wooden building. Several natives were sitting on their haunches
in front, playing some game in the dirt. They looked up and made a
kind of elbowing-in-imaginary-ribs gesture with their hairy arms.
Farthing made the same gesture to them. "Greetings," he muttered.
The sound of a saxophone floated out to us. We went inside.

We stepped into a large, dark room that smelled of wet earth—
well, wet dirt. It seemed to be some sort of antechamber. A few
natives were sitting by a broad doorway on the other side of the
room, their eyes glowing catlike in the dark. They all moved away
from the door when they saw us. "We are always given precedence," Farthing said with a degree of self-satisfaction. He went
over and squatted by the door. I followed.

Eventually a long-armed young native loped out and elbowed to
Farthing, then silently turned and headed back toward the interior of
the building. We arose and went with him, through a narrow
passageway to a small, tapestried room. The saxophone music
ceased abruptly, and the fattest native I had seen was standing in
front of us, working both elbows in greeting.

"Agt, you may be excused," she whispered to the boy, who
slipped quietly out of the room. Then to us: "So nice of you both to
drop in." The Anthorian language was a compendium of clicks and
glottal stops that still managed to convey a sense of genteel politeness.

"So nice of you to invite us," I clicked back. "Please accept this small token of my esteem." I handed her the Miles Davis cassette while Farthing gaped in astonishment.

"When did you learn their language?" he whispered fiercely.

"Don't be impolite in front of our hostess." Your confidence in my linguistic ability was not misplaced, Eminence. The compound's library was well-stocked, and I had plenty of free time.

Hver took the cassette reverently and placed it on a small table next to her. I noticed a battery-powered tape deck and a stack of cassettes beneath the table. "I shall treasure this gift always," she gushed. "Please be seated."

Have you seen pictures of these creatures—their long, sloping foreheads, bushy eyebrows perpetually knitted in a quizzical expression, beaked noses, soft fleshy mouths, bodies covered with thick brown hair? Hver was no different, except for her size, and except that the hairless portions of her face were pale and wrinkled. It occurred to me that perhaps she never left this tiny room. Around her shoulders was a mauve cape with gold trim.

"I am so pleased that you were able to come see me," Hver said as I tried to make myself comfortable in the straight-backed wooden chair. "I have been told that you are the leader of your people's religion. I would so very much like to hear about this religion." She settled back in her own chair and folded her hands over her broad belly.

Before I had a chance to reply, Farthing jumped in. "Father Crimmins is not the leader, but only the representative of one of many religions on Earth, Esteemed Hver. We have developed a brief description of its beliefs for you. . . ." And he went on to give my answer for me, talking in foggy generalities about the Supreme Being, the Golden Rule, Love Thy Neighbor, and the like. I realized that he had planned to give his own version anyway as he interpreted for me. My sneaky trick of learning the language had forced him to be blatant about it.

Esteemed Hver listened attentively, with the air, I thought, of someone who knew she was never going to get any Coca-Cola and had reconciled herself to this state of affairs. "Most fascinating," she murmured. "Quite remarkable."

Yes indeed. And what was I supposed to do? She asked me a couple of questions about sin and salvation, but as soon as my answers started to get too precise, Farthing would break in and cloud things up. So eventually I tried another tack and started asking questions myself. "As you can tell, Esteemed Hver, there is much that can be said about my religion. But perhaps you would honor me by telling me something of the religion of which you are the revered leader."

Her eyebrows went up and down in what I took to be animated agreement. "Yes, wonderful, nothing would delight me more." Farthing looked glum, but said nothing.

Hver reached behind her and produced a small flat stone, which she tossed onto the table with a clatter. "Here is God," she said.

Pause. "Er, in the stone?" I inquired.

"In the throwing."

Oh. She held the stone up to me. One side had a line on it. "Yes," she said. The other side had a circle on it. "No," she said.

I thought I saw the light. "Chance," I murmured.

Her eyebrows went up and down. "Chance," she repeated. "What cannot be understood, can only be accepted. Why this, and not that. Why I sit here, and you sit there. What cannot be understood can only be worshiped. Do you see?"

"I think so." And then the questions began to come to me. "Why are you the chieftain?"

She flipped the stone. It fell with the line face up.

"Do your people come to you for decisions?"

"People must decide for themselves. But if the decision is too difficult, or too important—" she flipped the stone—"God will help them."

I was fascinated. I had always perceived God in the rationality of things; this was a perception of God through the irrational—or, more precisely, the arational. "Is that how you decided to let us come onto your planet?"

She flipped the stone.

"But this stone is not perfectly formed," I said. "One side will come up more than the other. That takes away from the element of chance, doesn't it?"

"I have many stones. Which one I pick is determined by God."

"Is that why you like jazz—because it's so. . . . random, improvisational?"

"God speaks through your wonderful musicians. I wish God would speak as clearly through me."

I got in a few more questions before Farthing had had enough and interrupted. "Let us not weary the Esteemed Hver with our inquiries. I am sure she has matters of much greater consequence to attend to."

Hver did not disagree, although I'm sure she wouldn't have minded continuing with the interrogation. We all stood and made polite noises for a few moments. Then she reached down, picked up the stone, and handed it to me. "I give you God," she said.

"Oh no, I couldn't, I—"

"Plenty more," she said. "God comes in handy sometimes."

I did not disagree. On the way out I looked more closely at the game the Anthorians were playing in the dirt. They were all flipping stones—endlessly flipping stones.

I met Aronson and Fraser again that evening, and told them my tale.

"It's an intriguing concept, isn't it?" Aronson said. "It pervades their culture."

"But it must have terrible effects—I mean, what if God says not to plant crops this year?"

"They don't ask questions like that, though, because the answers are obvious. All sorts of religions on Earth rely on omens and the like. Some people would say all of them do. The Anthorians aren't harmed by it any more than the ancient Romans were harmed by the haruspex examining the entrails of goats."

"I think I disagree, Dave," Julie Fraser said. "There is a qualitative difference here. The Romans thought the entrails contained a message *from* God; these people would say the entrails *are*

God. The difference is subtle, but I think it might have far-reaching effects.''

"Actually," I observed, "according to Hver, it wouldn't be the entrails, but the act of looking at them, that would constitute the presence of God. I think."

I know how bored Your Eminence gets with theological speculation, so I will leave (reluctantly) that conversation, which lasted long into the night, and pass on to more difficult matters.

Things returned to their usual dull state for a while: the same faces at Mass, the same sins at confession, the same rain falling every day. Then one morning I was out collecting specimens for Tony Gammali, tramping through the thick underbrush of the nearby forest, when I felt a hand on my shoulder. I spun and glimpsed the hairy arm connected to it, and there was an instant of total panic, followed by the shamefaced realization that this alien would no more harm me than I would harm him. "Hello," I clicked.

"Hello," he replied.

Somehow he looked familiar—but perhaps every native would look familiar to me. He also looked nervous. "My name is John Crimmins," I said.

"Agt Kon." He was thin and short, with long arms. His head was tilted slightly as he looked at me, like a kitten appraising a ball of yarn.

Agt. My linguistic facility, Eminence. "You were at Hver's residence. You brought us in to her."

He raised and lowered his eyebrows, but remained silent, appraising.

"Er, can I do something for you?"

Indeed I could. "I am a student of the Esteemed Hver," he said in as soft a tone as his language could produce. "She chooses some of us to initiate into the mysteries of the God-stones. Someday, if God chooses, I may become a thrower myself, perhaps even a chieftain. I overheard much of your conversation with the Esteemed Hver. It is not right, but I am required to sit by the door and I cannot help but hear sometimes. What was said about your religion made me curious to learn more. Would you be willing to teach me about what you believe?"

I was not happy to hear this. "I—er—uh, I'm not supposed to talk with a native alone, Agt. Especially about religion."

"But I wish to learn—perhaps to believe as you do."

"People worship in many different ways, Agt. The way of your people may be a good one."

"But something must be either true, or not," he replied, quite Thomistically. "I wish to discover the truth."

"Won't you get in trouble with Hver if she finds out?"

"That is up to God."

Yes, I could see that it would be. I finally agreed to meet him two days later at the same spot. I would tell him then what I would do. I finished collecting my specimens, then went back to my little room and stared at the ceiling.

As you are probably aware, Your Eminence, the Church has not exactly rushed to make a decision on the question of whether aliens have souls. Most theologians agree that intelligent aliens do possess souls, but no official position has been taken. Not having answered that question, the Church has nothing to say about its follow-up: if aliens have souls, what should we do about it? Should the Faith be propagated among creatures with wings and antennae, or eyes in the back of their heads—or God-stones?

If the answer is yes, then there are still practical considerations. What would be the consequences of satisfying this young native's curiosity? If I was caught in flagrant violation of UNCEE's regulations, would that be the end of the Church's brief venture offplanet? Was the risk worth it?

Do you see my dilemma, Your Eminence? Do you understand the difficulty of the decision I faced? I walked like a zombie through my duties the rest of that day, and all of the next, as I wrestled with the problem. At night I prayed, but I have always had difficulty in knowing when my prayers have been answered. I thought of speaking to Aronson, or Tony Gammali, but what could they tell me about the situation that I didn't already know?

Finally, on the second morning, the decision was made. I donned my rain slicker and found my way back to the spot of our previous meeting. Agt was waiting, squatting on the soggy ground, head tilted as he watched me come. "Do you still want to learn?" I asked him.

"Oh, most certainly."

I squatted beside him. "Then let us begin."

Agt proved to be a sharp and stimulating catechumen. We would meet every few days for about an hour; he would listen attentively to my explanations, and then he would produce an endless stream of questions. Some were familiar to any priest:

"If God is all-merciful, then why does He allow so much suffering?"

"If God knows everything that we do, then how can we be said to have free will?"

"Original sin seems unfair. Why should a person be penalized for something he didn't do?"

And some of his questions were, perhaps, unique:

"Why is God so concerned with Earth people?"

"Do all living creatures share in Christ's redemption, or just Earth people?"

"If Anthorians are different, would the concept of what is sinful be different for them?"

I did my best. Often I would throw up my hands and say I had no answer for his question. Occasionally I would take a stab at it: "God is not more concerned with Earth people than He is with Anthorians, or any other race. I am just telling you how He made His will manifest on our planet. He might choose a totally different way on yours."

Agt took a stone out of his pocket and tossed it. "Like this?"

I threw up my hands. "I don't know."

Can you picture us there, in the eternal drizzle, sitting on rotting tree stumps, clicking, growling, gesticulating, as we tried to reach a common understanding of a faith he had never experienced, born in a race whose home he would never see? Of course I was doing no more than what others like me have been doing for over two millennia, but perhaps you will understand that I felt this was something special.

These clandestine meetings gave a constant edge of fear to my life. Surely Farthing could see my face turn red as we passed in the corridor. Surely that movement in the brush was an UNCEE patrol, come to take me into custody. More than once I was ready to tell Agt: you've learned enough, I'm not used to breaking rules, let's stop right now. But his eager questioning made it impossible: how could I deny him the knowledge he wanted so badly?

Agt, on the other hand, seemed to be little concerned by what would happen to him if he were discovered. "My people do not care especially about such things," he replied when I mentioned this to him. "I have heard the Esteemed Hver say that all your precautions are fruitless, that the two races will mingle as they wish, because that is the way of life."

"But much of what you hear or receive from us might be bad," I pointed out, agreeing at least in principle with UNCEE's regulations.

"That is not for you to decide. We are not stupid."

No, they are not.

Was I trying to convert him? I kept denying it to myself. I was merely providing him with information. I was merely answering his questions. But how can you merely answer questions about something you believe in so strongly yourself? If he disagreed with me about something, I would try to persuade him: look, this is the truth, this is what you need to know, how can I make you understand?

But I never really knew if I was making any progress. Intellectual arguments are not ultimately convincing in religious matters. A leap of faith is required. Usually (it is my experience) you can tell when that leap has been made: the questions start assuming belief (changing from "If God is all-good, why . . ." to "Since God is all-good, why . . ."); they start nibbling at the technicalities and the moral issues—the Virgin Birth, Infallibility, abortion—but don't worry about the larger matters. The person starts seeing the world through Catholic eyes.

This never really happened with Agt. His initial curiosity never seemed to deepen into commitment. Whenever I thought I saw a glimmer of belief, it would immediately disappear behind those cat's eyes, and the unrelenting questioning would continue.

One day I asked him. "You want to discover the truth, Agt. Do you think what I am telling you is the truth?"

He paused for a long time as the forest twittered around him. "What is truth?" he asked finally. Jesus had no answer for Pilate; I simply threw up my hands and continued my teaching.

And, of course, one morning Farthing showed up at my room, eyes burning laser holes through my skull. "You know a native by the name of Agt Kon?" he intoned, as if uttering a death sentence.

I nodded.

"Kon's parents are among the more influential farmers in the region. The other day they came upon some notes he had made. They couldn't make any sense out of them—there were mysterious phrases like Holy Trinity, Deposit of Faith, Immaculate Conception. They brought the notes to me."

"I see."

"I had to explain to them what the notes were about, of course. They became quite upset. It seems this fellow Kon is highly regarded by Hver, and the parents have had hopes that he would be her successor. They have gone to speak with Hver. Before I throw you off this planet, I think we had better go speak with her too."

"Very well."

Farthing's facade of righteous anger at my provocation barely concealed his intense satisfaction. All his darkest fantasies had come true, and now he had me where he wanted me.

We drove to Hver's residence in silence. Fog swirled around us, making me feel as though I were in some second-rate movie fantasy, heading toward the Pearly Gates. How would I be judged?

The same hangers-on were lounging outside the wooden building. Did they glance at us more curiously as we passed? The same eyes shone at us in the antechamber, there was the same unspoken agreement to move away from the door and give us precedence. No one came to greet us this time, however, so we walked down the passageway to Hver's room.

It was already crowded. Agt was standing in one corner, behind Hver. His parents, both tall, slim, distinguished-looking, were seated in front of Hver. They turned as we entered. If it occurred to them to show their anger toward me the impulse was quickly defeated. They stood and jabbed their elbows silently.

"So nice of you to come," Hver said cheerfully. "We were just talking about you, as a matter of fact. Please come in."

We scrunched in. I found myself next to Agt, who glanced at me briefly and then looked away. Farthing held out a cassette to Hver. "Ella Fitzgerald, Esteemed Hver. I hope you will be pleased with our humble offering."

Hver accepted it graciously. "Your generosity is legendary. I adore scat."

Farthing inclined his head in acknowledgment. "You are too kind. As you can see, I have brought this man Crimmins with me, so that he can apologize to you and to the parents of Agt Kon for his reprehensible interference in the religion and customs of your people."

All eyes turned to me. I took a deep breath, and addressed Hver. "I endeavored to give Agt information that he asked for," I said. "If this has given offense, then I am sorry."

"It is Agt's fault," the father said angrily. "What was he doing, bothering the Earth people like that? Doesn't he have enough to study, without learning their weird beliefs?"

"Crimmins is to blame," the mother responded. "It is against Earth laws to do what he did. He is older. He should know better."

"The boy is old enough. And he knew it was against Earth laws as well. He must be punished, and I would like the Esteemed Hver to determine the suitable punishment."

"Surely curiosity is no crime. Our society fosters it. And furthermore. . . ."

As the argument raged I glanced again at Agt. He was gazing now at Hver, and his gaze did not waver. Hver was listening, eyes half-closed, hands folded over her belly. Finally she made the barest flicker of a gesture with her right hand. Agt immediately reached down and got her a stone. She tossed it into the air. The clatter of its landing on the table stopped all conversation. She turned to Agt and pointed to the line on the stone. Yes.

Agt looked at it, then looked up. "I am sorry for any trouble I have caused. The Esteemed Hver asked me to find out what I could about this religion. I have done my best to obey."

End of climax. The parents fell all over themselves apologizing to everyone (evidently not disturbed that Hver had chosen to play a trick on them as well as me). Farthing asked plaintively why, if Hver had wanted more information, she had not simply asked. He would have been glad to provide it. I stared at Agt, but he was intently moving the stone this way and that on the rickety table. He would not look at me.

Am I to be blamed for feeling a bit betrayed? Surely if he had simply told me the truth he would have learned as much, without having to fool me and make me hope. . . .

But then again, perhaps not. I thought of how impassioned I had occasionally become as I sensed that I might be acquiring a convert. Surely Agt had learned more from those sessions than from a dry recitation of beliefs. They are not stupid.

Before we left, I asked Hver what she thought of my religion, now that she had made its acquaintance.

"A delightful set of beliefs," she said pleasantly. "I have no doubt that they are all true."

I did not ask her if she cared to be baptized.

"You're under arrest," Farthing informed me as we drove back to the compound.

And so I was, after a fashion. He couldn't exactly throw me off the planet until the transport arrived, which wasn't for a couple of weeks. So, like an angry father with a naughty child, he told me to go to my room and stay there.

There have been worse prisons. I managed to stay dry for the first time on the planet. I had access to the library through my viewscreen. My friends would stop by to chat and commiserate. But I was hardly in the best of moods. I kept seeing Agt's face, eyes wide and serious, following my every gesture as I strove to explain my faith to him. It would take time for me to get used to the hypocrisy behind that gaze.

The transport arrived, delivering its new experts and equipment and jazz cassettes. My time grew short. On the night before my departure Dave Aronson dropped by with a pint of whisky. He poured us each a drink and saluted me. "Boy, you sure screwed up good," he said.

"You are too kind," I responded, Hverianly.

He grinned. "Can you keep a secret until after your deportation?"

"I suppose so."

"I just got back from doing some field interviews about mating customs—chatting with young natives, mostly, along with the UNCEE rep of course. I was with a group today, and one of them got me alone when the rep was taking a leak. Seems this friend of hers had been talking to her about some strange Earth beliefs: things about three-headed Gods, wine turning into blood, people coming up out of graves. She thought he was making it all up, but just wanted to be sure."

"And you said—"

"I said no, he wasn't, some people on Earth actually do believe that stuff."

"Good of you. And she said—"

"And she said, isn't that strange, because my friend seems to believe the stuff too."

There was a pause. "Seems to," I repeated.

"Then the rep came back, so that's all I know. Take it or leave it."

"It looks like I'll be leaving it, whether I want to or not. But still—"

"But still, it looks like you've sown your seed. If Farthing ever finds out—"

"If Farthing ever finds out, I'm 7,000 light-years away, and the damage has been done. Cheers."

"Cheers."

Sowing seeds. Contamination, Farthing would call it. Depends on your point of view.

And, perhaps not surprisingly, it works both ways. I will not forget Agt's face, although now the memory of it will tantalize instead of infuriate me. And I will not forget Hver, or her gift. . . .

You see, I really could not make up my mind. Surely it was good to teach Christianity to an Anthorian, but surely it was bad to risk the Church's fragile place among the stars for such small hope of reward. How was I to decide?

God. In the gloomy morning, after a sleepless night, I tossed the stone into the air, and watched it land with a thud on my bedspread. Ashamed of myself, I looked. A circle. No.

And of course I forced myself to do the opposite. But God is in the throwing, Hver had said, and I had thrown it. I do not believe in it—perhaps Agt does not believe in Christianity—but perhaps the seed has been sown.

The stone sits in front of me now. Should I bother with this report, or will it only make things worse for me? Should I tell you how I really feel, or should I obscure everything in Vatican legalese? Do you see the temptation, Your Eminence? Only God knows, and it's so easy to ask Him:

Yes
No
Yes
No
Yes
No—

And there you have it. *Erase all.*

Instant With Loud Voices

Alan Dean Foster

Alan Dean Foster is perhaps best known as the novelizer of such science fiction media phenomena as Outland, Alien, *and* Clash of the Titans, *but he is also a successful novelist in his own right. I first encountered his work in a short story in a magazine and liked it enough to seek out more. His stories (such as those collected in* With Friends Like These . . .*) are marked by unobtrusively clever construction, an interest in the latest developments in science, and in the implications of those developments.*

"Instant With Loud Voices" arrived in my mail many months before the publication of Tracy Kidder's The Soul of a New Machine, *but they both deal with similar ideas, concepts to make us thoughtful about the tools we use so casually, everything from a pocket calculator to the word processor on which I'm writing this.*

How the devil was he going to tell Hank Strevelle that his life's work wouldn't work? As he hurried down the brightly lit white corridor, Ken Jerome tried to compose the right words as well as himself.

The remote unit via which he'd run the final check hung loosely from his right hand. His lab coat fluttered from his shoulders. The corridor was a football field of eggshell white, the remote unit a rectangular ball, and he was running, running hard and uncertainly toward the wrong goal.

There was nothing wrong with the concept of the question. It was the figuring that troubled Jerome. That, and the fact that no one knew if a machine could be mentally overstressed.

He'd spent a last hectic week reprocessing, rechecking. Wilson at MIT had confirmed his calculations, but at this late stage even Wilson's prestige might not be enough to get the question aborted.

He rounded the last bend in the main corridor. The guard smiled as he held up a restraining hand. Jerome had to wait impatiently while his identity tag was checked against the records. He was panting heavily. Forty-nine unathletic years old, and it was a long time since he'd run this far with anything heavier than a new equation.

The guard was smiling at him with maddening politeness. He was a handsome young man, probably a moonlighting theater arts student waiting for some visiting producer or director to stumble over his cleft chin.

"Nice day, sir. You should slow down. You look a little flushed."

Wait till you hit the archaic side of forty, Jerome thought. But all he said as he retrieved his ident card was, "I expect I do." The guard stood aside as the diminutive engineer hurried through the double doors.

Down another corridor, this one narrower and underpopulated.

Through another check station, four glass doors strong enough to have defeated Dillinger, and into The Room. The Room was the only one in the building. It *was* the building. It had been built to house a single important entity and its attendants. Jerome was one of the attendants. The entity was DISRA—Direct Information Systematic Retrieval and Analysis.

The Room was a modest three stories high and roughly the length and width of a football field (I must be going through male menopause, Jerome thought idly, to account for all these sports metaphors here lately). As human constructions went, it was not especially awesome. Nor was the physical appearance of DISRA overwhelming. What it represented was.

The flat sides of the three-story machine were transparent, allowing inspection of the exterior components. Yellow and white monitoring lights winked on and off, giving the epidermis of the machine the aspect of a captured night sky. They indicated to any knowledgeable onlooker that the computer was powered up and working on only minor problems.

If a similar machine had been built back in the 1950's it would have covered most of North America and still been inferior in capability to DISRA. Twenty years of effort, money and intelligence had gone into its construction. Jerome had been involved with the project for the last ten of those years.

Each year new techniques, new knowledge, were acquired and immediately integrated into the design of the machine. Its architect, Henry Strevelle, was no dogmatic, blind believer in his own omnipotence. He was as flexible as his creation and eager to adapt the best ideas of others into its framework.

If only he'll be flexible now, Jerome thought worriedly.

DISRA had been in operation for the past six years, answering questions, pondering hypotheses, dispensing immensely valuable opinions on everything from Keynesian versus Marxist economics to particle physics. When the Secondary Matrix was linked with the DISRA Prime two years ago, Catastrophe Theory had for the first time taken on the aspect of a real science. DISRA had shown itself capable of predicting major earthquakes as well as fish population stocks. Space probes of many nations and consortiums were now programed with previously unimaginable accuracy.

Six months ago construction on DISRA Prime itself had concluded. After a month of testing, Hank Strevelle had begun the task of programing the complex for a single question.

And, Jerome knew, DISRA was too valuable to mankind for that question to be asked.

He found Strevelle conversing with two technicians. The world's greatest computer scientist was six-four, thin as an oxygen tank and nearly as pale as the enclosing walls. His hair was brushed straight back and gave him the look of a man always walking into the wind. Jerome envied him the hair as much as the brain beneath. We are all frail, he thought.

Strevelle looked away from the techs as Jerome came over. He smiled tolerantly. He knew what was coming. Jerome had been badgering him with it for weeks.

"Now Ken," he said, "you're not going to hit me with your pet peeve again, are you? Now, of all times?" He glanced at his wrist. "Five minutes to startup. Give me a break, will you?"

Jerome conducted his words by waving the remote. "I've spent all night and most of the morning hooked up with the Eastern Nexus. Everything confirms what I've been telling you since the fourth of the month. You put this question to DISRA and we're liable to lose the whole works. A computer can be overstressed. Not a normal computer, but nothing about DISRA is normal."

"You're a good man, Ken. Best theoretical engineer I ever worked with. You'll probably be chosen to run DISRA operations when I retire."

"I can't run what isn't there."

Strevelle let out a resigned sigh. "Look, there are two and a half decades of my life and most of my reputation in this cube of circuits and bubbles and agitated electrons." He jerked a thumb back at the softly humming machine. "D'you really think I'd risk all that if I believed there was the slightest chance of losing capacity, let alone more serious damage?

"The machine runs twenty hours each day, four down for repair and recheck. Half the world depends on it to make decisions, or at least to offer opinions. Even the Soviets want it kept functional. They haven't experienced a single wheat or corn failure in the ten years they've been relying on DISRA's predictions."

"Wilson confirms my calculations."

For a moment the great man appeared uncertain. "Kenji Wilson, at MIT?" Jerome nodded. Strevelle mulled that over, then his paternal smile and eternal optimism reasserted themselves.

"Wilson's the best alive, Ken. I won't deny that. But he bases his calculus on DISRA's own information and DISRA doesn't seem disinclined to try the question. Besides which he doesn't know DISRA the way I do."

"Nobody alive does, Hank. You know that." He desperately tried another tack. "Look, if I can't get you to call this off, at least postpone it so I can refine the figures." He held up the remote, touched tiny buttons. A series of equations flashed across the small screen, hieroglyphs of a physics so advanced that fewer than a hundred minds in the world could comprehend it.

Strevelle shook his head. "I've seen your work for weeks, Ken. I don't buy it." He gestured toward the control booth, led Jerome toward it. "There are five senators there plus representatives from all over Europe and Asia. I can't put them off." His eyes gleamed from under brows tufted with fleece.

"You know what that group of senators promised me? That if we derive any kind of sensible answer to the question, anything at all, they're going to try and put through appropriations to double DISRA's capacity. *Double* it. I won't be around to see that happen, but I don't care. It'll be my legacy, the first computer that doesn't just approximate the ability of a human brain but equals or surpasses it."

"Run this program," Jerome said, "and you're liable not to *have* any legacy, Hank." I'm not saying it right, he told himself frustratedly. I'm not making my point strongly enough, emotionally enough. I'm a bland personality and I live with a calculator. Damn to the hundredth power! He's going to go through with it.

The equations weren't solid enough, he knew. Though given the glow of the great man's expression, Jerome wasn't sure the solidest math in the universe could have dissuaded him today. He resigned himself to the asking of the question.

Five senators. Jerome tried to tell himself that he was wrong, that Wilson was wrong. They could be. Certainly Strevelle knew what he was doing. They'd said DISRA couldn't be built and Strevelle had built it. He'd proven everyone wrong. Among his early detractors had been the youthful, brilliant theoretician named Kenneth Jerome.

I hope to God he proves me wrong again.

There were quiet greetings and introductions, idle conversation to cover nervousness. Only a couple of reporters had been allowed in, one from the New York *Times*, the other from *Der Spiegel*. Friends of Strevelle from the early days of derision and doubt. Now they would receive recompense for that early support. Strevelle never forgot a circuit, or a friend.

He folded himself into a chair next to the master control board, touched instrumentation, murmured to his ready associates. Jerome stood back among the curious. He was Strevelle's backup in case the great man had a stroke or forgot some item of programing. But Strevelle had the body of a man half his age and the mind of several. He would not collapse either physically or mentally.

"Quiet, please," a technician requested. The multilingual muttering in the booth faded to silence.

Strevelle thumbed a switch. "Condition?"

"Ready," replied a tech.

"Secondary Matrix?"

"On-line," came the quiet announcement.

Strevelle was too prosaic to construct a dramatic gesture. He just touched the button.

Banks of monitors sang in unison behind the watchers. Beyond the angled glass, out in The Room, thousands of tiny indicator lights suddenly flared green, red, blue. The inspiration was wholly mechanical, but it had the look of a hundred Christmas trees suddenly winking to life simultaneously, and provoked appreciative murmurs of admiration from the non-scientists in the group.

There were eight DISRA-2's emplaced in major cities across the

United States, four more in Europe, four again in Japan. The Japanese were not involved in the question because of time-sharing conflicts and other problems. Together, the sixteen constituted the Secondary Matrix. They would combine to ask the question which DISRA Prime would attempt to answer.

Six massive communications satellites were temporarily taken out of commercial service to shunt the constituents of the question to DISRA, shutting down half the communications of Europe and the continental United States for fully eight minutes. It was dark outside The Room and still not morning in London. The timing had been carefully planned to cause minimal disruption to the world's commerce.

Five months of laborious pre-programing now spewed in an electronic torrent from two continents into the waiting storage banks of DISRA Prime, filling them to capacity.

The eight minutes passed in tense silence. Jerome found that his palms were damp.

The digital clock on the wall marked time silently, continued past the eight minute mark as the technician on Strevelle's right said calmly, "Programing received."

In The Room DISRA glowed like some ponderous deep-sea monster, awaiting instructions. It's not human, Jerome reminded himself firmly. It's different, and in its limited way superior, but it's not human. Even Strevelle agrees to that.

Strevelle touched the button beneath the plate which read, "Process question," then sat back and lit a small, feminine cigar. The onlookers shuffled uneasily. A red light came on beneath another readout and the single word everyone was waiting for appeared there: WORKING.

Someone made a bad joke in French. A few people laughed softly. Everything was functioning properly. It was the import of the question that had been put to DISRA which was making them nervous, not any fear of mechanical failure.

DISRA worked on the question, digesting at incredible speed the immense volume of programing it had been fed. Normally, the most complicated inquiry took less than three minutes to solve. The digital on the wall counted.

Half an hour passed. The readout on the console glowed steadily red. WORKING. The lights behind the transparent panels of the machine flashed rapidly, efficiently. While they waited, the onlookers discussed science, politics, their personal travails and problems.

The power requirements for such processing were enormous, another reason for running the program at night. Demand in the city was way down. As it was, there was still barely enough power to meet the demand, but the local utilities had been notified well in advance and were prepared to deal with any possible blackouts. Extra power had been purchased from out-of-state utilities to help cope with the temporary drain.

Forty minutes. Jerome considered. Better that he be proven wrong, much better. Of course, even if he and Wilson were correct, nothing might happen. When it was all over he intended to be the first to congratulate Strevelle. Despite their disagreement in this, they were anything but rivals.

For the first time in several weeks his concern gave way to curiosity. After all, he was as interested as anyone else in the machine's answer.

To support DISRA's pondering, everything known or theorized about the Big Bang had been programed into it. That included just about the entire body of physics, chemistry, astronomy and a number of other physical sciences, not to mention all of philosophy and more. All in support of one question.

When was the Big Bang and what, precisely, did it consist of?

An equation for the Creation, Jerome mused. There were a few who'd argued against asking the question, but they were in the minority and outvoted. Many prominent theologians had helped with the progaming. They were as anxious for a reply as the astronomers. DISRA would answer first in figures, then in words.

Forty-five minutes. One of the technicians on Strevelle's right leaned suddenly forward but did not take his eyes from the console. "Sir?"

Strevelle glanced down at him. He'd gone through four of the small cigars and was on his fifth. "Trouble?"

"Maybe. I'm not sure. We're running at least two cyclings now, maybe more."

Jerome joined Strevelle at the technician's station. Cycling occurred when a component of a question could not be either solved or disregarded. Yet the machine was programed to answer. Its design demanded an answer. If not shut down or if the programing was not canceled, the same information would be run over and over, at greater strength and drawing on greater reserves. It was a rare occurrence.

"Four sections cycling now, sir. If the figures are right." He looked anxiously up at Strevelle.

"Cancel it, Hank," Jerome urged him quietly. "While there's still time."

"Eight sections, sir." The technician no longer tried to hide his nervousness. "Ten. Twelve."

There were forty sections comprising DISRA Prime. Forty sections devoted to Direct Information Systematic Retrieval and Analysis. Strevelle said nothing, stared stolidly down at the console, then out at the working machine.

"We've still plenty of capacity. Let it cycle."

"Come on, Hank," Jerome muttered intensely. "It's not going to work. You've reached beyond the machine's capacity. I told you."

"Nothing's beyond DISRA's capacity. We've asked it a perfectly logical question and supplied it with sufficient information to answer. I expect an answer." He put both hands on the console and leaned forward, his nose nearly touching the slanting glass.

"Twenty sections," muttered the technician. All the other technicians were watching his station now. "Thirty . . . thirty-five. . . ." Behind them something was buzzing, louder than the crowd.

"Forty . . . all sections cycling, sir." The technician's voice had turned hoarse.

Out in The Room there was no sign anything out of the ordinary was taking place. On the console WORKING continued to glow its steady red.

Then someone turned a spotlight on Jerome's face and just as quickly turned it out. . . .

* * *

The glass had missed him. So had most of the flying scrap. One of the support beams had not.

Still, he was one of the first out of the hospital, and the arm was healing nicely. He didn't need it for a while anyway, since there was nothing to work on for at least a month. Strevelle was already drawing up his new plans, dictating them from his hospital bed.

The roof was mostly gone, blown skyward to fall back in or to dust the campus, but the reinforced concrete walls had held. They'd been designed to withstand Richter scale nine earthquakes and near nuclear explosions. A little internal blowup had strained but not shattered them.

In the remnants of The Room workmen were cleaning up the last of the debris while technicians were already discussing where to begin rebuilding. DISRA resembled a cake that had fallen in on itself. About seventy percent of the machine was completely gone, scattered across the surrounding community in tiny pieces or else vaporized during the overload. So rapid was the final cycling even the safeties had been overloaded. The city-wide blackout had lasted two hours.

Jerome strolled around The Room, picking his way carefully over the remaining debris, chatting with those technicians he knew. There was no air of depression about The Room. An experiment had failed, that was all. Time to rebuild and try it again.

A slight figure near one of the walls was neither workman nor tech. Jerome squinted, thought he recognized the man, and made his way across to him.

"Hello. Hernandez, isn't it? From the *Times?* You were in the booth with us when she blew."

The man turned away from his examination of the concrete, smiled from beneath an afterthought of a mustache and extended a hand. "Yes. You're Dr. Jerome, aren't you? I understand the old man's already planning DISRA Prime Two."

For some reason Jerome felt embarrassed. "Yes. He's incorrigible. But we have to have a DISRA. The Secondary Matrix can only handle so many of the lesser inquirires. The world needs its questions answered."

"But not today's." Hernandez chuckled. "The astronomers will have to wait at least another generation."

"For that question? I don't think the government will let them try it again. Too much money for too little return."

"Oh?" The reporter was jotting notes down on a small pad. He's old-fashioned, Jerome mused. An odd trait to find in a science reporter.

Hernandez noticed his stare. "Tape recorders aren't right for every situation. There are people working here and I don't want to bother them. You're not bothered?"

"No. Just sore. It could've been a lot worse. Ninety-five percent of the energy seemed to go skyward instead of sideways."

"I know. I put that in my article."

"So I heard. Thanks for your kindness. We're going to need all the help we can get, despite the need for a new DISRA. Our public image isn't exactly at its most polished right now."

"Doesn't matter. As you say, the world needs a DISRA, and the public hardly suffered." He waved his pen at the wall. "A few people thought DISRA was the mechanical equivalent of a human being."

"A few people believe in astrology, too. DISRA was a brilliant machine, but that's all. Its superiority was limited to a few specific areas."

"Of course." Hernandez made some more notations, then indicated the wall. His voice lost some of its usual reportorial smoothness.

"Have you noticed the lines and markings on the concrete?"

Jerome had not paid much attention to the scorching. His attention had been centered on the ruined machine in the middle of The Room. But the source of the marks was obvious enough.

"You remember that most of DISRA's exterior paneling was transparent," Jerome said, "When she blew, the intense light was slightly masked by dark circuitry." He tapped the wall. "So we got these negative images seared into the walls, sort of a flash blueprint."

"That's what I thought." Hernandez nodded slowly. "I've seen such things before, only the outline was human and not mechanical.''

"Oh, you mean the Hiroshima silhouettes," Jerome said, "the outlines burnt into the streets and walls of people close to the bomb when it was dropped?"

"I wasn't thinking of them," the reporter murmured. He traced some of the circuit patterns with his pen. "These are much more detailed, more delicately shaded than just a plain outline."

"That's explainable." Jerome wondered what the reporter was driving at.

"You know," said Hernandez quietly, "there's intelligence, and there's intelligence. There are representations of man and representations of man. Sometimes you can ask too much of a man just as you can of a machine. It's taken us a long time to reach the stage where we could make a machine suffer like a man."

"If it suffered," said Jerome chidingly, "it didn't suffer like a man."

"I wonder," said the reporter.

"You said you've seen such markings before." Jerome tried to bring the conversation back to a sensible tack. "If not the Hiroshima markings, then where?"

Hernandez turned, sat down on a broken conduit and regarded the remnants of the machine the bulk of whose substance had vanished.

"On an old shroud, in Italy, in Turin. . . ."

Firestorm

Steve Rasnic Tem

Steve Rasnic Tem is a widely published poet who lives in Denver, Colorado, with his wife, writer Melanie Tem. He is a gentle, soft-spoken man whose manner belies the careful intensity of his stories. Those stories are much appreciated; since he made his first fiction sale to Ramsey Campbell's New Terrors three years ago, he has sold more than forty of them. He is currently editing an anthology of science fiction poetry with a grant from the National Endowment for the Arts.

"Firestorm" is his longest published story to date. It raises some harrowing possibilities about yesterday ... and some even more harrowing ones about tomorrow.

The flash that covered the city in morning mist
was much like an instant dream.
                              —Kyoku Kaneyama

*He was not very old, as gods go. He could still remember that
brief instant of his creation, and would remember it for all time. But
without the need for understanding.*

*The winds like silver and black hair for him, fire like speech,
uncontrolled, the power giving him wings, filling the sky with flame
as he rose into the air. Turning the ground below into fire and light,
discoloring concrete to a reddish tint. Granite surfaces peeled like
onion skin. A pedestrian incinerated, his shadow a bas relief on a
stone wall. Wide cracks in buildings, upturned faces gone white,
metallic ...*

*... like his own face, he somehow knew, and the word they were
thinking, the name they were giving him ... the "flashboom," Pikadon.
The new god ...*

September 14, 1965 ...

Tom woke up in his hotel room, feverish, shaking. Again he had
had the dream of burning up in the holocaust, only to rise phoenix-
like and spread the destruction outward, back to his home in
America. In the dream he tried to stop himself, but was completely
out of control. He was surprised at the depth of his anger toward his
country. He was beginning to understand how profoundly his father
had been affected by the war, the division in loyalties. And,
uncomfortably, he was seeing in himself signs of his father's
obsessions.

Tom had come to Japan to do a story on the "New Religions,"
the numerous sects which had sprung up since the defeat. He knew a

major reason he had been selected was his Japanese-American
ancestry. There had been another, more experienced, Religion reporter on his paper. This bothered him, but he thought the trip to
Japan might help him understand some things. It was a religious
quest, really. A search for context, for meaning.

Even though his family had been in the States almost a hundred
years, he felt some ambivalence about America's role in the war. He
dreamed about Hiroshima regularly. More than once he had screamed
himself awake, feeling his skin burning from his body. The most
disturbing aspect of those dreams, however, was that he was also the
pilot of the plane carrying the bomb.

In the dream he prayed before dropping the bomb. The bomb was
an offering, a gift to his god. A sacrifice. A return home. He wasn't
sure; the dream kept changing.

The last months of the war Tom, just a boy, had seen a dramatic
deterioration in his father's mental condition. He could not understand how his father could change so quickly. It seemed magical,
evil. He sometimes imagined his father had been kidnapped and that
the FBI had put this imposter in his place to spy on them.

It was a crazy time. There were rumors of hostile warships
cruising off the California coast.

His father had been a religious man. But toward the end he was
cursing the "white" god, and wouldn't allow his children to go to
white churches. He imagined he was under surveillance. Tom
remembered his father's shock and outrage when Japanese products
and art objects were burned or buried by angry neighbors.

His father clipped pieces out of the newspaper, hateful things, and
read them to the family at dinner. "This one says we should be
deported! This one that we are liars, barbarians, not to be trusted!"
Later Tom heard a violent argument between his parents, and
discovered by eavesdropping that his father was taping these articles
above his bed.

A Jap's a Jap . . . no way to determine their loyalty. You can't
change him by giving him a piece of paper.—Lt. General John L.
DeWitt, 1943.

California was zoned, the Japanese-Americans barred completely from Category A zones: San Francisco's waterfront, the area around the LA municipal airport, dams, power plants, pumping stations, military posts.

Earl Warren, California's Attorney General, said that the fact that there had been no sabotage on the Pacific Coast was "a sign that the blow is well-organized and that it is held back until it can be struck with maximum effect." He contended that the fact that Issei and Nisei had not committed sabotage was a sign of their disloyalty.

Dec. 7, 1941—Pearl Harbor. Executive Order 9066.

Germans and Italians were considered separately. It was believed their loyalties could be better judged.

They are cowardly . . . they are different from Americans in every conceivable way, and no Japanese . . . should have the right to claim American citizenry.—Sen. Tom Stuart, Tennessee.

The rumors of sabotage—setting flaming arrows in sugar-cane fields to direct the Japanese planes, blocking traffic to delay rescue efforts, arson—committed by the Japanese during the attack on Pearl Harbor proved to be totally untrue. FCC investigations discovered no illicit radio signals guiding Japanese submarines off the California coast. But their white California neighbors apparently did not hear of these refutations.

An old Japanese man, a survivor, had promised to lead Tom to the strangest religious group of all, a sect which practiced its rites in secret, so afraid were they of public reaction. The old man claimed he had actually seen this new deity, "a young wind with flaming hair."

"You are here . . . seeking this god," the old Japanese man had said to Tom that afternoon, with such certainty it disturbed him.

"Yes," Tom had said distractedly. Then unaccountably had added, "I guess I need a new god."

On September 14, 1965, Nagasawa Shino stood in front of her bedroom mirror, brushing her hair. She planned to visit her cousin Takashi Fujii. He had been a patient in the A-Bomb Hospital, Sendamachi, Hiroshima City, for three months suffering from leukemia. The early morning sun flashed through the blinds, filling her mirror with a white light. Kyokujitsu shoten, a gorgeous ascent of the morning sun.

She pulled long black hair away from her forehead, revealing a narrow, bright red, keloid scar. Her hair slipped loose of the brush, fell to her shoulders. Then one by one the strands eased from her scalp and fell like dark streamers to the floor. White patches were spreading on her bald pate. Tiny spots of red, green, and yellow bled like an exotic makeup into the skin of her face. Raised, puffy skin.

She reached frantically for a glass of water on the edge of the basin and it broke under her hand. Her hand rose slowly in front of her face, bleeding from the base of the thumb. It kept bleeding, the blood soon covering her hand, her forearm, creeping up the white silk sleeve of her robe. She knew the bleeding would not stop until her body had been completely emptied.

The spots on her face blended into a brilliant rainbow that flowed down her neck, across her breasts, staining the length of her body.

She remained silent, stared into the mirror growing muddy with her colors, searched out the young, unfocused features of her face hidden within the mirror. Thirty-four, but everyone always said she looked twenty; they often wondered aloud if the bomb had done that to her, kept her young.

Always so many silly rumors, tales of magic. She had always kept the scar hidden under her hair.

Too much light. Too much to be said. The mirror burned, looking rich and jeweled, much like Japan's imperial mirror, the mirror the sun goddess Amaterasu had seen when she was lured out of the cave. Shino even looked like Amaterasu, under the swirling colors, the light of the flashboom, the Atomic bomb. A goddess; she smiled despite herself. Shamefully. She imagined that thousands of people had just disappeared from the streets of the city.

The immense cellar stank of fish and stale grain. Tom leaned back against an old crate in the back of the chamber, breathing in the smell as deeply as he could, thinking of it as the atmosphere breathed by his ancestors, wondering if any of them might have known this cellar. It seemed so familiar, some space from a remembered past, perhaps from before even his father's birth.

He could see now that there had been no reason to hide. The hundred or so Japanese crowded into the room were intent on the service before them, or lost in trance. Many were dressed in his own western-style garb. An older man stood before them, head bowed, apparently praying. There was an altar behind him: a metal bowl on a table surrounded by flowers, and above that a stylized painting of a mushroom cloud.

Tom stared at the painting, mesmerized by the vibrant colors, the boldness and energy of the brushstrokes. He could imagine ground-zero, the leveled field that had once been city, the souls suddenly liberated in the flaming wind.

The bomb had been the climax of a series of humiliations visited upon his father, the memories of which would eventually unhinge him, leaving him saddened and diminished until his death in 1960. They'd taken away his small hardware business. The country he'd loved took him away from the house he'd spent much of his life building, and threw him and his family into a concentration camp in Colorado. Then they'd given him a new name, Nisei.

His god had forsaken him, and sealed this dishonor with a hell on earth.

His father could not believe the bomb; the first reports left him shaking in angry disbelief. Then as the truth became clear the old man fell into a depression from which he would never recover. He could not believe what his own country had done, what God had allowed, what evil power they had created and unleashed upon the world.

As an adolescent Tom had at first been confused and frightened by the changes in his father. Then frustrated, later angry. His father had been weak and silent when he had most needed him. He had let the American government defeat him as devastatingly as the Japanese homeland had been defeated. Tom was ashamed of his father and all the others who had let themselves be humiliated. He made a decision then that he would always be American, American in every way. They had the power. They had the bomb.

The old man was speaking to the congregation. "Pikadon brought a change all over the world; life will never be the same. One can gain power over the everyday problems of life by emulating the power of the great god Pikadon!"

The message was clear and simple. Tom could understand it even with his rough skills in the language. The theme, like that of most of the newer religions, was one of practicality: "Man built the bomb and brought a powerful new deity into being. This only confirms the great power latent in every man. If you meditate on the image of Pikadon, visualize the god within yourself, then you may utilize this power within your everyday life!"

Tom left the gathering secretly during the zadankai, a get-together after the ceremony for discussing specific problems and first-hand encounters with Pikadon. The old man who had told him about the group was speaking when Tom left. "The light, so brilliant. . . ."

Tom knew that soon he would have to visit the hospital.

Takashi Fujii tossed restlessly in his bed in the Atomic Bomb Hospital. The flash of light had moved east to west, as he remembered it, a curtain of pure white fire. It was August 6, 1945. He had been thirty-six, a journeyman welder at the time. His eyes had been giving him trouble, his lungs were congested, so he took the day off from his repairwork at the Fukoku Seimei Building and stayed in bed. After the flash there was a burning heat, then a violent rush of air that flattened his wooden home and buried him under planks, clothing, and heavy roof tile. He could not understand; the all-clear sirens had sounded but minutes ago. At the time his thoughts had returned to his biggest job: work on the domed Industrial Promotion Hall. Welder and rod had worked out of his padded arms like a cripple's hooks; but these were no handicaps. They spewed fire. And in the gathering darkness his fingers, arms, entire body became fire, welding metal and burning the superfluous to ash. Unseen people applauded; his children were proud. In his vision he could see his young cousin Nagasawa Shino approaching his bedside. She was fourteen, beautiful; he was very attracted to her. A bouquet of goosefoot and morning glories rose from her hand and floated down over the bedspread. Only a few flowers, but they covered the entire bed.

This is a race war . . . The white man's civilization has come into conflict with Japanese . . . Damn them! Let us get rid of them now!—Rep. John Rankin of Mississippi.

Religious men, all of them, Tom remembered.

Tom's family was given a week to pay bills, sell or store belongings, say good-bye, close up the house, get rid of the car, and assemble at a nearby center with other frightened, confused Japanese-Americans. He could still recall the intense anger he felt. An old man died while they were waiting. A woman said he had a weak heart, but young Tom knew better.

At first they lived in a converted horse stall at the racetrack Whitewashed, manure-speckled walls. Spiderwebs and horsehair carelessly painted over. April 28 to Oct. 13.

Folded spring cots, boiled potatoes, canned Vienna sausage and two slices of bread. A bag of ticking to be stuffed with straw for a mattress. Hot. The grounds a mud pit in the rain.

Then they were forced to move again. Colorado, they were told Some place out in the plains. Young Tom dreamed of tornadoes lifting him and his family up, casting them away. He dreamed that the Japanese-Americans had committed some terrible, secret sin, and that a great white god was punishing them. The Japanese nation had better watch out, he had thought, else this god would send tornadoes against them too.

"No Japs wanted here," the signs had said as they evacuated east.

The old man followed Tom out of the meeting hall. Tom watched as he gestured excitedly with both hands, his gray eyes feverish, rheumy. He motioned toward the alley and the dark, unmarked door in the shadows.

"Everything changed . . . so quickly!" the man said. "I had been sleeping, and in the dream . . . or after waking from the dream, I cannot be sure, I felt such a *power*, such a brilliant light consuming all the world! I'd been dreaming of defeat, defeat I was sure must happen, when this wonderful thing happened! You may think I'm crazy, *addled*, to call such a happening wonderful. But all had to be burned away, all had to be changed, before this new thing could come to be. Flashing eyes, bronze skin—I could *see* him! I've worshipped him since, always!"

Tom held him upright, the old man so overcome by religious fervor his legs had collapsed beneath him. Tom looked again into the alley's dark shadows, and around at the drabness of the neighborhood. It seemed an unlikely setting for a god.

Tom's family was sent to Granada in southeastern Colorado. Eight thousand Nisei there. The family lived in a 16' x 20' room, wood sheathing covered with black tarpaper. Furnished by a stove, droplight, steel gray cots and mattresses. Three hundred people packed into the mess hall. Soft alkaline dirt and sagebrush.

His father grew steadily worse. Insane, said the other boys. Tom got into many fights.

Dust under the loose-fitting window sash, dust under the doors, gritty floors, dusty bedding. People weren't meant to live in such desert. It reminded him of the Jews, when they had been cast out of Egypt. Why should the great white god punish them so? He could not understand. And where was their god? Didn't the Japanese have a god?

Earl Warren said that the release of the Nisei from WRA camps would lead to a situation in which "no one will be able to tell a saboteur from any other Jap."

Tom remembered his father bending over backwards not to offend. Bowing and apologizing to the sadistic young white soldier who had tripped him on the way back from the mess hall.

The American Legion wanted them deported. Tom could still see the windshield stickers: "Remember a Jap is a Jap." The *Denver Post* demanded a 24-hour curfew on "all Japs in Denver." There were rumors of bloodshed at the Tule Lake camp—the papers said it was full of disloyals.

His father was never the same. Tom couldn't really think of his father as a human being anymore. Almost as if he had never existed . . . wiped away in the conflagration . . . gone instantly from the face of the earth . . .

Shino's brown suit fit perfectly. Months of exercise had brought her down to her old figure. The spots of seconds ago had disappeared from her face; the mirror had flowed back to normal. She was startled to find a slight smile on her lips, as if the smile belonged to someone else, another woman hiding under her skin.

There was no pleasure in her anticipation of her visit with her cousin; she did not enjoy associating with other hibakusha, the survivors of the bomb. But her cousin was a nice man, and she had no other family left.

She kept her hair combed over the scar and pretended to know little of the bomb horror stories; she didn't want to talk about it. She didn't want people connecting her with the Hiroshima outcasts, those living dead. The bomb people, they all die, some people would say. She wasn't sure this was true, but why argue with common opinion? A dying woman was not meant to be loved; love belonged only to the living. She was a hibakusha, and those people, they never recovered.

She had never married. Her body had remained fallow; there had been no children, although she knew it was medically possible. At twenty-five she had loved a young man named Keisuke, a lawyer. But his old mother had objected to their marriage, said that she bore the A-bomb disease, that the babies would surely be deformed. After years alone Shino too had this fear, that she might give birth to something other, something never before seen on earth. Males gave birth to strange things through their extremities; she found it difficult now, even to have a man touch her.

She hurried out of the house. She would be late.

As the morning sun rose high over the treetops of Asano Park she remembered the park as it had been that day: the huddling corpses, the silent stares of the living dead, the fire raging in the distance, flame and dark smoke floating over the trees. Everything she had known had suddenly become nothing.

Shino opened her eyes and stared at the two old women huddled over her. She had fainted, and one lady was offering her water from a pink paper cup. The sky was clear again; the smoke had been long ago. It is 1965; she reminded herself, that was so long ago.

The other lady had brushed back Shino's hair and seen the scar; Shino saw her pass a knowing look to her friend.

One evening Tom went to a double feature of old Japanese science fiction films. *Gojira no Gyakushu*, Godzilla's Counterattack, and *Uchujin Tokyo ni Arawaru*, Space Men Appear In Tokyo. He had seen them both as a kid, but he found himself reacting to them quite differently this time. They had been fun then, although a little scary, and he really hadn't seen all that much difference between Americans and the Japanese based on the evidence of those two films.

Now he had to wonder what the reaction of the young Japanese must be to these two films. What must they think, watching the enormous Godzilla, a deliverer of monstrous and bizarre death and destruction, and who is described as a creature born of nuclear tests? Surely he must be a creature from their own childhood nightmares, comfortingly visualized and made concrete.

At least the *Space Men* movie seemed a bit more positive. In this invaders come to Japan for advice concerning all the nuclear tests being done on earth. The aliens are worried about them. Japan's unique knowledge of the bomb becomes a positive thing. And yet the aliens possess awesome power; Tom wondered if this was still another example of the Japanese feeling that they had all been guinea pigs, and that Hiroshima was an "experimental city."

The movies made the bombing seem even larger than before, mythic. Tom couldn't help thinking they were the stuff of which religions were made.

The water the women gave her was cool and reminded Shino of how different it had been twenty years before. There had been rumors that people were not to give water to the injured, or it would aggravate their sickness. Such a denial had been difficult to maintain; it was natural for the victims to request water. Water was thought to restore life by returning the soul to the body. The injured had been so polite: "Tasukete kure!" they had said: Help, if you please!

She could not forgive herself for ignoring them so, but she herself had been injured. She had walked as one in a dream, ignoring their pain. She had passed by the curtains of skin hanging off their bodies, her hands clasped over her own slashed breasts. She had been half-naked and cowered in shame. Even knowing what they were, she had walked upon human bowels and brains.

She would be late for her visit with Fujii, but she needed some time to rest. Across the street, they were performing a shinto rite at the grand opening of a new department store. They had done the same when she was a girl. But the military had fooled them into blind support with shinto, the religion and the country become one. How could it ever be the same again? How might she trust either?

She was hibakusha, a person of the bomb. A new deity had been born into the world, a deity born of the loins of little, petty men. But he was greater than they. Man had brought him from the sun at the center of the world for slaughter. He turned and faced her from the street in front of the department store, a slight smile on his lips. Amused by their petty nationalism. Appeared from the crowd, as if he had stepped out of their massed bodies. Flash off his teeth of metal and lightning and suns. He did not speak, but his loud breathing hurt her ears. Bright eyes and dark hair: very handsome.

She thought it strange that he looked only vaguely American; his face seemed to blur in and out of focus. Shaven eyebrows, almond skin. Sometimes he looked like her cousin Fujii.

The god thrilled her; how very handsome he was. Isamashii, brave. With him standing there, the breeze from the ocean lifting his long silver and black hair and laying it back against his shoulder, it seemed as if they were the only people really alive: she, the other hibakusha, and this new god. He spoke inside her head, and the power in his voice made her aware of the great responsibility they had; she could feel bombs exploding, giant mushroom clouds of red, yellow, blue and white, like flowers over the globe. People burned with an incandescent flame, then disintegrated into their basic elements, back into the earth to become trees, flowers, the very materials from which the bombs themselves had come. They would all be united; there would be no separation.

The dark-haired god smiled and this movement in his face seemed to harden his features, set lines firmly around his hawk nose, his black steel eyes. A square, mechanical jaw. Lines of sweat down the sides of his face.

A Coca-Cola truck passed, spraying dust in its wake. She realized the opening ceremonies were completed; the people had all left. That day . . . sometimes it seemed like yesterday. She had stayed home that day; she had told her mother she was too ill to go to school, but she had lied. Her class of girls had been assigned to clear fire lanes in case the American B–29's dropped incendiary bombs. She admired the way the people had accepted this; many tore down their homes and buildings because they were in the path of a designated fire lane. But all this destruction saddened her; she couldn't bear to help. Her mother left her at home with her sister, who knew she was faking but kept silent. It was just after breakfast, the hibachi stove was still smoldering. At 7:45 her mother left to catch a train downtown. The bomb must have struck when she was still on the train. Shino knew her mother had almost expected it, some disaster like this had worried her for a week, the way the American planes had flown over every day.

The dark-haired god smiled out in the street, people walking by. Shino couldn't remember what year it really was; she breathed noisily. Everything silent, all she could hear was her breathing, the god's breathing. What year was it? She imagined herself a girl again, at the side of the dark-haired god. He smiled and embraced her, searing her breasts with his flaming hands. Still, she did not cry out in pain.

Tom thought that Hiroshima looked much like any busy port city, although perhaps the setting was lovelier than most; the seven fingers of the Ohta river supported it, and it was ringed by low mountains. There still seemed to be much of the small, provincial town here in the people and their life styles. Certainly nothing to suggest the dramatic event which had once occurred here.

But the castle, shipyards, and municipal buildings had been rebuilt. The Aioi Bridge, target site of the *Enola Gay*, once more spanned the Ohta river. So many Tom talked to still expressed surprise that things could get better so soon.

The new downtown seemed western with its wide streets and attractive store-fronts, arcaded shopping areas. The new pride of the city was their baseball stadium and their team the Hiroshima Carps.

But he was aware of something else here, whose presence betrayed itself in an accumulation of small clues: a bit of fused metal, a warped post. Imprinted in the steps of Sumitomo Bank was the shadow of a man who had sought refuge that day twenty years before.

The god drifted in the pollution staining the rooftops, the pollution defiling the wind, the sea. All the old gods of sea and air, defeated so easily by people.

By people's creations, which they themselves could not even control.

The god sensed without thinking the great stupidity of people, their lack of control.

The god disdained the attempts of the followers of his own religion to influence him, seek his favors.

The new god Pikadon knowing something like incompleteness even in his instincts of stone. . . .

Anger. . . .

Tom spent the day in the Peace Park. The skeleton of the Industrial Exhibition Hall dome made an eerie backdrop. The park was full of children, and Tom thought how all that he had become obsessed with had happened long before any of them were born. He wondered what their parents must tell them.

He wandered around the Cenotaph, the official Atomic Bomb monument, where the names of those who perished, and continue to perish, are inscribed. Some had told him that the souls of the dead reside there. Tom stared at the sculpture, feeling like a survivor himself, drawn in to their horror, guilty. Many hibakusha, he knew, resented the nine-story office building which had been built behind the park, they thought it profaned this sacred place. There were conservatives in Hiroshima, however, who even wanted to tear the "Atomic Dome" down. Times change. People forget.

There is another statue in the Peace Park, an oval granite pedestal, symbolizing Mt. Horis, the fabled mountain of paradise. Atop this stands the image of Sedaho, a child who died. She holds a golden crane in her outstretched arms. Beneath her are tangles of colorful paper leis that people have left her, each lei consisting of a thousand paper cranes.

A crane can live a thousand years. If you fold a thousand paper cranes they will protect you from illness. At the base of her statue—"This is our cry, this is our prayer: peace in the world."

Tom spent a long time in the Peace Memorial Museum. A regular art gallery he thought. First the "Atomic Sculptures," twisted metal, tile, warped stones, fused coins and convoluted bottles, a bicycle wrenched into a tangled snarl, a shattered clock stopped at 8:10, a middle school boy's uniform that had turned to rags from the gamma rays of the bomb, rows of life-sized dummies modeling the remnants of clothing, a face black with ash, skin hanging from swollen faces . . . .

The paintings, the photos: victims packing the barracks and warehouses—all that death in a moment—eyeballs melted across a cheek, peeling skin, gutted torsos. . . .

There was a mechanical fountain in front of the peace museum, The Fountain of Prayers, offering fresh water to those who had died begging for it so long ago. Too late.

A few hundred yards downstream from the dome Tom discovered the Kanawa floating restaurant whose specialty was fine Hiroshima oysters. But he could not eat. He kept seeing the restaurant patrons as corpses, the people in the street as corpses, their stiffened forms accusing him, their eyes singling him out.

Tom looked into the stream and saw himself: his hair burned

away, his skin melting like tallow, and he began to weep. Even his own eyes accused him.

And the all-seeing eyes of an unknown deity, whose face Tom saw a moment in the water, but which disappeared with a passing ripple.

Shino had this fantasy. At last she has a baby, her own. A miracle! But the umbilical cord is rotten, and the skin peels off the face like decayed cloth. . . .

For a long time Tom was reluctant to visit the A Bomb hospital itself. He knew that most members of the cult visited there, seeking recruits. It was an essential part of the story. But he was afraid.

So he spent much of his time researching the hospital before making his first appointment at the hospital, with one Takashi Fujii. In the meantime Tom made many notes:

The A Bomb Hospital

A Bomb hospital completed 1956—120 beds—each admission disturbs the survivor community. Each death creates a new wave of hysteria. Local newspapers keep a faithful obituary list.

People suddenly dying—a bomb ticking within them. Severe anemia—need periodic blood transfusions. Depressed areas of the city often called Atomic Slums.

A reporter found all these abnormal children, all microcephalic with small heads and mental retardation. Mothers 3 or 4 months pregnant and within 2 miles of the hypocenter. Others, 24 yrs old, mental age of 3, size of a ten-year-old. The Mushroom Club—first the cloud, then they're all growing like mushrooms in the shade.

176 leukemia victims since the hospital's founding in 1956. Coming down suddenly with leukemia 20 yrs after, with no previous signs.

Failure to marry—many of those who are still living cannot find happiness.

Tom had made a long list of questions for Takashi Fujii, yet still he did not know what he could say to the man.

*   *   *

The young reporter . . . Tom . . . that was his name . . . had come to visit. He was a young American, but with a Japanese face. His curiosity irritated Fujii. He did not like to be thought of as someone odd. He was just a man, a strong man, like many others. But he admired Americans as a whole; he had to admit that. They had brought the bomb, and the bomb was a big thing. It had been like a new beauty in the world, a terrifying beauty that had changed everything. And he really did enjoy talking about the bomb; he had little else to do.

The young American turned on his tape recorder, and, after some fidgeting with his bed covers, Fujii began to speak:

"I was in the midst of a well-deserved vacation. There had been some repair work needed on the steel substructure of the Fukoku Seimei Building, and the owners knew I was the man for the job. But I did need a rest, so I told them they would have to wait. Of course, they held up the work just for me. They knew I was the right man. Unfortunate that I didn't get a chance to finish the job." Fujii twisted in the bed, a wide smile stretching his nose.

"I had been lying in bed, drinking some fine Suntory whisky. Then I was buried under my home. Much later I woke up, blood running from my nose. Much as it did recently, when I first discovered I had been stricken with leukemia. Ah, the bomb gets us all in the end. It hides in your body for years sometimes before it strikes. But I am a brave man; I don't complain.

"When I got out from under the house I saw many terrible things. The city, it was gone, smashed like a nest of insects. People ran about like beetles, pulling possessions, their fellows, out of the wreckage. The great atomic bomb had done this; Hiroshima was a great religious experiment for man.

"The great dome of the Industrial Promotion Hall was but a skeleton. Hiroshima Castle had been flattened. The entire western sector was a desert. A reddish-brown powder over everything. The Fukoku Seimei Building had only been 380 meters from the center of the blast; I certainly would have died if I had gone there.

"I saw many beautiful women naked, running around with skin hanging from their limbs. Sabishii! Sad! I helped bandage many of the half-clothed women. There was much shame; they would crouch and try to hide themselves, but they were in so much pain; they needed my help. The bomb had left terrible burns—they call them keloid—on their bodies. One old lady's face had grown together so that with the puffy red tissue I could not tell if she was facing me, or if her back was turned. There were many young girls from the secondary schools who had been out clearing fire lanes, most naked and terribly scarred and frightened. They reminded me of my young cousin Shino. I felt very sorry for them; I helped them with much affection. It was a terrible time.

"But sometimes, I would think that the bomb had left them with beautiful—perhaps that isn't the word—fascinating, yes fascinating, markings. Red, and yellow, and blue-green, and black stars and circles. Some so beautiful. The scars were like ornaments. I try to remember them, the women, as beautiful; I forget the disfigurement.

"The bomb was so large; I feel it has made me somewhat larger, stronger. For the first time, man had made a god, a god not...limited, like himself, but something part of everything, the dream that fills...everything. If I try, I can see him as a man. Multi-colored flames in his scalp; a bronze, naked body. He sleeps curled inside us, in our hearts, just waiting to be released through our working hands, fingers, genitals. I was never confused as to what this new weapon truly was. I knew it immediately. It was of man's interior, the Atomic Bomb."

Tom shut off the tape recorder and stared at Fujii's beaming, almost gleeful face.

"Everything collapsed," Fujii said. "My Buddhist neighbors, they thought that they were really in hell. They fell to their knees in prayer. Imagine! They really thought the world was ending...that it had become hell!"

He paused, and looked at Tom sadly. "I sometimes think it does no good for people to believe in a religion. If these Buddhists had not believed . . . they would not have been so mortally terrified. They would have seen this as an occurrence of war, not a sudden arrival of hell. Ours was an experimental city, nothing more.

"I could have done more. I must tell you, I know that now," Fujii said with tears in his eyes. Tom looked down, suddenly embarrassed. "Most of us, we acted selfishly. We were too frightened, our minds too full of this flash, this fire, to help each other. So we left people alone . . . left them to die. We shamed ourselves before whatever god there might be. I too, I admit it, feel a great shame. I did a terrible thing."

The dark-haired god of the gleaming skin, Pikadon, rested within a silver layer in the clouds covering the islands of Japan. He had just exhaled 1945, and breathing in 1965 left 1985 a mere exhalation away.

Hurricane force winds gathered in his hair indistinguishable from whiffs of cloud; fire settled into the corners of his imagined mouth like small red droplets of spit. He looked into the heads of his followers and imagined himself with silver and black hair flowing out into the horizon line, scarlet wings lifting him up into the sun, his bronze form scintillating with hot vapor. . . .

The god snatched a bird from the air and blackened it, swallowed it, cast it back through his anus. Concrete is discolored. Human souls turn to flaming wind. He is enraged, frustrated. . . .

Below, the Japanese islands appeared in the gaps of morning mist, divine children of the deities Izagagi and Izanami, along with the waterfalls, trees, and mountains. The fire god had been last, and killed his mother Izanami with burning fever.

A new fire god had come, and his rage could turn the islands back into the original oily ocean mass . . .

Takashi Fujii stared past his cousin, out the window to the parking lot. His cousin seemed strangely quiet. But of course she had said very little to him the last ten years, although they both had lived in the same house.

Shino thought about some of her dreams of the night before.

Dreams of white faces, keloid flowers on her body, the walking dead, undiscovered atomic bombs constantly overhead or imbedded deep inside her belly.

Shino remembered the way the red ashes rose out of the flattened rubble and took form as more survivors. Walking dead. No way to tell their fronts from their backs, arms dangling from elbows held out like wings. Ghosts wandering aimlessly. They couldn't bear to touch themselves. They walked very slowly, like ghosts. She had thought she had recognized an old friend. *Oh, my god*, she thought, *it is Okino!*

Shino had left her sister alone in the house. After a few hours, her sister had died. It made her feel very guilty; she had not stayed with her long. Shino's sister's wounds had oozed much pus and dark blood. She smelled so bad Shino couldn't stand to be near her.

She sometimes dreamed her sister would return some day from the realm of the dead to accuse her. She had failed her. Shino thought that perhaps that was why she no longer found solace in the old religions; they had died when all those thousands had died. They were religions for the dead. For memories. For ghosts.

It was a shame; he had never married. Neither had Shino; their family line would soon die out. Family was very important to Fujii; he didn't want the name to die. The family maintained one's immortality; this was man's central purpose in life.

Fujii thought much of religion these hours. Never particularly devout, but he was a strong patriot and nationalist. He believed in science, technology, little else. Shortly after the war he had become interested in various machine-age cults, religions based on the glories of technology. But that had been long ago; Japan needed a new religion, an object to unite behind.

He glanced over at Shino. "I truly did not know what it was. Remember, I used to believe it had been a Molotoffano banakago, a Molotov Flower Basket? I did not know it could do these things."

"He is a god; he burns up the sky," she replied quietly.

Shino thought of how the day was much like an earlier September, when green had crept over the rubble and along what had been barren riverbanks. Spanish bayonets, clotbur, and sesame had covered the ruins. It had been beautiful, and even the tiny hemorrhages the size of rice grains on her face and hands did not bother her. Insects had filled the air, rising in clouds over the city.

Fujii thought of the bodies and their final cremations. The people had not been able to dispose of the bodies properly earlier, and many corpses were already rotting. They burned with a smell like frying sardines; blue phosphorescent flames rose into the air. As a child he had been told they were the spirits of the departing dead, fireballs, and he imagined he saw some of his neighbors' and friends' faces in the smoke.

Tom drove through the city streets lost in thought, the cyclic changes from skyscrapers and other technological monuments to slums and ancient architecture having a mesmerizing effect on him, almost convincing him that he was time-traveling, surveying the lives of his ancestors and his progeny. A strange smell seemed to permeate the air, the smoke giving him a sense of great buoyancy. He decided to return to the church and talk to the old man about what he had seen, what the others had seen. He had a hundred questions.

First Street, Hell. That was what the survivors had called the city.

In the dream he had returned to Japan, land of his ancestors, to find god. No religion had ever answered his doubts before, none were identifiable within the context of the sometimes terrible and sometimes beautiful landscapes he saw inside himself. Every time, however the dream might begin, it always ended with the firestorm. With hell.

Violent inrushing winds . . . the air in his lungs seeming to combust spontaneously; he roared through the city like a part of the firestorm himself, aware of the moans of the burning, the asphyxiated in their shelters, but so caught up in his own fiery power he could not stop, for he was part of the flaming god himself, and the daily drama of frustration and loss undergone by people so similar to what he used to be . . . they were far removed from him. . . .

. . . the glorious flames spreading, Tom leapt into the air with them, spreading the destruction back to America like a contagion . . . .

. . . and the vengeance was a terrible one. Tom stood in his glorious cloak of flame, a few miles from each epicenter, one bombing after another, as eyelids ran, sealing the beautiful vision of himself forever within the eyes of all witnesses. Clothes melted into skin, bodies flew as if the law of gravity had been momentarily rescinded. The air filled with flames, brighter than any sun, brighter than anything an ancient god might concoct.

. . . as refugees wandered the streets in broken bodies wailing that God had forsaken them, but Tom was there, Tom in his God's form, welcoming all into his congregation.

. . . as stomach walls were ruptured, as eyeballs turned liquid and ran on cheeks like egg white. . . .

. . . as metal ran into glass ran into cloth ran into flesh and bone and brain and the end of all desire and the end of all thought. . . .

Tom smiled and took it all inside himself. The world had become truly one, flowing and intermingling, one within fire, one within God.

And all doubt, all loneliness was answered.

Fujii could almost smell the burning bodies of his friends and neighbors, the sweet perfume of their liberated souls, free of the body's gross control. He knew a man who talked of a new religion, a religion based on the bomb. Perhaps when he left the hospital. . . .

At last, Shino was seeing her lover again, the beautiful bronze face in the clouds, the endless streamers of silver and black hair reaching out toward the ends of the world. The god's beckoning wing. . . .

The smoke rose above the city of Hiroshima and spread to the surrounding islands, and out to cover the world. Tom watched the smoke mix into the clouds. The god Pikadon gathered the rising spirits within his scarlet wings. And his wings covered the world.

Be Fruitful and Multiply

F. Paul Wilson

F. Paul Wilson is a Georgetown-educated doctor who practices in a small community on the New Jersey shore. His writing demonstrates a deep interest in social and political questions, and he was the first recipient of the Prometheus Award for Literature given by the Libertarian Party. His best-selling novel, The Keep, *now being filmed, contains one of the most spectacular confrontations between Good and Evil in recent suspense/horror fiction.*

In "Be Fruitful and Multiply," he projects into the future several notable trends of our own world. "Orthodoxy and fanaticism," he wrote in the letter accompanying this story, "are almost always intertwined, both being products of rigid personalities, and can cause horrendous things to be done in the name of the most benign deities." He must have been reading the same newspapers you and I have been reading.

Saw God last week.

Or maybe it was just St. Bartholomew. Looked more like Bartholomew, but could have been God.

He came to me in the night, a vision dangling from my ceiling, twisting slowly in the air like a corpse hanging from a gibbet. Said the birth rate was down. *Down!* Told me to warn everyone, especially the Church Elders. Told me to warn them right away.

But I've been so busy lately.

Actually, I'm afraid.

(11:40 . . . about 20 minutes to spare)

They'll think I'm crazy. Paranoid, they'll say. But not if I can get everything organized. Not if I can show them in black and white that there's a plot afoot, a plot against the Church, a monstrous conspiracy that threatens everything generations of us have worked for. Been meaning to get organized for so long now, but can't seem to get going.

Maybe that's part of the conspiracy, too. Maybe. . . .

For Birth's sake, don't start blaming your own foot-dragging on someone else! Next thing you know, your stubbed toe is someone else's fault . . . then the pimple on your chin . . . then your backache. Soon you're crazy.

I'm not crazy. My church, the only church, the Church of the Divine Imperative, is in danger. God told me so Himself. I may be the only one who knows. But I can prove it. At least I think I can. With God's help and without too much hindrance from Satan and His minions, the Elders will hear and believe. And act.

But got to get organized. Got to sound sane. I have my folks' files and scrapbooks from the old days. That'll help. If I can put the plot in historical perspective, the Elders will be more receptive.

To work! Start with a quote from St. Bartholomew. That'll grab them. They can't turn away from the words of the man who was the inspiration for the Church. And his words are as timely now as they were forty-odd years ago:

. . . So I say again to you. The Divine Imperative was God's first command to the first man and woman: "Be fruitful and multiply." This was not a casual remark. God created the earth as no more than a staging area. This planet, this life—they are no more than a first evolutionary step toward the ultimate destiny God has planned for His faithful. Nothing more than a staging area. In all the troubles through which you will pass, never forget that.

Words to remember, to be sure. Especially now. After Bartholomew, how about some of this stuff from the Eighties. . . .

. . . these pictures . . . everybody's so plump-ugly. Population was so sparse back then I guess they had to eat more than they needed. Almost obscene to look that well fed. No worry about looking like that nowadays. . . .

Here's a magazine article from back then. The non-believers did a lot of empty speculation in the Eighties and Nineties as the movement started to take hold. This looks like a good one:

. . . and sociologists are at a loss to explain it. Most of the Church's members were raised in the one- and two-children family units that have been the norm. Yet the whole thrust of the Church of the Divine Imperative runs contrary to the trends of the past few decades. Instead of limiting family size out of concern for the environment and a desire to pursue more personal goals of self-fulfillment, the Procreationists, as they call themselves, have laid aside their cultural, religious and social backgrounds to band together in a compulsive drive to bring as many new lives as possible into the world.

It all started with a pamphlet called The Next Plateau *by an enigmatic man known only as Bartholomew who is believed to have sprung from the ranks of the now-defunct Moral Majority of the Eighties. He is the source of Procreationist theology—a dizzying mixture of right-to-life slogans, Far Eastern Mysticism, and rigid Fundamentalism. Bartholomew's writings and passionate speeches have fired a significant segment of a generation. Procreationism has caught. The Church of the Divine Imperative is spreading. Hopefully, for all our sakes, it will be short lived.*

Time, June 30, 1992

But we showed them—or at least my parents did. Being second generation Procreationist, I spent most of my life listening to my folks and their friends swap tales about the early days of the Church. Must have been exciting to be in the vanguard, to be shaping history. Wish I could have been there. The glory of it! They were outsiders in their day, struggling against the Satan-inspired population-control forces that ran the governments of the world. Hard to imagine today, with everybody Procreationist, but back in the old days they were a tiny, persecuted minority. The bureaucratic machinery and its allies in the media did their damnedest—an appropriate word, that—to curb the growth of the Church. Said we threatened to unbalance the environment, accelerate pollution, and trigger famines. Ha!

Goes to show they never understood us. Tried psychoanalytical parlor tricks to explain our growth. They were desperate for any explanation other than the truth: It was God's will!

Listen to this fool:

These people are scared. They want a way out—that is all there is to it. They look around and see shortages, unrest, economic and political uncertainty on all sides, and it scares them. But do they pitch in and help? No! They make things worse! They turn to mysticism and embrace practices that exacerbate the very conditions which frighten them. It's mass insanity, that's what it is! And it's got to be stopped!

Senator Henry Mifflin (D-Neb)
The Congressional Record
November 28, 1997

See? Never understood. The air is thick now, true, because the productive capacity of the entire race must be strained to the utmost to feed, clothe and house us all. Food is scarce, yes, but there's enough to keep us going until the life force reaches the critical point, the signal to God that we are ready to be transported *en masse* to a higher plane of existence. Even non-believers will be translated to the next plateau. *Then* they'll believe.

Coming soon. I can feel it. We all can.

(11:48 . . . better keep moving)

Getting side-tracked here. Let's see . . . The senator's remarks make a good lead-in to government attempts to control the Church. Knowing that the Church was doing God's work, the followers of Satan used the governments of the world to suppress it. Communist countries were the most successful—they simply outlawed us and that was that. But wherever there was a spark of democracy, we flourished. And once we were able to organize the faithful into voting blocks, no elected official could stand against us for long. Even after we had gained majority power, anti-Procreationist legislation was still introduced, but was consistently defeated when the final vote came around.

These headlines from some old newstats ought to be dramatic enough:

BIRTH CONTROL
BILL ABORTED

NY *Daily News*, November 7, 1998

DEFEAT OF POPULATION CONTROL BILL A CERTAINTY
President decries dementia sweeping western world

NY *Times*, May 17, 2002

I was born three days after that last headline. Government opposition to the Church folded completely during the first five years of my life. By that time, every head of state and virtually every elected official was a Procreationist. Governments of the free world no longer hindered us because we *became* those governments. Soon, even the inner circles of the Communist politburos came under our sway. The world was fast becoming Procreationist.

The media remained a problem for a while longer, probably because they were so full of queers. Queers feared us the most, and with good reason. They knew they were living in defiance of the Divine Imperative: they could not be fruitful and multiply, therefore they were an abomination. They offend God and all those who believe in God. But we soon put them in their proper place.

A golden age ensued. The Church continued to expand. Not enough to have most of humanity as members of the Church—we wanted *everyone*. We inducted new members constantly. Some were reluctant at first, but eventually they saw the Light. Had to. If you weren't with us, you were most certainly against us. The Divine Imperative was frustrated and the goal delayed by anyone who refused to reproduce.

A holy time was upon us. There were pockets of resistance—heretics, die-hard reactionaries who refused to change their ways, queers, feminists—but they didn't last long. All the world was soon one with the Church. Or so I thought.

Something sinister occurred around my ninth birthday. No one recognized it as a threat then, but looking back now I can see the hand of the Devil.

This is the earliest report I could find in the library files:

LEARNING DEVICE TO SEEK MASS MARKET
. . . London (AP)

Cognition Industries, Ltd. has announced development of a new microcircuit which will make mass distribution of its BioCognitive Learning Unit economically feasible. "It's a major breakthrough," said a spokesman for the Sheffield-based corporation. "Ten years from now there won't be a home without one."

NY *Times*, March 15, 2011

The company spokesman was wrong: Nearly every home contained a BioCog unit within *five* years, attached to the family vid set with up to a dozen headsets plugged in at once at the educational hours.

After a decade of widespread use, the results were astounding: ten-year-olds doing university level work, autistic minds reached, brain damaged kids formerly considered ineducable learning simple math and reading skills. Efforts were made to get BioCog units into as many homes as possible in every corner of the world. A triumphal time for the Church! Not only was the life force growing at an unprecedented rate, but our intellectual powers were increasing beyond our wildest dreams. All for the greater glory of God when He translated us to the next plateau.

Everyone was on guard, of course, for possible misuse of the BioCog device. Mind control was the big bugaboo at first, but that was proved impossible. On a subtler level, however, there was concern over the device's potential for influencing attitudes. Stringent laws were passed to assure the faithful that anti-Procreation ideas would never be put into their heads, nor into the heads of their children while they learned.

All went well until last year...

...last year... Gayle and I produced our fourth life last year, a boy. Still remember how I felt as I cradled him in my arms, knowing I'd helped add another tiny increment to the life force, bringing us all that much closer to our goal...

...side-tracked again. Have to concentrate.

Last year, by the time of our fourth, the BioCog unit had become a part of our daily lives. Like all devout Procreationists, we were learning all we could before Translation, to be better prepared for whatever the next plateau might bring. The educational programs were all uniformly effective. And uniformly dull.

Then *The Bobby & Laura Show* made its debut on the late-night vid.

(11:55 ... still some time left)

Warm in here ... palms sweaty ...

The show was controversial from the start. A young couple— Laura a sweet-looking blonde, Bobby darkly virile, both looking mid-twentyish and dressed in light blue kimonos—had been given an hour to explore methods of enhancing the emotional and physical responses of the procreational act. Discussion would take up the first half of the show; the final half would involve a demonstration via the BioCog unit.

Don't quite recall the details of the discussion that premiere night, but the demonstration was unforgettable. Remember the screen dimming as we were instructed to don our headsets. Could see vague shapes of Bobby and Laura disrobing. Then the shapes came together and my body was electrified. Could almost feel Laura's hands on me. Sensations built slowly to a crescendo that was almost unbearable, leaving me weak and limp afterwards. I remember turning to Gayle to find her staring at me with an odd expression on her face—she hadn't put her headset on.

Tried to explain it to her. Tried to convey the sensual and emotional warmth that flooded through me, but she just made a face and said it didn't seem right. Took her in my arms right then and showed her how right it was.

Gayle was hardly unique in her doubts about the propriety of the show. Many members of the Church felt there was something scandalous about it. The ensuing investigation revealed that Bobby and Laura were orthodox Procreationists with three lives—a little girl and a set of twin boys—to their credit. Their stated purpose was advancement of Church teachings into new areas. They wanted to explore all the roads of the procreational process in order to better follow the Divine Imperative. They had experimented and had discovered that the BioCog units could influence more than the cognitive areas of the brain, so they were employing the unit's abilties in the emotional and sensual areas as an educational adjunct to their discussions.

Their program was quickly cleared of any wrong-doing. It was, after all, discreetly staged and played only at a late hour. And besides, the reasoning went, weren't they merely doing God's work?

Aided by the notoriety of the investigation, the second *Bobby & Laura* drew the largest audience in the history of this country. Even Gayle put on a headset. She later agreed that it was a remarkably moving experience. It was. Such a feeling of warmth, of being loved, of being needed, of belonging.

With the blessing of the Church, the show quickly moved into all the foreign mass media, vidcast at midnight in every time zone around the world. Dubbing or subtitles were used in the first half; no translation was necessary for the second half. Billions began to look forward to the show each night. Crave it, in fact. Night shifts in factories were interrupted for *Bobby & Laura*. Even stories of hospital patients left unattended during the show.

I remember wondering about Bobby and Laura. Don't care how God-loving and righteous a couple is, they can't generate that level of emotional and physical intensity on a nightly basis. They either had a method of enhancing the signals they transmitted, or had recorded a library of their best procreational sessions and vidcast these to the eager billions wearing their headsets and waiting for the screen to dim.

So what? I'd ask myself. Only showed they were as human as the rest of us. The purpose of their show was not to set some sort of endurance record.

Still went through spasms of uneasiness, though. These would usually hit me after the nightly show was over and Gayle and I were falling asleep in each other's arms, spent without having moved a muscle.

Bobby & Laura had been on for well over a year when it came to me that we hadn't conceived our fifth life as planned. We both knew the reason: our procreational activity had ebbed to the point where the only thing we did in bed was sleep. That was wrong. Evil. Contrary to everything we believed in. Felt guilty and ashamed.

And confused. Couldn't understand what was happening to me. Loved God and the Church as much as ever. My faith was still strong. Hard for me to admit this, but I'd lost all desire for Gayle as my procreational partner.

Wanted Laura.

Noticed Gayle's righteousness slipping, too. Did Bobby fill her thoughts as Laura did mine?

(11:58 . . . better hurry)

Guilt made me keep all this to myself. Even noticed some hesitation about attending weekly services. Didn't feel as if I was doing my part to follow God's will. But forced myself to go.

Now I know I'm not alone. The vision told me the birth rate is down. Others have been afflicted as I have.

And I know why!

The Devil is sly and ever active. We thought the enemies of the Church had been eliminated. Thought them dispersed and discredited as heretics and blasphemers. Wrong! All Wrong! They merely went underground and have been insidiously undermining God's will all along.

And their master plot is *Bobby & Laura!*

Had my suspicions for a long time now, but last week's vision convinced me: We have all become sensually jaded and emotionally dependent on that show. We are exposed to such peaks of pleasure and intimacy via the BioCog unit that the human contact demanded by God seems flat and ordinary.

THE BIOCOG IS AN INSTRUMENT OF THE DEVIL! THROUGH IT WE HAVE BECOME ADDICTED! EMOTIONALLY, PSYCHOLOGICALLY, PHYSIO- LOGICALLY, AND NEUROLOGICALLY DEPENDENT ON BOBBY & LAURA!

But not for long. I'm going to expose this hellish scheme tomorrow. I'll put an end to *The Bobby & Laura Show* for good. I'll reveal them for what they are.

(Only a minute to go)

Exposure of the plot will mean no more Laura for me, but that doesn't matter. God's will is what matters! I can break this addiction and return to the True Path. We all can. I don't need the show. I can wash it away like sweat and dirt, leaving myself pure and clean for the coming Translation.

(Midnight)

Bobby & Laura is starting . . . Gayle's by the set . . . I'm going to join her . . . just for a few minutes . . . then I'll get back to this . . .

. . . promise . . .

. . . just as soon as the show's over . . .

(I'm coming, Laura!)

The Emigrant

Joel Rosenberg

Joel Rosenberg was born in Manitoba and lives now in Connecticut, but part of his childhood was spent in a place called Northwood, North Dakota, where, he says, "there were two kinds of people—at least according to the strict Lutherans who were the vast majority: 'Papists,' who were Catholics, and Protestants, everybody else, including, I suppose, Jews, Baptists, Moslems, and people who sacrifice bulls to Jupiter on their living room rugs."

Rosenberg began writing in 1980. "The Emigrant" is his second sale. It's the shortest story in this book, but it's among the most powerful.

After supper, and his announcement, and his older sister's almost hysterical recriminations and protestations over his desertion, Yisroel Cohen stepped out the back door, stood on the damp evening grass, and tilted his face toward the heavens.

He was not an old man, no more than thirty years of age, but he had the beginnings of gray in his hair and beard, and the hints of lines to come in his face that seem to characterize Hassidim, even when young.

Idly, Cohen twirled an earlock around his index finger as he squinted at the sky. Above his head, looking like a fourth star adorning Orion's belt, he saw a glint of light that might be the Colony—no, it was moving too fast; most probably a satellite in low orbit. He tilted his head back, accidentally dislodging the black wool skullcap from its top.

As he stooped to pick it up, he heard the back door whisper open, and the heavy footsteps of his brother-in-law thud on the steps.

"Sarah sent me out to talk to you," Alfred Morin said. As with most non-Jews—or most Jews, for that matter—Morin was uncomfortable around Hassidim, Cohen thought.

Morin shifted his feet in the grass, uncomfortably.

Cohen straightened easily, saying nothing, his thin face holding only a trace of expression, perhaps weariness, perhaps discomfiture. He had not been looking forward to this weekend.

"What are you doing out here?" Morin asked.

"Seeing if, perhaps, I could spot the Colony," Cohen said. "But," he sighed, "it's too early, I guess."

He turned to Morin. "My bags are packed. After Shabas I will be going to the airport."

"And the house? What are you going to do with the house?"

Cohen shook his head and shrugged. "It really doesn't matter. You and Sarah may do with it what you please. The papers are at my lawyers'." He walked over to the oak tree in the middle of the yard, turned, and leaned his back against its bulk. Morin followed, and faced him.

"And the butcher shop?"

"Avram is taking it over. . . . He's my uncle's son. I don't think you've met him."

"No," Morin shot back, "that part of the family still doesn't accept me." He kicked at the base of the tree with his square-toed shoes. "I thought you were different."

Cohen chuckled, a strange sound in his throat, something halfway between a laugh and a sob. "No, it isn't you. Now, mind you, for my parents, it might have been. They would have said *kaddish*—the prayer for the dead—over Sarah, and never allowed either of you in their house."

Cohen laid his slim hand on Morin's muscular arm, and led him over to a pair of wicker lawn chairs. They sat down.

"But me? No. I am of a different generation from my parents, as they were of a different generation from theirs, who died—many of them and may they rest in peace—at the hands of Hitler."

Cohen sat, silently. Morin reached into his jacket pocket for a pack of cigarettes, offered one to Cohen, who declined with a motion of a finger, and lit up.

The tip of the cigarette glowed in the darkness.

"No," Cohen went on, as though he hadn't paused, "I am not responsible for how my sister lives her life—although she seems, still, to feel responsible for how I live mine."

"She did raise you, after the accident," Morin said, brushing his limp blond hair into place with his free right hand. "Old habits die hard."

"This you're telling to a Jew? After all, because I am named Cohen, after the *cohenim*, the priests of ancient Judea, congregations are still, after two thousand years, in the *habit*," he bit the word off, "of letting me share, with other Cohenim, the privilege of first *aliyah*, of being first to go up to the altar for the reading of the Torah.

"Because I am a Cohen,"—he pronounced it Ko-hain—"I am

not permitted to marry a widow, or be in a graveyard except to bury a blood relative, or another score of piddling things."

"But," Morin said, gesturing with blunt, nail-bitten fingers, "you seem, except for the way you dress, so, so *modern*, in so many ways."

"Because I call myself a butcher, instead of a *shaychet*, like my father and grandfather? No, I am not a modern man; I am an orthodox Jew, and sometimes I feel very out of step with this year 5750, the two thousandth year of the Christian era. I still," he said, finger-flicking the fringes that depended from underneath his shirt, "wear the *tzitzit*, I pray three times a day, and I study with Reb Gershon—who, by the way, I suspect my sister blames for all of this, for my leaving."

Morin took his cigarette between thumb and forefinger, flicking it off in a shower of sparks into the darkness. "So why *you?*" he asked. "Why not everyone named Cohen?"

"Because I'm a Jew, and you're thinking like a Catholic." He raised a peremptory palm. "No, I don't mean that as a put-down. You are a good man, Alfred, and you treat my sister well.

"But . . . were I a Catholic, and had a . . . religious problem, I would ask a priest. If he did not know, he would ask a bishop, who, still puzzled, would ask a cardinal, I suppose, all the way up to the pope, who is the sole arbiter of what is right and wrong. For Catholics.

"But for a Jew? No, no final source, except the Law, and the Almighty. And the conscience.

"And," he sighed, "the possible. To wish for, or attempt the impossible," he said, warming to the subject, "is a sin against God, who reserves the impossible for Himself.

"The day my parents died in the crash," he mused, "and I wished it wouldn't have happened—I sinned." Cohen shook his head, wondering. "That I really don't understand."

"I don't either," Morin said, lighting another cigarette and shifting uncomfortably in the hard chair. "And I still don't really understand why . . ."

"Just so," Cohen said. "In there," he indicated the house with a shrug of his thin shoulders, "I stated the bare facts of my leaving—mainly to get it out of the way, partly for my sister's benefit, because she should understand. For you I will . . . trot out some history.

"Please understand, I am a butcher, not a historian, but this bit of history every Jew knows." He leaned forward, resting his elbows on thin, bony knees, and rested his forehead in his cupped hands.

"In 1933, the year that the Germans elected Hitler, there were ten million Jews in Europe.

"Between 1939 and 1945, the Nazis murdered millions of people in their death camps. Six of those millions were Jews." Cohen spoke slowly, carefully, as though each word were being written down.

"Some were forced to dig huge pits, lined up on the edge, and shot. Films—made by the Nazis themselves—survived the attempt to cover up in 1944 and '45 when the records were being burnt, when plans were made to destroy and cover the camps themselves.

"Most of the people, though, died in gas chambers, where they were told, half-heartedly by the sniggering guards, that they were going for 'decontamination.' They were crammed inside, the doors locked and barred, and crystals of Zyklon-B were dropped in through hatches in the ceilings.

"Their death was not a pleasant one. I have never been to Auschwitz—I am a Cohen, and may not enter a graveyard—but I have seen pictures of the gas chambers. The walls, the floors, and even the ceilings are marked with deep scratches from fingernails; people trying, in their last agony, to claw their way through the concrete of the room, perhaps to leave some mark of their passing.

"After the bodies were looted, they were burned." Cohen's voice was level, as always. Morin's eyes stung as he lit another cigarette. "Some in crematoria, some on open steel frames where the air could circulate more easily, as the corpses were splashed with gasoline, and set on fire.

"Some of the ashes were buried in deep pits, some scattered in the winds.

"And the winds blow across the face of the world. Every time we breathe, we breathe in traces of these people, murdered and burned."

Cohen sat silent again. Morin was almost sure that he had finished, and had opened his own mouth to speak when Cohen continued.

"And now, a quarter of a million miles from here, men build the Colony from aluminum and steel taken from the moon.

"I have applied for a job there—they will need butchers—and I have been accepted, and must go.

"For I am a Cohen, descended of priests, and to be in a graveyard is forbidden me."

Angel of the Sixth Circle

Gregg Keizer

Gregg Keizer teaches English in a junior high school in Salt Lake City. He has been writing for a couple of years now and has made one previous sale, to Omni.

It is sometimes said that the saddest words we can utter about the past are "if only. . . ." But suppose the future offered a way of reshaping the past. In "Angel of the Sixth Circle," Keizer draws a tense portrait of a future man, in a scientifically oriented Church, who is sent back in time on a religious mission and ends up confronting the one thing he least wants to find.

"Is there no one else who can do this?" I asked. But the Most Reverend remained calm this time, did not threaten to break the seals of his transparent chamber and infect me for my insolence.

"None with your experience or your skill," he said from his darkened room. "Only you can assume the bodies in the past and yet avoid those Sanction bastards. And you have the necessary requirement. Your faith is with you, DeVries." The tinny sound of his voice escaped the chip I held in my hand.

I shifted my weight, trying to remain steady. He was wrong, for I doubted my faith. How could I be sure, when it was weak from the fear of seeing hell? Not the fire and ice of Dante and the Catholics, but the Godless void of Calvin and the Orange Synod. Every time I killed in the past, I grew closer, for though they are not my own hands that close around the throats, it is *my* mind, *my* soul, that works them.

The Most Reverend has assured me that I need only ask forgiveness. Christ died for me, he has said, died so that I may live. I believe that, yet images of the deaths I have caused stay with me. My duty is a necessary evil, the Most Reverend has said. I cannot help but wonder if Christ would have died, not so that I might kill, for we have always killed and been forgiven, but so that I might enjoy killing. That is what I fear; that I am drawn to murder, that I like it, and that I have lost my faith because of it.

"I was hoping to rest before going out and down again," I said. "I would like to get reacquainted with my own body."

"No, no, that is impossible. You must return with the THIEF as soon as arrangements can be made."

"Did something go wrong?" I asked, seeing the face of the dying priest in my mind, feeling his throat with fingers that hadn't really been mine. I had killed him before he could become bishop, by going back into time with the THIEF. I did not want to go back and kill again.

"No, nothing went wrong," the Most Reverend whispered. "You are sure he died? The priest, I mean."

"Yes." After all his power, he still had to trust my word when I told him what I had done. Only those who actually alter time can know more than one reality. *I* was the one who had killed the thin-faced priest who would have become bishop. *I* was the only one who could know both realities; original and altered. Before and After. I was supposed to count each reality I'd known by numbering the times the dying had breathed in my face. The Most Reverend, like the rest of the world, knew but one reality. To him, as to everyone, the altered reality was the only world that had ever existed.

I was *supposed* to remember both realities after I'd killed someone in time, but yet I could not. I *felt* that the world was different, but when I studied the records, I could find nothing that stood out as being unfamiliar, inconsistent. It was as if the probability calculus made my murders necessary.

I sometimes wondered if time changed at all. Perhaps my work dissipated under the press of centuries. Perhaps I eliminated the wrong people. Perhaps I imagined it all.

But it was the way it was done; both by us and the Jesuits, the Catholic killers in time. We wanted to alter reality to eliminate each other, but were afraid of killing those too important. So we danced at the edges of time, not knowing what the world would contain if Luther or the Apostle Paul was killed. At the periphery of events, people died; important only to the probability computers, seemingly not vital enough to actually alter reality. It was a curious way to campaign, but it was the way it was done.

"You've done well, DeVries," the Most Reverend breathed. "Thirty-four thousand Catholics no longer alive. An eighty-one percent chance of that. All because you clicked that priest. Excellent, DeVries, excellent."

I felt no remorse for the death—no, the non-existence—of those thousands. I really didn't believe that I'd killed anyone but the priest. The memory of his face was enough.

"You must go deeper than the Point of Reformation," the Most Reverend said. I looked up, toward the dark shape of his hidden face. Deeper than the Point? Impossible. "You are the most skillful, DeVries. The Synod chose you."

None from the Synod had gone deeper than that day in 1517 when Luther tapped his ninety-five theses on the church door in Wittenberg. And none of the Elders, the ones like myself, who hunted Catholics. If the world was altered before the Reformation, it might be so altered as to be without the Orange Synod and Protestants. The Synod dared not take that chance. Time deeper than 1517 was abandoned, left to the Catholics and their Jesuit time killers. What they did with it no one knew.

"Probability claims the Papists will kill someone vital to the Reformation. We have no definite idea who, so the Elders are being sent down to protect the best targets." The Most Reverend's whisper had risen to a hoarse normalcy. "See to it that none of the Jesuits get by you, DeVries. If one does, the world may change too much and you may find yourself burning as a heretic when you return." He paused. "As may we all be burned."

"Who?" I asked, glad that I was not to kill this time, only protect. My soul would suffer no additional sin.

His fingers edged into the light. One was merely a stump, its tip livid white; the other was hard and rigid. There were rumors that he'd created the leprosy-like affliction himself, years ago, by killing the wrong person in the past.

"Thomas de Torquemada," he said. "You must make sure that Thomas de Torquemada, Inquisitor-General of the Spanish Inquisition, lives. Do not let that butcher die, DeVries."

The technicians were waiting in the THIEF room when I walked in, my orientation for the trip already completed. I sat on the couch that was actually the machine which pushed minds into bodies in the past, felt the hard, yet yielding surface, and watched while the technicians fastened the arm and leg securers. The life-support console was pushed beside me and the drip tubes were slipped into the sockets near my wrists. My body had to be fed, even though my mind would not be in it.

"Feeling her?" a tech asked as she snapped the THIEF's input lead into the implant behind my left ear. I nodded as the peculiar static filled my head. Then the soft female voice of the THIEF reached me, gradually growing in volume.

"Good day, Elder DeVries," the computer-like voice said, whispering to me. I wondered if the Jesuits had a female voice for their THIEF. Perhaps a young boy's instead.

"Drop me now," I said, not whispering, and heard the echo of my voice even through the drugs the life-support console was pushing into me.

"You do not wish the briefing on the time-spot?" the THIEF asked, its voice sounding petulant. I'd already read the printed briefing.

"Drop me now," I said again.

The darkness of the THIEF came to me, pulled my mind from my body and dropped it into another's, all in one infinite moment of time. I was deep in time once more.

The marketplace was crowded, noisy and dirty. I stepped back toward the wall I was near, then leaned against it. My vision blurred briefly, then cleared, as the THIEF left me. I looked down at the body I inhabited, saw that it was male, had dark, rough hands, and seemed healthy. The last was important, for dying in this body would be as fatal as dying in my own. My own body, on the THIEF couch centuries in the future, would live only as long as this body I inhabited lived. One dies, so does the other. And me.

I let the body work itself, making sure I did not consciously think of being within it. As long as I did that, I would understand and speak the language, would move gracefully and normally through this world. Above all, not stumble or stutter, for if the Sanction Team was here, then they would find me, click me, kill me, for being a time tamperer.

For that is what I really am, a time tamperer, and thus a criminal in the eyes of Sanction. Once the thought of being a tamperer had disgusted me, but no longer. Although I tried to change time without approval, tried to alter reality with every action, it was for a just cause. At first, the Synod had been anxious about the theological implications of changing time, but then there was no choice, for the probability computers spat out figures that said the Catholics had already altered time. A seventy-eight percent probability, they said.

Though I am not a common criminal, like the ones who go deep and steal paintings, buy precious metals, take artifacts that they hide in a safely remembered place where they can be found later, in Realtime, I am still sought by the Sanction Team. They are the ones who go deep into time and set things right again, according to the probabilities, by killing the tamperer who had altered the world in the first place. All they have to go on are a set of probabilities and the knowledge that tamperers are clumsy in their borrowed bodies. I fear Sanction and watch carefully for them, but I am good at what I do. I am as graceful deep in time as one from the Sanction Team itself, who are supposed to be the best at using others' bodies.

I stepped from the shade of the wall into the bright glare of the marketplace. The smell of rotting fruit was strong, almost overpowering the stench of the people who stood near me. I sniffed gently, thankful I could not smell myself.

"Señor Ordienta, are you coming?" asked a voice near my ear. I turned and saw a shorter man, his smile obviously false, his hands spread wide, palms up. I looked for the strange gleam of detachment Sanction Team members are said to have, but his eyes were vacant. I did not know him, although he certainly knew me, but he was definitely a *familiar,* for he wore the long black cloak of that office of the Inquisition. He was a guard, sent to find me, perhaps.

"We will be late for the interview," he said, his smile even wider and even more false. He touched my shoulder, briefly, before I could step away. His smile left him and for a moment I felt the fear of discovery. But it left me quickly as I reassured myself that this man was neither a Jesuit time killer nor a stalking Sanction Team member. He was strange, but in his own right, not because another's mind inhabited his body. I reminded myself that I could not afford to be overly suspicious, for I would not accomplish anything if I was constantly glancing at everyone's eyes and suspecting Sanction Team members in every odd bit of behavior.

Squinting against the harsh white glare of the open square, I followed him across the plaza and into the cool darkness of a squat building. The walls were smooth, then rough, then smooth again as I touched my hand to them while we walked through the dim corridors. Once, I turned to see if anyone followed us, but there was no one. I heard only the quick footsteps of the *familiar* in front of me.

I closed my eyes and let the body move itself. It knew this place, for it walked comfortably down the corridor, the steps sure and rapid. I wondered what this body had done before I came to it. As I felt myself stride down the hallway, I had time to think of what I was to do here in fifteenth-century Spain.

The Catholics, through their Jesuit killers, were going to eliminate Torquemada, even though he was Catholic himself. That is what the calculus computers had, would someday, say. It was brilliant, for who would suspect the Jesuits of killing one of their own?

The possibilities were many, but the prevailing thought of the computers had been that the Jesuits expected the death of the Inquisitor-General to dampen the effect of the coming Reformation. With Torquemada dead, the Inquisition might falter, even expire. There would be one less excess of the Church to rebel against when the Reformation came. Thousands of faithful Catholics, who would die in Torquemada's autos-da-fé in this reality, would live and bear other Catholics if the Inquisitor-General died in their place. The central authority of Rome would not be questioned as Torquemada's work had been, the Papal rule would be a bit tighter, and when the time came to crush Luther and his movement, there would be no hesitation, as there had been in this reality. Even allowing for the probability computers' usual caution and understatement, it was a brilliant idea. I wondered why the Most Reverend had not thought of it.

I realized my body had stopped walking. I saw a room, men seated at a long table, the pale face of a man in the solitary chair at the other side of the table. I recognized the pinched look of Thomas de Torquemada, Inquisitor-General, from a portrait I'd seen. He stood off to one side. I glanced at the faces nearest me and satisfied myself that none of them were Sanction members or Jesuits.

"We are pleased you have joined us, Señor Ordienta," Torquemada said, his voice surprisingly soft. But the sarcasm remained when his voice disappeared. I bowed slightly, my hands nervous at the fabric of my shirt. I let them work themselves, wondering why this body was so afraid of the Inquisitor-General. I was not one of the accused, but one of the accusers. I sat in the offered chair, across the table from a black-robed man, his jowls thick and loose on his face. I noticed that my escort had stayed near the door and seemed to be guarding it.

"We will proceed with the reading of the evidence, now that Señor Ordienta is here," Torquemada said. I listened to his Spanish, quietly marveling at my ability to understand it. But as I did, the words he spoke became foreign and I was lost. I quickly forced conscious thoughts from my mind.

". . . has been called to give testimony on this case," Torquemada said. "Señor Hadida, remember truth and be mindful of your soul." Torquemada smiled gently and the man in the chair became even paler. His eyes were drawn to the crucifix on the far wall.

I kept my eyes searching for someone who didn't belong, someone sent by the Jesuits to click Torquemada.

"My godmother is a Christian," the man, Hadida, stammered. His fear was visible on his face and I knew he stuttered because he was afraid, not because he was a time traveler. "I have seen her go to mass many times," he said, his speech clearer.

"Did she not refrain from working on Saturdays?" Torquemada asked. The rest of the men in the room were silent, staring dully at the witness. I heard my own breathing through the softness of the Inquisitor-General's voice.

"Yes," the man said. "No. Wait." He hesitated, his eyes searching the faces around him. "She ignored the Jewish Sabbath. I saw her working on many Saturdays."

"Is your godmother not a Jew, in all fact, though not in name?

Has she not reverted back to her Jewishness, does she not merely hide it, and only pretend to be a Christian?''

The witness was silent. A man who had been slouching against the far wall stood and moved a step or two toward Torquemada. I ignored the continuing questions and tried to watch the man without actually looking at him. Perhaps he had a wire in his clothes and would step behind the Inquisitor-General and strangle him. Though part of my mind wished me to remain quiet and not rise and kill this man, the thought was shoved away as I felt my hands flex under the table.

The man I watched leaned over, and when his hand moved into view again, he was lifting a cup of water, its sides glistening with droplets. I was half out of my chair before I realized he was handing the cup to Torquemada, who took a long sip before handing it back. The man across the table from me, the one with the heavy jowls, glared curiously at me as I sat down again. The man with the cup had not been a Jesuit and I had only drawn attention to my strangeness.

But I had been ready to kill. The thought swept through me as I caught fragments of the questioning and Hadida's answers.

''I know nothing about anything that went on in my godmother's house. I know nothing,'' Hadida said, his voice nearly a whisper. I listened to him, but my mind thought only of my readiness to kill. I would burn for my eagerness, and my soul would be forever lost because I wanted to kill, desired it, with such relish.

''Come now, do you expect us to believe you know nothing, Señor Hadida?'' Torquemada asked, his face wide with a smile that showed too many teeth. ''You have known her all your life, is that not so?''

The man nodded, his hands shaking as he held them in his lap. ''Yes, yes,'' he breathed softly. I had to strain to hear him.

''Did she not observe the Jewish Passover, Señor Hadida?''

Hadida shook his head slowly. ''I know nothing of anything that went on in her house. I know nothing.''

''You would not lie to us, would you, Señor Hadida?'' the fat man across the table from me asked. I was surprised to hear him speak, for I had assumed that only Torquemada could ask questions here. Perhaps I was also expected to ask questions of Hadida. I found the idea repulsive; asking questions in a Catholic inquisition.

Hadida blanched even more and swayed slightly in his seat. I thought he would fall, but one of the guards reached out and put an arm on his shoulder.

"No, no, no, no," the man said. He was weeping now. I glanced at Torquemada and saw that he was smiling still, his eyes hard in the dim light of the room. He was enjoying all this immensely.

"Do we not have the information we need?" I asked, my voice sounding too loud in my ears. "Can we not let Señor Hadida return to his business?"

Torquemada nodded, his face still smiling but his eyes betraying his surprise at what I'd said. The fat man's jowls flapped as he opened his mouth to say something, then obviously thought better of it.

Hadida was pulled from the chair by one of the *familiars* and led to the door. As he passed Torquemada, I could see his body stiffen. But Torquemada only watched him through half-closed eyes, the gentle smile still on his lips.

"Perhaps we shall see you again, Señor Hadida," Torquemada said as the man reached the doorway. I glanced carefully at everyone in the room, still expecting to see a Jesuit or Sanction Team member behind each pair of eyes. But I found only fellow members of the Inquisition.

"I know nothing, sir," Hadida said, his face slack.

"I certainly hope so," Torquemada said, and waved the guards and Hadida from the room. The door closed silently behind them and the candles on the table fluttered for a moment, threatening to throw the already dim room into complete darkness.

"The woman was lying to us," the fat man said. "That man knew something of his godmother. There is heresy here, Inquisitor-General."

"Yes, one of them is lying to us. We must find the truth in this," Torquemada said. "If we do not, then a soul will be lost to us. To Christ. That is what matters most, is it not? The body is unimportant, after all." As I saw the fat man nod his head, Torquemada's smile widened until I could see his teeth again. The man was so obviously insane.

"Please leave me," Torquemada said, and the guards began to file from the room, the sound of their robes against the stone floor sounding like wind through curtains. The men at the table stood too, and one by one they walked from the room. "No, do not go, Señor Ordienta," Torquemada said as I rose from the table. "I have some matters that must be discussed." I vaguely heard the door shut and felt my hand twitching again. I knew if I consciously tried to stop it, it would only get worse. This body I was in was frightened of Torquemada. Or was it me?

"Why do you continue to oppose me, Ordienta?" Torquemada asked, his fingers paging through the Bible on the pulpit. I wondered if he was looking for anything specific.

"I was only trying to help," I said, hearing the voice as though it were my own, fluent and smooth. At least I was still in control of that.

The Inquisitor-General's face became flushed and he seemed to be having trouble breathing.

"You dare assume that you can aid me in this matter? You are but an apprentice. What right have you to presume such things?" Torquemada asked, his voice so near a whisper that I had to lean forward to catch it. I noticed my hand was moving even more than before.

I glanced up at him and our gazes met for the briefest instant. He exploded again.

"You will not look at me that way," he said, his voice now rising in volume. "You do not know your place here, that is evident."

"But the man was telling us the truth—"

"That is for me to decide, not you!" he shouted, the echo of it ringing off the stone walls. I looked away from him and my gaze fell on the crucifix. I had never gotten used to the Catholic custom of portraying Christ on the cross, the red paint on the wounds at the side and limbs. I much preferred the simplicity of the bare cross of the Synod.

"Even our own are not exempt from heresy," Torquemada said. He had seen the object of my glance. "Heretics come in many shapes, not only converted Jews."

"Are you immune, Inquisitor-General?" I asked, looking into his eyes again. I knew I was making a mistake, drawing out his anger, since it was rumored Torquemada had Jewish blood, but I could not stop myself.

He stared at me for a long time, then suddenly laughed, a short, sharp bark. "I forget myself, Ordienta. After all, we both search for the same thing. Truth. Truth in Christ." He was smiling again, but this time I was unsure of what was behind it. It seemed so different from when he'd grinned at Hadida.

I must have been mad to believe he could be changed, could be reasoned with, I thought. He would remain the same, always. Just as my Most Reverend would never change.

"I have business with the Queen," Torquemada said, turning his back to me. I took the signal as one of dismissal and walked toward the door. My hand was on it when he spoke again.

"Do not oppose me," he said. "Never again." I saw his smile as I turned, the same smile he had shown Hadida. It took all my skill to keep from trembling as I closed the door behind me.

As I walked into the brightness of the marketplace, I knew I could not watch Torquemada closely. He would become suspicious if I was always near. For a moment, I cursed the THIEF for giving me this body, instead of one of the ubiquitous *familiars,* the bodyguards of the Inquisition. But I knew this body was better. I was more important, able to move freely without arousing curiosity. No one was foolish enough to question an Inquisitor, even an apprentice. Not in this time, this place.

I would have to go looking for the Jesuit the computers claimed would be here. It would be stupid to assume he would try to assassinate Torquemada only when I was near. What I would do with the Jesuit once I found him—and I was certain I would—I did not yet know. My duty was clear; I was to kill him, as I'd killed all the others marked by the probability machines. But I was afraid that if I killed once more, I myself would be lost. I would never be able to stop, never keep myself from liking the feel of the dying in my hands. I had to stop sometime.

I would decide what to do when the time came, when I actually found the Jesuit the Catholics had sent here. It was all I could think of at the moment.

No one looked at my face as I walked across the square, past the small tables spread with vegetables and fruit. The smell of the produce was strong, almost overwhelming. I picked an orange from a solitary table, as if it were my right. The man behind the table proved me correct, for he said nothing as I peeled off the rind and threw it on the ground. The juice tasted good as I bit into the orange, glancing around the marketplace at the same time. The cathedral loomed over the square, dominating everything. It was opposite the squat building which housed the Inquisition, and I couldn't help but smile at the foresight of the Catholics.

I stepped back into the shade of a nearby awning, standing at the fringes of the crowd, watching the people go by. Torquemada came from the dim doorway, looked around for a moment, then walked to his left, a group of *familiars* trailing behind him. The Inquisitor-General was afraid of assassination. I wondered if he would believe that one of his own, not a *converso* Jew, was the one who sought him out. Not only one of his own, but one from his future.

I watched carefully for anyone who seemed to be following the Inquisitor-General, but seeing no one, walked after him myself. Even if I could not stay next to him, perhaps I could still stop any attempt, or at least discover who the Jesuit was.

I walked through much of the city, following Torquemada and his bodyguards. At first I thought his path was aimless, but then I saw that he was gradually traversing all the busiest sections of the city, showing himself to the people, perhaps as a warning, perhaps to console them, I did not know. No one made a sudden move for the Inquisitor and I saw no one who might have been a Sanction Team member or Jesuit. I kept to the rear of the party that followed Torquemada, sure that he did not see me, just as sure that I could get to him if necessary. But nothing happened and before dark he walked back to the now-empty plaza and went into the squat building. I could not follow him without passing the *familiars* who guarded the doorway, for they were sure to announce my presence to Torquemada. I remained outside, not sure of what to do next. The voice behind me solved my problem.

"Señor Ordienta, please follow me," the voice said, and I recognized it as the short *familiar* who had escorted me to the Inquisition chambers earlier. Presumably he was my guide and servant while I was here.

"I am surprised to see you still here, Señor," the man said as he began walking. I followed him, not knowing what else to do now that he was with me. "You must need refreshment, Señor. Have you forgotten the way to your guest house, Señor?"

I nodded, and grunted a vague reply.

"Yes, yes, one can become lost in Castille. I will take you there now, Señor." He led me through streets that were unfamiliar to my mind but not to my body, for I walked quickly and comfortably, often edging ahead of my short guide. I should have thought of this before; it would have prevented this man from seeing my confusion and indecision.

The house was huge and I was the only one in it, except for the pair of *familiars* who were the caretakers of the house. It seemed to be a residence regularly used by members of the Inquisition.

"I will call for you in the morning, Señor Ordienta," the short man said quietly, bowing slightly and showing his smile again. It reminded me of Torquemada's smile, the way the Inquisitor-General had grinned at Hadida when the suspect had been taken from the room. That was why this man's smile made me so uncomfortable.

Nevertheless, I slept soundly that night, for I had tired my body with the walk around the city after Torquemada. I woke only once, when I thought I heard someone in the courtyard below my window, but when I went to look, there was only the darkness and the sound of a breeze.

My *familiar*, whose name was Sanferaz, came for me early in the morning and I left my breakfast half-finished to follow him to the Inquisition's chambers. The walk through the dim corridors felt the same as the day before, and again I turned to see if anyone followed. There was no one. I was still too paranoid, I thought.

The room of Inquisitors was the same too, with the tapers glimmering on the table and Torquemada standing behind the pulpit, his Bible open in front of him. The only differences were that I was not the last to arrive and there was a new suspect, a woman, in the chair at the table.

Torquemada did not glance up when I sat at my place, opposite the jowled man who still looked at me strangely, perhaps seeing something odd in my behavior or personality. I tried to let the body do as much as possible on its own, hoping that any interference from me, from my own mind, would be quieted. I wished that the THIEF would come for me now, take me home, to my own time and body, and leave this place for another Elder. I was suddenly tired of inhabiting another's flesh, wanted to see my own reflection instead of an unfamiliar face. But the THIEF would not reach out for me until my job was done, and I had to live here for the duration. And if I was not careful, a Sanction Team member or Jesuit would click me and then I would be dead, both here and in the future.

Torquemada finished shuffling the sheaf of papers on his pulpit, straightened, and looked at the woman in the chair. "What is your name?" No emotion, no inflection in his voice. Strictly business.

"Maria Pampona, Excellency," the woman said. There was more confusion than fear in her eyes and she acted as if she had been here before and knew the procedure, for her answers to Torquemada's questions were quick.

"Do you know why you have been brought to us?" Torquemada asked.

"No, Excellency. I have already confessed before you that I was forced to practice the customs of Jews. Surely you—"

"Do you have any enemies?"

"Not that I know of, Excel—"

"Do you attend confession? Each week?" Torquemada asked, still not looking at the woman, keeping his eyes on the papers before him. I pulled my gaze away and looked around the room. I may be paranoid, I thought, but at least I am alive still.

"What is your diocese? Who is your confessor? When did you last make confession?" Torquemada asked. He was following the Instructions he himself had written for his questioning. I recalled the briefing I had read before dropping out and down with the THIEF. He would continue to fire a rapid series of questions at the woman, hoping she would become confused and confess something.

"I have confessed before *you*, Excellency. My husband beat me and forced me to follow the customs of Jews. I came to you, of my own will, and I was absolved of sin. Surely you remember?" Maria Pampona said, her voice now wavering slightly as she glanced from one Inquisitor to another. I dropped my gaze to the table when she looked at me.

"You are a false penitent!" shouted the jowled man across the table from me. I looked up quickly and saw that he was standing, pointing a finger at Maria. Now Torquemada glanced up from his papers and looked at her, smiling gently. He looked almost fatherly.

"No, Excellency," Maria said, her face white. "I confessed to you, truly and freely."

"Are you sure you have not forgotten something, perhaps, Maria?" Torquemada asked. "Some point that you neglected to tell us of when you were here two months ago? Perhaps there is a small thing that you have forgotten. Tell us now, Maria. Confess. You will be forgiven, as before."

"I confessed all to you," she said. She was stubborn in her defense, something I knew Torquemada would eventually overcome, whether here or in the darker chambers below this one.

"We have evidence that you are still a Jew, Maria," Torquemada said quietly, his voice dropping so low that I could just hear him. I wondered if Maria, who sat farther away, made out what he said. "We have testimony that you are following the laws of Moses yet, Maria. From many people. From your godson, Señor Hadida."

Though I knew that was a lie, having heard Hadida's testimony, Maria did not. She was shaken by the news and I wondered if there was some truth to what Torquemada accused her of. Perhaps she was a heretic after all.

I realized with a start what I had been thinking. I was here, part of the Inquisition, and I was becoming like those who sat next to me at the table; an Inquisitor, suspecting everyone of heresy. I was not here to look for Catholic heresy. I was here to protect Torquemada, this man who stood before me and whispered grimly to frightened women. He enjoyed this. It was so obvious. His smile, his lowered voice, his glances that seemed to be looking at the far wall while actually looking at the witness in the chair.

I had to leave this room before I became any more like the Inquisitor-General. I felt contaminated, as if the Most Reverend had stepped from his sealed chamber and touched my face with his infected fingers. My body shuddered involuntarily at the thought.

"Please excuse me, sir," I mumbled to Torquemada, and stood from the table, scraping the chair over the stone floor. The Inquisitor-General's expression was one of surprise, then confusion. "I am not feeling well, not well at all. Please, excuse me." And I rushed from the room, not wanting to control this body any longer, sick of inhabiting someone else, spying from his eyes, watching the past for enemies. I am afraid that was when I lost what faith I yet had, felt it slip away in the dim corridor through which I raced. I did not have to worry about being forsaken for liking death any longer. I would be cast down for a more important reason. I no longer believed. Not in the Orange Synod, not in the Most Reverend, not in my task. Perhaps not even in Christ.

I had become like those I hated, like the Catholics I had killed. The Most Reverend should have known the danger of contamination, yet he had forced me here, where I would lose my faith. I had been called to this, he had told me long ago, but he had lied. He had only used me, and in so doing had caused my loss of faith.

I walked through the plaza, weaving around the stalls, wanting only to get far away from the Inquisition. I let the body work itself, finding its own way to the guest house. I would remain there until the THIEF came for me, even though I was to guard Torquemada from the Jesuits. I no longer cared if he lived or died, or even if his death altered time. I felt betrayed by my religion and did not care if it vanished with Torquemada's demise.

Sanferaz found me that night, drinking from the second bottle in my room at the guest house. He bowed again, though not as deeply, and again showed his smile that duplicated Torquemada's.

"You are better?" he asked, the smile still there. I nodded. "You may find it interesting that Maria Pampona was declared guilty of heresy, being a Judaizer and false penitent. She will burn tomorrow at the auto-da-fé."

I nodded again, my mind foggy but still in control of my borrowed body.

"She finally confessed, though the Inquisitor-General had to turn her over to the rack and the water," Sanferaz said. He enjoyed his job too, just as Torquemada did. They had both probably watched while water was poured down Maria's throat until she gagged and began to strangle. That was probably when she "confessed."

"Get out of here," I said hoarsely.

"I am to bring you to the auto-da-fé in the morning," he said, not moving. "The Inquisitor-General was most displeased that you left the interview without permission."

"Get out!" I believe I screamed it as I hurled the half-empty bottle at him. It missed, but it had its effect, for he left hurriedly, not smiling any longer.

When I awoke, light was just beginning to come through the half-shuttered windows. Empty bottles lay around me on the bed, their contents stained into the blankets. I sat up slowly, my head humming. The pain was there, but not unbearable. I would live.

I called for the caretakers and had bread, fruit and cheese brought to me. I was determined to stay in this house until the THIEF came for me. I had no wish to see Maria, or anyone else, burn at the auto-da-fé. I knew I would face punishment when I returned to my own time, for not following instructions of the Synod, but I did not care. If it came to the worst, I could always lie about my actions. There was really no easy way for the Most Reverend to check on my word. After rebuking my faith, I would not be damned any farther by a lie.

A soft knock interrupted my meal. I ignored it, but it sounded again, and then again, louder each time. The door was shaking with the blows before it burst open, the frame splintered. Sanferaz and two of Torquemada's bodyguards stood in the doorway. Sanferaz was smiling.

"You are asked to accompany us to the auto-da-fé, Señor Ordienta," he said. I looked over the glass of wine I was sipping and shook my head.

"The Inquisitor-General made his wishes quite specific, Señor. There is not room for interpretation, I am afraid."

The two guards, *familiars* dressed as Sanferaz was, moved into the room and stood beside me.

"And if I do not wish to attend?" I asked, not looking at the men next to me.

Sanferaz smiled his Torquemada smile and spread his hands wide in front of him. "That will be impossible, Señor." They would pull me to my feet and drag me to the plaza if they had to. So I drank the last of the wine, set the glass on the floor and stood from the bed.

The sun was already hot in the plaza when we arrived, Sanferaz and the two *familiars* beside me. People stepped out of my way and looked down at the ground when we passed. Sanferaz had brought a ceremonial robe for me which I had pulled on over my clothing. Its shiny blackness and stiff collar were impressive, I had to agree.

"Am I to join the procession?" I asked Sanferaz.

"Whatever you wish, Señor," he said, smiling at me all the while. But the two guards did not move and I knew they would force me into the parade. I shrugged my shoulders, knowing that contact with the Inquisitor-General would not do me further harm, for the harm had already been done.

I walked through the crowd, parting it as I went, and made for the red silk banners of the Inquisitors. I could see the sign of the Inquisition emblazoned on the side facing me; the rough cross with the olive branch on one side, the straight sword on the other, both pointing to the heavens. I finally reached the Inquisitors, led by Torquemada himself, resplendent in his official costume. He saw me shove my way into the group, but only nodded to me. I wanted to call out to him, but thought better of it when I noticed the file of soldiers beside him, halberds on their shoulders.

My escort had left me and I stood on my toes, looking over the heads of those in front, and saw the procession stretched out before me. I could see a green cross draped with black bunting waving over the heads of everyone, along with the green poles that held the effigies of those declared heretics who had had the good fortune to escape before arrest. The remainder of the parade was a mass of hats, the shapes and colors marking who was who. The tall caps, like the mitres the priests wore, pointed out the accused. I remembered the caps were called *coroza*, and the red cross on each declared the wearer a heretic. On either side of each *coroza*, I could see the flowing black hood of a Dominican priest, ironically trying, even now, to edge the accused into repentance. It would do Maria Pampona no good, I knew, for she was declared a false penitent, and thus had no option but to burn at the stake. Others, more fortunate, could repent and be strangled before the faggots were lit.

The Inquisitors in front of me began to step forward and I automatically followed, the pace terribly slow at first, then faster as everyone in the procession began to move. Torquemada was two ranks in front of me, his black robe seeming to soak up the bright sunlight. Looking to my side, I saw that no one in the crowd dared raise his eyes toward the Inquisitor-General.

Then I saw the Jesuit. He watched Torquemada carefully, while everyone else looked at the ground. That was his error.

He was in the rank of Inquisitors between myself and Torquemada. His face was unfamiliar. He had not been in the chamber during the interviews with Hadida and Maria Pampona, for I would have noticed his gasping breath and his stumbling walk. He was not an experienced time traveler, I knew, for he was most awkward in his borrowed body. He did not take a step that was not hesitant or clumsy. Continually, he trod on the heels of the man in front of him. He was not directly behind Torquemada, but off to the Inquisitor-General's right, close enough for a strangling wire. How he planned on escaping the procession and the ranks of soldiers I did not know. Perhaps he was a one-way traveler, ready to die to complete his mission. I had heard of Elders like that from time to time.

The procession was nearing a corner where it was slowly turning toward the center of the plaza. I could see the high platform decorated with black crepe where the Inquisitor-General would take his seat for the auto-da-fé. There was a large group of sightseers at the corner, pressing against the soldiers. As we neared the crowd, I reached out my hand and grabbed the Jesuit by the back of his head, my fingers clutched in his long hair. Sliding to my left, dragging him through the files of Inquisitors, I pushed him through the mass of people and quickly followed. It was all over in a few seconds and the procession moved on, seemingly not missing us.

The Jesuit was on the ground, his hands splayed out in front of him to break his fall. He was trying to get to his feet, but I kicked him in the small of the back and he was flat on the pavement again. A small circle had been made for us by the people around. They weren't even bothering to look at either the Jesuit or myself, wisely believing it was none of their business what two members of the Inquisition were doing here, fighting in the street.

I was on top of the Jesuit now, my hands wrapped around his neck, lifting his head and twisting it so that he could see my face.

"Jesuit," I hissed. "Pray to your pope, Jesuit." I started to twist his neck even more, but he made sounds as if he wanted to speak. I loosened my grip slightly.

"Señor, what are you doing?" he gasped, the noise of his breathing almost masking his voice.

"Do not try to trick me, Jesuit. I know who you are."

"Please, I don't know what you are saying. Please release me, Señor, I beg you," he whispered.

"Admit that you are a Jesuit and I will let you live," I said. I was aware of no one else, only the man on the ground beneath me. The crowd had vanished, as far as I was concerned. "Tell the truth and you will live."

The man said nothing. I closed my hands tighter around his neck, then slackened them again. He nodded quickly. "Yes, yes, I am Jesuit. Are you Sanction, or—"

He did not finish, for I twisted his head until I hear his neck snap. His eyes glazed over and I let the body slide out of my hands and to the ground. Turning him over, I loosened his robe and pawed his waist until I found the length of wire intended to strangle his victim.

I stood slowly, the cleared space now larger than before. I looked at the people around the open area, but they all looked away.

I had killed again, without even thinking of what I was doing. It was so simple, so automatic, that it was over in a matter of minutes. The Jesuit was dead at my feet, though I had sworn I would never kill again. I had been afraid of losing grace for liking murder, yet my experience had killed this man without thought or meditation.

"What are you looking at?" I yelled at the people who stood around me, *not* looking at me. "Why don't you watch, why don't you look at me?" My voice was out of control now, stuttering and stammering as it climbed higher and higher. "What are you so afraid of? Look at me!" I was screaming now, my voice singing far into the plaza, for mass was now being said from the platform where Torquemada sat.

I collapsed on the ground, next to the dead Jesuit, the clumsy Jesuit. I shook from anger and frustration. I would never be able to stop killing, I knew.

I sat there, weeping aloud, while the mass was read. Eventually, I got to my feet. None of the people around made a move to aid me, but I slowly straightened and pushed through the crowd, saying nothing.

The mass was finished and the heretics were being led to the stakes at the far side of the square. The *sanbenitos* they wore were bright yellow, red crosses and flames drawn on them in garish paint. Some had flames painted on upside down; these were the ones who would be strangled before the fires were lit. I saw Maria in the group of those who would be burned alive, their hands bound behind them and the marks of torture still on their faces from the night before.

By the time I reached the platform, the fires were just being set, the green faggots smoking thickly. If she was lucky, Maria would succumb to the smoke before she felt the heat of the flames.

"You look fatigued, Señor Ordienta," Torquemada said as he stood and moved to stand next to me. His voice was as soft as the first time I heard it, in the Inquisition chamber, a mere two days ago.

I watched the lighting of the fires and Torquemada turned to look that way also. "Do you pity them?" he asked.

I said nothing, still catching a glimpse now and then of Maria through the smoke that encircled the stake she was bound to. "Though their bodies are lost, their souls are so saved. That is what is important, don't you agree, Ordienta?" the Inquisitor-General asked.

"I once believed that," I said, still looking at the fires, trying not to listen to the screams.

"You are not sure of your faith, Señor Ordienta?"

"Do you know of the Sixth Circle, Inquisitor-General?" I asked, ignoring his question, still looking at the fires that smoked and occasionally burst into open flame.

He did not answer for what seemed like minutes. "Ah, Dante Alighieri, you mean. Yes, I have read him." He looked to the smoke and fires. "You refer to the Circle of Hell where heretics are punished. Am I correct, Señor Ordienta?"

"They were made to lie in open tombs, red hot tombs," I said.

"And the lids of those tombs will be put into place on the Day of Judgment. I have read it, Señor. What is your point?"

"They will have a death within a death, closed away from God," I said, knowing now why I feared contamination from the Inquisitor-General. Why I felt I had lost my faith, not by liking murder, but by becoming what I fought.

"Do you enjoy this work of God, Inquisitor-General?" I asked.

"It is not a matter of liking what I must do. It is the work of God and it has been given to me to complete. It is my duty to root out heresy that can destroy the Church. I do it for that reason. I need not like what I must do." He pointed toward the fires, where the screams were growing louder and louder. I could hear the crowd's murmuring as the flames touched each of the heretics in turn.

He was lying. I could see the gleam in his eye as he stood and watched those he had sent to their deaths. He would rationalize what he did, just as I had done, but it would do no good. He could not hide the fact that he enjoyed it.

"We are both heretics, Inquisitor-General, and will burn in the Sixth Circle," I said quietly. "Because you murder in the name of God," I said, pointing to the crowd and the burning women and men, "and I have done the same. But you will be shut within your iron box because you like what you do *and* because you will not admit it. Heresy within heresy, Inquisitor-General; death within death."

I hated myself almost as much as I hated Torquemada at that moment. There was too much of myself in him, too much to look at and compare. My fear of desiring murder and my fear of contamination from the Catholics were two parts of the same emotion. The Inquisitor-General enjoyed death, just as I did. I feared my own hunger for death, thus I feared Thomas de Torquemada. Until now, for I realized that I was not as lost as he. At least I could admit my hunger.

I should not have been thinking, but watching instead. Perhaps that was why I was caught off guard, though perhaps it was because I had never heard of *two* Jesuits dropping out and down to the same time and place.

Before I could react, a wire had been slipped around the Inquisitor-General's neck and begun to bite into the skin. I saw the face of the Jesuit behind him and noticed only that it had no expression. The Jesuit felt nothing as he killed the Inquisitor-General. By the time I reached the Jesuit, Torquemada was dead and I had failed my mission for the Synod. The wire, still twisted around Torquemada's neck, made the Jesuit clumsy. It was easy to kill him. I thought nothing as I strangled him with hands that are not really mine. It was automatic, yes, but I knew what I was doing. It was not like when I killed the first Jesuit in the street, the one who had been only a diversion for the real murderer. The Catholics were clever.

The sudden death of Torquemada had cleared away an open space on the platform. Even the *familiars* did nothing. It was as if time had stopped.

For me, it had, for I felt the THIEF reach out for me, its blackness beginning to envelop me. It must have been keyed to pull me out the very instant my mission was fulfilled, or failed. It was both, actually.

For that infinite moment of time between bodies, I could see the corpses on the platform, the wire still around the Inquisitor-General's neck, and hear the dwindling screams of the people burning at the auto-da-fé. I could still feel my hands around the throat of the Jesuit and I smiled to myself, knowing that I liked the feeling, and not caring that it pleased me.

The Most Reverend granted me the leave of absence I asked for when I woke in my own body. I spent the year he gave me on the pleasure islands and I only killed two people during that year, one of them a young woman who believed I was the Angel of the Lord. I kept the name, but not her.

Nothing had changed. The world was as it had been before I left for Castille and Thomas de Torquemada. His death had altered nothing. Oh, the probability machines said that people had never existed, but the computers had always said that. Nothing would ever change, no matter who was killed in time. Nothing affected reality.

When I finally returned to the Most Reverend's sealed chamber and stood before its transparent walls, squinting into the dimness of his room, I was sure I had made the correct decision.

"I have lost the faith of the Synod and my soul as well, Most Reverend. I must ask to be relieved of my duty," I said softly into the chip I held in my hand. I knew how he would answer. Just as I would have known how Thomas de Torquemada would have answered.

"Yet you have faith of a sort, Jan DeVries," he said simply.

I nodded. "Yes, Most Reverend." My faith was no longer in my religion, in my Most Reverend, not even in my God. It was in myself, the knowledge that I could kill with impunity, wanted to kill, and that here I had an outlet for that, a place where it was sanctioned. Indeed, revered.

"Then you will continue to serve God," the Most Reverend whispered. Perhaps by now the new-leprosy *had* affected his voice.

"Your soul means nothing to the Synod. But as long as you have a faith, you will continue to do God's bidding."

Indeed, I could not help thinking, and smiling to myself at the same time. Indeed.

Judgment Day

Frank Ward

Frank Ward teaches English and a course in science fiction in Louisville, Kentucky. He has sold several stories to amateur publications; "Judgment Day" is his second professional sale.

Among man's noblest features is his constant desire to quest for things beyond his reach, to stretch himself as far as he can. At the same time, history and literature have long warned us of the crime of hubris, pride, overweening ambition. At what point does one become the other? "Judgment Day" offers an answer ... and another question.

The cherub floated into the cabin and hung silently between floor and ceiling, waiting patiently until I looked up from the autoscript.

"You've got it," he said. The Dresden doll face never matched the telepathic bass that came into my head every time Herschel spoke.

"When?" I asked, flipping the mike away. It drifted out to the length of the cord, then made a slow arc into its Velcro cradle.

The angel's expression remained unchanged but that inner voice acquired a slight tremble.

"At your convenience, Maxwell. He's in no hurry. But it's considered good form to have an audience before evening worship. Otherwise, nightfall is delayed. That upsets the seraphim a great deal."

Herschel continued to hover. After a moment, I remembered protocol and made a hasty sign of the cross. In a flurry of wings and pink baby flesh, he left.

So we finally get a chance, I thought as I turned back to the autoscript and randomly plucked some of the text sheets off the track. For four weeks I had sweated blood over that machine. Pleas, logic, rationalizations. Dozens of empty threats and a handful of real ones I thought we might be able to muster. Every conceivable argument that might weigh in our favor formulated, revised and restated until there was a tidy stack of 35,000 words of text in the retaining cage. It was a hundred-page defense, and He would probably consider it objectively, in spite of the fact that from the beginning of time He had known everything I would say in it.

"Damn omnipotence." I made no attempt to lower my voice. After all, He knew everything that was going on anyway.

For a few minutes I considered calling Herschel back. He hadn't brought word about Kruger's promised resurrection in days and that had done nothing for the state of my nerves. It was all just too much. Suicides, angels, mortal sins in the middle of a saddle-curved universe, appeals and reprieves and perdition, all strung along the length of a kilometer-long testimony to man's collective scientific skill. The only thing I wanted at that moment was to wake up and find out it had all been nothing more than a bad reaction to residual suspension fluid.

I decided that some physical exertion might clear my head. Unfortunately, with that imposing archangel still looming over the hatchway to the control center and steadfastly refusing entry to anyone long enough to activate ship's gravity, the gym and rec center were out. That left a tow, the push-pull lunging through the ship on the emergency tethers we had rigged. Two complete trips down the length of the central stem worked up the sweat I'd hoped for. It didn't help.

At the end of the second leg, the short, stocky figure of Parkins, my executive officer, dropped out of one of the tubeways. The crew had seen Herschel, he said, and they wanted to know what was going on. I told him about the appointment. He seemed actually relieved.

"Let's get it over with." His voice sounded as tired and disgusted as I imagined mine did at the end of every shift. "If we don't move on, there are going to be shore leave problems."

It was the first humorous thing I had ever heard Parkins say, raising the image of a navy cutter with ensign waving as it puttered across the eternity of space to the nearest shore. Unfortunately, the rest of his comments weren't so amusing

"Captain," Parkins added after a slight hesitation, "we're going to have trouble if we don't move soon. The Kruger business has everybody on edge and now there's Peel and that angel. It may not be a woman, but you try and convince him of that. As it stands now, we'll have to tie him down when we leave or he'll go right after it, vacuum notwithstanding."

I had seen the object of Peel's love and could understand the sentiment. It was hard to believe that figure could belong to anything but a gorgeous female, even with the thirty-foot wingspan. She was striking, of course. They were all striking. Men, women, children;

all of them right out of the greatest religious paintings of two and a half millennia. It was going to be a problem. I told Parkins to ban all forms of supernatural beings from the crew quarters. We both politely ignored the fact that I'd given that particular order twice before.

I continued the workout until exhaustion came on, then floated back down the lines to my cabin. The thought of dinner had no great appeal and at first I gave up the idea of eating altogether. But tomorrow I would be in no condition to eat, I decided, and every condemned man deserves a final meal.

I cleaned up while the galley worked, and came out just as Ensign Biddle delivered a meal basket for me. The dinner was a waste of time; the taste of everything was drowned in the fact of tomorrow.

Later, I zipped up the lining of my door and threw the security clearance light. At least it guaranteed that I wouldn't be bothered with anything less than a minor emergency. For a minute the thought of taking one of Kruger's sleeping pills crossed my mind. They had been a help in the first few days but now they had begun to bring on nightmares. Instead I wrapped myself in the free-fall netting and tried to sleep.

Oddly enough, I succeeded. After a few hours, most of it faded away. Herschel, Peel's affair with an angel, Kruger's death and promised resurrection. Every problem eased out of my consciousness with one small exception; tomorrow I had a meeting with God.

The next morning cycle, Herschel appeared in the air lock just as the EVA crew finished checking over the module. He made a few quick passes over the equipment, occasionally touching various points on the stark white finish with his chubby fingers. Each time, the paint team floated forward, crowding around the spot for half a minute, then drifting on to the waiting cherub's next location. After a quarter of an hour, Herschel pronounced the job done. At least two dozen figures dotted the surface, from the outline of a fish to a Byzantine cross. Satisfied with the transformation of the module into an icon, he motioned for me to enter.

We went through the normal check-out procedures, Herschel

hovering over my right shoulder the entire time. Eventually the crew left the lock and I cycled the computer for disembarkation. With only the mildest shudder, the umbilicals separated and I took over manual control.

It was a glorious day. The lock hatch opened to the sight of vast cumulus walls a hundred kilometers distant, majestic as any painting. The cloud walls terminated in the azure sky that you dream about constantly when you're under suspension, that never-ending fragile blue.

No matter what the instruments said, the view was strictly planetary. There *was* an up and down. Every experience as a human being and an interstellar confirmed that somewhere below was the ground—ground that pulled flying objects to itself. Your reaction was to start the engines and leave them on. No matter how many times the readouts said *space*, it was always an immense *sky* you were flying through.

The module cleared the ship's nose and for the first time I had a totally unobstructed view. We were moving through a trough, the gigantic walls breaking quite evenly kilometers below into a cloud cover that formed the floor. It was without a break, a billowing carpet of white that you might see on a dozen planets and never glance at as you slid through the atmosphere. It was common, normal, totally without significance until you looked up into those towering walls and that infinity of blue which every sensor, every instrument, and every moment of your own training told you just couldn't be there. Then you realized it for the first time: the inescapable conclusion came before you even had a chance to rebel against it. Kruger had been right: a likely impossibility was preferable to an unconvincing reality. Truth was what fit the circumstances and brought forth the conclusion, no matter how unpleasant. The problem was not the conclusion, but the acceptance.

Herschel's presence eased into my mind and gradually took over motor control of my hands. I sat back, at least mentally, and tried to enjoy the ride. The first few times I had watched my own fingers operating the controls with smooth efficiency and without a single impulse from me had been very upsetting. But Herschel obviously enjoyed this form of flying and I was used to it by now. After all, he was certainly a more qualified pilot—at least by natural inclination..

As the panorama flowed by, I thought, thank God *(poor choice of words)* that Kruger had never been EVA. Just the view from the observation gallery had been enough to convince him that we were in paradise. I dreaded thinking what he might have done after looking at those exquisite cloud mountains with a Sistine Chapel infant spirit hovering at his side. Probably would have tried to fly out there himself, like the scores of angels we saw every day through the ports, and gotten the shock of his life when the vacuum snuffed him out. No matter what it looked like, it was still the same emptiness of space that fills the universe between galaxies. The visual contradictions didn't change the realities.

Too many contradictions. From the first moment I'd awakened to the sight of a chubby two-year old with wings staring at me intently, they had been piling up. At first glance, everything fit the image of celestial territory: the angels, the sky, the sense of unlimited power that pulls a probe out of hyperspace with the same disinterest with which you might remove a sliver of metal from your thumb. It was enough to convince you that here was the one and only Supreme Being: Jehovah, Odin, Zeus, Brahma—the Creator.

But there were little things that didn't fit. Herschel, for one. From the moment he spoke to me for the first time, there was that name, as improbable as the entire situation. And his voice. It had all the angelic quality of a slabber when the forms don't set properly. He may have been a cherub on the outside but there was decidedly something else inside that pink head.

Then there was the delay. If the sin we had committed was so immense, why hadn't He simply exercised His legendary skills and flicked us off to some eternal damnation? Even Milton's God didn't require Lucifer to summarize his rebellious inclinations in writing, much less wait a month for the final draft.

In the very beginning, Kruger had suggested that we were creating the scene ourselves: our own minds were adapting sensory data alien to our experience into shapes we could recognize. Kruger had dumped that particular theory the first time a passing member of the

Host casually mentioned that here resurrection was a fact. He had thrown away a dozen years of training and as many of actual flight time on that one little point. We were still spotting tiny globules of his blood in the ventilation system.

Off to port, a gleaming pinpoint of light appeared in the distant cloud bank. Herschel turned sharply and headed for it; apparently this was our destination. The fact that it was over two hours before he actually set the little module down on a ledge may give some idea of the size but not of my reaction. What I saw was so natural, so fitting in this situation, that I suppose I should have expected it, but my first reaction was just too human. My laughter must have offended Herschel greatly, because he was still not talking to me when we got out and started to climb that golden staircase marching upward through the clouds.

Hours later, I demanded a break. The muscles in my legs were cramping and my respirator light glowed ominously amber. Those stairs were a great deal of work for a man who hadn't been in a gravity field for months.

Herschel reluctantly agreed. He was still upset with my earlier response and only spoke after some insistent prodding. Finally his gravel voice emerged from behind the telepathic block.

It wasn't until then that I truly realized how completely I had hurt his feelings with my laughter, and he was now offended even more because I hadn't thanked him for the gravity. He informed me with a series of mental images darkened with sullenness that he had had to make a special request for that particular feature of our audience and he left no doubt that it had been supplied only because of his reputation for frugality. I suppose it was my own fault, after constantly harping about the gossamer-winged lummox in the control center, that Herschel would think I'd appreciate the sensation, even when trying to climb a staircase that gave every indication of going on forever.

In the most contrite tones, I projected my thanks. The cherub body-blushed in embarrassment and hastily agreed to an extended break.

For a while we talked lightly about our respective human and angelic responsibilities. Herschel let slip a small piece of information which gave me a new insight into the daily lives of the Heavenly Host. Peel's lady friend was the talk of the neighborhood, Herschel whispered, and under even more pressure to break things off than Peel himself. The distinct impression Herschel left me with was that the community felt it was a scandalous step down. It was even rumored that *He* was going to step in and take a hand in settling the matter.

I found it hard to believe that the Lord God Almighty would stoop to solving a domestic *faux pas*. Perhaps He acted as the ultimate counselor, patiently listening to thousands of complaints about who failed to be home for supper on time, or had an affair with which celestial secretary. I suppressed the laughter that was building up inside me. Nowhere in the vast multiplicity of religions scattered throughout the universe did it say that being God didn't come with its own set of drab, uninteresting problems.

Herschel finally relaxed enough and I gingerly suggested that he might reduce the gravitational force, at least until we reached our rendezvous point. Waves of apologetic sympathy poured into my thoughts and he readily agreed to see what could be done. Flying up the line of stairs faster than I had ever imagined he could travel, he disappeared in a matter of moments; I was alone for the first time that day.

Ours was certainly a peculiar relationship. I still couldn't decide if Herschel was an ambassador or a guard. Certainly after our second meeting there could be no doubt that the latter was at least partially true.

At first Kruger and I had found ourselves alone with the *Edmund Babel* in automated free-fall, apparently the only ones whom the powers-that-be felt necessary to revive. A frenzied thirty-six hours of work had accomplished the awakening of most of the crew. The two of us had just compared notes and come to the realization that the illusionary cherub of our first few moments of consciousness was a common experience when Herschel flew into the stateroom.

He spoke then for the first time, the telepathic voice announcing in the most somber tones to every mind on board that we must *come to judgment.* That was the exact phrase: *come to judgment.* As if we were a boatload of medieval peasants obsessed with dying so we could escape the misery of life. We, the cream of an exploration program covering two dozen human colonies—the amassed knowledge of mankind filling our heads and our computers; the power of atomic fabric twisting the universe itself to move us out of our own galaxy—here being addressed in a tone of voice that suggested we were too naive to understand our situation.

"You must realize that you have presumed." Even as Herschel spoke, Kruger began to drift toward the doorway. He must have hoped to cut the cherub off before he had a chance to do his disappearing act again.

I tried to keep the cherub talking. "Presumption seems to be your specialty, not ours. We certainly didn't intend to stop here. That was your idea."

"Not mine," he said. He floated to within an inch of my nose and stared hard into my eyes. *"His."*

I was beginning to feel like one of those awful characters out of the ancient space operas, confronted with some disgusting lime-colored monstrosity with Napoleonic delusions on a universal scale, Ming the Merciless with legions of heavenly minions, one of whom flew before me and tried like the devil to sound imposing.

"And who is *He?"* It was a stall, but an interesting one.

It was that question that gave me my first lesson in cherub physiology. He actually turned white with shock. His entire three-foot-long body paled and a small twitch developed at the base of his left wing.

"The Creator." It was a mental whisper, spoken in a hush that mixed respect and fear in equal portions. He was far too serious to laugh at, so I tried to project the same sense of propriety.

"You mean *your* creator?" I tentatively suggested.

The response was immediate and agitated. "There is only one Prime Cause. He Who sets all things in motion: the Word, the Light. Our Creator, your Creator. The Almighty who reigns in Oneness." For a moment, his face took on the deepest sense of sorrow. "And you have presumed against Him."

The conversation had taken on such outlandish implications that I forgot Kruger until it was too late. He had managed to position himself on the cabin wall directly opposite Herschel. He suddenly pushed away, arms wide in a scooping gesture. I never did understand what he was trying to accomplish. Certainly he had better sense than to hope to catch the angel in some sort of flying tackle. Later, when he was conscious again, he muttered a few broken sentences about illusions and mass psychosis.

In any case, what he planned was a moot point the moment he was two feet from the wall. Frankly, I had to admire the skill of whoever was running the show. In two hundred years we had never been able to produce a gravity field small enough to encompass anything less than a medium-sized asteroid, but the one that grabbed Kruger and froze him to the floor plates was tailor-made for his body. It was strong, too. Kruger could bench press 150 kilograms in an Earth field, but at the moment he could barely force himself off the floor for a few seconds before collapsing.

The strain on his internal organs must have been near the critical point before the field cut off and he began to drift off the floor with the air currents.

"Still more of your presumption." The angel's telepathic voice projected vast pity, as if he were watching the antics of a poorly trained animal act. With ritualized formality he pulled a glowing scroll from out of the air and handed it to me. "He sends you a list of your failings."

With a few stately movements of his wings, Herschel turned, drifted around Kruger's waking form, and floated away.

The scroll was a beautiful piece of work. Kruger later said that it was superior to the medieval ones, the labor of dozens of years of monkish obsession, that he had seen in a Hamburg museum on Earth. Certainly the combination of script and gold leaf was breathtaking.

Sadly, the text itself was far less pleasant. The cherub had been completely truthful. The sin was indeed presumption, and not just ours, the crew of the *Edmund Babel*, but that of the entire human race. Apparently we were to justify the ways of man to God and to show just cause why man (or we—the terms seemed interchangeable as far as the scroll and *He* were concerned) should not be punished.

And the final irony was the case in point, the immediate act which had brought the wrath of *Him* down on us. Kruger and I each read the last passage over and over again, looking for any other interpretation. We even called in Parkins, the least imaginative officer in the interstellar service, hoping that the implication was imagined and not real.

"It says we violated Heaven." Parkins didn't even flinch at the statement he had made. "We showed up where we weren't supposed to be without His permission."

After that, Kruger insisted that we move down to Medical and produced what was perhaps the only bottle of scotch in at least two dimensions. Of course he was right. That certainly was the time for a drink.

So there was no doubt that Herschel was warden of the jail. But it wasn't until later, the next appearance and the ones after, that I began to see him as our liaison, our guide, and oddly enough, our supporter.

It became clear that this particular angel was impressed with us. His third visitation, while filled with vast reams of instructions on how to respond properly to the indictment before us, was also the occasion for a request to tour the ship. He seemed fascinated by the mechanics, the relays and links, chips and microcircuits that comprise the heart of any ship designed to reach through the curve of the universe.

"It's all so *material*," he cooed in awed tones after we emerged from the last engineering section.

I tried to sound pleased. After all, we needed all the friends we could get in this situation and Herschel was definitely showing signs of becoming a reluctant supporter. He fluttered about, obviously hoping for more.

"Would you like to see the drive itself?" I suggested.

It was inconvenient to break the seal on the generator core and even more inconvenient to replace it, but the result was well worth the effort. Four hours later, after peering into every force curtain and macrochannel, Herschel was positively ecstatic. From that point on, if Herschel was in command of the watch, it was a relaxed tour of duty.

In the end, if the document stuffed in the storage pocket of my second skin did any good, it would be due to the aid and assistance of our peculiar ally. It was from him that I began to sense the reasoning of the *One* Who had brought us here, and it was Herschel who timidly suggested still one more defense for what we had done.

"You must argue compatability with the image and likeness." That had been his only response after a four-hour review of the first draft of our rebuttal to the scroll. After all, presumption favors godliness, he had said and left without explanation as to how that would save us. I had to fit it somehow into the jigsaw puzzle of our situation.

Sitting there on a literal reproduction of a stairway to paradise, I hoped I had gotten it right.

A small dot appeared, swelled, and finally filled out into the figure of Herschel returning. Even before he reached me, I noticed the gravitational pull lessening. As always, the cherub had come through.

It may have been hours or days before we reached the final step. For me time simply ceased to be gradations on a clock, and became only the lifting of one foot after another, the pushing of a step down and away into an infinite pile of rubble that I had begun to imagine was behind me.

No wonder I stumbled when I reached the last step. I found myself standing on an endless plain of gold beneath a sky of miracle blue. The view was broken by only a single object. Perhaps a hundred meters from us was a small, raised platform molded from the same material as the floor. On it was a throne.

I suppose the simplicity of the whole scene was what threw me off guard. Of the myriad possibilities that had crossed my mind over the past few weeks, this had not been one. Slowly the majesty of the scene, its directness and understatement, took hold. There was something fitting and proper about an almighty being that could appreciate the mood created by this meeting place.

Then, as if to complement my thoughts, *He* came forth.

He walked out of the distance as if He had been out for a stroll and had decided to rest in the gazebo of a small garden. With a casual air, He mounted the platform and languidly stretched himself upon the throne.

I started forward. Herschel instantly fluttered in front of me and made it perfectly clear that the audience would be long distance. So I stayed where I was, and the show began.

Against a universe of sky that could have swallowed entire nebulas, I was given the history of my species in a panorama. Not just the massive, civilization-shattering events, but the entire summation of every creature that had shared the label of human since the beginning of the world. Those lives filled a vast, pulsating canvas. Races, wars, Caesars and Khans, the births and deaths of a thousand cultures flared in the foreground. The history contained in countless textbooks and museums was nothing more than sparks that burned for a moment, then faded to minuscule insignificance when faced with that breathing, massive background. No single human achievement was more than a momentary pinprick of energy. The story of man lay in the shifting mosaic of life that beat out its billions of births and deaths. The rest, the thousands of moments and events that had always been labeled history, were nothing more than frivolous detail.

But it all said the same thing: the irritation of a parent whose child refuses to obey or offer respect. Man presumed to think, to feel, to change and adapt the natural order not only on his own world but a dozen others. Now he presumed to touch upon the very fabric of his Creator.

The last scene was a view of the *Edmund Babel*, hanging in the clouds as I had left her. But she wasn't beauty nestled in beauty now. Now she was a shriveled piece of mute metal and plastic dwarfed by clouds that spoke of their own greatness and the pathetic size of this intruder.

Then the sky cleared. Even with the distance between us, I recognized the gesture as *He* rose and raised his arm. Present what defense you can muster, *He* commanded.

I took the manuscript from my pocket and handed it to Herschel. With great dignity, he soared away toward the figure on the platform and gingerly laid it at His feet.

He stood motionless as each page swirled upward and blossomed to fill the sky from horizon to horizon, my arguments transformed into images of sight and sound. They rose and stood for a brief instant, then were swept away like dust. Each explanation, each plea, vanished before me in total insignificance. Even I had to recognize their weaknesses. Our hints of retaliation were laughable, our demands for justice and due process ridiculous. Nothing could withstand the indictment of man's collective disaster that had just been presented.

There was only one point left, the only interpretation that I had ever made of Herschel's advice. It lay now as the last pages of the manuscript, those few pages holding the fate of myself and my people.

They rose as the others had and exploded into full realization. It was a short, single image, somehow not at all what I expected. Suddenly the sky was filled with a reflection of my own view at that moment: the plain, the throne, the hazy figure standing there—Him, the One, the Word. The scene was a mirror image of what I was seeing through my own eyes.

Then the perspective changed, zooming in close enough for me to make out each detail, each feature of Him.

There could be no mistake. From the metallic, silver glow of the suit to the small crimson officer's stripes that had taken me twelve years to earn, everything was the same. It was I myself there, the image and likeness of both creature and creator.

He still stood motionless, as if considering the outlandishness of the idea. Yet if this was all the real thing, if *He* was what He appeared to be, then to condemn us for acting like gods would be as foolish as punishing a child because he had learned his father's trade.

I have no idea how long we waited. Neither of us spoke, each awaiting his own individual fate.

Finally there was movement on the platform. He raised both hands very slowly, then brought them together in a clap of thunder. A huge fireball sprang from those clasped hands and enveloped both of us in blinding light.

The last thing I remember before slipping into unconsciousness was the sound of deep, strangely human laughter echoing in my head.

I woke up in the *Edmund Babel*, stretched out on the cot rather than the free-fall net. Obviously, some decision had been reached. With my head throbbing, I staggered to the hallway and down to the Control Center.

It didn't take long to find that the entire ship was deserted. Peel, Parkins, all the others, gone; their rooms neatly arranged and tidy as if we were back at Orbital-1 ready for disembarkation. Even the angels themselves weren't in sight. It was the same in every section. No person, no sound but that of equipment purring to its own internal rhythm. The suspension hold gaped empty like a dry well, the hundred individual cubicles patiently waiting to cool the life out of bodies that no longer seemed to exist, pantries filled with endless rows of consumables that would last a single man hundreds of years. Everywhere the same. There was no one.

For some reason, it all seemed appropriate. There was nothing to do but prowl around and eventually sit watching, hours upon hours, in the observation gallery for something to move between the sky and clouds.

And eventually something did. The angels, in their usual stream of traffic, again began to float by. After a week they were back to their normal flow, busily traveling from one destination to another across my field of vision. Even Herschel materialized finally. He appeared while I sat eating my makeshift breakfast today.

He wants me to settle a dispute between two archangels over territorial rights. And render a decision on the fate of some race of intellectually animated insects that are about to push two piles of uranium a bit too close together for their racial good. He also left a schedule for tomorrow.

Six cases of pre-amino acid dispersion; a miracle visitation to a chosen race of silicone cubits; one intercession in the natural order of a nova; four saviors to be selected, and at least one Final Judgment.

I suppose it will help pass the time. Herschel tells me that the throne is still available and I suppose I shall use it to help create the proper atmosphere. Getting used to the idea of being an Ultimate Essence depends a great deal upon the mood you set, or so it seems to me. But it still leaves me without an answer to the question, the one that caused the cherub to turn pale for the second time since I have known him and to leave me until tomorrow, I suppose. So I sit here, letting it echo through the ship's intercom on a loop tape, hoping for the final answer to come from the metal itself. With the irony of my own voice, it booms out the single, nagging query that is probably the least important of all things now.

Is this the punishment or the reward?

The Theology of Water

Hilbert Schenck

Hilbert Schenck won instant acclaim a couple of years ago with his first short stories, collected in Wave Rider *in 1980. His first novel,* At the Eye of the Ocean, *was published in 1981 and reinforced his reputation as a fine and thoughtful writer whose work is solidly grounded in both hard science and a deep sensitivity for the fragile humanity of his characters.*

In "The Theology of Water," Schenck presents an isolated group of scientists with a scientific question that may or may not have a scientific answer.

NASA had finally come to the Titan Mission as a desperate, final throw of the dice. The robot Mars landers, with their little automatic diggers and warmed and watered flower pots, had grown nothing. The probes to Venus, Jupiter and the asteroid belt all sent back discouraging messages: sterility and either violent surface conditions or utter barrenness. But then the big Saturn orbiter, an expensive wonder in itself, had turned its instruments on the moon, Titan, and a tiny hope was born. Titan had a thick atmosphere, mostly methane and other hydrocarbons but some oxygen, the surface pressure at almost seven-tenths Earth normal. Pasadena altered the orbiter's flight to let it free-fall around Saturn near Titan and several surprises appeared. There was ice, seas of it, in fact. Although the surface was at a horrendous mean temperature of minus one-hundred-and-twenty Celsius, the bolometer at the prime focus of the onboard reflecting telescope told of substantial warm spots—volcanic, radio-active, or both—where the temperature estimated beneath the ice sheet was actually above zero C. Most exciting, there were electrical storms that scorched the atmosphere of Titan and actually set high-altitude ''sky fires,'' where the local oxygen concentration was high enough for ignition with methane, and these further warmed the satellite. The exobiologists of NASA, who for years had been trying to make life in their labs from methane and electrical discharges, were filled with hope, and though the public had mostly lost interest in the life-in-space hunt, NASA slowly began to assemble the Saturn-mission manned vehicle in orbit, panel by panel, appropria-tion by appropriation.

After almost fifty years, NASA had finally concluded that the number of consecutive push-ups and miles-run-per-day were irrele-vant criteria for selecting deep space crews. The four persons on the Titan lander were thus the oldest and most expert astronauts ever to travel beyond the Moon. Mission Commander David Brunel, pilot and astronomer, had years of deep space activity, as did Dr. Gregory Bateson, a professor of chemistry at a distinguished New England university. Dr. Thomas Feeney, S.J., often referred to in the press as "God's Astronaut," had walked on the moon and had flown ten months in synchronous Earth orbit making geophysical measurements. And the tiny, fifty-year-old Japanese-American exobiologist, Dr. Anna Takoa, dean of her odd profession, was the ultimate hope for the lords of NASA in their search for other life. Veteran of half-a-dozen flights, this small woman, less than five feet tall and weighing ninety pounds, was the only scientist who had actually created a "pseudo-life" in the test tube, though she had never been able to get her chemicals to assemble duplicates of themselves. As a handsome bonus, Dr. Takoa required only sixty-three percent of the life support used by the other crew.

The gigantic Earth-Saturn transit vehicle took almost a year to make the trip, but once near Titan, the actual descent of the lander from its storage bay turned out to be simple. The cold, soupy atmosphere of Titan readily and safely absorbed the lander's potential energy and Brunel was able to drift his vessel across Titan's surface and pick his spot. They set down on a flat, volcanic plane, adjacent to a great lake or sea of ice that stretched to the horizon. And though they had all seen wonders not even imagined by most persons, they now stared, transfixed, out the lander's ports and up through the deep, blue-black sky of Titan to huge Saturn and its brilliant ring structure.

Father Feeney, his large, red face momentarily illuminated by the thin sunlight reflected from Saturn, stared in wonder. "Well, Anna," he said finally. "It's awfully cold, but the view alone ought to be enough to stir up some life out here."

The little woman peered up at the stocky priest and smiled gently. "What a nice idea, Tom," she said, "that life might emerge in response to beauty. If only it were true."

Suddenly a lightning-set sky fire went off in Titan's upper atmosphere where gravitational separation increased the molecular oxygen concentration, and the flat, rocky ground around them was fitfully bathed in an even redder light. They heard the thunder and then felt the ignition boom as the lander shuddered.

"I'm glad those things don't happen on the surface," said Commander Brunel half to himself. "Where do you think the O_2 comes from, Tom?"

"Out of the rocks, Dave," said Feeney at once. "I can't see how the ice could ever disassociate at these temperatures. There must be a continual fall and accretion of water and hydrocarbon compounds from those ignitions."

The Titan lander, its stubby wings jutting out on each side, sat on four eight-foot legs. The little craft had only two crew compartments, the upper one for sleeping, eating, and piloting, the lower one for lab work. The crew had known from the orbiter data that the ground-level atmospheric disturbances on Titan would be small. The high gas viscosity at these cold temperatures, coupled with the small contribution of heat from the distant sun, damped any weather activity. Their protective suits thus needed to resist only the bitter cold, but were flexible and non-armored, operating as they did at Titan's surface pressure.

First priority was the search for life. Dr. Takoa and Brunel went off in the electric, three-wheeled land-runner to search along the shores and out onto the ice sheet near them, while Tom Feeney and Bateson poked around the rocks and dirt of a nearby "warm spot" they had located while flying across Titan's surface. The NASA exobiologists, led by Anna Takoa, had developed an arsenal of marvelous, life-seeking instruments; devices that could detect the smallest bit of heat from the metabolic activity of microscopic, one-celled animals, protoplasm detectors that reported the weak radio waves emitted by all living cells undergoing certain kinds of biological activity, hydrocarbon probes that acoustically detected "large" or "complex" molecules such as might be associated with living matter.

Houston had designed the mission for a sixteen-day stay on Titan, to correspond with one complete orbit of the satellite around Saturn. Everyone had agreed before the start that if these four specialists could not find some kind of life on Titan in that time, it did not exist. And so, when they were not eating or resting, they went out on Titan's dark surface, peering, measuring, digging, and hoping for some tiny sign of warmth or irritability.

After several days of continuous search, their disappointments began to grow. Titan seemed as sterile as Earth's moon. There was ice with water under it. There was some oxygen and there were various hydrocarbons in the weathered "dirt." But it was a chill, flat, dark world, and finally Father Feeney and Professor Bateson decided to spend a day in the lander organizing and assimilating their data and specimens. While Tom Feeney tried various plotting methods to separate and locate Titan's two magnetic poles, Bateson worked in the chemical hood with some of the dirt and water from the surface.

"Hey, Father. Can you spare a minute?"

Tom Feeney, glum and disheartened, sighed and walked himself across the lab floor to the hood on his wheeled, aluminum stool. "Amoeba?" he suggested in a rumbling, hopeful voice.

Bateson shook his long, craggy head, but he was grinning. "No, but something weird anyway, Tom. I hacked out about a gallon of ice from the edge of the lake." He had both hands in the enclosed hood and he pointed with a slick, latex finger at the properties analysis box. "There's a sample melted from that ice in the magic box, Tom, and I'm getting a freezing point of minus 67.1 degrees Celsius."

Feeney frowned. "Quite a depression! Salty?" he suggested.

Bateson shook his head. "What I thought. So I distilled half a liter." He pointed to a compact apparatus stuffed in one corner of the long hood. "Not much residue, mostly dust. I'll look at it later. That material in the magic box now is distilled Titan water."

"It's not water, Greg, if it freezes at minus 67 C," said Father Feeney, frowning harder. "What is that stuff? It's absolutely clear?"

Bateson's grin turned sly. "If the audience will now direct its attention to this corner of the stage." His plastic-covered finger indicated a small electrolysis apparatus. "Notice that we have gas traps over the two electrodes, busily collecting gas from the electrolytic decomposition of this . . . ah . . . stuff. Note especially that one gas appears in just twice the volume of the other. Clue one. Now I take this glowing stick, ignited in the bunsen flame, and plunge it into the gas appearing in the lesser amount." He lifted the glass cover off one of the collection burettes and plunged the glowing stick into the colorless gas. It glowed whitely, then flamed up. "Clue two," said Bateson, peering sideways at Father Feeney's round mouth and eyes. He then took the flaming stick, lifted the cover off the other burette, and held the fire at the mouth. A blue flame and a loud pop immediately followed. "Clue three," said Professor Bateson, taking his hands out of the gloves.

But Tom Feeney's initial surprise had been immediately replaced by something else, a wariness coupled with an excitement. "Greg, what else is odd about that . . . water?" he asked in a tight voice.

"Let's see what we get for specific heat." Bateson put his hands back in the hood and fiddled with the controls of the properties box. In a moment the monitor screen beside the hood flashed some numbers. "About 20 percent higher," muttered Feeney thoughtfully. "Greg, can we get its density curve? Let's see if the extremum at 4 degrees C is still around anywhere."

The box heated and tested the sample as requested and soon a full data curve of liquid density against temperature appeared on the monitor. Tom Feeney blinked at the output. "Look at that, Greg! The extremum is much deeper and at least 20 degrees above the freezing point."

"Let me check that nutty thing with some real water," grunted the chemist, but when he did, the curve exactly matched the Earth water reference line.

"Why is the Titan curve stopped at 28 C?" asked Feeney.

Bateson peered at the monitor. "Because that's the boiling point, Tom. I didn't ask it for steam properties."

"Of course!" breathed Tom Feeney, and it suddenly seemed to Professor Bateson that Feeney was peering right out through the side of the lander.

At that moment they heard the *whiss* of the gas into the air lock. In a minute the hatch in the center of the circular lab compartment opened and a small, silver figure climbed up. Anna Takoa was both tired and discouraged. The finding of life, any life, on Titan would be the ultimate triumph in the career of any exobiologist. The hateful sterility of the place, cruel and harsh as it was, upset her. Titan wasn't much but it was now the only hope left in the system. And she, the greatest of her exobiologist tribe, would eventually have to pronounce it a lost hope to the world press. Her science simply did not exist, at least in this system.

Dr. Takoa was followed immediately by Mission Commander Brunel in a much larger suit. And even this extrovert seemed quiet and lost, an investor who had gambled years of effort in an enterprise now seen to be without gain or profit.

Still, they could both sense that something had changed in the lab. Tom Feeney had showed that same, slumped resignation when they had left on the electric vehicle for another life search, but now he was standing straighter and his large face was flushed and tense. Even Gregory Bateson's New England reserve seemed frayed and his hands were twisting together.

The priest stared at the arrivals as they hung up their suits and connected them for recharge. "Greg," he said, turning, "give them the same magic act you gave me. But start with the electrolysis."

Nodding, Bateson pushed his hands back into the gloves and explained where he had found the water, how he had distilled it, and what he was doing now. After the flame-up and the little blue pop of an explosion, Bateson turned to Commander Brunel. "What would you say that stuff was, Dave?"

Brunel smiled at him. "Hey, you'll have to ask harder ones than that to flunk *me* out. It's water, Professor, just like in Chem 101."

"Exactly," said Bateson drily. "Anna, what are your thoughts?"

The little Japanese woman crinkled her eyes at him. "It is obviously *not* water. Otherwise you wouldn't be going through all of this," she said with a small laugh.

"Now that's not fair!" said Bateson. "Anyway, I now place a sample of the water in the magic box and give you . . . freezing point, density of the liquid, and boiling point at one At."

They stared long and silently at the curve until Anna Takoa turned to look at Father Feeney. "Father Tom," she said lightly, "do you understand this?"

Feeney sat facing them. "I may. Some of it, anyhow. But I think we should look at whatever other properties the analysis box can give first. I have to tell you a story that I think may relate to this, but you'll believe it more after you see for yourself how this material acts."

Brunel peered shrewdly at the older man. "Is it water, Father?"

Feeney nodded. "Yes, I believe it is Titan water."

"What other . . . changes . . . in its properties do you expect?" asked Brunel, his cool eyes peering at Feeney.

The priest smiled. "Yes, you should test me that way, Dave. All right. I think the solid phase will not only float, but have an unusually low density."

Greg Bateson put his hands back in the hood and soon the monitor showed numbers and uncertainties. Brunel read off the ice density himself. "Point-six-two. I'll say it's lighter!" He whistled, then said more loudly to the chemist, "Greg, I know that super little properties box cost NASA a couple of million, but would you actually float a little Titan ice on a little Titan water for us to see?"

Bateson immediately filled a beaker with water and opened the door to a small refrigerator at the back of the hood. He removed a sliver of ice with tongs, chopped it roughly cubical with deft knife strokes and popped it into the beaker.

There was no doubt about it; the Titan ice floated far higher than normal ice. And as it floated, it rapidly melted, runnels of water appearing throughout the underwater part. This caused the cube to topple over, but as it turned upside down, it kept on rotating, over and over, faster and faster, growing steadily smaller and less cubelike. They stared, astonished.

Finally Gregory Bateson rubbed his fingers into the corners of his eyes and said to the exobiologist, "Care for a couple of those ice cubes in your before-bed nip of bourbon, Anna?"

But Tom Feeney was intently watching the ice turn and melt.

"Greg, is there any substance that when it melts has an ordered, molecular momentum exchange, say from recoil effects, as the molecule leaves the solid phase?"

Bateson shook his head. "No way, Tom. No solid is ordered like that. And the distances are too small. . . .

But the priest was muttering, lost in thought. "We never even thought of that. A high-level ordering during solidification. But what use is it?"

"All right," said Brunel to Tom Feeney with a rueful grin. "I give up on this property. Tell us another, Tom."

Feeney pursed his lips and thought for a moment about Titan. "The vapor pressure curve should be steeper at the high end. Normalize the two curves, Greg, zero to 100, then superimpose them."

Indeed, the Titan water curve was much steeper near its boiling point than the curve for Earth water. Encouraged and excited, Father Feeney rattled off a few more predictions. "Thermal conductivity of the liquid is probably about the same, as is viscosity. Specific heat of the ice, the solid phase, will be higher. Latent heat of fusion also larger but boiling latent heat lower, way lower maybe. The ice probably has different absorptive characteristics to electromagnetic energy with infrared penetrating deeper."

Almost an hour later, after all these statements were shown to be correct, the three of them stared silent and baffled at the priest, whose face now twitched with excitement. "I think we'd better hear that story, Tom, before I go completely nuts!" said Brunel.

"All right," said Tom Feeney, settling his large bulk squarely on the small stool. "Understand, it was a painful time for me and I never thought. . . . Well, as you know, I went to Notre Dame grad school after I joined the Society of Jesus. The Jesuits have always been big on physical science, sort of 'keeping an eye on the enemy,' I suppose, and I was a star in the geophysics department. So I became a professor there after my doctorate, and wrote my books and did all that business. I didn't like academic life much. NASA has some stupid people and does some stupid things, but at least nobody is claiming they're some kind of unique humanistic seers while behaving like hypocritical phonies.

"I was on the doctoral committee of a student named Elias Fullerton. He was a priest, a Jesuit too, so he immediately asked me to be his major professor since his other committee members were two laymen and a stuffy old Dominican who was department chairman. Fullerton was tall and scrawny, had a huge Adams apple, was nervous, jerky, what Freud would have seen as a classic neurasthenic.

"His dissertation topic was as odd as he was. He wanted to study, really optimize, the characteristics of water in relation to the climate of the Earth. Oh, many people had noticed how the stranger properties of water—for example its high heat capacity, density extremum, and floating of the solid phase on the liquid—related to climate and ocean behavior. But fifteen years ago it had just become possible to run computer simulations that could actually predict climatic changes with hypothetical changes in the properties of air or water. Before then we didn't have the knowledge or the equations. Too much was empirical. Also, the machines couldn't access the memory fast enough to do a complete Earth.

"The dissertation title was some typically academic jargon, 'Climatic parameter variations of real and simulated Earth-type planets as a function of the liquid and solid phase properties of water.' Something like that. Around the department, we called it 'The theology of water.'

"Well, the thing interested me. It was certainly a project with some scope to it, so Fullerton wrote the proposal and we all signed it and we were off. He did the study both ways. That is, he both varied the water properties for our given Earth, then tried the true water properties on planets at different locations, with different masses and so on. That's how I guessed out the trends for Titan's water. I tried to remember what was the best kind of water for small planets far from the sun."

"And the Earth's water and the Earth itself optimized together?" asked Anna Takoa.

The priest nodded. "It was striking. For example, if you simply assumed a continuously increasing liquid density with cooling, without our water's highly unique extremum at 4 degrees C, all kinds of drastic things happen. The cold water now lies stagnant in the deep oceans and the mean Earth temperature is over 20 Celsius degrees lower. Storms, wind and heavy cloud result. It's even worse if you make the ice sink instead of float. The oceans permanently freeze to within a couple of hundred feet of the surface. The rapid air temperature changes lead to massive storm systems. Fullerton's simulation predicted winds averaging over 300 miles an hour. If you monkey with the vapor pressure or the huge latent heat of vaporization, you get either too much cloud or none at all; either way, it's disaster. Try reducing the high specific heat of water, and remember there are few other substances that are that high, and you lose the stabilizing effect of the ocean surface and get more storms, colder average days. Virtually everything he tried either had very little effect, as with viscosity and conductivity, or else drastic effects in either direction."

"Then they were true optimums, Tom?" asked Dr. Takoa.

"Both ways," answered Feeney. "Whether you tilt the Earth up straight or lean it over to roll around like Uranus, you need another kind of water. Up straight, our water gives too much thermal stability and you get complete cloud cover and ice caps down to latitude 40 north and south. With the polar axis down flat, you get wild storms because of the source-sink effect of the hot and cold, poles. To moderate this, you need a lower freezing point, lower specific heat so the storms are more localized, and other changes. In fact, it was the angle of tilt of the Earth's axis that optimized most sharply with the properties of water."

Commander Brunel sighed. "And what was the optimizing parameter, Tom?"

Father Feeney shrugged. "It was some complicated thing that Fullerton had worked out. He went to the biologists and your gang"—Feeney pushed a finger at Professor Bateson—"to decide on a mean Earth temperature at which metabolic, hydrocarbon activity would best be served, then figured in a statistical number that expressed the severity of wind and climatic variations, kind of a standard deviation for lousy weather.''

"It was geared to us, Tom, to human life?" asked Brunel, frowning.

Feeney nodded. "Yeah . . . us, Dave . . . not snakes or ants. Things that run at 98.6 Fahrenheit.''

But Commander Brunel was already wondering what he could possibly tell Houston in the next transmission.

Father Feeney continued. "What happened next, I have no excuses for. I don't know how much you remember about the university situation fifteen years ago, but it was a discouraging, demoralizing time. I know I wasn't thinking clearly. I hated the school, but I didn't know what else to do, or to put it in the language inside my head, what God *wanted* me to do.

"Fullerton had already done three dissertations' worth of work and neither he nor I was satisfied with what he had. Oh, it would have been another story three or four hundred years ago. They would have made him a Prince of the Church. How Rome would have delighted in all his simulation output as a counter to nasty old Copernicus. 'Look,' they would have said, 'so what if we aren't the center of the system? We're even more unique and unusual, and thus more God-centered.' Elias and I didn't see it like that. Planetary systems form in statistically allowed ways, as you well know, Dave. How freaky were we? That was the question Elias wanted to look at next. He wanted to go on and make a statistical study to determine the probability of planets that fell within the several limits apparently expressed by the properties of water. That is, planets of our mass, solar constant, tilt, primary star type . . . Yes, he had even looked at the sun's spectral class. You see, natural ocean water has a kind of spectral window to the most intense solar spectral region. . . . Oh, rotation speed was another critical parameter, and related to specific heat and latent heat of evaporation.''

Commander Brunel smiled thinly. "It came out a damn small chance, didn't it, Tom?"

Father Feeney nodded. "The chance of a water-optimized Earth occurring in our own galaxy varied between one in ten-to-the-seventh to one in ten-to-the-ninth, depending on how far you were willing to let Elias's optimum 'life parameter' slip. In the visible universe, it was higher, a chance of one in ten to one in a thousand that a single Earth might appear.''

He looked around at the others, his face heavy with remembered distress. ''To understand what happened next, I have to tell you a little about what was going on then in the university. Oh, Notre Dame was nothing special; half the big schools and most of the private ones were on strike that year in one way or another. It isn't very priestlike to say it, but I'd really had a gut-full of that faculty. It was obvious that the country faced serious difficulties, changes in jobs, retrenchment, but all they wanted was more money and fewer hours to do the same, tired old stuff. The most despicable thing about them was the fact that they all knew their own students could never aspire to the kind of leisure and affluence they had lived through themselves, yet they were prepared to withhold grades, teaching and degrees to continue their own pleasant and unhurried lives.

''At first the students fell in with the faculty militants . . . It wasn't that they were stupid, just young and bewildered by the canniest con men of all time, full bulls on the liberal arts faculty. But a graduation missed because no grades come in tends to concentrate one's mind, like a hanging, as Samuel Johnson once said.

''By the time Elias finished his last calculation, the students were in court after restraint and had begun to picket the faculty pickets. It was ugly enough, all right, in and out of school. Shouting, curses, old men who had once lectured on Chaucer and Aquinas and John Locke spitting venom and hate at young persons who responded with rocks, shouts, and open cans of paint. That morning was especially bad, a car afire at one campus entrance, local and state police between the various groups, tear gas, and filthy, abusive language everywhere.''

Feeney looked around. ''If that was what universities had become, it seemed to me that we were lost and society ended. Where was the source of renewal or sanity? Of course they didn't bother me much. Some of the students cheered as I went through the lines in my clerical collar while the faculty pickets turned their backs. Still, I got phone calls all the time . . . threats and hatred . . . shouts about dirty scab Catholic finks . . . all that kind of phony talk the faculty had learned from reading about the earlier days of labor war, when real men fought for real rights. I'm telling you this so that you'll understand what comes next.

"Elias came to my office at about nine that day. His face was white and he seemed very disturbed. I was disturbed too, and when he showed me his results, I went into a kind of funk. What he was saying was that we, we on Earth, were all there was anywhere . . . an improbable oddity. A dreadful, small, selfish, hurting people, beset by greed and violence, and still . . . the absolute lords of the known universe! It was really shocking, unbelievable. I spent the whole day going over his stuff, assumption by assumption. We found one mistake and it only made the probabilities a little higher, a little worse.

"By five that afternoon there was loud chanting from the campus entrances and sirens were all about us. Elias Fullerton stared at me and his bony face was a mask of white distress. 'Are we really God's creatures?' he asked finally.

"I nodded, feeling sick. 'We are imperfect, Elias,' I said.

"He pointed out toward the sounds of riot. 'Those men and women represent the culmination of three thousand years of humanistic scholarship and philosophy. And all they can think about is greed and grossness . . . greed above all!'

" 'Elias,' I tried to say, 'there are good men yet. They are silent now, but they are all around us.' But I didn't really believe it and he could see that. The mistake we were both making was in assuming that if people with PhD's could turn into bums, the rest of the world was already gone." Father Feeney chuckled. "As though Saint Francis or the folks who faced the lions had PhD's. Not likely!

"There really were good, steady citizens, millions of them, and in the end they muddled the country through to where we are now. That fuss at the universities was just a kind of specialized decadence, local, and the old bulls were really more to be pitied than hated.

"But back then everything seemed ended and awful. I have no excuse for what happened next. I should have seen that Elias was in deep trouble, but I was like those people out on the picket line, thinking of my own philosophical problems, my own alienation. I never really knew him. We should have had a drink together or gone to a movie sometime. He walked out into that wild night, white-faced, his hands shaking in rage and dismay, and all around us were sirens, violence, the flicker of fires across the campus.

"I decided to sleep in the department office that night. We had some cots set up in the basement corridor. Why didn't I keep Elias with me? I still think about that now and then. I certainly wasn't much of a priest. There were plenty of devils whispering in your ear at the university then!

"The next morning I was in my office early, thinking about what Elias had found and trying to make some other interpretation of it. There was still noise of riot, but old Father Ryan, the Dominican head of the department, walked in, sat down, and stared at me. 'Father Fullerton killed himself last night, Tom,' he said evenly. 'He went off a bridge into the river. He tied two flatirons to his ankles.'

"He had chosen death by water, the same way Quentin Compson killed himself in Faulkner's story. Elias liked Faulkner; it was about all he read outside of geophysics. I couldn't answer Father Ryan and the old man went on. 'He cleaned out his office, Tom, all his dissertation stuff. Apparently burned it all . . . plenty of fires last night for that, I guess.'

"I began to shake; my hands, my head. I suppose you three have never had that happen to you? If NASA had ever heard of it, I wouldn't be here now. My head seemed huge, expanded. My jaw muscles were absolutely locked, rigid, and I couldn't control the shaking. I began to cry and tried to speak. Finally I said, 'Father . . . Father . . . I can't go through those lines . . . I'll kill the bastards . . . Kill . . . I hate them . . . Father. . . .'

"That old man was stooped and wrinkled, but he was tough. He got up and came behind my desk and took my arm and actually stood me up, like unfolding a jackknife.

"'I'll get you off the campus, Tom,' he said to me in a low voice.

We walked to the campus police offices. I don't know what Ryan said to the head of Campus Security but within minutes we were in a police car, driven by a youngster who wore a gun, the red lights spinning on top, the siren screaming. We went through the faculty pickets at sixty miles an hour, like a cannonball, and I only caught a glimpse of shaken fists. A rock bounced off the trunk.

"We drove six hours that day, Father Ryan, the young cop, and I. In another state they left me at a Dominican retreat. They didn't give me food or sleep when I got out, still shaking, trying to weep from eyes long run dry. They took me into the chapel and I fell onto my knees with them and we were there a very long time.

"They got me through the worst of it, somehow, and a week later a young Jesuit in a rented car arrived and in two days I was at an exclusive retreat high in the mountains of New Mexico. They valued me, the Society, and they weren't going to flush their efforts and investments down the drain without a fight. I never went back to the university. They bought me a place on an eclipse expedition and I did some good things there. Then came NASA and all the rest of this. I've never told you folks the story for obvious reasons, though I guess by now I probably won't start shaking again."

Dr. Takoa put her small hand on Father Feeney's arm. "Dear Tom," she said, "how too bad that you and Father Fullerton could not see then this other interpretation of his finding." She shook her head. "Yet, how could you? How could anyone?"

Commander Brunel frowned at the small exobiologist. "What 'other interpretation,' Anna?" he asked darkly.

She winked at him. "Why, the obvious one, Dave. Water evidently has variable properties. The reason Father Fullerton found an exact optimization is not that the Earth is 'lucky' or 'statistically unusual.' The Earth's water was specifically designed for it. Titan's water, if Tom's predictions mean anything, was designed for it as well."

Brunel stared at the floor of the lander and grunted. He looked with a pleading expression at Professor Bateson. "Greg, for heaven's sake. How can water be different here from on Earth? I mean . . ."

Bateson shrugged. "The thing is, Dave, why not? This Titan

water is actually closer to the way you would expect our water to behave if it followed similar compounds like hydrogen sulfide. It still has too wide a liquid range, but at least it boils lower on the temperature scale. Theoretically, water should boil at about minus 100 Celsius." Brunel started shaking his head but the chemist went on. "You see, all the theories of boiling, freezing, vapor pressure, whatever, depend on measurements. I mean, we know that water boils when the energy of molecular agitation exceeds the attractive forces between the liquid water molecules. So we calculate those bonding forces from kinetic theory. But if Earth water had been like this stuff, we certainly wouldn't have found it any more novel than what we have now. We'd just compute constants for the binding forces and go along with them. The point I'm making, Dave, is that there's nobody who can prove from, say, the laws of thermodynamics, that water *must* behave the way it does for us. Its behavior is a given, an experimental starting point."

The chemist rubbed his chin thoughtfully. "Let me ask you something, Dave. Did they ever test the properties of Mars water, or bring any back?"

Commander Brunel tried to remember all the experiments. He shook his head. "The robot diggers really never found any in the temperate zone. They tried to incubate any encysted life in the soil with water they brought along."

Anna Takoa chuckled to herself. "The poor Martian bacteria, Dave! Oh, dear! I suppose surface tension, capillarity, and osmotic pressures must be very different between these different waters. If there was any life in the Martian dirt samples, we probably either exploded it—" she suddenly puffed out her cheeks—"or shrank it away to nothing. . . ." And now she sucked in until her lips poked out like a guppy's. "No, Greg. I don't want *any* of that ice in my bourbon!"

"Wasn't there a Martian polar cap probe, Dave?" asked the chemist.

"Yes, but it was mainly for seismic and weather measurements. Think about it, Greg. Why use up room and power on an expensive space craft to run high school experiments on water?"

"Which they wouldn't have believed from that distance anyway," continued Bateson in a thoughtful voice.

"Look. Do any of you have an explanation for this?" said Brunel in exasperation. "Are you willing to just accept that the damn stuff changes at will from planet to planet?"

Professor Bateson shrugged again, but he spoke quietly and seriously. "Dave, what else have we got but Tom's story? If this isn't a theological matter, then what else is it?"

Feeney's large, ruddy face was beaming at them now. "Think of it!" he said excitedly. "We're just talking about water. But what about carbon? Or silicon? Their properties aren't even completely known yet. Imagine what other world-to-world adjustments may also exist!"

Brunel shook his head fiercely. "Now wait a minute, all of you! Let's back off from the metaphysics and get back to physics. Greg, what if we disassociate the Titan water and burn its O_2 and hydrogen with our hydrogen and O_2? Do we get some kind of intermediate or average property?"

They all thought about that. Finally, Father Feeney frowned and rubbed his hands together. "Dave, I don't know. Do we want to try that right now . . . ?" His voice trailed off as Brunel peered at him in puzzlement.

Anna Takoa patted Tom Feeney's hand and cocked her head. "Tom, I think Dave has proposed a crucial experiment. We *must* go forward with this."

Feeney suddenly grinned at them and leaned back on his stool. "Of course we must. We've gotten this far following what we think is the path to truth. Now, if ever, we should go ahead," and his smile became radiant. "But, Greg, I do suggest that we test the decomposed and recombined Titan water first, to make sure we're not doing something by breaking down the molecule."

Professor Bateson clapped his hands in mock applause. "You know, I really do like being on a geriatric crew. Young kids never think of things like that. They just want to go ahead as fast and spectacularly as possible."

They formed a tense line in front of the hood, each on a stool, while Professor Bateson added catch tubes to his electrolysis apparatus, then led the gas flows to a combustion chamber and condensing apparatus that allowed the recombined water to drip into an analysis-box specimen-holder. Bateson turned up the juice on the electrolysis, and lit off the combining gas so that a blue flame flickered steadily and water droplets condensed and ran down the cooled glass of the condenser. Minutes passed and finally the sample holder was full. Bateson took a deep breath and shifted the water specimen to the analysis box. "Okay, here's good old density-versus-temperature again." The monitor screen flashed up a curve.

Commander Brunel exhaled and blinked. "Now . . . it's just water, our water." Indeed, the density curve lay exactly over the Earth-water reference, starting at zero C instead of minus 67 as before.

But Tom Feeney's eyes were wide and bright. "Greg . . . Greg . . ." and his voice was so tense that they all turned and stared at him. "Test some of the water from the beaker that didn't go over."

Bateson stared. "We've done the distilled Titan water three times already, Tom."

"Again, Greg. Please!"

Bateson turned without a word, put his hands in the gloves, and drew a sample from the original flask of distilled Titan water. He placed it in the analysis box and they silently watched as the data flashed up on the screen. Now it too was identical with the previous sample and the Earth reference curve.

Commander Brunel's cheeks turned dead white. "Now . . . hang on here! We weren't hallucinating! Those other experiments are all on video tape. That camera goes on every time Greg shoves his hands into the gloves!"

Tom Feeney stared at them in wonder. "Don't you see it yet? Any of you? He . . . He *designs* each world . . . to be as *gentle* as He can make it! It didn't work on Titan, maybe not on Mars either. Nothing came to live. But now *we're* here! And we're searching! *We're* the life on Titan! He's *given* Titan, its water, everything, to us! Think of it, Dave! He's like Johnnie Appleseed, preparing orchards all across the universe. And then changing them when a different seed comes by. How beautiful! Oh, Anna, think of the variety, the endless kinds of life! Ah . . . the love . . ." And Tom Feeney dropped to his knees on the floor of the lander and lifted his hands in prayer. He remembered a summer moment when he was fourteen as though it were an hour ago. He had gone with some Protestant friends to a Presbyterian song service on a Sunday night in the summer resort town where his family spent two weeks each year. They had a new minister, a bearded young man, who had organized a musical program with a choir and some soloists. The part of it that Tom Feeney remembered was a thin, plain girl who stood and sang in a sweet, round, innocent voice a song called 'The Saints of God.' Tom Feeney did not remember most of the verses; they were about different saints. . . . "One was a doctor, and one was a thief, and one was devoured by a fierce, wild beast. . . ." But he had never forgotten the refrain. . . . "And there's no real reason, no none in the least, why I shouldn't be one too," sung in that pure, lovely voice. Kneeling on the floor of the Titan lander, Father Thomas Feeney, S.J., suddenly, finally, understood how you became a saint. You *knew!* It was that simple. *You knew!* And the intensity of his prayers bloomed like sudden flowers.

But the rest of them were not yet ready. Anna Takoa peered intently at the two other men. "Send out the land runner! See if the ice sheet has changed too! Quickly!"

They darted over to the control station for the robot vehicle and soon they were watching a TV view of the runner scooting out on the ice sheet. They braked it over a smooth spot they had surveyed before and the digger descended and pulled a plug of ice up into the runner's innards. Brunel's hands moved over the console and they watched a density curve move upward on the screen. Earth water again!

The little woman's eyes were wide. "Have it put down the acoustic probe, Dave! That changed water must be freezing on the bottom right now!"

The acoustic profiler immediately extended and tracked the thickening ice sheet. There was no doubt about it. The water was rapidly freezing solid in the hot-spot bottom pools. The ice cover was thickening while they watched, at a rate of half a meter per minute.

The bolometer monitors they had planted in deep bore holes in the ice were registering sudden, intense thermal output from the latent heat released by the solidifying ice.

Commander Brunel shut his eyes and let his head fall back to the steel wall behind him. "Greg . . . Anna . . . Tom. Good God! While we were testing a half liter of its water, something has changed the whole planet!"

But Anna Takoa had finally seen and heard enough to understand it. She fell to her knees in front of Tom Feeney and pressed her thin hands up between his. Her eyes filled with tears of joy. She said to him in her soft voice, "The Lord Buddha can appear as a running, tinkling brook as well as a man, Tom."

Feeling her hands between his, Father Feeney bent toward her small face. "Monet, the painter, knew that God lived in the pond and the lilies. Oh, think of a billion different ponds and lily pads, dear, dear Anna!"

"And frogs on them, Tom. Fat, green, croaking. All different. All beautiful!"

Their souls swooned together then and their prayers pierced the metal of the lander and flew outward into the great spangle of stars that lay in every direction.

And at just about that same time, hundreds or maybe thousands of other, more or less similar, groups were making these same discoveries and responding in nearly identical ways. So that for those who could see and delight in it, the entire universe was constantly pierced by bright new arrows of surprise and love and joy.

Hamburger Heaven

Nicholas Yermakov

Nicholas Yermakov's first several novels appeared in rapid succession, beginning in 1981 with Journey From Flesh *and* Last Communion. *His writing is characterized by a high energy level and a grim and gritty view of reality. He departs somewhat from this pattern in the story that follows.*

We have all speculated at one time or another about the nature of heaven. Mark Twain used to tell a tale about a man who died and went to heaven, only to find it filled with people he'd been hoping all along had gone to the other place. "Which just goes to show," he concluded, "heaven for climate, hell for society."

The gates did not seem to be actually pearl, but they were pearly. They were also rather small, like the gates in wrought iron fencing around the front lawns of suburban homes. Except that this material was not wrought iron. Brewster had no idea what it was at first. It was smooth to the touch and it had a glossy sheen. It felt like plastic.

"Fiberglass," said the little old man who sat on a stool (rather like a bar stool) by the entrance. He was dressed in a white robe. Once it must have been pure white, but now it was sort of off-white, as though it had been washed too many times or gone dingy with age. The old man wore sandals, expensive European sandals that appeared to be the sole concession to fashion in his otherwise spartan apparel. He had a halo, too. It wasn't a ring over his head, like Simon Templar used to have at the beginning of each episode of *The Saint;* this was a flat golden disc, just like the kind seen in Eastern Orthodox icons.

"Saint Peter?" said Brewster.

"But of course," said the little old man.

The corners of Brewster's mouth turned up in a wry smile. He felt a little foolish. It was all true, then. No doubt there would be angels with harps of gold and heavenly choirs, as well. As a child, he had always pictured it this way, but the other kids had laughed at him and he had given up the notion.

He knew he wasn't dreaming. There was no question of that. He recalled his death quite vividly and there had been nothing dreamlike about it. In fact, the whole thing had been a rather drawn out and extremely unpleasant process. All those years spent smoking three packs of cigarettes a day had finally caught up with him. It wasn't only lung cancer; his kidneys had been shot, his liver was little more than a memory, and his arteries had been almost completely calcified. But it was the lung cancer that killed him. He had spent his final days as the subject of some bizarre medical augury, stuck full of tubes and needles, hooked up to machines and plastic bags as, bit by bit, they cut pieces of his vitals out of him. As if in protest at a lifetime of overachievement, his body had quit the race before his mind had reached the finish line. At least, that was the way Robert Brewster would have phrased it.

"I'm not sure I ever really believed in you, you know," he said to Saint Peter. He was still a little skeptical. Some things never die. After a lifetime of thriving in the cutthroat competition of the business world, Robert Brewster was always on the lookout for deception. Brewster wasn't taking anything on faith. He never had.

"Just have a seat," Saint Peter—or the man who said he was Saint Peter—said to him, waving Brewster over to a contoured orange plastic chair that suddenly appeared from out of nowhere. Perhaps he was Saint Peter, after all.

"I'll be with you in a moment," he said, and consulted a humungous book that rested on a lectern before him.

Brewster was reminded of his childhood, when he had spent many afternoons sitting in the principal's office, waiting fearfully as Mr. Freed consulted his records. Mr. Freed had kept a lot of records. The principal's office had functioned like the F.B.I. Each and every transgression, no matter how minor, was dutifully recorded and filed away, indexed and cross referenced. Brewster had been a difficult child. His teachers never intimidated him, not even Mr. Pulaski, who taught shop and yelled a lot. But Mr. Freed terrified him. Mr. Freed never raised his voice. Not even a little. The way he used to look at Brewster made him feel like an insect about to be dropped into a jar of alcohol. The procedure had always been the same. Even though Brewster had been a frequent visitor to the principal's office, Mr. Freed always made him sit down in front of the massive desk while he checked the records. He must have known them all by heart, but he checked them anyway. And the longer Brewster was made to sit, the more frightened he became. Later on, when he was something of a principal himself, Brewster had done the same thing with his employees. He would wave them to a chair, telling them to wait while he checked the records. And, from time to time, he would glance up from his papers to give them Mr. Freed's look.

"I see you've been very successful, Mr. Brewster," said Saint Peter.

Here it comes, thought Brewster. They won't let me in. "What's your excuse?" Mr. Freed used to ask him. Brewster tried to think up some good excuses.

"And you made an excellent hamburger," said Saint Peter.

He said it as though it were an epitaph. Perhaps it was. The thought made him recall his funeral. It had been a simple affair, just family and friends. His wife, who had inherited the business, a chain of fast food restaurants called Hamburger Heaven (ninety-nine varieties!), had wept unabashedly. Marcia was a wonderful woman and he would miss her, despite the fact that she had been cheating on him for years. All in all, a very nice funeral. He was glad he had been allowed to see it. The tombstone had not read, "R.I.P., Robert Brewster, 1916—1982. He made an excellent hamburger." It would have been nice, though.

"I see you were a real go-getter," said Saint Peter, stroking his long white beard. "Very tough on the competition. Ruthless, in fact."

Brewster sighed. He might have known. Fight and scratch your way to the top and everybody holds it against you.

"Still, you weren't a sinner," said Saint Peter. "I mean, it *was* business, after all, right?" He smiled at Brewster.

"Right," said Brewster, feeling very much relieved.

"Hmmmm," Saint Peter said, leafing through his book. "I don't think we can say the same for *Mrs*. Brewster, I'm afraid." He shook his head as he scanned the records. "Did you know she was unfaithful to you? But of course you knew. Still, an occasional lapse is one thing, but...."

He turned a page. And then another. And another. And another. And another.

"That many?" Brewster said.

Saint Peter shrugged.

"Jesus!"

Saint Peter held up an admonishing finger.

"Sorry."

"I'm afraid that unless Mrs. Brewster does something absolutely terrific between now and next Thursday, she won't be joining you."

"Next Thursday?"

"Yes, she's scheduled to die next Thursday."

"I see," said Brewster. "Will it be painful for her?"

"That's very considerate of you," said Saint Peter. "No, it will not be painful. It will only take an instant. She's going to have a heart attack while she's in bed with your next-door neighbor."

"*Harvey?*"

"Yes, I believe that's his name."

"But he's half her age!"

"And married, too," Saint Peter said. He made a clucking noise with his tongue. "I'm really very sorry about your wife, Mr. Brewster."

It was only then that Brewster realized that Saint Peter was going to let him into heaven.

Thinking of his wife, he said, "Is . . . that other place . . . terribly unpleasant?"

"Well . . . it's hell," Saint Peter said. "I mean, what can I say? It can't be helped. She made her bed, so to speak, and now she's going to have to fry in it."

Brewster winced.

"Sorry," said Saint Peter. "It's just that I'm getting to be a bit of a curmudgeon lately. You might say the competition seems to be getting most of the business these days."

"I understand," said Brewster. And he did, too. When he'd brought one of his major competitors to his knees, the fellow with the clown, Brewster had given him a position on the board of Hamburger Heaven. The only thing worse than a sore loser, Brewster believed, was a graceless winner.

"Well, I'm pleased to say that we'll be very happy to have you with us, Mr. Brewster," said Saint Peter. He rang a little bell on his lectern and a very young angel suddenly appeared at his side.

"The boy will take you to your room," Saint Peter said. "You'll be issued your wings during orientation."

Brewster cleared his throat anxiously.

"Yes, Mr. Brewster?"

"Will I get to see God?"

"But of course you will. At the Final Judgment."

"You mean I haven't been officially admitted?"

"The Lord does have the final Word," said Saint Peter. "But that's going to take a while. Backlog, you know. Still, no need to worry. I'm sure you'll do just fine."

"Your Honor?"

"Just Peter will do. What is it?"

"What about Jesus Christ?"

"Oh, yes, Him. He'll be around."

"How will I know Him?"

"Oh, you'll know," said Saint Peter. "Trust me."

The first thing that struck Brewster about heaven was that absolutely no one looked like Charlton Heston. They all looked like themselves, and no one looked particularly beatific. The fact that they all had wings and wore white robes seemed purely incidental. And only the saints had halos. That seemed appropriate. His room was bright and cheery, with a muted orange rug and chrome-and-plastic furniture. In fact, the color scheme reminded him of the one he had selected for his restaurants.

"I want nice, bright, happy colors," he remembered himself saying when the time came to design the interior of his first establishment. "I want it to look cheery, but I don't want it to look expensive. I'd like the atmosphere to be comfortable, but still let my customers know that they're not paying for the decor. I don't want it to look cheap, you understand, but I do want to convey an impression of frugality. The people who come to Hamburger Heaven should know that they're paying for the best hamburger in town, period. No fancy decorations, chandeliers or artsy menus. I want my place to be a happy place and people are happy when they know they're saving money."

He learned a great deal during his first few days in heaven. For instance, he learned that there *were* days in heaven. And nights, too. He also learned that clothes were no big deal in heaven. Everyone made do with the white robes, and the sandals seemed optional. And there were harps, of course. He was told that he could have one if he wished. It occurred to him that he had all the time in the world—in the universe, in fact—to learn how to play a harp, but then he also had all the time in the world to change his mind and do it later if he chose, so he passed on it.

One of the first things he'd noticed was the lack of toilet articles in his room. He also noticed the lack of a toilet. When he commented on that, the little angel who had taken him to his room merely asked why he felt he needed them.

"Well, don't people brush their teeth in heaven?" Brewster said.

With a slightly injured air, the little angel told him that there was no tooth decay in Heaven. Nor was there any dirt, so there was no need to wash, although there *was* a laundry. Some angels liked the feel of freshly washed robes. Brewster couldn't get his hair mussed unless he wished to, nor would he need to get it cut. It wouldn't grow, either, unless he wanted it to. The same applied to his nails.

"But what happens if you have to go to the bathroom?" Brewster asked.

The little angel, whose name was Frank, rolled his eyes.

"Really, Mr. Brewster," he explained, "this *is* heaven, after all. Angels have no need of going to the bathroom. It's positively *unangelic*. Still, if you feel you must, a bathroom could be provided, but I assure you, the whole thing would be pointless. There is no waste in heaven. Of any kind."

That appealed to Brewster. He always hated waste of any kind.

"I don't think that will be necessary, Frank," he said. "Still, I do like to brush my teeth. It's a nice way to start the day."

Frank said he would arrange it, although he clearly didn't understand. Frank didn't like to brush his teeth. He had died when he was only ten and his greatest joy on entering heaven had been discovering that he would never, ever, have to wash his hands or brush his teeth again.

Before Frank left, Brewster asked him what people *do* in heaven.

"Why, anything they want to do," said Frank. "It's even okay to curse once in a while, so long as you don't do it all the time. And you can't take the Lord's name in vain. That's a definite no-no around here."

"I'll remember that," said Brewster. "But I'm really not sure about what I'm going to do. I loved my work. My whole *life* was my work."

"What did you do?" asked Frank.

"I made hamburgers," said Brewster. "I made the best hamburgers in the world."

"That's the sin of pride," said Frank.

"Well, it's true," said Brewster. "And is it a sin to take pride in your work?"

"Oh. Well, I guess that's okay, then," said Frank. "I love hamburgers. And french fries. I especially love french fries."

"I make terrific french fries," Brewster said. "Great big thick ones."

"The really meaty kind?"

"The meatiest."

"Oh, boy!"

"Don't they have hamburgers and french fries in heaven?" Brewster asked, astonished.

"Well, we do have a lot of gourmet cooks," said Frank, "but they frown on hamburgers." He sounded wistful.

"Frown on hamburgers?"

Frank sighed. "I know. I just don't understand it, but there's no fast food in heaven. I guess all those people went to the other place."

And seeing the expression on Frank's face, the look of sadness on the little angel, Brewster knew exactly what he was going to do in heaven.

After he had been in heaven for a while, Brewster ran into Amy Harris. Actually, he *flew* into Amy Harris, as he was having a hard time adjusting to his wings. They fell gently to a cloud in a flurry of feathers. The last time Brewster had seen Amy Harris was in grade school, but he recognized her instantly. Brewster never forgot Amy Harris. She was the first girl he ever had a crush on, the prettiest girl he had ever seen, with dark hair and sparkling eyes, a stunning smile and dimples. She also had some terrific giggle. Brewster loved to hear her giggle. But the boy who made her giggle was Wayne Wyckoff, the class clown. He sang, told jokes and did impressions.

One day, Brewster passed a note to Amy and Wayne intercepted it. As Brewster watched, chagrined, Wayne unfolded the little piece of paper and, with a flourish, read the note out loud.

"*I-love-you!* To Amy, from Bobby Brewster!"

The entire class burst out laughing and Brewster died inside. He raised his desktop and hid behind it, surfacing only when Mrs. Glaze put her heavy hand on his shoulder.

"Bobby, go to Mr. Freed's office."

It was to be the first of many trips down the hall to visit Mr. Freed, with his records and his looks. And it was then that Brewster had decided that no one would ever laugh at him again.

When the feathers settled, Brewster looked at Amy and grinned.

"Hi. Remember me? Bobby Brewster?"

Amy smiled her stunning smile.

"Yes, I remember."

"I can't get over it," said Brewster. "You look just the same! You haven't changed a bit!"

And then a horrifying thought occurred to him.

"No, I didn't die young," said Amy, guessing what he thought from his expression. "I died in my sleep when I was sixty-two years old. I had six grandchildren."

"But you haven't changed at all!"

"Of course I've changed," she said. "It's only that you see me as you want to see me."

"How can that be?" said Brewster, frowning slightly.

"Well, this *is* heaven, after all," said Amy with a smile. "This is your just reward for having lived a good and moral life. It's paradise. But everybody has their own idea of what paradise should be, so there's a certain amount of flexibility in how you perceive reality up here. You remember me as a pretty girl in Mrs. Glaze's class. I'm really very flattered. Such a strong memory can only mean that I was someone very special to you. I wish I could have appreciated your feelings back then, but I was actually a very superficial little girl. I must have been very unkind to you."

"You laughed at me," said Brewster. "But I don't think you meant to be unkind." He wondered if it was possible to blush in heaven. "I felt hurt at the time, but I never really held it against you. You were so pretty and so lively and I was fat and I guess I looked kind of funny as a kid."

"Well, maybe," Amy said, "but you grew up to be a very attractive man. So distinguished looking. I grew up fat and dumpy. I'm glad you see me as I was."

Brewster was puzzled. "But you mean you don't see me as Bobby Brewster now? The way I was back in the second grade?"

Amy shook her head.

"How do I look to you?"

"I'd say you appear to be in your fifties, husky but not over-weight, with a high forehead, a strong jaw, and salt and pepper hair," she said.

Brewster realized that what Amy was describing was the way he had looked on the cover of *Business Week* magazine, fully fifteen years before his death. That same photograph hung in the manager's office in each and every Hamburger Heaven restaurant. He felt a momentary twinge of sadness that Amy's memory of him was not as strong as his of her, but then he realized that she saw him as he was at his best. It was paradise, indeed, he thought. He would not have wanted her to see him as tubby Bobby Brewster.

"Listen, Amy, if you're not very busy, would you like to have dinner with me?"

Brewster felt a little awkward in her presence, though he wasn't quite so overwhelmed as he had been in the second grade.

"Busy?" Amy giggled. "In paradise?" She giggled again. It was that same wonderful sound Brewster had thrilled to when he was a little boy. "Goodness, where on earth did *that* come from?" said Amy.

"We're not on Earth," said Brewster.

She giggled once again.

"I haven't laughed like that since I was little," she said. "That giggle always got me into trouble. I worked so hard to change it and now I'm doing it again. How strange."

"I like it," Brewster said. "So you'll have dinner with me?"

"I'd love to have dinner with you, Robert," she said, "but we really don't have to eat up here, you know. It isn't necessary."

"Don't you like to eat?"

"I *love* to eat," said Amy. "It's just that we don't have to. But it's wonderful to stuff your face and not worry about gaining weight."

"Watch it," Brewster said. "That's gluttony *and* vanity."

"And in the same sentence, too," said Amy. "It's so hard to be angelic. It takes a lot of getting used to."

Brewster offered her his arm and together they flew off to a special place he had in mind. When Amy saw the white building with the sky blue roof and shutters, she gasped.

"Why, it's a Hamburger Heaven restaurant! How marvelous! But where did it come from?"

"It's mine," said Brewster, feeling very pleased with her reaction. "My own version of paradise. After all, what's heaven without hamburgers?"

And it was then that Amy learned that he had been *that* Robert Brewster, and she was delighted. While she was alive, Amy used to love taking her grandchildren to Hamburger Heaven. She had used them as a convenient excuse to load up on Brewsterburgers, the house specialty: a hamburger with everything on it, even a sliced hot dog. It was so big you had to eat it with a knife and fork.

The place was doing a brisk business. Everything was free, of course, but that wasn't why everybody came. They came because Brewster still made an excellent hamburger and even an angel likes to pig out occasionally. Over by the window, Amy saw a famous gourmet cook; he was eating the Wellingtonburger. At another table, Mahatma Gandhi was digging into a Paisanoburger, able to enjoy it because in heaven it wasn't necessary to kill a cow to have a terrific meal. Next to him, Florence Nightingale sipped a banana malted. John Keats was thoughtfully pouring ketchup on a plate of french fries and Thomas Beckett was sharing a basket of onion rings with little Frank. Lao-tze looked up from a Chiliburger and waved.

When they sat down, a waitress wearing a white minirobe, high heels, and a small metal halo attached to a golden headband came and took their order. Brewster ordered a Plainburger, as he always had, and Amy said she'd have a Mushroomburger. Over ice cream sundaes, they talked about old times and everything that happened to them since. Everything. It took a while, but they had lots of time.

Amy's life, it turned out, had been painfully ordinary in every detail, right down to the husband who'd left her for a younger woman.

"So then, you're all alone?" Brewster said when she finished.

Amy shrugged. "I guess you might say I'm available."

"Are angels allowed to get married?"

She smiled. "Robert," she said, "some marriages are made in heaven."

They settled down together on an orange cloud. Their house was a split-level, painted white with sky blue shutters. They had a nice front lawn that never needed trimming and a slate walkway which led up to the powder blue front door. The door had a chime that played "Hark the Herald Angels Sing." Inside the house, they had lots of chrome and plastic furniture, wood-panelled walls and muted orange carpeting.

One day, while Amy was doing a crossword puzzle, Robert was watching *Let's Make a Deal*. Carl Jung was dressed like a giant moth and Sigmund Freud was exhorting him to choose between what was in the box or door number one, door number two, or door number three. The chimes rang and Brewster got up to see who was at the door. The moment he opened it, he knew.

"Hello, Mr. Brewster," Jesus said. "May I come in?"

"Please do," said Brewster. "Amy! Amy, look Who's here!"

"I hope I'm not interrupting anything," said Jesus.

"Oh, no, of course not," Amy said. "Please, make Yourself

comfortable. Would You like some coffee and a piece of apple pie?"

"Yes, thank you, Mrs. Brewster," Jesus said, "that would be very nice."

While Amy went into the kitchen to make a fresh pot of coffee, Jesus went into the living room with Brewster. The TV set was turned off and they sat down together on the vinyl couch.

"Nice place you have here," Jesus said, shifting around a bit uncomfortably.

"Thank you," Brewster said, feeling a little nervous. "What brings You to our little orange cloud? Is my Final Judgment coming up?"

"Well, yes, that's part of it," said Jesus, "but that really isn't what I came to talk to you about."

"Is something wrong?" asked Brewster, suddenly alarmed.

"Well, yes and no," said Jesus. "About your Final Judgment. I don't really think you have anything to worry about. You were a very good man, Mr. Brewster. You were a tough businessman, that's true, but you weren't a sinner. I don't think there's any question about your belonging here. But that's part of the problem."

"Oh?"

"You see, Mr. Brewster—may I call you Robert?"

"Please."

"Well, Bob, how shall I put this? The whole idea of heaven is that it should be a paradise, the Celestial City, all that sort of thing."

"Yes, I know, it's wonderful," said Brewster. "Everything up here is simply perfect."

"Perfect for *you*, Bob. And that's just the trouble. To a large extent, paradise is what you make it. And, well, please don't get upset, but you've made it rather tacky."

"*Tacky?*"

"Well, yes, in a word. Take this house, for instance. It's a nice house, but it belongs in Levittown, not here. And this orange cloud. And the blue one next to it, where your neighbors live. Heaven was never meant to be suburbia, Bob. I realize that suburbia is paradise for *you*, that devoting your time to your restaurant is your idea of heaven, but the trouble is that your tastes are contagious. Whoever heard of vinyl clouds? People are getting rashes. We've never needed to use talcum powder here before.''

"I'm sorry," Brewster said.

"No need to look like that," Jesus said, "you couldn't help it. You're a good man, Bob, but I'll be blunt. All your taste is in your mouth. You make one terrific hamburger, but there's got to be more to paradise than french fries and secret sauce. You've got the Heavenly Choir singing things like "Chances Are" and "Feelings" and all the angels are going bowling every Friday night and, believe me, nothing looks more ridiculous than a saint in hush puppies. It might be your idea of heaven, but it's *boring*."

Brewster felt even worse than he had that day when all the kids in Mrs. Glaze's class had laughed at him. He wished he had a desk to hide behind.

"I realize this is hard to take," said Jesus, "and I hate to be the one to tell you, but somebody had to. You know how it is. Every time a rough job comes up, I'm the one who has to do it. I'm sorry."

"I don't know what to say," said Brewster. His voice sounded very small. "What do you want me to do?"

"I don't really know," said Jesus. "You're entitled to your paradise, of course, but we can't have a *nouveau plastique* heaven, it just won't do. We've had complaints. It's gotten so bad that several angels have requested a transfer."

"You mean—"

"Yes, to *there*. Bob, when you first came here, the heaven that you first perceived was what you imagined in your childhood. Well, okay, that wasn't so bad, but since then, your adult sensibilities have taken over and it seems that no one can resist them. The same strength of personality that made you such a success during your lifetime is making you the dominant force up here, and it just isn't fair to all the others. Michelangelo sat down to paint the other day and what came out was an Emmett Kelly clown. If he wasn't already dead, I think he would have killed himself."

Amy came out from the kitchen with a tray of coffee and apple pie. She set the tray down on the chrome and plastic coffee table.

Beside the coffee and the pie, there was a jar of non-dairy creamer and a glass bowl full of pink packages of Sweet'n'Low.

"Maybe I should refer this back to My Father," Jesus said.

It was a beautiful day and the park was full of angels. Some were roller skating, some were jogging, a few were jumping rope. Two little angels were playing with a Frisbee. The musicians in the bandstand were playing "The Days of Wine and Roses."

"I've tried, I've really tried," said Brewster.

"I know," said God.

They were sitting together on a park bench, throwing pieces of Wonder Bread to the pigeons. God was looking very dapper in a Botany 500 suit. He was wearing Bali shoes and a silk tie and He wore a tasteful diamond on His pinkie. Brewster thought He looked a great deal like Rex Harrison.

"I mean, is this really so terrible?" said Brewster.

Queen Victoria rode by on a bicycle, tooting a squeeze bulb horn. The Lord wished her a pleasant afternoon.

"I must admit, it has a certain plebian charm," said God. "But I'm glad you got rid of the vinyl clouds."

"Is Michelangelo still mad at me?" said Brewster.

"No, he got over it. Besides, he's moved on past clowns. He's doing kittens on black velvet now, matadors with bulls, that sort of thing. He rather likes it."

Not far away, the Four Horsemen of the Apocalypse were sitting at a folding table in the shade of a large oak tree. They were playing bridge. Every once in a while, one of them would glance over at God and start to rise, but God would only shake His head slightly. Looking disappointed, the Horsemen would resume their game.

"I suppose I could get used to it," said God. "After all, it *is* My handiwork, in a manner of speaking."

"I guess it is," said Brewster. "But I don't want anyone to be unhappy. All I ever wanted was to make people happy. And Jesus said—"

"I know what Jesus said," said God. "I told Him to say it. I thought you'd take it better if you heard it from Him."

"Well, my feelings were a little hurt," said Brewster, "but I tried my best. I'm sorry if it wasn't good enough."

"Don't worry about it," said God. "I've figured it all out, anyway."

"You have?"

"Um hmmm. I'm going to start all over. Why not? After all, I'm God. I can do anything I want to. Earth's about had it, anyway. In fact, the entire universe has become rather tiresome, expanding all the time, who needs it? Yes, I believe that's what I'll do, I'll start all over."

God nodded to the Four Horsemen and they threw down their cards.

"A whole new universe. And as long as I'm going to do a brand new universe, why not a brand new heaven? Why not a brand new hell?"

"Why not a franchise?" Brewster said.

"I beg your pardon?"

"You know, a franchise. Why not expand the operation? Set up another heaven and appoint someone to run it. Each heaven can be different. A heaven for every taste."

"Interesting slogan," said God.

"You can have ninety-nine varieties," said Brewster. "You can have ninety-nine *million* varieties! You can have a universe franchise, all run by the home office! You can set up a management training program and have district supervisors and—"

"Let's not get too carried away," said God. "Still, you might have something there. What say we discuss it over lunch?"

Brewster smiled.

"I know just the place," he said.

A Green Hill Far Away

Michael P. Kube-McDowell

Michael P. Kube-McDowell is a fine new writer, the best of those making their first appearances in the recently revivified Amazing. His stories have been appearing there regularly since 1979, as well as in Analog and other magazines. He lives in Goshen, Indiana, where he teaches middle-school science. Before college, he attended a "now-defunct" Catholic high school in Camden, New Jersey, although he was raised Lutheran ... "now largely lapsed," he adds.

"A Green Hill Far Away" is one of several stories in Perpetual Light that present a view of a future Church. Kube-McDowell focuses on a future man of that Church who is caught in a tangled crisis of faith, a universal problem in a set of circumstances unique to his time.

"We may go deeper into space than anyone, for we know we will not be alone."

St. Abbenew the Galactic

I

At night in the garden of the monastery on Retreat, Subabbot John Moretti, Order of St. Benedict, did not regret leaving Earth.

The garden was quiet, and the brothers had managed a wonderful blend of lushness and careful grooming. Above the garden, the skies blazed gloriously with hundreds of minus-two magnitude stars. Most were a hot blue-white, though there was an occasional yellow or red scattered among them. They seemed to hang close overhead, and some did; a half-dozen of the brighter were less than a light-year away.

By comparison, the night sky of Earth, Moretti's birthplace, was a dim memory of a pale imitation. Even the best of the Jesuits' telescopes in the abbey observatory could not pick out the pinpoint that was Earth's star against the glare of the mighty young suns. Only in places such as this, in the heart of a globular cluster, did such a sight exist and, surveying it, Moretti felt closer to the God he had hoped to find here.

Settling on a white stone bench, Moretti brushed at the wrinkles a busy day had etched in his vestments. *The sky, at least, is as they promised*, he thought. *It should have been possible to find Him here.*

But save for a few blissful months at the beginning, it hadn't been. There were too many stars—too many metal-rich or deep-soil planets, Population III children—too many people with plans for those planets—

That *is where the problem lies*, Moretti thought forcefully. *The intruding secular world—twenty thousand light-years of privacy wasn't enough. The present echoes the past: they followed us here, just as they once followed the monasteries into the wild and isolated places of Earth. Too many simple-minded, spirit-poor people. Too many covetous of riches, or yearning for their private fief on a new world. Too many who cut off their concern for the future at their own deaths. Too many to whom sin was not a digression but a tactic against life.*

Yet Moretti could hardly blame them—he was having trouble enough holding on to his own faith. *If it weren't for the people,* Moretti thought, *I might have managed—*

A piercing chirp intruded on his reverie, and he reached inside the folds of his robe to retrieve the pager.

"Subabbot Moretti," he said.

"Sorry to disturb you, Subabbot." Morretti couldn't identify the voice, though it was bound to belong to one of the several Pauline Fathers in the Provender branch. "The abbot wishes to see you directly."

"He's up a bit later than usual, isn't he?" Moretti asked, standing and moving toward the gate in the garden wall. "Is there trouble?"

"I'm afraid so—Father Pasquale just requested emergency support on Alpheus. My guess is the abbot will ask you to take out the Second Monastic Court."

Moretti's spirits sank still lower at the news. "You may tell the abbot I'm on my way," he said heavily.

Regrettably, the Pauline Father proved to be right.

Moretti's discomfiture must have shown on his face as he listened to the assignment, for the abbot cocked an eyebrow and asked, "I something wrong?"

Moretti wanted to scream an answer: *I won't go! I won't ge; drawn into that again!* But he managed to quell that impulse, and said in measured tones, "That isn't why I came to Retreat."

"That, I think, would be true of all of us. But we cannot shirk our responsibility for Moral Enforcement." The abbot's voice was gentle but firm.

Moretti hesitated before responding. He had had difficulty speaking openly with the abbot since meeting him aboard *Pilgrimage II* two years ago; Moretti found the older man's unwavering contented self-assurance daunting, a challenge to his own ever-present doubts. "I don't wish to shirk my responsibilities to the order. But I wonder if there isn't some other way I can discharge them. Must I be the one to go to Alpheus?"

"Father Noyes and the First Court will be tied up on Sarandi for at least another ten days. The Rule—"

"There are others here trained in Moral Enforcement."

"None with your experience—and the situation on Alpheus would seem to demand our best. John—what is the problem? Why *did* you want to come here?"

Moretti averted his eyes, studied the spines of the books on the abbot's desk. "In the histories—they spoke of a time when our people enjoyed a quiet contemplative life. Service to and close communion with God. I—had difficulty finding that on LaLande."

"Ah. You questioned your faith."

Moretti nodded. "When I took my vows on LaLande, all the new novices were being assigned to supervise penances imposed by the Court—and even so, we were always short-handed. Moral Enforcement was growing so quickly. I never really had a choice of vocation. Perhaps if I had spent some time in the Missions, or Provender—I might have been stronger. . . ."

"You found the contact with sinners draining?"

"Yes."

"Have you thought about why?"

"A great deal—both then and since."

"With what result?"

"I—I realized that I couldn't be secure in my faith until I could see more of worth in His greatest creation." There. It was said—more easily than he had thought.

The abbot gestured toward the window, a motion which took in the canopy of stars over the monastery. "Does the quality and perfection still escape you?"

"I was speaking of man."

"I know you were," said the abbot, rising. "But what persuades you that man is God's greatest creation—or that He would suffer His works to be ranked by you?" He moved around the corner of the desk toward Moretti. "Did your histories also tell you what happened on Earth when Moral Enforcement was left to secular authority? About the horrors committed in His name, or committed against His creations and never repented?" The abbot's tone had not changed, but challenge had replaced compassion nonetheless.

"I know something of those things."

"And are we discussing the past or the present? How is your faith today?"

"My faith is strong," Moretti lied.

"Good. Because your fears are not enough to exempt you from this duty. Sometimes we are tested. One either grows in God or one leaves Him. This cluster is growing, changing. If we cannot grow and change to meet these people's needs, we will have failed them."

"Yes, abbot."

"On your way, then. Gather the Court and leave at once."

"Yes, abbot," Moretti said, angry at himself for his own servility. He headed for the door, only to be called back.

"John," said the abbot. "Something to remember when you confront the sinner." He quoted from the New Writings: "'Even a master potter's clay may crack, without blame to the potter.' Keep that in mind, will you?"

"I'll try," Moretti said without enthusiasm.

The monastery's shuttle field was bathed in enough starlight for Moretti to see clearly the squad of First Fathers standing at parade rest outside the *Chalice*'s angular shuttlecraft. They wore the standard brown Benedictine Infantry robes, though the red chevrons on the left sleeves looked grey in the starlight. As Moretti neared them, one stepped forward and greeted him with the salute of the cross.

"The squad is prepared for departure and ready for your orders, Subabbot."

"Have them board."

The squad leader turned and barked an order in Latin, and the rank of First Fathers turned smartly and began to ascend the short boarding ladder. "Who will the adjudicator be, sir?"

"Brother James O'Toole," said Moretti.

"One of the Jesuits," the squad leader said approvingly. "He'll do well."

"Yes. As soon as he and Brother Andrew get here, we'll be on our way." Moretti peered into the shadows at the edge of the field.

"Brother Andrew will be the assistant prosecutor?"

"Yes. There's Brother James coming now, if I'm not mistaken."

The gaunt figure of the adjudicator melted out of the shadows of the trees and advanced on the shuttle. He strode past Moretti and the squad leader without speaking or in any way acknowledging their presence. Neither man took offense. It was dictated by the Rule that the adjudicator spend the period preceding a trial in contemplation.

"Go on in and see that everyone's ready," Moretti directed the squad leader. "We'll lift as soon as Brother Andrew shows up."

"Knowing Brother Andrew, that may be some time." The glowering look Moretti sent his way told the squad leader he had gone too far, and he hurried into the shuttlecraft.

Sighing, Moretti began to pace the smooth fused-rock surface of the field. Fifteen minutes later, having almost decided to send the squad to remove the biologist forcibly from his lab, Moretti heard the swish of cloth against cloth behind him.

"Evening, John," said an affable voice. "Sorry if I held you up. You should have known I was in the middle of some work—"

"I didn't ask for you. The abbot did."

"Oh." Brother Andrew digested this information, then smiled. "In any case, I had to arrange to have one of the novices continue my observations."

Moretti dismissed the subject with a wave of his hand. "Let's get on our way."

Moretti paused just inside the hatch and poked his head into the pilot's compartment. Brother Andrew brushed past him and took a seat in the empty back row. "Ready, Friar," said Moretti to the pilot. "*Chalice* is waiting for us."

He turned to the rest of the Court, which half-filled the shuttle's main cabin. "In case all you've heard are rumors, here are the facts." The shuttle lurched into motion, and Moretti grabbed for a seat back before continuing. "This will be a short trip—join up with *Chalice*, then four days to Alpheus, where Father Pasquale has asked for our assistance. We received this message from him two hours ago: 'Fifth Commandment. Sinner has refused the offices of the Church. Please dispatch the Monastic Court at first convenience.' That's all I know so far—you'll know more when I do." Their faces showed that the last comment was unnecessary. The Court was content with what they had heard.

The shuttle was picking up speed, and Moretti joined the Dominican in the back row. "Murder, eh?" said Brother Andrew, yawning. "That's the first one out here."

"If the sin is confirmed."

"That explains why you're the prosecutor, and not Father Hegarty. You have all that experience from back on Ross 128."

Moretti's face twisted into a mask of distaste at the reminder. "LaLande," he corrected.

"And why I'm here," Brother Andrew continued. "Though how much use a biologist will be, I don't know. You might have done better with a freehealer on Alpheus. Though I am looking forward to this."

Moretti sighed. "I'm not."

"Why?"

"I don't know how we can presume to sit in judgment of other men. I never have known," Moretti said tiredly. "The old writings expressly forbid it."

"You'll forgive me if I point out an inconsistency? You're here."

"Granted." After a pause, Moretti tried to explain. "I learned early on that it worked best if I didn't try to make up my mind whether they were sinners or not. I simply treat it as though I were speaking for the affirmative in a seminary debate—just for the sake of argument. I leave the judgment to the adjudicator."

Brother Andrew's skepticism showed. "The old writings are called that because they've been superceded, not because of their age. And who will judge, if we don't?"

"God—at a time of His choosing."

"You don't really believe that, do you?" The biologist squinted at Moretti. "That's just the jargon of our profession."

If Moretti hadn't heard the same sentiment from a score of lips, he might have been indignant. But it was familiar enough to rouse no emotion.

"I really believe it," said Moretti.

But even as he said it, he wondered if he did.

Moretti's reservations were irrelevant. He was on his way to Alpheus despite them, thanks to the Rule. It was also the Rule which had made his brief explanation to the Court almost excessively detailed.

The full name—the Rule of St. Abbenew the Galactic—was rarely used. The full document—540,000 words, seven volumes in script or one-and-a-half memory modules—was even more rarely read. But any explanation of the existence and work of the Unified Galactic Orders which ignored the Rule missed the point completely.

At heart, the Rule was simply a prescription for the religious orders in the age of spacegoing man. It borrowed heavily on the Rule of St. Benedict, which had influenced most orders since it was written in the sixth century A.D. But there were also elements from dozens of later Roman Catholic monastic traditions, flavoring from the Buddhists—though not their pessimism—and hints from nearly every denomination whose religious orders had survived into the 21st century. The Rule carried forward the growing freedom to personally interpret ideology, theology, and the monastic ideal. It welded together an unlikely and occasionally volatile mixture of believers in the same way that the Global Council had welded together Earth's nations: by identifying a common goal powerful enough to transcend the differences. For the Global Council, the goal was human survival. For the U.G.O., it was justice.

St. Abbenew had been a Jesuit, a member of the Global Council, and a lawyer. He had seen clearly from his perspective on the Council that, for a time at least, the exploitation of deep space— beyond Pluto—was in the hands of individuals and small concerns.

The governments of Earth had no interest, nor did the great multi-national corporations. There was enough for them to do on the inner planets and the Jovian moons, and study after study had "proved" that both importing wealth from and exporting mouths to deep space were practical impossibilities.

But the scientists still went, and the adventurers still went, and those stifled by Earth's carefully tuned society and economy still went. For them, the Rasmussen drive's .7 lightspeed was fast enough, and a dozen or more stars close enough: Wolf 359, Sirius, Ross 154, 61 Cygni—after a time, the catalog was boringly familiar. There were more than a hundred thousand people on nine assorted planets when St. Abbenew decided that men of God should go out from Earth as well.

His Rule, and the Vow of Justice taken by U.G.O. members on top of their other vows, dictated three great purposes: spiritual ministry, the contemplation of God and His universe, and policing the anarchistic frontier worlds. The organization of the U.G.O. paralleled those three purposes: Missions, largely made up of fierce-ly independent free-roaming mendicant friars; Scholarship, which attracted both the most and least dogmatic thinkers; and Moral Enforcement, with its rigid structure and Benedictine Infantry. A self-service branch, Provender, saw to food, communications, trans-portation (the "Flying Fathers"), and the maintenance of the monasteries.

The U.G.O. worked hard from the very beginning to establish a reputation for firm, fair judgments, and when the Slipdrive pushed speeds beyond *c*, bringing the pioneer worlds into Earth's backyard and awakening the latent interest of the Earth's monolithic financial and political organizations, the Monastic Court was firmly entrenched. For most people, there was something humbling about being one of only 5000, or 500, or 50 humans on an entire planet. The pioneers did more than accept the U.G.O.'s presence; they seemed to crave it. When the first Rockwell Slipship reached Proxima Centuri, the U.G.O. and its Monastic Court were political, social, and moral forces to be reckoned with. Some historians opined that, in the explosive growth and struggle for control which followed, the religious concerns became window dressing for the U.G.O.'s secular role.

But before it all, and beneath it all, was the Rule.

In his cabin on *Chalice,* John Moretti squirmed to a new, equally uncomfortable position on his bunk, and lowered the screen brightness of his Datapad to a more agreeable intensity. He paused to yawn, then continued reading.

. . . the revisionists held sway, in the end. The infallibility of the Bible, made vulnerable by the fallibility of its interpreters, expired under an unending onslaught from biology and archaeology. Those faiths which took the change in stride survived. Frailer, less adaptable faiths panicked and descended into dogmatic cultism. After a brief reactionary renaissance, they were gone . . .

A noise from the direction of the open doorway distracted Moretti from the text. He looked up to see Brother Andrew standing in the hallway.

"Alpheus tomorrow," he said cheerfully. "Ready?"

"More or less. Come on in—sit a minute." Moretti waved a hand at his Datapad. "I've been skimming Carpelli's *Genesis of the Rule.* Ever read it?"

" 'Fraid not," said the slender Dominican, crossing his arms and leaning against the doorjamb. "I can't even keep up with my journals and the abbot's missives."

"You should make the time. Here—listen. 'Many changes were required of those denominations that survived,' " he read aloud. " 'Humanism won out over theism. Open-eyed commitment won out over blind faith. People-centered won out over Bible-centered. Psychology won out over theology. Service won out over salvation.' " Moretti looked up. "That's when it happened. We really lost something along the way."

Brother Andrew shook his head in polite disagreement. "Gained something, I'd say. Perspective. Balance. Purpose. I would never have taken vows in those days."

Moretti's surprise was apparent. "I don't understand you," he said flatly.

"I know," Brother Andrew said agreeably.

"Tell me about your God."

Brother Andrew smiled. "Oh, I have a lot of ideas about God. Sometimes I think the idea of God is just the personification of the awe we feel when we confront the universe."

Moretti was scornful. "Whose God is that?"

"Dobzhansky's—Teilhard de Chardin's—Spinoza's—Einstein's."

Moretti shook his head in dismay. "You come from a whole different world than I."

"True—and no condemnation of either of us. Goodnight, Subabbot. Sleep easy."

But as it had every night since *Chalice* had left Retreat, sleep came very hard indeed.

II

Flat and grassy Alpheus seemed, at least from the air, to have scarcely noticed its 12,000 human passengers. The spaceport at Kennon, the largest village, hardly deserved the name.

The shuttle was met by Father Pasquale, who squinted out at the newcomers through a face that was puffy and purplish.

"Good Lord, what happened to you?" asked Moretti as he neared, turning the monk to face the sunlight.

"As I reported, the sinner refused the offices of the Church."

"Rather pointedly, I'd say."

Father Pasquale reddened with embarrassment. "I've been so busy, I've let my hand-to-hand training slip. You know, I've been asking for months for a second priest to help with the ministry. I've got my hands full with Moral Enforcement—"

"That's all right, Father," Moretti said soothingly. "What of the sinner?"

"Perhaps we could remove to my house? The faithful have provided food and drink for the Court."

Moretti nodded agreement. "Most gracious of them."

A short time later, Moretti and Brother Andrew were seated in the sparsely furnished but comfortable study of Father Pasquale's small home. "It was the spaceport manager who brought the story to me," said Pasquale. "The sinner is a local man named Hollis Grubb. The deceased—technically she's only missing, but that's a moot point— is Kelly Henderson. She has a large estate about a hundred klicks to the southwest of Kennon, but she kept her deep-yacht *Gloria* berthed up here."

Moretti was jotting notes on a small pad. "Go ahead."

"A week ago yesterday, Grubb left *Alpheus* in his skiff—an hour before Henderson lifted in *Gloria*. Thirty hours later, Grubb touched down in *Gloria*, alone."

"What did he say had happened?"

"He claims to have taken over the ship as a derelict. He said he had gone up with the intention of committing suicide—until God intervened."

"By presenting him with *Gloria?*" asked Moretti.

"Yes. It's a good tale—you'll have a chance to hear him tell it."

"How do you know he's lying?"

"I have no proof. It's a judgment I had to make—as you will have to, and Brother James also. I've known people whose lives had been touched by God. They're humbled by it. Grubb is smug, as though everything we say and do was scripted for us by him."

Brother Andrew spoke for the first time. "Did I miss it, or haven't you said? Where's the body? I should get to it as soon as possible—"

"There is no body—yet."

"Did you search the *Gloria?*" asked Moretti.

Pasquale pointed to his face. "I tried." He smiled tolerantly as the others chuckled, then went on. "Grubb has a dome a few klicks from here. He hasn't been seen in town, but the faithful who have business that way have kept an eye on him."

"I don't understand why he's still here," said Moretti. "Why didn't he skip out in his new ship?"

Pasquale smiled through his swollen lips. "My standing with the spaceport manager is rather better than Grubb's. *Gloria* will go nowhere unless we release it—unless Grubb can find a way to run a Slipdrive without hahnium." ˙

Moretti nodded his approval. "Can you provide us with some ground transportation?"

"A wagon and horse, if that will do."

"It will." Moretti stood. "It's time we met the sinner."

It was the marvelous inconguity of the pioneer planet—to climb out of a Slipdriven spacecraft and into a horse-drawn cart. Subabbot Moretti and Brother Andrew sat together on the pitching, swaying back seat, while Father Pasquale, reins in hand, perched comfortably on the front bench. On either side of the vehicle trotted a half-dozen First Fathers in single file—the squad leader had spurned the offer of another wagon.

The Kennonites were accustomed to the comings and goings of their mendicant friar, but the Benedictine Infantry was new to them, and drew the attention of children and adults alike. The former were amused, and ran alongside in clumsy imitation of the BI stride. The latter were amazed, and questioned the propriety of paramilitary monks in whispered conversations.

But any one of the Infantry, had they cared to stop, could have recited a list of precedents. In the 12th century, aristocratic Knights Templars had protected pilgrims traveling to and from the Holy Land. In Tibet, the lower Buddhist clergy once acted as a police force to defend the higher clergy and the monastic territory. The quasi-monastic order of Sikhs known as the Nihang Sāhibs fended off Muslim invasions of the Punjab region of India for four hundred years. The Benedictine Infantry was not troubled by the seeming contradiction; if anything, their morale was the strongest in the U.G.O.

"Clear something up for me?" Moretti asked his benchmate as the buildings of Kennon fell away behind them.

"If I'm the one who obscured it."

"On board *Chalice*—"

"I remember."

"What *do* you believe in? What do those words mean to you—God, sin, judgment?"

"To dispose of the second question first, very little," Brother Andrew said, shrugging. "I believe that the universe which I perceive is real. I believe that it operates by orderly processes which can be described by the rational mind. I believe I'm alive, but that that's a temporary state—with a permanent ending."

"What kind of meaning does that give your life? It strikes me as cold—empty."

"I prefer a language like Pa'i, where questions about the meaning of life are unaskable." Brother Andrew pursed his lips. "Man needs the moral force we represent. Isn't that enough meaning?"

"Not for me," said Moretti. "Not for me."

To which an eavesdropping Father Pasquale added a silent amen.

The moment Grubb's home became visible on the plain ahead of them, the First Fathers surged forward at a double-time pace. By the time the wagon came to a merciful stop a hundred meters from the dome, the squad leader had deployed his men in a circle around it as though laying siege to a fortress.

"Your permission, Subabbot, to secure the building."

"Permission denied, Father. We are not yet at war." He moved with long strides toward the front entrance, and Brothers Pasquale and Andrew trailed behind him.

The dome fit the image that Moretti had been constructing in his mind. It was an Efrons S-7: light-duty, a single room, meant for temperate regions and gentle weather—the sort of home a man of modest means would bring with him to a new world, keeping an eye toward replacing it at first opportunity. The dome needed washing—even to the solar unit that capped it. Had the shell not been made of maintenance-free alloys, Moretti was convinced it would need painting as well.

Grubb greeted them without surprise and received them as guests. "Ah, the U.G.O. in defense of its own," he said cheerfully, while peering over Moretti's shoulder at the First Fathers. "Father Pasquale, you seem well—no permanent damage, I trust? Abbot, I hope—"

"Subabbot," Moretti corrected quietly.

"Whatever. I hope you've reviewed the concept of private property with your local representative. Come on in, and we can talk—but let me say that I have no regrets about what I did. A man has a right to—"

Moretti ignored him and stepped through the doorway, taking in the contents of the dome at a glance. Much of the furniture was improvised. Shiny cargo modules, now dented, had been covered or padded to serve as tables and chairs. A compact muscle-conditioning rig in the center of the room gave the appearance of being in regular use.

Moretti turned to the younger man. "You are Hollis Grubb?"

"Yes."

"You have been charged before the Monastic Court with the sins of violence, murder, and theft. If our examination finds any merit to these charges, a trial will be convened. In the Rule of St. Abbenew a fifteen-day period is specified for the resolution of these matters, during which you are asked to place yourself in the protective custody of the Court. I commence this period now. Do you accept the protection offered?"

Grubb's face darkened momentarily. "I deny the sins and I deny your right to accuse me," he said frostily. But the smile quickly returned, and Moretti realized why he didn't care for it. It was the smile of a grown-up being tolerant of a noisy children's game that had briefly engulfed him. "Still, some of the townies have had the same garbage on their lips. When I've explained things to you, they'll see they were wrong—and I can be on my way. I accept the protection of the Court."

"And the authority of God?" demanded Pasquale.

Grubb shrugged. "If you expect me to be afraid of you, you'll be disappointed. God has shown me which way my path leads."

"It leads to Retreat and penance!" snapped Pasquale.

"Father!" Moretti said disapprovingly.

"That's all right," Grubb said, his face serene. "I know that Father Pasquale's grudge will not prejudice your findings. It's truth that counts, not one man's belief. Father Pasquale forgets—but God remembers."

*   *   *

"When he talks like that, I want to smash him," fumed Father Pasquale. "His tongue is quicksilver—beautiful poison."

"Find your patience," chided Moretti.

"That was your first exposure," retorted Pasquale. "Wait. You'll see. You'll feel it, too."

Slow-turning Alpheus offered seventeen hours of sunlight, for which Moretti was grateful. There was much to be done, and the fifteen-day deadline seemed already too close.

While the First Fathers escorted the sinner back to the town, Moretti and the others continued on to Kennon's spaceport. With Grubb's keydisc, they boarded and searched the *Gloria*. Even Moretti's guarded optimism proved too hopeful: there was nothing there to find, except a glimpse or two into Kelly Henderson. She kept no formal log, any more than Father Pasquale would for his travels by wagon. There was a navigation recorder, but it could only tell them where she had gone, not why or when she had left the ship.

And left it she unquestionably had. The only part of her that was still aboard was inside her voice-capable word processor, which took up the space normally reserved for a communications recorder. Brother Andrew scanned the memory module they found in it, but it was a trying experience; it was filled with semi-pornographic stream-of-consciousness poetry.

The spaceport manager brought them two cargo modules of women's clothing and personal effects. "I kept everything he tried to throw out," the manager said pridefully. "She was a good woman. He can't just make her disappear."

So far he has, thought Moretti. "No," he agreed diplomatically. "Where is Grubb's skiff?"

"Presumably still up there, somewhere," said the manager. "We don't have deep radar, so we didn't track it."

"Any particularly bright meteors in the last few days?"

"None that I heard of, but if you'd like, I can check with some amateur astronomers I know."

"I'd like," said Moretti.

They inspected the personal effects with great diligence and little real hope, and learned only that Henderson's tastes were eclectic and that she had more than a passing interest in physical pleasure. Then they excused themselves from the manager and stepped outside. Following Moretti's lead, they walked slowly toward the shuttle.

"I have serious doubts," Moretti announced. "Without a body or a witness, confirming the sin will be impossible. Barring confession, of course."

"And that means no penance," Father Pasquale said worriedly. "If he goes free, my work here is going to be much more difficult."

"I'm aware of that, Father." Moretti chewed thoughtfully on his forefinger. "She's up there, somewhere. The turnaround on *Gloria*'s last flight was 500,000 klicks out." He stopped, and turned to Brother Andrew. "I'd like you to take *Chalice* and look for her—first on the skiff, then in vacuum."

"She won't be on the skiff," Brother Andrew said. "Grubb's not that stupid. She'll be all alone—"

"Even if he finds her there, that doesn't make it murder," Father Pasquale pointed out unhappily.

"It does if she's *sans* spacesuit."

"There is such a thing as suicide."

"Perhaps we can find out enough about Henderson to rule that out," suggested Moretti.

"To our satisfaction, yes. But that won't be enough for Brother James."

"I know," Moretti said, annoyed. "But I don't know where else to take this." He looked to the biologist. "How much can the body tell us?"

"A lot—if he actually did something to her. But if he didn't kill her himself—if he just abandoned her—we won't be able to tell accident from suicide from murder," Andrew said grimly. "And from what I've seen of Grubb, that would be his style." He hesitated, an odd expression on his face. "But maybe *she* could show us which it was."

Moretti's look was skeptical. Pasquale seemed befuddled. "Explain."

"Well—ever since neural mechanics locked down the mechanisms of human memory, it's been theoretically possible to 'read' the chemical engrams that make up a memory trace."

"Read their mind?" demanded Pasquale.

"In a way. But since the brain has to be destroyed, layer by layer, to do it, and since the engrams decay unless the body temperature is dropped to minus 70 C, it's not very useful. Also, it only works on certain parts of the memory. I think it's only been done three times with humans—twice for aural memory, once for visual. Thoughts and emotions are out of the question."

"Praise God, that's it!" Moretti cried, grasping the biologist's arm. "We'd see what she saw just before she died. She's the witness *and* the victim."

"Maybe. Or maybe her body heat kept her warm enough to break down the engrams. Or maybe all she was seeing and thinking of when she died was blackness, or the disc of the sun."

"That's no reason not to attempt it."

"I agree. But don't overlook the biggest problem—finding her. He could have dropped her off anywhere along 500,000 klicks—or brought her back to burn her up in the atmosphere. You may as well ask for divine intervention—a squad of angels to help in the search."

Moretti raked the biologist with a scathing look.

"It'd be no squad of angels," said Pasquale, "but there are three or four of the faithful who might join a search with their sprints."

"See about it, Father," said Moretti, the anger still creasing his face. "I need to speak with Brother Andrew before he leaves."

Father Pasquale nodded and started away.

"Divine intervention—that's a joke to you, isn't it?" demanded Moretti.

"I suppose so."

"How can you live with such beliefs? How can you wear that cross?"

"I wear the cross with pride. As for the first question—I don't see very much choice." Father Pasquale, a dozen meters away but still within earshot, reached for his crucifix and deliberately snapped the cord that held it, scattering beads across the tarmac. As he knelt to retrieve them, he strained to hear the rest of the exchange. "You alluded to it on *Chalice*," Brother Andrew was saying. "There's been less and less for God to do all the time. It used to take His personal intervention to open a flower, or make the sun come up each day—or so we thought. Now auxins and simple physics will suffice. Only an ignorant man can read the old writings literally. And neural mechanics explains man's self-awareness without resort to the soul."

"So—in your opinion, God is unemployed?"

"All that's left for Him to have done is create hydrogen, with all its properties. Or quarks, if you prefer. Everything else—even us—follows in due course. Not by chance, or by constant tinkering, but by the rules written into matter. I find it much more elegant than the shazam-and-special-effects creation we once promoted. But, John, I think you've missed the point. I'm not sure it matters how I—or you—see God."

"That requires explanation."

"The moral force we represent fills a vacuum on these worlds. We stand for something—something of value to people. Freedom from fear. Freedom from the need to be the strongest and meanest Homo sapiens on the block." He cocked his head. "Of course, you've already said it—you're not happy with that role. You really don't want to be here."

Moretti looked away. "No. Not here—or on Retreat—or anywhere else where men do things like spacing another human being." He exhaled heavily. "Good-bye, Andy. Find her."

He turned and stalked off toward the wagon at the edge of the field. Picking up the last of the beads, Pasquale hurried to follow.

Four long days. The first two had been spent at Kelly Henderson's estate, where they found her caretaker, a dried-apple caricature of an old man, in an agitated state.

"What will happen to me?" he asked nervously, time and again. "This is all I have."

What Henderson's papers couldn't tell them, the caretaker could.

Henderson had been a self-described poet and adventurer, whose visit to Alpheus was no more than a well-financed extended vacation. According to the caretaker, her periodic excursions in *Gloria*, slow cometary-orbit trips, were to "reestablish communion with the creative energies of the universe." Remembering the contents of the shipboard word processor, both Pasquale and Moretti withheld comment.

When they had run out of both questions and answers, they took their leave. Moretti assured the caretaker that, though Henderson's relatives had five years to assume her land claim, it was doubtful they ever would. His happy face was a sharp contrast to the sober expressions of the priests.

Two more long days were spent interviewing the people of Kennon. The priests found that neither Grubb nor Henderson had been tightly bound to the social life of the town. For every person who had actually known one of them, the priests found a dozen who had known neither but were eager to publicly bemoan the terrible sin and run down the sinner. When they returned to Pasquale's house the evening of the fourth day, neither seemed willing to give voice to what they both knew to be true: that all their work had produced depressingly little of substance.

"I find righteous anger wearying," was all Moretti would say. Pasquale was quick to agree.

In part hoping for encouraging news and in part to update Brother Andrew, they contacted the *Chalice*.

"Howdy down there," Brother Andrew said cheerfully at their call. But his mood did not reflect his news. The skiff had been located; it was empty. Nothing else had been uncovered by *Chalice* and her five tiny escorts. "Not to despair. We still have time."

"Not a great deal. And not a great deal of evidence, either. Grubb came here about four years ago, his skiff piggy-backed to a deep-ship heading farther into the cluster. He wasn't a success as a farmer—hard on this planet, I understand—and does odd jobs to keep himself in food. Everyone agrees that he's desperate to leave here, but most of it sounds like after-the-fact wisdom—if he has any real friends, they've gone into hiding."

"So what's the agenda?"

"Tomorrow we'll present the Court with the evidence for the sin of violence—the attack on Father Pasquale. The penance is trivial, but that should consume two or three days."

"We can use the time, up here."

"I know." Moretti sighed. "After that, we'll have to take up the sin of murder with whatever evidence we have. We won't be able to wait much longer, or we're looking at day fifteen and the end of the resolution period."

"'Justice delayed is justice denied,'" Andrew quoted from the New Writings. "Saint A. might have given us a bit more leeway when he set this up."

"He might have," Moretti agreed tiredly.

It was not a good night for Subabbot Moretti.

In praying, he felt self-conscious, for the first time in a decade. He fought off but could not entirely escape the idea that in praying he was merely talking to himself. Then sleep would not come, and neither the unfamiliar bed nor the thirty-one-hour day would accept the blame.

Quietly, Moretti left the house and began walking along the dirt road that led away from Kennon. The sky was as brilliant as on Retreat, and the silence of night nearly as total, broken only by the occasional cry of a night flier and the faint *ka-chung* of machinery from the direction of the town.

What I need, thought Moretti as he walked, *are some of the features of Earth's civil courts that St. Abbenew was so careful to avoid—a backlog of cases, for instance. Then Brother Andrew would have time for a proper search. Or a jury, so we could spend weeks wrangling over who will stand in judgment. Or a complex legal code, plus lawyers, to obscure the gaps in our evidence. Or an open court, so that public opinion might have a chance to rewrite the judge's definition of objectivity.*

Moretti came to a stop in the middle of the road. *But I don't have any of that,* he thought unhappily. *I have fifteen days. I have a well-educated adjudicator with a discerning mind. And I have a sinner with enough wit to protect himself while appearing not to.*

Turning, Moretti began walking back toward Pasquale's house, and bed. His robes swept the ground, kicking up a faint cloud of dust behind him. Perhaps he wouldn't sleep; still, he had heard somewhere that an hour's quiet rest is almost as beneficial as an hour's sleep.

By morning he knew that to be false.

III

Brother James had chosen the U.G.O. sanctuary in Kennon as the site for the Court proceedings. As Moretti neared it the next morning, he found Father Pasquale waiting for him at the front steps.

"Good morning, Father. How did the sinner pass the night?"

"The First Fathers say he slept the sleep of the blessed," Pasquale said, scowling. "Subabbot, I was hoping for a chance to speak to you before the trials begin."

Moretti nodded assent.

"First, I must confess two indiscretions against your privacy, one inadvertent and one conscious. I refer to your conversations with Brother Andrew in the wagon the first day and, just before he left, on the runway."

"Forgiven. Go ahead."

"I understand that you may count Brother Andrew among your friends. Even if that is so, he is *wrong!*"

"Oh?"

"Those clerks regular—the Jesuits—*anybody* in Scholarship—they have a funny way of seeing things. They're too secular. Too many teachers and scientists. Not enough contemplation."

"Make your point, Father."

"Sins against God we leave for God to resolve. But sins against man call for penance here in the world of matter-energy. It's not just a favor we do them—their eternal life is at stake. If there's no justice here, it casts doubt on justice in the next world."

"Yes. I have noted that," Moretti said, his face unreadable.

"Thank you, Father—for your concern. But Brother Andrew speaks only for Brother Andrew. We'll see if we can't help this sinner see his error."

Satisfied, Father Pasquale followed the Subabbot up the stairs and into the sanctuary.

Moretti left the sanctuary that evening doubly shocked. The first shock was that the trial for the attack on Brother Pasquale was over. Moretti had expected—hoped—it would last at least two days, perhaps three. But Grubb had conceded the details of the fight and offered only a brief explanation that was at the same time defiant and contrite.

The second shock was the lightness of the penance—a donation of fifty credits to the U.G.O.-Alpheus treasury. It meant that Brother James had been favorably impressed with Grubb on a personal level. St. Abbenew had warned against the dangers of emotional response for sinner and prosecutor alike, but he had been unable to remove the possibility of it with his Rule.

The news from Brother Andrew did nothing to lift Moretti's spirits. "A body is just about at the lower limit of resolution for the deep radars," Brother Andrew reported. "We've had to piddle along at a few dozen meters per second and use the proximity and collision radars. A few of the brothers are even using scopes and binoculars. Personally, I don't think the body will have a high enough albedo to be picked up visually, unless we happen to run right on top of it."

"How far are you from the point where Grubb took over *Gloria?*"

"About three hours. Friar Elon plans a 3-D spiral search pattern when we get there."

"Those are awfully time-consuming."

"She can't have gotten very far with whatever tiny velocity she had. Don't give up, John. Just give us some time."

The request was unnecessary; Moretti knew what he had to do. Unfortunately, there would be few opportunities to slow down the work of the Court. Only summary trials during revolutions and wars were simpler and more straightforward than the Monastic Court.

But one of those opportunities would present itself in the morning—

the prosecutor's Discourse on the Sin. Moretti had the right, when mortal sins were involved, to speak in general and historical terms on the sin that was before the court, for whatever length of time he chose. The ordinary goal was to inspire the sinner to a free and open confession. There was no hope of that, Moretti was certain, but with proper preparation, he might gain back the two days he felt he had lost. Determinedly, he fell to the task of assembling references.

Short of sleep but otherwise eager, Moretti began his Discourse at nine the next morning. By the time the adjudicator suspended the Court for the evening, Moretti's voice was gone but his references were not. Somewhat heartened, he returned to the rectory to check on Brother Andrew's progress. But Brother Andrew had found nothing, and Moretti's lightly entrenched optimism vanished.

The next morning, their fourth day on Alpheus, Moretti resumed his statement. Grubb, seated a few meters to his right, yawned openly and often. Brother James was more polite, but no more attentive—whatever he thought of Moretti's discourse, it was clear he had decided it did not require his close attention. But Brother James had no standing to interrupt, and Moretti went on. Even so, as they neared the midday break, the prosecutor found himself repeating old writings for the third time, and reluctantly closed his Discourse with the traditional appeal:

"For the sake of your soul, your conscience, your community, and your standing with God and in the next world, I call upon you to make an open confession of your sin." His voice was a croak.

Grubb sat forward and rested his elbows on his knees, his chin in one hand. His expression was amused. "I have no sin to confess. But if I did, I certainly would, after such a display of inspired rhetoric. I stand—no, I correct myself, I sit—in awe, Abbot."

Moretti had no doubt the mistitling was deliberate.

"We will suspend for one hour," pronounced Brother James. "On our return, the prosecutor will present evidence for the sin, and against the sinner."

Hollis Grubb was smiling broadly as the First Fathers led him from the room.

*   *   *

"If your news isn't good, perhaps you'd better keep it to yourself. Amen," said Moretti, seated at the communications console in the rectory.

Four seconds of silence followed: time for the wave to propagate across space to *Chalice,* and for an answer to return. Four seconds that made Moretti feel very alone. "Sorry to disappoint you," said Brother Andrew. "All we've found is an occasional bit of rock. How is Sir Grubb behaving? Amen."

"More arrogant than ever. He treats the First Fathers as servants, rather than guards—demands food at odd hours, books, other comforts. Amen."

"How much more time do I have? Amen."

"I can't say with certainty. I can't give you the full seven days, I suspect—not and retain credibility with Brother James. Another day or day and a half to present my evidence—and that's talking slowly and drinking a gallon of water an hour. Then his side—twenty minutes on the last sin!—my rebuttal, and adjudication. And at this point, I don't think Brother James will have too much trouble deciding. I really think I'm going to lose him if you come up empty-handed. Amen."

"We'll be working while you're sleeping," Brother Andrew promised. "Lord keep you."

Moretti slumped back in the chair, his fingers curled around the body of the microphone. It was there that Father Pasquale found him a half-hour later.

"Yes?"

"The sinner has asked to see you, Subabbot."

Moretti dragged himself up to a normal sitting position. "Why?"

"He wants you to hear his confession." Pasquale's face voiced his contempt.

"Has he ever attended services at the mission?"

"No, Subabbot."

"Called on you for spiritual guidance?"

"No."

"Shown *any* outward sign of being one of the faithful?"

"No, Subabbot—though I would hesitate to deny him—"

"Have someone else hear his confession," said Moretti with finality, turning away.

"Yes, Subabbot. But who? The First Fathers aren't permitted, any more than an altar aide would be. Brother James is in contemplation, and the other Court priests are with the *Chalice*."

"That would seem to leave you."

"Yes—and despite my feelings toward the sinner, I would have already done so—if he would accept me as his confessor. In the last two days, I've given him six chances to do so."

"Well, I can't hear it," Moretti said defensively. "I can't compartment off one part of my memory to hear his confession, and not know that I'm the prosecutor. What if he said something about the woman? I can't keep it confidential from myself now, can I?"

"That would be difficult," Pasquale agreed.

"Tell him he'll have to wait or accept you."

"Yes, Subabbot," said Pasquale, pleased. "I'll tell him. But I doubt he'll trouble to have it heard by anyone else."

Pasquale was in the doorway when Moretti called after him, "Wait."

"Sir?"

Moretti sighed. "I set out to be a priest, not a prosecutor. Sometimes I forget where I started. I will be there in twenty minutes to hear what he has to say."

The First Fathers had set up a confession screen in the basement of the rectory, though with its small size and the circumstances it hardly seemed necessary.

"Mr. Grubb, Father Pasquale passed your message to me," said Moretti, settling on his side of the screen. "If you wish to make a general confession of your sins, I am prepared to grant you absolution. But I must warn against your naming specific sins because of our special relationship—"

"Thank you for coming, Father," said Grubb as though Moretti were not speaking. Moretti resisted the urge to correct the title. "As you probably know, I'm not a regular—I don't know the right answers and rituals. I just wanted to talk to you about what I've done.''

''The contrite heart means more than a ritual response. For a general confession, you need only—''

''I killed a woman, Father.''

There was an ugly silence, as Moretti prayed furiously to be transported elsewhere, anywhere. *I didn't want to hear that*, he protested in vain. *I offered a general confession—*

''It was that or suicide, Father. Which is worse? And killing her was easier. She wanted so much to help, once she received my signal—I said it was appendicitis, and I couldn't pilot my skiff. After that—do you know the kind of person whose eyes are so wide open that they can't see? That was Henderson. It was very pretty, actually, the sunlight shining off her—''

''To take pride in a sin doubles your debt to God—''

''What I was really wondering about, Father, was this—which *is* the greater sin, do you think? Suicide or murder?''

''It's not my place—''

''I think it's suicide. After all, you don't have a chance to make it up to God when you kill yourself. But I'm told that no matter what the sin, you'll be forgiven—even if you wait till the day you die to accept Him.''

''Can we know our day of death, and blithely sin until we reach it?'' Moretti said sharply.

''You might say I've already been in hell, here on Alpheus. I made a mistake in leaving Earth. Actually, I ran away—from other people's expectations of me, from being a failure. It's a long way to run, I know. But I thought it would be different here. I forgot I had to bring myself along.''

For a moment, Grubb seemed serious, and Moretti had hope. ''Then perhaps you have learned something from this great sin.''

''Oh, everything's working out fine, now. I'm going home, to take another crack at things. I'm getting away from here—going back where there's enough people to make a real human society.''

On the other side of the screen, Moretti held his bowed head tightly in his hands. "An evil act always promises gain, my son. But the gains are illusory, and the price paid too high. Think not of this world, but of the next." The words slipped out from between clenched teeth.

"Oh, I don't know. What is it they say? 'It's an ill wind that—' "

"Folk sayings are small comfort for a soul condemned to hell!" thundered Moretti. "There is only one road that can lead you back to God's grace. You must make an open confession of your sin to the Court, and contritely accept the penance it imposes."

Grubb chuckled. "And spend another ten or fifteen years out here, running little monk errands on Retreat? Not likely. You say a lot of silly things, Father. Condemned souls—what nonsense! When you're dead, you're dead. My time is precious, and I won't waste it with you simpletons. Oh, there I go—that's another sin. Sin of murder, sin of pride, sin of theft—think of anything else, Padre? I want to get the slate clean."

Moretti squeezed his eyes shut, his body rigid, then fled toward the stairs, the sound of his sandals betraying his departure. "I guess some of this is blasphemy, too, isn't it?" Grubb called after Moretti. "Say, Father, where are you going? You forgot to grant me absolution!"

Moretti did not turn back, and Grubb fell back in his chair, consumed with laughter.

Father Pasquale was waiting in the room where Moretti had been sleeping. "What happened?"

"A sacramental confession is not for discussion."

"All right, I'll tell you. He confessed to the murder, knowing it'll drive you crazy to know he did it and then see him go free."

"Please leave," Moretti said tersely.

Father Pasquale shook his head angrily. "This is one of those times I'd like to forget my Vow of Justice and ask for forgiveness later."

"Father!"

"I don't know why you did it. He just wanted to twist the knife in you. Why protect him now? He wasn't sincere."

"Aren't I a priest?" Moretti asked, his voice brittle. "Doesn't he have a soul?"

Father Pasquale looked away.

"That's all right," Moretti said in a softer voice. "Your feelings are understandable. Ask God for forgiveness for your weakness."

"Yes, Subabbot."

When the door closed behind Father Pasquale, the subabbot flung himself on the bed and cried.

Moretti himself was not conscious of the change that showed when he appeared to present the remaining evidence. But Father Pasquale saw it—the tension in his posture, the way he avoided even the briefest glance at Grubb. As they left the sanctuary for the midday break, Father Pasquale took the prosecutor firmly by the arm. "Come on, Subabbot, you need a break. If I ever saw someone who was a bomb waiting to explode, it's you."

Moretti protested, but Pasquale did not relent, guiding him toward the wagon. "You need to get away from here and remember some of the old monastic tricks for peace of mind. Here, up you go. Slide over."

"But the trial—"

"We'll be back in time."

By fits and starts, Moretti became aware of the knots in his back muscles, and the aching of his clenched jaw. The swaying of the wagon and the faint breezes distracted him, and he began to relax. When he let out a sigh, Pasquale looked his way and smiled.

"You're looking better already."

"And feeling better. Thank you, Father."

"I just try to minister to anyone in my territory who needs me."

Moretti laughed lightly, experimentally. It felt good. "Where are we? What road is this?"

"Swings around to the south of town—below the port." He pointed across the field to the right. "See?"

"I was wondering what those buildings were," said Moretti. "I hadn't seen it from this angle before. There—there's part of *Gloria*." He frowned. "Wait—what's she doing rolled out? She was in the hangar when we arrived."

"I don't know—" Father Pasquale said uncertainly.

"Take me over there."

"But—"

"Take me over there, I said! Across the field. Quick, now."

Reluctantly, Father Pasquale complied, sending the vehicle across the grassy field at a bone-jarring pace.

"Where's Brother James?" Moretti barked at the First Father seated on the doorstep of the rectory.

"Upstairs, in contemplation—" He stopped, as Moretti was already past him and charging up the stairs, robes streaming out behind him. The house resounded with the force of his ascent.

At the top of the stairs, Moretti threw open the door. "Brother James, I would speak with you."

The Jesuit turned away from the window. "Then do."

"Did you give permission for the *Gloria* to be prepared for a flight back to Earth?"

"I did."

"In God's name why?"

"They asked if I had any objections. I did not. Such preparation is time-consuming, and Mr. Grubb is eager to leave at the first opportunity."

"Then you're going to absolve the sin."

"That remains to be seen. But if we can forget our roles for a moment, Subabbot, your case is weak."

Grubb's confession shouted in Moretti's ears: "It was very pretty, actually, the sunlight shining off her—" But he could not speak, though the wish to speak nearly strangled off his breath. Listlessly, Moretti turned and slowly descended the stairs.

Grubb enjoyed his stage in the afternoon session, telling stories, laughing at his own jokes. "God reached out and touched my life, kept me from ending it before my time," he said theatrically. "He said, 'Hollis, don't quit yet. I'm going to give you another chance.' And there it was, the most beautiful sight, a deep-ship, empty and waiting for me, the sunlight shining off her—"

He looked at Moretti, a smirk playing at the corner of his mouth.

After a moment, he went on, seemingly disappointed at the lack of reaction from the prosecutor. But Moretti was unaware of it until later; he sat in his chair, looked straight ahead at the wall and the simple cross, and the time passed as though he were sleeping.

The glazed expression on Moretti's face was most apparent to Brother James, who, out of consideration, ended the afternoon session an hour early. Even so, Father Pasquale had to tell Moretti it was over, and lead him back to the house.

"Do you want to talk about it?" Pasquale offered when they reached Moretti's room.

Moretti closed his eyes and shook his head, and Pasquale respectfully withdrew.

Twenty minutes later he returned, and had to call Moretti's name three times to get the prosecutor to look up. "The *Chalice* is returning to Alpheus, Subabbot. Do you want to speak to Brother Andrew?"

Moretti's face showed puzzlement, the first emotion that had appeared there in several hours. "Coming back?"

"That's what they said, sir. They're waiting for you." He hesitated. "Can I help you?"

Moretti shook himself like a dog rising from a nap. "No. No, I'm coming. Tell them I'll be right there."

"Then you found her. Amen." This time, the final word was both functional and heartfelt.

"Keep a tight hold on your excitement," cautioned Brother Andrew. "I know you were hoping for a decompressed body—but she was in a suit—light-duty model. She died when her air ran out. No bruises or marks of any kind. There's no sign that she did anything but get careless on an EVA. Older than I would have thought—though I suppose everyone looks older dead. Amen."

Moretti's head suddenly seemed heavy. "That's very hard news to take. What about the other? Her memory? Amen."

"I don't know. We're preparing the brain tissues now. But I'm not very hopeful. Oh, her body is in good enough condition—but she would have been out there for an hour at least, judging from the suit's air capacity. Who knows what she was looking at, thinking about? And I'm going to need time—a lot of it. We virtually have to peel back her cortex in layers a cell thick—locate, identify, and map the neurotransmitters—interpret the patterns. And with this equipment—I don't mean to be unnecessarily negative. I'll get something. But I don't know how much and how fast. Amen."

"Can't you give me an idea on the time? Amen."

"At least thirty hours. Amen."

"We don't *have* thirty hours. Grubb will finish tomorrow morning, I'm sure. I can respond to his testimony, but what's there to say until you get here? We agree on nearly every point, except whether Kelly Henderson was on *Gloria* when he got there. Amen."

"Find *something* to say," Andrew said firmly. "I don't know what I'll bring you, but I'll bring you something. But I need that thirty hours. I'm getting back to work. Lord keep you."

Moretti sat still for a long moment, gathering up the threads, then stood and shouted, "Father Pasquale!"

The mendicant came running. "Father, get me a complete history of this colony. As detailed as possible. Logbooks, diaries, I don't care. I need them by morning. And a set of technical manuals for *Gloria*, as complete as you can find. And its service history. Get a couple of the First Fathers to help you. Hurry, now! The eternal life of Hollis Grubb may rest on it."

"Pressure values in the secondary thrust chambers are controlled by a two-position differential-gap controller," Moretti read aloud from the screen of the microviewer. "If at any point the given values exceed the safe operating pressure criteria established by the manufacturer, the final controlling element moves to the second position and will not return until the variable has passed through the differential gap in the opposite direction. A lumped-constant wavemeter linked to the bridge servo interpreter will provide diagnostic data."

Moretti extracted the memory module from the 'viewer and replaced it in the case. The table was crowded with binders and memory mod cases: the town meeting minutes, the sanctuary log, back issues of the irregularly published town newspaper. He had been reading for twelve hours, and his voice was threatening a strike. Sipping at a tumbler of water, he took up the next module—fourth of nine—from the *Gloria*'s tech manuals.

Grubb leaned toward him and whispered harshly across the aisle, "You've blown both fuses, Padre. Why don't you let them take you back to Retreat and wire you back together?"

Moretti ignored the gibe, as he had those that had preceded it.

"You do yourself no service," Brother James admonished Grubb, then turned toward the prosecutor. "Your choice of evidence is fully your concern, Subabbot, but I feel you should know that the point is lost on me."

"Other Control Systems, Slipdrive, Subsection IV-B," read Moretti in answer. Grubb groaned.

Another hour passed, during which Moretti's voice became a characterless drone even to himself, and then the doors of the sanctuary flew open. Charging past the surprised First Fathers stationed there were Brother Andrew and one of *Chalice*'s tech friars. The latter carried a microprojector and wordlessly began to set it up, while Brother Andrew slid into the seat beside Moretti.

"I didn't have time to really clean up the engrams," the biologist apologized earnestly. "And since the memories are stored as schemata, I had to use a computer to recreate the sense data in a digital analog—but I didn't have as sopisticated a program as I'd have liked—"

"*Do you have it?*" hissed Moretti, grabbing the Dominican by the wrist.

"I have it."

The tech friar was finished, and Moretti released Brother Andrew. "Then let's be done with it."

"I'll present it," Brother Andrew said, standing. "Brother James! What you are about to see is the testimony of Kelly Henderson concerning the sin of murder—her own murder. I took this testimony from her personally, and on my vows stand behind its authenticity and accuracy." He stepped toward the adjudicator and handed him a memory module. "I have collected for you the research that made this possible, the details of the process, and the statements of six brethren who assisted and were witnesses to what I've done.''

Grubb gaped.

Brother James's eyes widened as he took the module. ''I will have to review this material before I can view the—testimony.''

So saying, the adjudicator turned away and placed the module in a 'viewer that one of the First Fathers hastened to provide. Grubb, his composure regained, shrugged and stretched out on the floor, closing his eyes for an apparently untroubled nap. Moretti took to folding and refolding the corners of the newspapers until they crumbled in his hand.

Forty-five minutes later, just as Moretti had begun to fear waiting overnight for a decision, Brother James turned back. ''Very well,'' he said without fanfare. ''Present your evidence.''

Under the friar's hand, the sanctuary lights dimmed and the microprojector flashed a flat image in midair: brightness, then grey snow, then brightness again. The only sounds in the church were the faint hum of the overhead fan and, from time to time, a whimper from Grubb.

The images were disjointed and marred by ''noise,'' keeping those in the sanctuary spectators even though they were seeing with Kelly Henderson's eyes. There were moments of great clarity: the skiff alongside *Gloria*, a bubble helmet settling over Kelly's head, a gloved hand tugging at a safety line. Then, for a long three minutes, James, Moretti, Andrew, Pasquale, even Grubb, *became* Kelly Henderson.

They wrapped their arms around a doubled-up, space-suited stranger to bring him across the void to *Gloria*. Their eyes stared, incredulous, as the sick man suddenly straightened and unclipped their safety line. They looked for explanation into the impassive face of Hollis Grubb. And, at the end, they were hurled out of the hatch by powerful arms, tumbling end over end as the *Gloria* and Alpheus below her steadily grew smaller and ever more permanently out of reach.

Grubb came to his feet, his face ashen. ''Where did that come from?'' he screamed. ''Where did you get that?''

"From Kelly," Brother Andrew said calmly. "From the memory chemicals in her brain, preserved by the environment to which you committed her. If you know any neurophysiochemistry, I'll be happy to explain—"

"Liar! *Liar!*" Grubb cried, moving toward Brother Andrew with clenched fists. "It was an actor—a mask"—he turned toward Moretti—"You! You used my confession to make that—you broke your own vows—" Two of the First Fathers rushed forward to halt his advance, and they dragged him back to his seat, still shouting angry words of protest.

In the midst of the tumult, Moretti stepped up to the adjudicator's pulpit. "For God and the faithful of Alpheus, I close my case against the sinner Hollis Grubb."

Brother James made the sign of the cross. "The sin is confirmed. Penance will be done by service to God on Retreat. In accordance with the Rule of St. Abbenew, the costs of the Court will be charged to the estate of Kelly Henderson."

Grubb's protests became a wail as they took him away.

IV

With the microviewer and the tech friar aboard, Pasquale's wagon was full. The ruts and bumps in the road threatened to bounce one or the other of them out at any moment.

"How are you this morning?" Brother Andrew asked Moretti.

"Better," said the prosecutor forcefully. "Not good, but better. I feel I should thank you again—"

"Twice is sufficient. Besides—aren't you directing your thanks in the wrong direction?"

Moretti scrutinized the scientist's face. "If anyone else had said that—"

"You'd have thought they were ridiculing you. Well, I meant it."

Moretti nodded. "You're very tolerant of those who don't share your beliefs."

Brother Andrew shrugged. "I thought we were supposed to be."

The wagon turned in at the spaceport, and Brother Andrew looked ahead to see the shuttlecraft and *Gloria* side-by-side on the tarmac. Spaceport workers were completing final inspections on both.

"We won't have to change *Gloria*'s name," Moretti observed. "Just its meaning."

"What are we going to do with her?"

"Ferry her back to Retreat, for now."

"For now?"

The wagon was slowing, and Moretti hopped out without answering. He walked toward *Gloria*, and Brother Andrew followed. "Did it ever occur to you that the sinner and I are very much alike?" Moretti asked as the biologist came up beside him.

Brother Andrew glanced at *Gloria*, then back at Moretti's face. "No. How?"

"In what that ship represents to us. He was desperate to leave the cluster because there are too few people here—and I, because there are beginning to be too many."

"You're going to ask the abbot for *Gloria*—that's why we took her in payment," Brother Andrew realized suddenly.

"No need to—he offered her to me, last night. He said I could leave from here, if it suited me."

There was an uncomfortable silence, broken at last by Moretti. "I've long had a fanciful image of striking out alone, into the heart of God's universe. Last night, it was stronger than ever. I kept thinking, perhaps when I'm alone, I'll finally hear His voice clearly." His soft chuckle was self-aware. "This morning it seems a bit silly. I know that you take yourself with you, wherever you go—all the strengths, all the flaws. But I'm not quite ready to give up my vision."

"Well—I hope—." Brother Andrew stopped. Uncertain what to say, he said nothing.

"I told him no," said Moretti.

"Pardon?"

"I said the abbot had *offered* me *Gloria*. I turned him down," Moretti said. "He seemed pleased."

Brother Andrew's confusion showed plainly. "I would have thought—"

"Even a sinner can be a teacher," Moretti said, his smile an epigram for painful understanding. "Perhaps it's time I stopped trying to force God into a compartment I designed." He tugged at Brother Andrew's sleeve and started toward the shuttle. "Come on, Brother. I don't expect to become a convert, but I'd like to hear a bit more about God and—what was it? Hydrogen?"

Small Miracles

Mel Gilden

Mel Gilden's gentle and understated stories have graced a large number of anthologies and magazines in recent years, ranging from Twilight Zone to More Wandering Stars. Besides writing fiction, he is also a frequent contributor to the Los Angeles Times Book Review.

"God moves in mysterious ways," we are often told—and told too often in times of crisis. In "Small Miracles," Gilden has come up with a new treatment of the idea, as well as a character you're likely to remember for a very long time—if indeed you don't know him already.

The night that his unfortunate daughter went out with Morrie Rabinowitz, David Resnick fell asleep in his chair and had a dream.

He dreamed that he was in a dark oppressive room. The smells of camphor and death were in the air. His mother, gray and wrapped in a shroud so that only her face showed, was sitting up in bed. David thought, even as he dreamed, how his daughter Devorah took after her. She had the same nose that was too long and pointed, the same mouth that was too big, the same eyes that were too small. Devorah was a fine girl—smart, good natured, but it was remarkable how she resembled a bear when she moved.

Sitting on the edge of the bed was Morrie Rabinowitz. He was a handsome boy, David thought as he wondered what Morrie was doing in his mother's room. Morrie was a slim muscular fellow, so unlike Devorah's other suiters—pimply-faced boys, either thin as starvation or grossly fat.

Morrie was feeding David's mother chicken soup with a silver spoon from an enormous bowl. When his mother put her lips around the spoon, her mouth was distended into a grotesque grin.

Rabinowitz looked at David with warm even eyes and said, "I can make your daughter happy too."

David woke up sweating. He had been startled by something, but did not know what it was. He was alert, waiting in the darkness. He heard the ticking of the clock, the vague conversational rhythm that came from the television his wife Lila was watching upstairs.

His father had sat on his mother's bed like that the night she died. He remembered the strange conversation he and his father had that night while sitting in big leather chairs in the darkened study just off the sick room.

David's father sighed and then smiled as if he'd resigned himself to doing something that was only partially unpleasant.

He said, "David, I have to go away. You must make sure your mother is put to rest with the proper dignity, make sure all the proper ceremonies are observed."

David was amazed. He said, "What can possibly be important enough to drag you away at a time like this?"

"I have to go. That is enough."

"But *now?*"

"Will you listen to me, David? I haven't got a choice. Do you think I'd leave your mother, whom I love even more dearly than I love you, if I didn't have to?"

David shrugged.

His father said, "You know, even when she was young and well your mother was never a beautiful woman."

"I'm surprised to hear you talk like that."

"It's time to be honest. Oh, she's a good woman, intelligent and kind—I never questioned that. But even now, when women are becoming emancipated, it's not easy for one who is ugly."

David nodded. "So?"

"Your mother, when not yet thirty, was fast becoming an old maid when I arrived." Old Mr. Resnick stopped and his mouth formed that odd smile again. He said, "Do you know what a *batlan* is?"

"I've never paid as much attention to the folklore of my people as I should have."

"No matter. A *batlan* is a man who is not much good for anything but taking up space. In the old days he was paid to be the tenth man in a *minyan* or to say the Kaddish for a family that was without a surviving male relative. He could study and perhaps debate, but do neither well.

"There are *batlans* even among the angels. They are never involved in the arguments over fine points of Talmudic law. When they listen they don't understand. They are not without intelligence or willingness, but merely talent. Their miracles are like week-old seltzer water."

David laughed, looked through the doorway at his mother, and once more became serious.

"These *batlans* are sent out by the Holy Presence to do certain things."

"Things?"

"Things. They make small adjustments to life on Earth. Maybe marry an ugly woman so she might have a little happiness—so she might have a son who will be a doctor."

The son and the father stared at each other—the father expectantly, the son with understanding that matured gradually into disbelief. The son said, "What are you telling me?"

Mr. Resnick looked at the floor. "Your father is one of those angels."

"A *batlan* angel."

"Yes."

They talked for a while longer. Mr. Resnick got up and walked into the room where his wife lay dying. David followed, almost on his heels.

When David crossed the threshold his father was already gone. David looked out the window and checked the closet. He was alone in the room with his mother, who had died only moments before.

The mystery of his father's disappearance was momentarily blotted out by David's sudden grief. He had been prepared for his mother's death for months. Still, it was a shock when it actually happened. Trembling, he called the doctor. He sat in the dark, thinking gravely on the fact of his father's disappearance without venturing to look for an explanation. The people from the mortuary came and took his mother away.

The next morning, David had found his father lying dead in his own place in the big bed where he had slept next to David's mother for 50 years.

Now married, and with a daughter who took after his mother, David sat up for most of what remained of that night trying to decide if he really knew who Morrie Rabinowitz was.

Lila had done her part as prospective mother-in-law and invited Rabinowitz to dinner the following weekend. He had accepted happily. As a legal student who worked summers on an ice cream truck, his funds were limited, and he was, he admitted, always ready to eat a free meal.

Devorah seemed more comfortable with Rabinowitz than she had the week before, and they joked up and back while they ate. David made small talk but said nothing about his dream. He was much less certain now of his suppositions than he had been on the night he'd made them. Yet, there had to be some reason Rabinowitz made him feel so awkward.

After dinner David asked Rabinowitz if he'd like to go for a walk. Rabinowitz nodded solemnly.

They left the house and while they walked, they discussed the beauty of the weather and how it related to the ice cream business. Rabinowitz went on at length.

David said, "You know, I had a dream about you the other night."

"I'm flattered, sir."

David told Rabinowitz what he'd seen, and he finished by remarking, "My daughter is not a great beauty."

"There are other things besides physical beauty."

"The poor girl takes after her grandmother."

"Why do you say these things? You want to chase me away?"

"No, no. Let me ask you something. Do you know what a *batlan* is?"

"*Batlan?* No."

David explained and Rabinowitz nodded. David told himself not to go on. Where would Devorah be if he chased the boy away? But David said, "My father told me there are also *batlan* angels. They are sometimes sent to Earth to work small miracles with understanding and compassion rather than with spectacles."

Rabinowitz said, "Does this relate somehow to Devorah and me?"

"Doesn't necessarily relate to anything. I'm just talking." David laughed and shook his head. "My father, may he rest in peace, told me just before he died he was a *batlan* angel."

Rabinowitz didn't laugh. If anything, he looked worried. He said, "You believed him?"

"My father was one of the kindest men I knew. He could have been an angel."

"I suppose stranger things have happened."

"You are remarkably like him."

"I take that as a great compliment."

They completed their circuit of the block. Just before they went back into the house, David said, "We don't have to talk about any of this to Devorah or my wife."

"If you like," Rabinowitz said.

Devorah found another young man. His name was Sammy Katzman. And while David thought he was not the prize that Rabinowitz seemed to be, he was nonetheless a substantial young man with a good job.

"Here's a problem I never thought I'd have," Devorah said. She laughed.

"A nice girl like you?" Lila said. "I'm surprised there are not more young men." David watched his wife and his daughter talk across the breakfast table. In his wife's every line and curve was grace; it was too bad the fortunate chromosomes had not been deposited in their offspring.

Katzman came over to visit. He looked as if he were made of two hard-boiled eggs, a smaller one for a head and a larger one for a body.

David said, "So you're a bookkeeper."

"Yes, sir."

"Ladies' ready-to-wear."

"Yes, sir."

"You're going to school?"

"No, sir."

"I suppose there's nothing wrong with that." David wished he had a pipe to light, but he had given up smoking years before.

"We have to go, Daddy," Devorah said.

"So soon? I want to talk with Sandy, here."

"Sammy," Lila said.

"Sammy, of course." David looked at the floor between Katzman and himself.

"Where did you say you were going?"

"Miniature golf," Katzman said.

"I understand there's a good movie at the Baxter."

"Daddy," Devorah said.

"What's the matter?"

"Maybe we'll see it next time," Katzman said. He stood up. Devorah and Lila followed him to the door. David sat wishing he had not given up his pipe.

When Katzman and Devorah were gone, Lila hurried back into the living room and confronted David. "What are you doing?" she said. "I've never seen you act so unpleasant toward one of Devorah's friends."

"Excuse me for living." He folded his arms and looked away.

"It's Rabinowitz, isn't it?"

"What?"

Lila sat down across from him and leaned in his direction. "When Rabinowitz comes over, you're all smiles. I agree he's a nice boy, but no nicer than Katzman."

David shook his head and said, "I don't understand it myself. I only know that he reminds me of someone."

"Rabinowitz? Who?"

David did not say anything.

In a gentler tone, Lila said, "Who, David?"

"My father."

She nodded, said, "Ah," and leaned back into the corner of the couch. He told her about his dream, and his discussions with Rabinowitz.

"Maybe you should see a doctor."

"No. I don't need one."

"Then let nature take its course."

"We are talking here about the best man for your daughter. Such things should not be left to chance."

"You're talking like a man who was born in Europe somewhere instead of Chicago."

David smiled. He said, "I am, aren't I."

The front door chimes rang. Lila went to see who it was. She stood aside, and Morrie Rabinowitz entered the room. His eyes seemed to have sunken into his head and his face was lined. He seemed to have aged by years since the last time David had seen him. "Mr. Resnick, can I speak to you?"

David stood up and said, "Of course." To Lila he said, "We'll be back in a minute." Lila stood to one side as they walked out the door. "Be careful," she called after them.

They walked for a few minutes before Rabinowitz said, "I have to leave. I should be gone already."

"Why?"

"I . . . I am no longer needed."

"Needed for what?"

"Your daughter doesn't need me."

"You know about Katzman?"

"I know. Don't ask how."

"What is there about Katzman that makes you feel like giving up?"

"It's not a matter of giving up. I should never have been here in the first place."

"I don't understand," David said, though the fact that he perhaps understood too well excited him.

"I think you do," Rabinowitz said.

David wondered if the man was reading his mind.

Rabinowitz said, "Marriages are made in heaven, you know." He smiled. "I lost faith for an instant, and came here thinking that God had forgotten something and I should take care of it."

David put his hands in his pockets because the night was turning chill. He looked at the young man beside him and could not help but see a physical resemblance to his father. David had not noticed it before. Perhaps it was an illusion brought on by the occasional pale light from the street lamps.

"You know," David said, "according to my mother, my father came out of nowhere and married her just when everybody thought she would die an old maid."

"In a universe as big as this one, good things can happen as well as bad."

David shook his head. "My mother, my daughter. A funny coincidence."

Rabinowitz shrugged.

"I think you're a *batlan*. A *batlan* angel like my father was."

Rabinowitz had been looking at the ground all this time. He walked with his hands behind his back, like an old man returning home from *shul*.

"You take a long time to answer," David said.

"It's an unusual thing you want me to admit," Rabinowitz said.

"Don't be coy, please. You've as much as admitted it already."

"Be content then."

Angrily, David said, "If you persist in being mysterious, why did you come to see me?"

"I didn't want to leave without saying good-bye."

"Say good-bye to Devorah, if you can."

"She has Katzman. I never should have come in the first place."

"So you said."

They rounded a corner under a streetlight and David saw their shadows stretch out before them and fade into the darkness where the lamplight did not reach.

David said, "You like Devorah?"

"As if she were my own granddaughter."

David looked sharply at Rabinowitz.

Rabinowitz smiled and shrugged.

David said, "You're playing with me."

"I'm . . . Perhaps. Why do you ask if I like her?"

"I don't know what you are, Morrie Rabinowitz, but I ask you now a favor, as my father's son and as my daughter's father. Stay here. Court Devorah. I am sure it would be only a matter of time before she forgets Katzman."

"Impossible."

"Even a *batlan* angel should be entitled to an impossibility or two."

"I've used my quota, just being here. Believe me."

"A *batlan*, as I said."

Rabinowitz said nothing. He did not even shrug. He stopped suddenly and looked at the sky, his arms spread wide, imploringly. His hands came together with a slap, and he looked at the ground.

David waited, wondering if all this mystic posturing was sincerely felt, or if it was for his benefit. At last Rabinowitz said, "All right, I'll stay."

"What changed your mind?"

"Strength or weakness. You tell me."

"You seem very human for an angel."

"A *batlan* angel. You said it yourself."

"It's true, then?"

"I didn't say that."

David turned and walked back the way they had come. Rabinowitz caught up with him, and they walked together. Neither of them said another word until they stood in front of David's house. Rabinowitz said, "Are you certain that it is for Devorah's sake that you are asking me to stay?"

"I want the best for her."

"It's not the same thing."

While David thought about this, Rabinowitz got into his old but well-kept Chevrolet and drove off.

Lila was waiting for David in the house. When she asked him what happened, he said, "He said he wanted to see her again. I gave my permission."

"Why does he suddenly need permission?"

David shrugged and said, "A young man sometimes needs reassurance."

Rabinowitz called the next day and made a date with Devorah for Sunday. When David asked her what was going on between her and Rabinowitz, Devorah sighed and said, "Oh, he's a nice boy, I suppose." David could not lead her into saying more.

Between the phone call and Sunday, Devorah went out for coffee a few times with Sammy Katzman. When he brought her home, she was always laughing or staring romantically into space. David cursed Rabinowitz for not coming over sooner. If he was not going to make a wholehearted play for Devorah, Rabinowitz might as well stay away, as he'd intended.

When Rabinowitz came to pick up Devorah on Sunday, he looked even more haggard than he had before. David said, "Where have you been?" but Devorah came into the room before Rabinowitz had a chance to answer. She smiled at him in an offhandedly friendly way, but seemed to be thinking of something else. Rabinowitz politely ushered her out the door. "Have a good time," David cried after them.

An hour later, David was in his study reading a news magazine when he heard talking at the front door. He came out to find Lila entertaining Sammy Katzman in the living room with coffee and cookies. Katzman stood up when he saw David. "Good afternoon."

"Good afternoon. Devorah isn't here."

"So your wife has told me."

"She's out with another young man."

Katzman looked stricken. Lila glared at David. David said, "It's true, isn't it?"

Katzman, already on his feet, said, "Perhaps I should go."

Lila said, "Please sit down, Mr. Katzman. I'm sure my daughter will be happy to see you."

Katzman looked uncertainly at David, but sat down. His finger involuntarily hammered on the arm of the chair. David poured himself a cup of coffee and took two cookies. He said, "You still working in ladies' ready-to-wear?"

Katzman nodded.

There were footsteps on the walk outside the house. Seconds later the front door was unlocked and opened, and Devorah came in followed by Rabinowitz. Her face was a blank, as if she were bravely bearing some great trial as well as she could. When she saw Katzman, she smiled immediately and crossed the room to greet him. Rabinowitz was left standing at the door.

"Come in, Mr. Rabinowitz," David said.

Rabinowitz walked into the room, nodding from one person to the other. David introduced Rabinowitz to Katzman. They shook hands warily and let go as soon as they could.

When Rabinowitz was seated, Katzman said, "Frankly, Mr. Rabinowitz, I am not pleased to see you. I have an important question to ask Devorah and I didn't want to do it in front of an audience." Katzman was on his feet again.

"Please stay," Rabinowitz said. "I feel that I am intruding."

"No, no," said David, and suddenly felt ridiculous.

"Perhaps," said Lila, with the air of a woman working out a difficult problem, "Devorah and Sammy would like to talk in the den."

"I will leave," Rabinowitz said, and stood up.

"Sit down," said David. Rabinowitz made no move.

"I'm sorry to have caused you trouble," Katzman said. He walked toward the door.

"Wait," said Rabinowitz, his voice full of command. "Ask your question."

Katzman stopped and looked at him. Moments passed during which the two suitors did nothing but study each other. At last Katzman said, "All right, I will." Rabinowitz sat down.

Katzman turned to Devorah and after inhaling deeply, said, "Will you marry me?"

Devorah reddened. David and Rabinowitz exchanged looks. Lila looked questioningly at David. At last, Devorah stood up and said, "Yes."

David suddenly heard the peal of bells that seemed to be so far away he could not tell if the sound perhaps was his imagination. Rabinowitz stood up slowly. Devorah, Lila and Katzman stayed just as they were, as if suddenly frozen.

Rabinowitz said, "You see? God takes care of everything."

David said, "What happened to them?"

"Nothing. I will leave and they will be fine." He walked toward the door.

"You can't be giving up."

"You always were stubborn, David. But no. Perhaps I am not so much giving up as I am finished with my assignment."

"What do you mean?"

"I mean that God moves in mysterious ways. Perhaps I was allowed to come here not to marry Devorah, but to teach you a lesson."

"Which is?"

"You tell me."

David thought for a moment, opened his mouth to speak, but did not. Then he said, "This is not much of a miracle, as miracles go."

Rabinowitz said, "Next time have a bigger problem."

The door opened for Rabinowitz. When he went out, the door closed behind him. The faraway bells stopped ringing and Lila leaped out of her chair to hug Devorah. Katzman held out his hand to David. David, still dazed, shook it rapidly and said, "But what about Rabinowitz?"

Everyone stopped and looked at him. Lila said, "What about him?"

"But he was just here."

"Where?" Devorah said, and laughed as she bent to look under the couch.

David felt very small in the vastness of space while stars and pinwheels of galaxies poured through him as if he were a funnel. He solemnly gave his daughter and his new son-in-law his blessing.

Relativistic Effects

Gregory Benford

Among the writers who have firmly established their careers in the field of science fiction over the last decade, Gregory Benford is arguably the most likely to reach a wide general audience. His prize-winning novel, Timescape, *was hailed in 1980 as a "towering success" by the* Washington Post Book World, *and shows every evidence of becoming one of that handful of novels that science fiction readers offer their friends as proof of what the genre can produce at the top of its form.*

Benford is a practicing scientist and his work is filled with a genuine love for the marvels of science and the possibilities of the future. But he can see the people too, in minute detail, and the human relationship to major events. Witness "Relativistic Effects."

They came into the locker room with a babble of random talk, laughter and shouts. There was a rolling bass undertone, gruff and raw. Over it the higher feminine notes ran lightly, warbling, darting.

The women had a solid, businesslike grace to them, doing hard work in the company of men. There were a dozen of them and they shed their clothes quickly and efficiently, all modesty forgotten long ago, their minds already focused on the job to come.

"You up for this, Nick?" Jake asked, yanking off his shorts and clipping the input sockets to his knees and elbows. His skin was red and callused from his years of linked servo work.

"Think I can handle it," Nick replied. "We're hitting pretty dense plasma already. There'll be plenty of it pouring through the throat." He was big but he gave the impression of lightness and speed, trim like a boxer, with broad shoulders and thick wrists.

"Lots of flux," Jake said. "Easy to screw up."

"I didn't get my rating by screwing up 'cause some extra ions came down the tube."

"Yeah. You're pretty far up the roster, as I remember," Jake said, eyeing the big man.

"Uh huh. Number one, last time I looked," Faye put in from the next locker. She laughed, a loud braying that rolled through the locker room and made people look up. "Bet 'at's what's botherin' you, uh, Jake?"

Jake casually made an obscene gesture in her general direction and went on. "You feelin' OK, Nick?"

"What you think, I got clenchrot?" Nick spat out with sudden ferocity. "Just had a cold, is all."

Faye said slyly, "Be a shame to prang when you're so close to winnin', movin' on up." She tugged on her halter and arranged her large breasts in it.

Nick glanced at her. Trouble was, you work with a woman long enough and after a while, she looked like just one more competitor. Once he'd thought of making a play for Faye—she really did look fairly good sometimes—but now she was one more sapper who'd elbow him into a vortex if she got half a chance. Point was, he never gave her—or anybody else—a chance to come up on him from some funny angle, throw him some unexpected momentum. He studied her casual, deft movements, pulling on the harness for the connectors. Still, there was something about her. . . .

"You get one more good run," Faye said slyly, "you gonna get the promotion. 'At's what I'd say."

"What matters is what they say upstairs, on A deck."

"Touchy, touchy, tsk tsk," Jake said. He couldn't resist getting in a little gig, Nick knew. Not when Jake knew it might get Nick stirred up a little. But the larger man stayed silent, stolidly pulling on his neural hookups.

Snick, the relays slide into place and Nick feels each one come home with a percussive impact in his body, he never gets used to that no matter it's been years he's been in the Main Drive crew. When he really sat down and thought about it he didn't like this job at all, was always shaky before coming down here for his shift. He'd figured that out at the start, so the trick was, he didn't think about it, not unless he'd had too much of that 'ponics-processed liquor, the stuff that was packed with vitamin B and C and wasn't supposed to do you any damage, not even leave the muggy dregs and ache of a hangover, only of course it never worked quite right because nothing on the ship did anymore. If he let himself stoke up on that stuff he'd gradually drop out of the conversation at whatever party he was, and go off into a corner somewhere and somebody'd find him an hour or two later staring at a wall or into his drink, reliving the hours in the tube and thinking about his dad and the grandfather he could only vaguely remember. They'd both died of the ol' black creeping cancer, same as eighty percent of the crew, and it was no secret the Main Drive was the worst place in the ship for it, despite all the design specs of fifty-meter rock walls and carbon-steel bulkheads and lead-lined hatches. A man'd be a goddamn fool if he didn't think about that, sure, but somebody had to do it or they'd all die. The job came down to Nick from his father because the family just did it, that was all, all the way back to the first crew, the original bridge officers had decided that long before Nick was born, it was the only kind of social organization that the sociometricians thought could possibly work on a ship that had to fly between stars, they all knew that and nobody questioned it any more than they'd want to change a pressure spec on a seal. You just didn't, was all there was to it. He'd learned that since he could first understand the church services, or the yearly anniversary of the Blowout up on the bridge, or the things that his father told him, even when the old man was dying with the black crawling stuff eating him from inside, Nick had learned that good—

"God, this dump is gettin' worse every—lookit 'at." Faye pointed.

A spider was crawling up a bulkhead, inching along on the ceramic smoothness.

"Musta got outta Agro," somebody put in.

"Yeah, don't kill it. Might upset the whole damn biosphere, an' they'd have our fuckin' heads for it."

A murmur of grudging agreement.

"Lookit 'at dumb thing," Jake said. "Made it alla way up here, musta come through air ducts an' line feeds an' who knows what." He leaned over the spider, eyeing it. It was a good three centimeters across and dull gray. "Pretty as sin, huh?"

Nick tapped in sockets at his joints and tried to ignore Jake. "Yeah."

"Poor thing. Don't know where in hell it is, does it? No appreciation for how important a place this is. We're 'bout to see a whole new age start in this locker room, soon's Nick here gets his full score. He'll be the new super an' we'll be—well, hell, we'll be like this li'l spider here. Just small and havin' our own tiny place in the big design of Nick's career, just you think how it's gonna—"

"Can the shit," Nick said harshly.

Jake laughed.

There was a tight feeling in the air. Nick felt it and figured it was something about his trying to get the promotion, something like that, but not worth bothering about. Plenty of time to think about it, once he had finished this job and gotten on up the ladder. Plenty of time then.

The gong rang brassily and the men and women finished suiting up. The minister came in and led them in a prayer for safety, the same as every other shift. Nothing different, but the tension remained. They'd be flying into higher plasma densities, sure, Nick thought. But there was no big deal about that. Still, he murmured the prayer along with the rest. Usually he didn't bother. He'd been to church services as usual, everybody went, it was unthinkable that you wouldn't, and anyway he'd never get any kind of promotion if he didn't show his face reg'lar, hunch on up to the altar rail and swallow that wafer and the alky-laced grape juice that went sour in your mouth while you were trying to swallow it, same as a lot of the talk they wanted you to swallow, only you did, you got it down because you had to and without asking anything afterward either, you bet, 'cause the ones who made trouble didn't get anywhere. So he muttered along, mouthing the familiar litany without thinking. The minister's thin lips moving, rolling on through the archaic phrases, meant less than nothing. When he looked up, each face was pensive as they prepared to go into the howling throat of the ship.

Nick lies mute and blind and for a moment feels nothing but the numb silence. It collects in him, blotting out the dim rub of the snouts which cling like lampreys to his nerves and muscles, pressing embrace that amplifies every movement, and—

—*spang*—

—he slips free of the mooring cables, a rush of sight-sound-taste-touch washes over him, so strong and sudden a welter of sensations that he jerks with the impact. He is servo'd to a thing like an eel that swims and flips and dives into a howling dance of protons. The rest of the ship is sheltered safely behind slabs of rock. But the eel is his, the eel is *him*. It shudders and jerks and twists, skating across sleek strands of magnetic plains. To Nick, it is like swimming.

The torrent gusts around him and he feels its pinprick breath. In a blinding orange glare Nick swoops, feeling his power grow as he gets the feel of it. His shiny shelf is wrapped in a cocoon of looping magnetic fields that turn the protons away, sending them gyrating in a mad gavotte, so the heavy particles cannot crunch and flare against the slick baked skin. Nick flexes the skin, supple and strong, and slips through the magnetic turbulence ahead. He feels the magnetic lines of force stretch like rubber bands. He banks and accelerates.

Streams of protons play upon him. They make glancing collisions with each other but do not react. The repulsion between them is too great and so this plasma cannot make them burn, cannot thrust them together with enough violence. Something more is needed or else the ship's throat will fail to harvest the simple hydrogren atoms, fail to kindle it into energy.

There— In the howling storm Nick sees the blue dots that are the keys, the catalyst: carbon nuclei, hovering like sea gulls in an updraft.

Split-image phosphors gleam, marking his way. He swims in the streaming blue-white glow, through a murky storm of fusing ions. He watches plumes of carbon nuclei striking the swarms of protons, wedding them to form the heavier nitrogen nuclei. The torrent swirls and screams at Nick's skin and in his sensors he sees and feels and tastes the lumpy, sluggish nitrogen as it finds a fresh incoming proton and with the fleshy smack of fusion the two stick, they hold, they wobble like raindrops— falling—merging—ballooning into a new nucleus, heavier still: oxygen.

But the green pinpoints of oxygen are unstable. These fragile forms split instantly. Jets of new particles spew through the surrounding glow—neutrinos, ruddy photons of light, and slower, darker, there come the heavy daughters of the marriage: a swollen, burnt-gold cloud of a bigger variety of nitrogen.

Onward the process flies. Each nucleus collides millions of times with the others in a fleck-shot swirl like glowing snowflakes. All in the space of a heartbeat. Flakes ride the magnetic field lines. Gamma rays flare and sputter among the blundering motes like fitful fireflies. Nuclear fire lights the long roaring corridor that is the ship's main drive. Nick swims, the white-hot sparks breaking over him like foam. Ahead he sees the violet points of gravid nitrogen and hears them crack into carbon plus an alpha particle. So in the end the long cascade gives forth the carbon that catalyzed it, carbon that will begin again its life in the whistling blizzard of protons coming in from the forward maw of the ship. With the help of the carbon, an interstellar hydrogen atom has built itself up from mere proton to, finally, an alpha particle—a stable clump of two neutrons and two protons. The alpha particle is the point of it all. It flees from the blurring storm, carrying the energy that fusion affords. The ruby-rich interstellar gas is now wedded, proton to proton, with carbon as the matchmaker.

Nick feels a rising electric field pluck at him. He moves to shed his excess charge. To carry a cloak of electrons here is fatal. Upstream lies the chewing gullet of the ramscoop ship, where the incoming protons are sucked in and where their kinetic power is stolen from them by the electric fields. There the particles are slowed, brought to rest inside the ship, their streaming energy stored in capacitors.

A cyclone shrieks behind him. Nick swims sideways, toward the walls of the combustion chamber. The nuclear burn that flares around him is never pure, cannot be pure because the junk of the cosmos pours through here, like barley meal laced with grains of granite. The incoming atomic rain spatters constantly over the fluxlife walls, killing the organic superconductor strands there.

Nick pushes against the rubbery magnetic fields and swoops over the mottled yellow-blue crust of the walls. In the flickering lightning glow of infrared and ultraviolet he sees the scaly muck that deadens the magnetic fields and slows the nuclear burn in the throat. He flexes, wriggles, and turns the eel-like form. This brings the electron beam gun around at millimeter range. He fires. A brittle crackling leaps out, onto the scaly wall. The tongue bites and gouges. Flakes roast off and blacken and finally bubble up like tar. The rushing proton currents wash the flakes away, revealing the gunmetal blue beneath. Now the exposed superconducting threads can begin their own slow pruning of themselves, life casting out its dead. Their long organic chain molecules can feed and grow anew. As Nick cuts and turns and carves he watches the spindly fibers coil loose and drift in eddies. Finally they spin away into the erasing proton storm. The dead fibers sputter and flash where the incoming protons strike them and then with a rumble in his acoustic pickup coils he sees them swept away. Maintenance.

Something tugs at him. He sees the puckered scoop where the energetic alpha particles shoot by. They dart like luminous jade wasps. The scoop sucks them in. Inside they will be collected, drained of energy, inducing megawatts of power for the ship, which will drink their last drop of momentum and cast them aside, a wake of broken atoms.

Suddenly he spins to the left—*Jesus, how can*—he thinks—and the scoop fields lash him. A megavolt per meter of churning electrical vortex snatches at him. It is huge and quick and relentless to Nick (though to the ship it is a minor ripple in its total momentum) and magnetic tendrils claw at his spinning, shiny surfaces. The scoop opening is a plunging, howling mouth. Jets of glowing atoms whirl by him, mocking. The walls near him counter his motion by increasing their magnetic fields. Lines of force stretch and bunch.

How did this— is all he has time to think before a searing spot blooms nearby. His presence so near the scoop has upset the combination rates there. His eyes widen. If the reaction gets out of control it can burn through the chamber vessel, through the asteroid rock beyond, and spike with acrid fire into the ship, toward the life dome.

A brassy roar. The scoop sucks at his heels. Ions run white-hot. A warning knot strikes him. Tangled magnetic ropes grope for him, clotting around the shiny skin.

Panic squeezes his throat. Desperately he fires his electron beam gun against the wall, hoping it will give him a push, a fresh vector—

Not enough. Orange ions blossom and swell around him—

Most of the squad was finished dressing. They were tired and yet the release of getting off work brought out an undercurrent of celebration. They ignored Nick and slouched out of the locker room, bound for families or assignations or sensory jolts of sundry types. A reek of sweat and fatigue diffused through the sluggishly stirring air. The squad laughed and shouted old jokes to each other. Nick sat on the bench with his head in his hands.

"I . . . I don't get it. I was doin' pretty well, catchin' the crap as it came at me, an' then somethin' grabbed . . ."

They'd had to pull him out with a robot searcher. He'd gone dead, inoperative, clinging to the throat lining, fighting the currents. The surges drove blood down into your gut and legs, the extra g's slamming you up against the bulkhead and sending big dark blotches across your vision, purple swarms of dots swimming everywhere, hollow rattling noises coming in through the transducer mikes, nausea, the ache spreading through your arms—

It had taken three hours to get him back in, and three more to clean up. A lot of circuitry was fried for good, useless junk. The worst loss was the high-grade steel, all riddled with neutrons and fissured by nuclear fragments. The ship's foundry couldn't replace that, hadn't had the rolling mill to even make a die for it in more than a generation. His neuro index checked out okay, but he wouldn't be able to work for a week.

He was still in a daze and the memory would not straighten itself out in his mind. "I dunno, I . . ."

Faye murmured, "Maybe went a li'l fast for you today."

Jake grinned and said nothing.

"Mebbe you could, y'know, use a rest. Sit out a few sessions." Faye cocked her head at him.

Nick looked at both of them and narrowed his eyes. "That wasn't a mistake of mine, was it? Uh? No mistake at all. Somebody—" He knotted a fist.

"Hey, nothin' you can prove," Jake said, backing away. "I can guarantee that, boy."

"Some bastard, throwin' me some extra angular when I wasn't lookin', I oughta—"

"Come on, Nick, you got no proof 'a those charges. You know there's too much noise level in the throat to record what ever'body's doin'." Faye grinned without humor.

"Damn." Nick buried his face in his hands. "I was *that* close," so damned near to gettin' that promotion—"

"Yeah. Tsk tsk. You dropped points back there for sure, Nick, burnin' out a whole unit that way an' gettin'—"

"Shut it. Just shut it."

Nick was still groggy and he felt the anger build in him without focus, without resolution. These two would make up some neat story to cover their asses, same as everybody did when they were bringing another member of the squad down a notch or two. The squad didn't have a lot of love for anybody who looked like they were going to get up above the squad, work their way up. That was the way it was, jobs were hard to change, the bridge liked it stable, said it came out better when you worked at a routine all your life and—

"Hey, c'mon, let's get our butts down to the Sniffer," Faye said. "No use jawin' 'bout this, is 'ere? I'm gettin' thirsty after all that, uh, work."

She winked at Jake. Nick saw it and knew he would get a ribbing about this for weeks. The squad was telling him he had stepped out of line and he would just have to take it. That was just the plain fact of it. He clenched his fists and felt a surge of anger.

"Hey!" Jake called out. "This damn spider's still tryin' to make it up this wall." He reached out and picked it up in his hand. The little gray thing struggled against him, legs kicking.

"Y'know, I hear there're people over in Comp who keep these for pets," Faye said. "Could be one of theirs."

"Creepy li'l thing," Nick said.

"You get what you can," Faye murmured. "Ever see a holo of a dog?"

Nick nodded. "Saw a whole movie about this one, it was a collie, savin' people an' all. Now that's a pet."

They all stared silently at the spider as it drummed steadily on Jake's hand with its legs. Nick shivered and turned away. Jake held it firmly, without hurting it, and slipped it into a pocket. "Think I'll take it back before Agro busts a gut lookin' for it."

Nick was silent as the three of them left the smells of the locker room and made their way up through the corridors. They took a shortcut along an undulating walkway under the big observation dome. Blades of pale blue light shifted like enormous columns in the air, but they were talking and only occasionally glanced up.

The vast ship of which they were a part was heading through the narrow corridor between two major spiral galaxies. On the right side of the dome the bulge of one galaxy was like a whirlpool of light, the points of light like grains of sand caught in a vortex. Around the bright core, glowing clouds of the spiral arms wended their way through the flat disk, seeming to cut through the dark dust clouds like a river slicing through jungle. Here and there black towers reared up out of the confusion of the disk, where masses of interstellar debris had been heaved out of the galactic plane, driven by collisions between clouds, or explosions of young stars.

There were intelligent, technological societies somewhere among those drifting stars. The ship had picked up their transmissions long ago—radio, UV, the usual—and had altered course to pass nearby.

The two spirals were a binary system, bound together since their birth. For most of their history they had stayed well apart, but now they were brushing within a galactic diameter of each other. Detailed observations in the last few weeks of ship's time—all that was needed to veer and swoop toward the twinned disks—had shown that this was the final pass: the two galaxies would not merely swoop by and escape. The filaments of gas and dust between them had created friction over the billions of years past, eroding their orbital angular momentum. Now they would grapple fatally.

The jolting impact would be spectacular: shock waves, compression of the gas in the galactic plane, and shortly thereafter new star formation, swiftly yielding an increase in the supernova rate, a flooding of the interstellar medium with high energy particles. The rain of sudden virulent energy would destroy the planetary environments. The two spirals would come together with a wrenching suddenness, the disks sliding into each other like two saucers bent on destruction, the collision effectively occurring all over the disks simultaneously in an explosive flare of X-ray and thermal brems-strahlung radiation. Even advanced technologies would be snuffed out by the rolling, searing tide.

The disks were passing nearly face-on to each other. In the broad blue dome overhead the two spirals hung like cymbals seen on edge. The ship moved at extreme relativistic velocity, pressing infinitesimally close to light speed, passing through the dim halo of gas and old dead stars that surrounded each galaxy. Its speed compressed time and space. Angles distorted as time ran at a blinding pace outside, refracting images. Extreme relativistic effects made the approach visible to the naked eye. Slowly, the huge disks of shimmering light seemed to swing open like a pair of doors. Bright tendrils spanned the gap between them.

Jake was telling a story about two men in CompCatSynch section, rambling on with gossip and jokes, trying to keep the talk light. Faye went along with it, putting in a word when Jake slowed. Nick was silent.

The ship swooped closer to the disks and suddenly across the dome streaked red and orange bursts. The disks were twisted, distorted by their mutual gravitational tugs, wrenching each other, twins locked in a tightening embrace. The planes of stars rippled, as if a huge wind blew across them. The galactic nuclei flared with fresh fires: ruby, orange, mottled blue, ripe gold. Stars were blasted into the space between. Filaments of raw, searing gas formed a web that spanned the two spirals. This was the food that fed the ship's engines. They were flying as near to the thick dust and gas of the galaxies as they could. The maw of the ship stretched outward, spanning a volume nearly as big as the galactic core. Streamers of sluggish gas veered toward it, drawn by the onrushing magnetic fields. The throat sucked in great clouds, boosting them to still higher velocity.

The ship's hull moaned as it met denser matter.

*   *   *

Nick ignores the babble from Jake, knowing it is empty foolishness, and thinks instead of the squad, and how he would run it if he got the promotion: They had to average 5000 cleared square meters a week, minimum, that was a full ten percent of the whole ship's throat, minus of course the lining areas that were shut down for full repair, call that 1000 square meters on the average, so with the other crews operating on 45-hour shifts they could work their way through and give the throat a full scraping in less than a month, easy, even allowing for screwups and malfs and times when the radiation level was too high for even the suits to screen it out. You had to keep the suits up to 99 plus percent operational or you caught hell from upstairs, but the same time they came at you with their specifications reports and never listened when you told them about the delays, that was your problem not theirs and they said so every chance they got, that bunch of blowhard officers up there,. descended from the original ship's bridge officers who'd left Earth generations back with every intention of returning after a twelve-year round trip to Centauri, only it hadn't worked, they didn't count on the drive freezing up in permanent full-bore thrust, the drive locked in and the deceleration components slowly getting fried by the increased neutron flux from the reactions, until when they finally could taper off on the forward drive the decelerators were finished, beyond repair, and then the ship had nothing to do but drive on, unable to stop or even turn the magnetic gascatchers off, because once you did that the incoming neutral atoms would be a sleet of protons and neutrons that'd riddle everybody within a day, kill them all. So the officers had said they had to keep going, studying, trying to figure a way to rebuild the decelerators, only nobody ever did, and the crew got older and they flew on, clean out of the galaxy, having babies and quarrels and finally after some murders and suicides and worse, working out a stable social structure in a goddamn relativistic runaway, officers' sons and daughters becoming officers themselves, and crewmen begetting crewmen again, down through five generations now in the creaky old ship that had by now flown through five million years of outside-time, so that there was no purpose or dream of returning

Earthside any more, only names attached to pictures and stories, and the same jobs to do every day, servicing the weakening stanchions and struts, the flagging motors, finding replacements for every little doodad that fractured, working because to stop was to die, all the time with officers to tell you what new scientific experiment they'd thought up and how maybe this time it would be the answer, the clue to getting back to their own galaxy—a holy grail beloved of the first and second generations that was now, even under high magnification, a mere mottled disk of ruby receding pinprick lights nobody alive had ever seen up close. Yet there was something in what the bridge officers said, in what the scientific mandarins mulled over, a point to their lives here—

"Let's stop in this'n," Jake called, interrupting Nick's muzzy thoughts, and he followed them into a small inn. Without his noticing it they had left the big observation dome. They angled through a tight, rocky corridor cut from the original asteroid that was the basic body of the whole starship.

Among the seven thousand souls in the ten-kilometer-wide starship, there were communities and neighborhoods and bars to suit everyone. In this one there were thick veils of smoky euphorics, harmless unless you drank an activating potion. Shifts came and went, there were always crowds in the bar, a rich assortment of faces and ages and tongues. Techs, metalworkers, computer jockeys, manuals, steamfitters, muscled grunt laborers. Cadaverous and silent ale-soakers, steadily pouring down a potent brown liquid. Several women danced in a corner, oblivious, singing, rhyming as they went.

Faye ordered drinks and they all three joined in the warm feel of the place. The euphorics helped. It took only moments to become completely convinced that this was a noble and notable set of folk. Someone shouted a joke. Laughter pealed in the close-packed room.

Nick saw in this quick moment an instant of abiding grace: how lovely it was when Faye forgot herself and laughed fully, opening her mouth so wide you could see the whole oval cavern with its ribbed pink roof and the arcing tongue alive with tension. The heart-stopping blackness at the back led down to depths worth a lifetime to explore, all revealed in a passing moment like a casual gift: a momentary and incidental beauty that eclipsed the studied, long-learned devices of women and made them infinitely more mysterious.

She gave him a wry, tossed-off smile. He frowned, puzzled. Maybe he had never paid adequate attention to her, never sensed her dimensions. He strained forward to say something and Jake interrupted his thoughts with, "Hey there, look. Two bridgies."

 And there were. Two bridge types, not mere officers but scientists; they wore the sedate blue patches on their sleeves. Such people seldom came to these parts of the ship; their quarters, ordained by time, nestled deep in the rock-lined bowels of the inner asteroid.

"See if you can hear what they're sayin'," Faye whispered.

Jake shrugged. "Why should I care?"

Faye frowned. "Wanna be a scuzzo dope forever?"

"Aw, stow it," Jake said, and went to get more beer.

Nick watched the scientist nearest him, the man, lift the heavy champagne bottle and empty it. *Have to hand it to bioponics*, he thought. *They keep the liquor coming.* The crisp golden foil at the head would be carefully collected, reused; the beautiful heavy hollow butts of the bottles had doubtless been fondled by his own grandfather. Of celebration there was no end.

Nick strained to hear.

"Yes, but the latest data shows definitely there's enough mass, no question."

"Maybe, maybe," said the other. "Must say I never thought there'd be enough between the clusters to add up so much—"

"But there *is*. No doubt of it. Look at Fenetti's data, clear as the nose on your face. Enough mass density between the clusters to close off the universe's geometry, to reverse the expansion."

Goddamn, Nick thought. *They're talking about the critical mass problem. Right out in public.*

"Yes. My earlier work seems to have been wrong."

"Look, this opens possibilities."

"How?"

"The expansion has to stop, right? So after it does, and things start to implode back, the density of gas the ship passes through will get steadily greater—right?"

Jesus, Nick thought, *the eventual slowing down of the universal expansion, billions of years*—

"Okay."

"So we'll accelerate more, the relativistic rate will get bigger—the whole process outside will speed up, as we see it."

"Right."

"Then we can sit around and watch the whole thing play out. I mean, shipboard time from now to the implosion of the whole universe, I make it maybe only three hundred years."

"That short?"

"Do the calculation."

"Ummm. Maybe so, if we pick up enough mass in the scoop fields. This flyby we're going through, it helps, too."

"Sure it does. We'll do more like it in the next few weeks. Look, we're getting up to speeds that mean we'll be zooming by a galaxy every *day*."

"Uh huh. If we can live a couple more centuries, shipboard time, we can get to see the whole shebang collapse back in on itself."

"Well, look, that's just a preliminary number, but I think we might make it. In this generation."

Faye said, "Jeez, I can't make out what they're talkin' about."

"I can," Nick said. It helped to know the jargon. He had studied this as part of his program to bootstrap himself up to a better life. You take officers, they could integrate the gravitational field equations straight off, or tell how a galaxy was evolving just by looking at it, or figure out the gas density ahead of the ship just by squinting at one of the X-ray bands from the detectors. They *knew*. He would have to know all of that too, and more. So he studied while the rest of the squad slurped up the malt.

He frowned. He was still stunned, trying to think it through. If the total mass between the clusters of galaxies was big enough, that extra matter would provide enough gravitational energy to make the whole universe reverse its expansion and fall backward, inward, given enough time . . .

Jake was back. "Too noisy in 'ere," he called. "Fergit the beers, bar's mobbed. Let's lift 'em."

Nick glanced over at the scientists. One was earnestly leaning forward, her face puffy and purplish, congested with the force of the words she was urging into the other's ear. He couldn't make out any more of what they were saying; they had descended into quoting mathematical formulas to each other.

"Okay," Nick said.

They left the random clamor of the bar and retraced their steps, back under the observation dome. Nick felt a curious elation.

Nick knows how to run the squad, knows how to keep the equipment going even if the voltage flickers, he can strip down most suits in under an hour using just plain rack tools, been doing it for forty years, all those power tools around the bay, most of the squad can't even turn a nut on a manifold without it has to be pneumatic *rrrrrtt* quick as you please nevermind the wear on the lubricants lost forever that nobody aboard can synthesize, tools seize up easy now, jam your fingers when they do, give you a hand all swole up for a week, and all the time the squad griping 'cause they have to birddog their own stuff, breadboard new ones if some piece of gear goes bad, complaining 'cause they got to form and fabricate their own microchips, no easy replacement parts to just clip in the way you read about the way it was in the first generation, and God help you if a man or woman on the crew gets a fatal injury working in the throat crew, 'cause then your budget is docked for the cost of keeping 'em frozen down, waiting on cures that'll never come just like Earth will never come, the whole planet's been dead now a million years prob'ly, and the frozen corpses on board running two percent of the energy budget he read somewhere, getting to be more all the time, but then he thinks about that talk back in the bar and what it might mean, plunging on until you could see the whole goddamn end of the universe—

*   *   *

"Gotta admit we got you that time, Nick," Jake says as they approach the dome, "smooth as glass I come up on you, you're so hard workin' you don't see nothin', I give you a shot of extra spin, *man* your legs fly out you go wheelin' away—"

Jake starts to laugh.

—and livin' in each others' hip pockets like this the hell of it was you start to begrudge ever' little thing, even the young ones, the kids cost too, not that he's against them, hell, you got to keep the families okay or else they'll be slitting each other's throats inside a year, got to remember your grandfather who was in the Third Try on the decelerators, they came near to getting some new magnets in place before the plasma turbulence blew the whole framework away and they lost it, every family's got some ancestor who got flung down the throat and out into nothing, the kids got to be brought up rememberin' that, even though the little bastards do get into the bioponic tubes and play pranks, they got not a lot to do 'cept study and work, same as he and the others have done for all their lives, average crewman lasts 200 years or so now, all got the best biomed (goddamn lucky they were shippin' so much to Centauri), bridge officers maybe even longer, get lots of senso augmentation to help you through the tough parts, and all to keep going, or even maybe get ahead a little like this squad boss thing, he was *that* close an' they took it away from him, small-minded bastards scared to shit he might make, what was it, 50 more units of rec credit than they did, not like being an officer or anything, just a job-jockey getting ahead a little, wanting just a scrap, and they gigged him for it and now this big mouth next to his ear is goin' on, puffing himself up in front of Faye, Faye who might be worth a second look if he could get her out of the shadow of this loudmouthed secondrate—

Jake was in the middle of a sentence, drawling on. Nick grabbed his arm and whirled him around.

"Keep laughin', you slimy bastard, just keep—"

Nick got a throat hold on him and leaned forward. He lifted, pressing Jake against the railing of the walkway. Jake struggled but his feet left the floor until he was balanced on the railing, halfway over the twenty-meter drop. He struck out with a fist but Nick held on.

"Hey, hey, vap off a li'l," Faye cried.

"Yeah—look—you got to take it—as it comes," Jake wheezed between clenched teeth.

"You two done me an' then you laugh an' don't think I don't know you're, you're—" He stopped, searching for words and not finding any.

Globular star clusters hung in the halo beyond the spirals. They flashed by the ship like immense chandeliers of stars. Odd clumps of torn and twisted gas rushed across the sweep of the dome overhead. Tortured gouts of sputtering matter were swept into the magnetic mouth of the ship. As it arched inward toward the craft it gave off flashes of incandescent light. These were stars being born in the ship-driven turbulence, the compressed gases collapsing into firefly lives before the ship's throat swallowed them. In the flicker of an eyelid on board, a thousand years of stellar evolution transpired on the churning dome above.

The ship had by now carved a swooping path through the narrow strait between the disks. It had consumed banks of gas and dust, burning some for power, scattering the rest with fresh ejected energy into its path. The gas would gush out, away from the galaxies, unable to cause the ongoing friction that drew the two together. This in turn would slow their collision, giving the glittering worlds below another million years to plan, to discover, to struggle upward against the coming catastrophe. The ship itself, grown vast by relativistic effects, shone in the night skies of a billion worlds as a fiercely burning dot, emitting at impossible frequencies, slicing through kiloparsecs of space with its gluttonous magnetic throat, consuming.

"Be easy on him, Nick," Faye said softly.

Nick shook his head. "Naw. Trouble with a guy like this is, he got nothin' to do but piss on people. Hasn't got per . . . perspective."

"Stack it, Nick," Faye said.

*   *   *

Above them, the dome showed briefly the view behind the ship, where the reaction engines poured forth the raw refuse of the fusion drives. Far back, along their trajectory, lay dim filaments, wisps of ivory light. It was the Local Group, the cluster of galaxies that contained the Milky Way, their home. A human could look up, extend a hand, and a mere thumbnail would easily cover the faint smudge that was in fact a clump of spirals, ellipticals, dwarfs and irregular galaxies. It was a small part of the much larger association of galaxies, called the Local Supercluster. The ship was passing now beyond the fringes of the Local Supercluster, forging outward through the dim halo of random glimmering-galaxies which faded off into the black abyss beyond. It would be a long voyage across that span, until the next supercluster was reached: a pale blue haze that ebbed and flowed before the nose of the ship, liquid light distorted by relativity. For the moment the glow of their next destination was lost in the harsh glare of the two galaxies. The disks yawned and turned around the ship, slabs of hot gold and burnt orange, refracted, moving according to the twisted optical effects of special relativity. Compression of wavelengths and the squeezing of time itself made the disks seem to open wide, immense glowing doors swinging in the vacuum, parting to let pass this artifact that sped on, riding a tail of forking, sputtering, violet light.

Nick tilted the man back farther on the railing. Jake's arms fanned the air and his eyes widened.

"Okay, okay, you win," Jake grunted.

"You going upstairs, tell 'em you scragged me."

"Ah . . . okay."

"Good. Or else somethin' might, well, happen." Nick let Jake's legs down, back onto the walkway.

Faye said, "You didn't have to risk his neck. We would've cleared it for you if you'd—"

"Yeah, sure," Nick said sourly.

"You bastard, I oughta—"

"Yeah?"

Jake was breathing hard, his eyes danced around, but Nick knew he wouldn't try anything. He could judge a thing like that. Anyway, he thought, he'd been right, and they knew it. Jake grimaced, shook his head. Nick waved a hand and they walked on.

"Y'know what your trouble is, Nick?" Jake said after a moment. "Yer like this spider here."

Jake took the spider out of his jumpsuit pocket and held up the gray creature. It stirred, but was trapped.

"Wha'cha mean?" Nick asked.

"You got no perspective on the squad. Don't know what's really happenin'. An' this spider, he dunno either. He was down in the locker room, he didn't appreciate what he was in. I mean, that's the center of the whole damn ship right there, the squad."

"Yeah. So?"

"This spider, he don't appreciate how far he'd come from Agro. You either, Nick. You don't appreciate how the squad helps you out, how you oughta be grateful to them, how mebbe you shouldn't keep pushin' alla time."

"Spider's got little eyes, no lens to it," Nick said. "Can't see further than your hand. Can't see those stars up there. I can, though."

Jake sputtered, "Crap, relative to the spider you're—"

"Aw, can it," Nick said.

Faye said, "Look, Jake, maybe you stop raggin' him alla time, he—"

"No, he's got a point there," Nick said, his voice suddenly mild. "We're all tryin' to be reg'lar folks in the ship, right? We should keep t'gether."

"Yeah. You push too hard."

Sure, Nick thought. *Sure I do. And the next thing I'm gonna push for is Faye, take her clean away from you.*

—the way her neck arcs back when she laughs, graceful in a casual way he never noticed before, a lilting note that caught him, and the broad smile she had, but she was solid too, did a good job in the blowback zone last week when nobody else could handle it, red gases flaring all around her, good woman to have with you, and maybe he'd need a lot of support like that, because he knows now what he really wants: to be an officer someday, it wasn't impossible, just hard, and the only way is by pushing. All this scratching around for a little more rec credits, maybe some better food, that wasn't the point, no, there was something more, the officers keep up the promotion game 'cause we've got to have something to keep people fretting and working, something to take our minds off what's outside, what'll happen if—no, *when*—the drive fails, where we're going, only what these two don't know is that we're not bound for oblivion in a universe that runs down into blackness, we're going on to see the reversal, we get to hear the recessional, galaxies, peeling into the primordial soup as they compress back together and the ship flies faster, always faster as it sucks up the dust of time and hurls itself further on, back to the crunch that made everything and will some day—hell, if he can stretch out the years, right in his own lifetime!—press everything back into a drumming hail of light and mass, now *that's* something to live for—

Faye said pleasantly, "Just think how much good we did back there. Saved who knows how many civilizations, billions of living creatures, gave them a reprieve."

"Right," Jake said, his voice distracted, still smarting over his defeat.

Faye nodded and the three of them made their way up an undulating walkway, heading for the bar where the rest of the squad would be. The ship thrust forward as the spiral galaxies dropped behind now, Doppler reddened into dying embers.

The ship had swept clean the space between them, postponed the coming collision. The scientists had seen this chance, persuaded the captain to make the slight swerve that allowed them to study the galaxies, and in the act accelerate the ship still more. The ship was now still closer to the knife-edge of light speed. Its aim was not a specific destination, but rather to plunge on, learning more, studying the dabs of refracted lights beyond, struggling with the engines, forging on as the universe wound down, as entropy increased, and the last stars flared out. It carried the cargo meant for Centauri—the records and past lives of all humanity, a library for the colony there. If the drives held up, it would carry them forward until the last tick of time.

Nick laughed. "Not that they'll know it, or ever give a—" He stopped. He'd been going to say *ever give a Goddamn about who did it*, but he knew how Faye felt about using the Lord's name in vain.

"Why, sure they will," Faye said brightly. "We were a big, hot source of all kinds of radiation. They'll know it was a piece of technology."

"Big lights in the sky? Could be natural."

"With a good spectrometer—"

"Yeah, but they'll never be sure."

She frowned. "Well, a ramscoop exhaust looks funny, not like a star or anything."

"With the big relativistic effect factored in, our emission goes out like a searchlight. One narrow little cone of scrambled-up radiation, Dopplered forward. So they can't make us out the whole time. Most of 'em 'd see us for just a few years, tops," Nick said.

"So?"

"Hard to make a scientific theory about somethin' that happens once, lasts a little while, never repeats."

"Maybe."

"They could just as likely think it was something unnatural. Supernatural. A god or somethin'."

"Huh. Maybe." Faye shrugged. "Come on. Let's get 'nother drink before rest'n rec hours are over."

They walked on. Above them the great knives of light sliced down through the air, ceaselessly changing, and the humans kept on going, their small voices indomitable, reaching forward, undiminished.

God's Eyes

Craig Shaw Gardner

Craig Shaw Gardner and his wife, writer Francess Lin Lantz, together know more about obscure music, and silly novelty songs in particular, than anyone I know. She writes strange stories for children. He writes strange stories for adults who act like children. More than a dozen of them have been published recently in a wide variety of magazines and anthologies, most of them fantasies marked by wild inventiveness and sharp wit, such as those about an unfortunate wizard named Ebenezum who has terrible sneezing spells when exposed to magic.

But Gardner has written darker stories too, and "God's Eyes" is definitely one of them. Sometimes when the world ends, a man's trials are only beginning.

"Thus are we cursed by the ones who come from the stars."

The preacher's voice cracked, and he turned away, toward me and Eb at the front of the crowd. He stared blankly at us for a dozen heartbeats. It was the first time I'd noticed how deep the lines were on his face. His eyes flicked across the members of the congregation, his hands pulling at opposite sides of a battered black hat.

"May he find peace," he said in not much more than a whisper, then, louder, "May we all find peace." He strode away from it then, through the congregation.

It was time all of us left. After we had strung Ben out to die, we had to move on. That's what the preacher told us. The consecrated ground upon which we had formed our church had been tainted by Ben's return. Not that I didn't believe, then, what the preacher said. I was one of the strong hands of the church. It was up to Eb and me and a couple of the others to catch Ben and tie him down, no matter how I felt about it, how I wished there was a way to let Ben live. I can still remember the head, where Ben's head used to be, but looking now like no head any human had ever seen before, mewling and crying as we dragged Ben's body over to the rock on which he was to die.

They had touched Ben, you see. He hadn't let on, hoping the stories wouldn't be true for him. But he changed, like all the others they had gotten to.

QUESTION: What was the name you used?

ANSWER: We tried not to call them anything, as if mentioning them would bring them straight to our doorstep. When we had to, we called them the Kuth.

The questioner repeats the name.

ANSWER: You almost got it. To say it just right, you have to spit before your mouth forms the "K." *He laughs.*

*   *   *

So we moved, fast. We never carried many worldly things. The people were our church. There were twenty-three of us, then, once Ben was gone.

Up until then, I had never seen one of the Kuth.

The move wasn't easy. We lived in the valley for close to three years, far longer than anyplace else I can remember. It was spring and everything was green. The bushes that surrounded the clearing where we had built our homes were heavy with berries, and the spring grasses and flowers threatened to overgrow even the path from the houses to the stream. Our snares up on the forest hill rewarded us with a pair of rabbits and a possum, and on our last trip out Ben had spotted a silver fox running across the shallow creek.

We took what food we had saved. We had to abandon the planting we had finished just the week before. But, as the preacher said, where one Kuth showed, others were sure to follow.

We left in the early morning, the sun still not fully over the valley's edge, a thousand birds crying welcome to the dawn. The hill to the top of the valley was steep and crowded with trees. I helped my mother, getting her to hold on to me when there was no other support, actually lifting her bodily when the congregation had to climb a small cliff face halfway to the top. Eb did much the same for Auntie Flora. Eb surely got the worst of that trip.

Flora had gotten on in years and was quite infirm. It was all she could do to totter along the well-worn paths of our village. But the preacher wouldn't leave her for the Kuth, and "Auntie"—everybody called her that, even though, as far as I know, she wasn't related to anybody—had certain abilities that were of value to the congregation. But I'm ahead of myself.

We climbed out of the valley and onto a ragged plateau, as bleak as one of the preacher's sermons. Scrubgrass grew in the rock crevices to remind us of the new season, but the wind blew so much you could swear it wanted winter back.

We made dinner that night from the rabbits and possum and the few roots and potatoes left over from the winter stores. I took a portion to my mother, then another to Auntie Flora. The old woman stared out beyond me, out over the plateau. Her hand closed around the tin plate I gave her, but she made no other acknowledgment of my presence.

I stood there for a minute, watching the sky where Auntie Flora stared.

"So far," she said to the horizon. "So far." She looked at me then. "Why do we have to move?"

I didn't know what to answer. Because no one has ever spoken to the Kuth? Because the preacher tells us? Because moving gives us the best chance of survival in a world that's been taken away from us? None of these were answers.

"Perhaps there is another way," I said for lack of something better.

"Then we will be shown it," Auntie Flora said. She smiled then, and rocked gently back and forth as she turned back to the fading sunlight.

We had to rig up shelters out of what odds and ends we had. I fixed up what I could from blankets and old clothes for Ma and Auntie Flora. Eb and I slept just outside, piling up whatever we could find as a wall against the wind.

That night, Auntie Flora had a vision.

I jumped awake, on my feet before my eyes could open. I heard her screams, louder than the wind. Others were awake around me, the preacher running across the campsite with his great, black-booted strides. I pushed my way into the makeshift tent, the preacher right behind me.

Someone, my mother, probably, had lit the light inside. Auntie Flora stared at me with the clear blue eyes of age.

"The cross." She smiled at me, then looked past my shoulder to the preacher. "I have seen it. This boy is for the cross."

"We don't follow the cross, Aunt Flora," the preacher replied in a voice just loud enough to carry across the tent. "That came from before. Your old god has forsaken us. What else can you tell us?"

But the old woman had nodded into sleep.

Two days later, we found it. We had finally descended from the rocky plateau, into a region of gently rolling hills, mostly grassland, with an occasional stretch of forest. I think it made us all happier to be back among growing things again, even though the region was different from the one we were used to. It was so much more open. The distant, rolling horizon was almost too vast to accept after one's eyes had become accustomed to the narrow vistas and hidden ways of the valley we'd just left.

"The cross!" Eb saw it first. It stood atop the third hill, dark against the evening sky. The preacher wiped the sweat from his forehead and smiled at Auntie Flora. "Maybe this is your dream, Auntie."

Flora frowned as Ma and I helped her up the hill.

The cross stood in a corner of a ruined building. The day's last sunlight cast mountainous shadows across the rubble. We had to pick our way carefully over the last hundred yards. In the fading light, we weren't able to see the man nailed to the wood until we were halfway there.

I called it a man, but it was really just the figure of a man. The others hung back, even the preacher, but I went up and touched it. The bleeding feet looked smooth close up, and were cold under my fingers. The whole body was too smooth to be real, too perfect; even the nails in the figure's hands and feet were too polished and perfectly centered. The bearded face was all wrong, too. A man nailed to a pair of boards should be suffering. This one looked like he was asleep.

"Amazing it's still intact," the preacher said behind me. "Surely one of the miracles Auntie always goes on about." He squinted one eye in the way he had. "This is a holy place, for all we've left the symbols behind. And the hills are green here." He turned, so his gaze encompassed all of the congregation. "This is where we will settle."

I looked across the meadows spread below us. From the crest of the hill you could see some distance, just as the ruined church had been visible from miles away. I didn't think about it then. The preacher's wisdom had kept us alive for seven years. I hadn't learned to doubt it, yet.

*   *   *

Q: So you had no idea as to the motives behind those you called the Kuth?

A: None. Like I said, we even avoided bringing up the subject. I never even knew the real date of the invasion. Just before I was born, I guess. That's what my mother said. The preacher used to say the Kuth had been with us always, that they had been visited upon us by God for our sins.

Q: Didn't that make you doubt the preacher's word?

A: Never. If I had done that, my mother would have beaten me.

Eb found the woman, too. I was chopping wood, cutting down trees to build the new village, when I heard him shout. I ran, the axe still in my hand.

He held her arms together from the back, so I got a good look at her face first thing. Her brown hair was cut off just above her eyes, then fell over her ears, framing a slightly long face, a very frightened face. She was thin, and taller than Eb, almost as tall as me. She struggled uselessly against Eb's grip. If anything, Eb was stronger than me.

"I found her running across the woods," Eb said in that flat voice of his. You could have elected Eb king of the world and he wouldn't have raised an eyebrow.

"Let me go!" the woman cried. "I have to get out of here!"

I tried smiling at her, but she was beyond reassurance. Understandable, I thought. If her living experience was anything like the cloistered existence of our church, Eb and I would be the first new faces she had seen in years.

"There's nothing to be afraid of," I said. "You're with the church now. You can stay if you like."

"You don't understand. We all have to get out of here!" She sobbed. "I saw them coming after me! The aliens! The aliens!"

Of course she meant the Kuth.

"Should I let her go?" Eb asked.

What would the preacher do? We were over half an hour from camp; we'd get no help there. It would have to be my decision.

I nodded. "If she promises not to run. If the Kuth are coming, it might be better if we stayed together."

Eb let her go, and I took my first real look at her. In other circumstances, I would have found her pleasant to look at.

"Now," I continued, "where did you see them?"

She looked downhill. "They were there, all at once. I don't know what happened to the others. I ran." From the way her body was tensed, I could tell it took all her will power to keep from running again.

"We should get back to the church," I said. "I think we'd be safer there."

We heard the scraping sounds before we reached the top of the hill. They seemed at first to be above us and slightly to our right. I stopped, then waved to the other two to follow me quickly to the left.

The sound again, like something heavy dragged across gravel, in front of us this time. The woman spun around and ran the other way.

She screamed when she saw the Kuth. I would have too, had I been the first to look.

It was the strangest thing I'd ever seen, part plant, part machine, like some tree had got it in its mind to grow nuts and bolts. The limbs on the thing, and there were more than two of them, were about the length and thickness of a young willow, but they moved, and they were coated with what looked like a slippery grey mud. In the middle of all this movement was something shiny. I think it was round, too; I remember it that way, but your mind tries to make sense out of what it doesn't understand.

I swung my axe at it. There was a flash of light, and heat. I thought I heard other scraping sounds behind me.

I don't remember anything else until I awoke at the foot of the cross. Eb and the woman, whose name I later learned was Sara, lay to either side of me. It was night time, but all the church was gathered around us. Closest was the preacher, frowning down at me.

"Have you been touched?"

I told him what I remembered. Eb and Sara said much the same. The preacher said he wanted to talk to me alone. My mother was crying as we passed her to go into the preacher's cabin. The preacher took off his hat as we entered.

He had me sit on a bench Eb and I had fixed up only the week before. He stood and looked out of the cabin's only window.

He said my name, but did not turn around. "You are one of the pillars of the congregation. You and Eb and a handful of others are the ones we depend on. It is because of you that we survive." He coughed. "For the sake of God, and everything I've ever told you about God, if you have been touched. . . ."

He paused, and his indrawn breath seemed to make his body shake. "If you know you have been touched, please, by God, get as far away from this camp as you can. Because, if the change comes, I cannot save you."

"I have no memory of being touched."

"I believe you. Stay if you must; your mother depends on you. Whatever God wills will happen." A laugh escaped from the back of his throat. It sounded low and hollow in the tiny room.

The next day I contracted a high fever. I felt a great constriction in my chest, and became delirious. My mother wrapped me in blankets, and she said I rolled about in them for hours, screaming and crying, as if I were fighting devils. Then the fever left me as quickly as it came, and I slept for a full half day.

I woke when my mother screamed.

The blankets had been pulled down to my waist. I sat up and looked at my mother. She was pressed against the far wall of our small hut, her eyes wide, her mouth working silently. A pair of words sputtered out.

"Your chest."

I looked down at what had been my bare chest. There was some sort of lump there now, some sort of growth. Without thought, I swung my hand to touch it.

The growth moved underneath my hand. I pulled my hand away and leapt to my feet, thinking, somehow, that if I moved fast enough, I could leave the thing behind that had sprouted on my chest.

It was still there, of course. Half-nauseated, half terrified, I walked the few steps to the mirror we had salvaged years before.

In the cracked reflection, I saw that the growth on my chest looked like a bearded face.

Q: How did you react to the change?

A: I didn't, except to allow events to go on around me. Events, I guess, triggered by the change. One must accept one's lot, the preacher told us. Auntie Flora had a story about the changes. Others told it, too, but I think Flora started it. It seems, according to her, that the Kuth play a little joke on Death with the changed, parading before it the deformed bodies and facial cancers of those the Kuth have touched. Death cries: "These are not men! They are none of my concern!" Thus, not only are the changed deserted by humanity, but by Death as well, so that they may live forever in agony.

Q: Why are you telling me this?

A: Many of Flora's fancies turned out to hide the truth. I was wondering if this was another.

Q: It's a good story.

A: Is that all? Then I must know a great many good stories.

I had to run. There was nothing else to do; the preacher had even suggested it in his way. Otherwise, no matter what Auntie Flora said, I would be staked out and left to die of the elements while the congregation moved on. I tried to think of the church without me, how they would survive. I probably allowed myself too much importance.

But what about Eb and the new woman, Sara? Had the changes come over them as well? I slipped out of our hut in the still dark of early morning, and crept across the way to the dormitory where all those without families stayed. If Eb and I went together, we might stand a better chance.

The door to the dormitory slammed open before I could reach it. I had to squint against the light to see into the room. Everyone seemed to be standing. The preacher was there, too, his black form etched against the others. He pulled someone from the crowd, thrusting him outside.

It was Eb. The preacher and some of the others followed him out, carrying lamps. Somebody kicked him.

I felt like they had kicked me instead. Eb didn't make a sound, but fell to his knees. I ran across the clearing to him, and the lamplight told me why he was silent.

Eb no longer had a mouth. The lower half of his face wasn't even flesh. It was smooth, and shone in the artificial light.

"You are unclean!" the preacher cried. He raised the thick oak branch he held over his head. "Contaminated! And you dare bring your filth to the church!"

Eb didn't move. He just looked back at the preacher with quiet eyes.

My name roared from the preacher's lips. His eyes, two great pools of black in the darkness, caught me and held me.

"What have you done?" he cried. "What have you brought among us?" His tone lowered, almost conversational. "Do you carry the curse, too?"

All my courage left me in that instant. I shook my head dumbly, wanting to deny the truth.

But the preacher had turned back to Eb, and brought the oak branch down with force on Eb's face.

The face on my chest let out a high, mournful howl.

"No!" I cried and tried to run, but the congregation was all around me, angry faces, hard fists and elbows and shoulders pushing me. They tore my shirt away.

And I saw the crowd around me twice. Once, with my true eyes, I saw the people I had lived with all these years, changed by fear. But the face on my chest had eyes, too, and they were open now. The figures these eyes saw were bright shadows against the darkness, silhouettes of humans in blue and red, moving against a void.

Everything stopped for a while. Whether my new eyes changed my time sense, or my second gaze froze the congregation, I don't know. My next actual memory is Auntie Flora's voice.

"Do nothing to them!" Her thin voice carried well in the still night. "This is the meaning of my dream! This will be our salvation!"

The preacher leaned on his bloody branch. "What do you mean, Flora?"

"My dream. It's the sign of our redemption." She pointed to me. "Look closely at what's on his chest. It is the face of Christ!"

The face of the plaster man on the cross. I had seen no such resemblance when I looked at my chest in the mirror, but then I hadn't looked for any.

I had no control over my second face. Did it smile at Flora's revelation? Its eyes sent me strange signals. Was it working on my brain in other ways? I shivered in the night air.

The preacher spat. "What kind of redemption is this? Don't talk of holiness—" He stooped. His words hung in the air. I heard the sound behind me, gravel on gravel, great weight dragging across the earth.

"Kuth!" I shouted, and the lamps swung outward.

They encircled us. Forty or fifty of them, moving closer with their willow legs.

The congregation huddled together, shrieking and crying. I was left alone before the approaching Kuth.

The face on my chest spoke, if the sounds it made could be called speech. Strange gutturals, with odd shifts of tone and cadence, fell from my second lips. The Kuth stopped their advance.

My other voice rose, its chant alternately hypnotic and startling. I saw the Kuth through my other eyes: orange flames, so unlike their physical forms that I would not have connected the two if my two sets of eyes had not combined them in my mind. The voice was crying out now, a high, singing sound that filled the air just before dawn.

And my eyes saw the orange flames kneel before me.

Q: The expedition overreached itself.
A: Perhaps your goals were unattainable.
Q: That is not at issue here. We wanted to understand humans, a sentient race, before they died out completely.
A: Died out? Did you think of saving them?
Q: That was impossible without communication.

A: But you achieved communication, and more than communica-
     tion.

There is a pause in the conversation.

A: Your "dying race," as you call them, seems to hold more
     resources than you could manage in your experiment.

Q: Again, that is not at issue here. We are involved in an
     ongoing process, and all problems will be corrected.

A: What would you do if I had my eyes?

The voice in my chest spoke for some time to those before it,
kneeling flames in one sight, still and silent Kuth in the other. At
first I had no understanding of what my second voice said; it came
from a brain as new as the face on my chest. But soon that new
mind began to feed images behind my real eyes, stories of wherever
the Kuth had come from, and stories about the Kuth and men.

I knew when the voice was finished. The kneeling flames knew as
well, for the Kuth turned and left the congregation untouched.

"Our salvation," Auntie Flora said when the aliens had left. But
most of the rest of the congregation fled for what little safety their
homes had to offer.

When the sun rose, we saw that the Kuth had not entirely left us.
A dozen of them ringed the village in a large circle at the foot of the
hill.

Eb and Sara and I were the only ones still in the open. Auntie
Flora and my mother had left our side at dawn to finally get some
sleep, and there was no sign that any of the others would risk
showing themselves. I wondered what had happened to the preacher.
He had never been the kind to hide.

We watched the Kuth for a while, but they stood as motionless as
the trees they half resembled. Eb fell asleep in the shadow of the
ruin by the cross, and Sara and I were left more alone than we had
ever been.

Sara had been touched, too, although her change was not as
drastic yet as either Eb or me. Slender green shoots sprouted from
either side of her neck, and they drifted back and forth in the early

summer breeze that blew across the hill. I knew already they would grow into the willow arms of the Kuth, far more unwieldy than either Eb's or my deformities.

The silence of the night before had followed us into the day. The camp had never been so quiet. Even the birds had left the surrounding trees, scared away by the Kuth.

"Why did this happen to us?" Sara asked.

"Why were we chosen by the Kuth?" I told her that I didn't know. In my mind, it related somehow to the preacher's concept of how we of the congregation were the chosen people, the survivors, left to rebuild the world. I told Sara about some of the preacher's sermons, and how I never quite understood how I myself had become one of the chosen.

Sara sighed and looked out beyond the Kuth at the distant rows of hills, blue in the early morning light. "It's just because we're here, then, in this time and place?"

I nodded. It was as good a reason as any, better than most.

She touched my new face. It was a strange sensation, feeling a hand run along something my human brain didn't want to accept as part of me. Her hand traced the eyebrows, nose, lips, chin.

"Does it hurt?" she asked.

"Not anymore. It's part of me." I felt one of her green tendrils. It was cold to the touch. "Yours?"

"No. It should, somehow." Her gaze shifted to my real face. She looked very human, then. What's human? Intellect, body heat, emotion, all jumbled together. Who knows? But we were both very human then, the only humans, way up on a hill that topped the world.

So we made love. To prove our humanity, I think, as much as anything, especially in front of the silently watching Kuth. I had never done that sort of thing before, protected by the church as I was, but she had, and she showed me what to do. I can explain it to you if you like.

We lay exhausted afterward, the face on my chest still sucking at one of her breasts.

I scrambled up when I heard the shouting, pulling my pants on as I ran. The preacher and three others rushed from a copse of trees on the hillside, torches in their hands. They ran toward one of the motionless Kuth.

The face on my chest cried out a warning.

The Kuth retreated as the four men fell upon it, then, as suddenly, it seemed to double in height, throwing two of the men into the air. One fell on the grassy knoll and scrambled away, the other hit a patch of rock and didn't move again. The Kuth's willow limbs swung about wildly, knocking the torch from the third man's hands and hitting the preacher across the face. The preacher reeled back, his hat lost to a strengthening wind, forgotten. The survivors of the assault scrambled back up the hill, toward the spot where Sara and I stood.

The preacher stopped when he saw me. His face bore a dark red mark from his left eye to his chin.

"Judas!" he cried. "You brought this upon us! You have destroyed the church!" He looked at the smoldering torch. "Would that I could burn you from our memory!"

I heard voices behind me. The preacher's cries had brought the congregation from hiding. I tried to think what I could say to them, how I could keep them from doing something foolish.

The voice on my chest spoke to the Kuth. And the Kuth moved, up the hill toward the village.

"What are you doing?" the preacher cried. He lifted the smoking torch, then flung it to the ground and knelt before me. "I'm sorry for my anger. I know you control them. Stop them, please, before they destory the church."

There were tears in my human eyes. "I can't!" I cried over the gutturals pouring from my chest. "This growth is no part of me! I can't control anything!"

"Don't be afraid," Auntie Flora called. "He will save us again. Come with me, and join hands, and we will greet the Kuth as they come up the hill."

She spread her arms and offered her hands to any who would take them. My mother smiled at me and took one of Flora's hands. No one else joined them.

The Kuth scraped their way up the hill. The voice in my chest kept calling to them, and my second eyes saw them as marching flames.

"We welcome you!" Auntie Flora called as the Kuth approached. "We can talk now, learn to live—"

She broke off and screamed as the Kuth rose above her, heavy trunks, whipping limbs. She and my mother ran, but they were both old, and the Kuth moved with great speed for their size.

I saw them both crushed, and my human voice screamed as my other voice called the orange flames on.

What could I do? My second eyes locked on the flames, beckoning them forward. I clawed at my chest, but the voice kept on spitting out its foul syllables. Whatever it was doing, it would destroy everyone as the flames danced for my second eyes.

Somewhere in there, I had what the preacher would have called a revelation. The mouth on my second face exhorted them, yes, but I felt the Kuth really obeyed my other eyes, eyes that saw inside of them and could manipulate that sight; eyes neither good nor evil, but committed to some purpose beyond me.

The voice in my chest rasped something over and over. I tried to turn away, but the Kuth were all around us, heeding the voice and eyes. I was sure everyone would die because of me.

I saw the preacher's torch then with my human eyes, and grasped it with my still human hands, and thrust it against the eye sockets of my second face.

Both my voices screamed, and I fell to the ground, my body burning in agony. I rolled in the dirt, but the searing pain stayed. And the second eyes could no longer see.

The Kuth rolled away then, back down the hill. I don't remember any more.

Q: Were you convinced then you were no longer human?

A: No, I have always been human. I was simply unable to control the new functions of my body.

Q: You think of those new parts as facets of your humanity? These new things caused your so-called Kuth to kill people.

A: I somehow doubt that was purposeful. Rather, it was the total newness of my second face. Like a baby trying to walk, I had to test out these new features before I could put them to the best use.

Q: And have you?

A: Of course. How else could I talk to you like this? Somehow, once I lost my second eyes, it was easy to bring the voice under control.

Q: You manage very well.

A: I'll do better. I understand, now, that it's a part of me. It comes from inside me.

I woke to look down on the congregation. While I was unconscious, they had removed the plaster figure from the cross and strapped me in its place.

The preacher stared up at me. The red mark of the Kuth still crossed his face. The dozen or so other surviving members of the church stood around him.

"You have damned the church!" the preacher said, glaring up at me with his single eye. "And the church damns you in turn. Auntie Flora, who was killed through your actions, said that you wore the resemblance of Christ on your chest. Therefore, I thought it only fitting that you should die on the cross, as Christ died."

He turned away, and they left me there, in the chill wind of the hilltop. Through the pain, which still washed over me in waves, I watched the pitiful remnants of our congregation straggle down the hill. Only thirteen remained, a couple of them lame from their encounter with the Kuth. The end of our church's strength. The preacher had blamed me, although I had been acted upon much more than actor in the events of the last three days.

I had changed. The change had left me different, somehow greater than I had been before.

The church could not accept the changes. I looked down on the thin black figure of the preacher. His balding head was bare against the sun, now that he had lost his hat. His dream was fading, too. It had to be that way. The preacher's church was really dead before my mother and I ever joined it. Humanity had to change if it were to exist in a world with the Kuth.

After the preacher and the congregation had marched out of sight, Sara and Eb came out from hiding to cut me down. Sara asked what we would do next. I told her it was time to visit the Kuth.

Q: So you came here.
A: Again, yes. Haven't I repeated my story enough?
Q: You are part of a study. That's why you are allowed to speak.
A: How long have I been here?
Q: Your conception of time is impossible to correlate with ours, at least with the available data.
A: The others?
Q: They are unharmed, and can be reactivated when needed.
A: So I came to talk to you, and all you tell me about are "studies" and "reactivation"!
Q: At first we were amazed that you could talk at all. There were those among us who wanted to suspend the project before you came, and finally rid the planet of what indigenous life forms still remain.
A: You'd kill us all then? My ability to communicate means nothing?
Q: It is good for research.
A: And my eyes?
Q: An aberration. A chance occurrence. It was well for your own survival that you blinded yourself. Otherwise, we might have had you destroyed.
A: I did not gain my second eyes by chance. And you could not destroy me.

The creature who sat in the space with me (You could not call it a room. It had no real walls or ceiling, only a place where the illumination ended.) became agitated again. My interrogator was mostly metal, save for three brown, wood-like bands evenly spaced top-to-bottom along its body. The aliens had different forms for different functions; that was one of the things I had learned.

"You are obtuse again," the alien's voice box rattled. "Your ability to communicate has held our interest. We have therefore allowed you to retain your consciousness. Do not force us to repeat ourselves too often. If you fail to communicate, you fail to interest us."

I looked at the creature with my human eyes. Its metallic arms twisted in great loops, a reaction I now knew signified anger, and a reaction I could now elicit easily. I had come to know a great deal about the aliens during the length of the investigation.

I did not respond to the creature's statement.

Sound came from the flexible space between wood and metal. "You must cooperate. You remain here for our amusement, but you are no longer amusing. Speak."

I made a rough noise with my larynx, my human voice, the voice the alien could not understand.

"Enough of this!" my second ears heard. "I should destroy you now!"

It was time. I removed the bandage that hid my second eyes. The alien stopped, and a yellow flame knelt before me.

"My eyes have healed," I said in the alien tongue. My first mouth, dry from disuse, whispered "I have work to do." For the first time, both my voices spoke together:

"I am reborn."

St. Joey the Action

Shariann Lewitt

"St. Joey the Action" is Shariann Lewitt's first short story sale. "Somehow," she writes, "the idea of dicing with the Devil has always interested me, but when I think of dice, I think of Nathan Detroit. Directing Guys and Dolls in upstate New York one summer must have warped my imagination." Lewitt attended the Yale School of Drama and saw her first play produced in New York when she was nineteen.

The ghosts of Nathan Detroit, Damon Runyon, and, I suspect, St. Dismas, were all hovering over her shoulder as she wrote this. Saints, it turns out, seem to look a lot like you and me.

It's like I told that Monsignor from the Vatican, Joey wasn't really different from any of the others in his class. You know, Moran and Capone here in Chicago, he ran this city with them when he was still alive. I don't mention them guys in New York. One of them tries to call himself the Boss of all Bosses, like all bosses was in New York. Like New York was the center of the earth or something. But we had it good in Chicago, good money, dames, everything. And Joey wouldn't have liked what was done to him last week, which is why I'm telling it so as to defend his image.

Like I told the Monsignor, if he did happen to win the nightie and the harp he wouldn't be singing no hymns. Joey, the Boss, that is, couldn't sing a note. Which is what got him thrown out as a choirboy and got him started in his career. No, if they're right about him being a saint and all, he's upstairs right now running a clean game with St. Dizzy-what's-his-name. You know, the one the nuns was always talking about. A clean game was his style.

"You can't fleece them more than once if you've got a bad reputation," the Boss always said. And we had a lot of what he called repeat customers. The Boss was real educated, he had a whole year of night school and Dale Carnegie, too.

When I think of what they're calling him now—St. Joseph Valenti, the Active, I think—I could weep on my sister's grave. And she ain't dead yet.

But that's all done now, like they took out a contract on his soul or something, and it's up to me to set the record straight.

Maybe if you was born too late you don't know much about Joey the Action, but I was with him from the beginning, me and my piece, and I never forgave myself for not protecting him in the end. The Monsignor said it was God's will, but I think it was that snake Bugsy Dees what was faster than me and I don't make no excuses, not to the Vatican, not to nobody. But that's the end and it's in all the papers and *Time* magazine. They don't talk much about the beginning.

There was three who ran Chicago back in the old days when we was rumrunning from Canada: Capone, Moran and the Boss. The Boss inherited from Caprisi after Rothman in New York took out a contract on the old man. All neat and legal-like with little folding bills to the right guys at City Hall. Caprisi didn't have much, his customers were not always well satisfied.

In the first year the Boss took care of that. The games was always clean and the bourbon wasn't watered. And when someone paid us for protection he got protection. Honest service for good money, the Boss always said, and we gave honest service. Business went crazy and we had to recruit. And no matter what we did, how many employees we had, the business was always more than we could handle.

Now, Capone and Moran didn't like it, seeing as how they had always seen Caprisi as a small fish, nothing to worry about. And if they hadn't of hated each other so bad they'd have got together and offed the Boss right then. But the Boss was too good for that, he just kept them at each other's throats and took the profits down the middle. Like I said, nothing to get too excited about.

The stuff they write up in the papers, that all happened later. See, the Boss was just overburdened. He needed some assistance, someone to maybe help out in running things. But none of us guys from the old days was smart enough for that. Now me, I'm good with a piece and the Boss, he was like my brother. But I wasn't no good at arithmetic and there wasn't no one else the Boss could trust. So he found Angelo.

The Boss never did say where Angelo come from. Angelo never said, neither, so maybe the Boss didn't know, but two days after Thanksgiving there's Angelo in the Boss's office. And the Boss said to me, he said, "Frankie, this is my new assistant and I want you to listen to him like you listen to me."

And then Angelo says, "Francis. For St. Francis of Assisi?"

I was amazed. No one ever asked me that before. But I was being charming and I says, "Yeah. He liked birds, right? I like birds. I got a canary." That canary died and I got another one, only this one don't sing so much.

Anyway, the Boss just smiled at Angelo, like it was a joke or something, and I patted my belt. I don't like jokes that I only hear the punch line.

But Angelo, who ain't mentioned in the papers, he was different. At first I thought he was a little funny, you know. He always wore this white suit. And he could eat four helpings of spaghetti and never get a spot on it. And it ain't no joke.

So we was in the Boss's office and here was Angelo. And the Boss didn't tell me nothing so I just stood over to the right like I always done and was real quiet. They was talking about bringing in a lot of gin from Canada. Angelo knew about the supplier.

The Boss wasn't real happy, this not being top quality commercial stuff, but some kind of homebrew. Like the Boss said, we didn't deal in bathtub gin. We charge a stiff price and we deliver the goods. Angelo didn't say nothing, just listened to the Boss. I heard this kind of stuff before so I didn't bother to listen too hard, till I heard them decide how to run it across the lake.

There it was, Angelo's first job. And the Boss said I was supposed to keep an eye on him, on account of how the Boss trusted me like I was his own.

Well, you read what the newspapers said about that, and the Vatican, too. But they only had some of the story and never mentioned Angelo. We got to Canada all right and picked it up, four hundred cases. And we opened and spot checked right there like we always done. The Boss didn't pay for low quality stuff. Well, I tested it myself and it was good. Not as good as some of our shipments, but it was the goods, all right. I tasted it myself and I know. So we loaded it on the boats and paddled across and stocked it in the warehouse, like we done a million times. And Angelo never got his suit wet even in the motorboat which was going one way when the police was going the other.

Then the Boss came down to test the shipment, to set the price before the final sale. They appreciated that, the personal touch, that the Boss always made sure of things himself. And there was Angelo with a smile wider than a watermelon on his face. I didn't trust him then and I never trusted him again. I seen too many guys looking like that.

Well, the Boss opened the first crate and opened the first bottle and tried a taste. And his face all screwed up and he looked like he was about to hit the mattresses against Capone and Moran together. "What the hell is this?" he screamed.

I pulled my gun out and waved it at the employees standing around, in case they had something on their minds. But they all looked as innocent as lambs and as confused. So the Boss asked again, "What is this?"

And then Angelo come over and without a by-your-leave he tastes the gin and says, "This isn't what we picked up in Canada." He takes another sip to be sure, and then he says, "Boss, this isn't gin."

And the Boss yells, "I know that! What is it and what happened?" His face was real red and he was talking slow. I never seen him so angry before.

"I think," Angelo said, "I think, Boss, but don't quote me, that this is sacramental wine. Church wine."

The Boss stood still, like he didn't even want to see the stuff. But he took another taste and nodded his head. It just bobbed up and down like an apple in a dunking contest. "We are going to have a lot of disappointed customers," he said, and I knew what he was thinking. The other bosses, they ordered their best stuff from Joey the Action. He had a reputation. And it wasn't smart to have Moran and Capone mad at you. Like I said before, they hated each other like cat and dog, but they was men of business. And if that meant getting the Boss, they would do it. My hands itched. I was at least as good a shot as any of their muscle, once some newspaper even called me the Legs Diamond of Chicago. So let them try, I was ready.

"No, Frankie," the Boss said, and he laid a hand on my arm real brotherly like. "We're calling a council meeting. And I'm going to talk to them. Negotiate first."

"Boss," I said, "they'll eat you alive. Let me hit them first and it's all done."

Angelo looked sour, like he ate too many unripe tomatoes.

"Don't worry, Frankie," the Boss said, "I've got a plan."

You gotta give it to the Boss, he was educated and he always had plans. "You go and tell them to meet at Dolly's at ten tonight," he said. "If there's any problem, let me know. But I think they'll be there. And Frankie, be nice. Don't do anything you don't have to do. Let me decide when and what and where."

They met at Dolly's because it was neutral territory. Dolly paid protection to everyone, she could afford it. And she paid in favors and information as well as money, too, so everyone respected her. If she'd had more than one cat house in the city she'd have had some real problems, being in the competition. But having only the one she was in real good shape, and she only kept the best kind of girls and bought her liquor from everyone. So they always met at Dolly's if they had to meet at all. And Dolly always laid a good spread; I never had such good sandwiches again as I had at Dolly's.

The Boss took me to Dolly's since all the others bring their bodyguards. We are a special group, we get to sit in on high policy meetings, and if we're not wanted we go down and get the sandwiches Dolly fixes. And we talk business. After all, the Boss always told me we was in business, and that's how the others felt, too. And if one of us had to take care of another, well, that was business too and nothing personal. Everyone understood.

Angelo went to Dolly's too. I don't know why the Boss took Angelo. Well, sometimes the successor shows up at these type things, but Angelo had only done one job and he'd botched that. Then I realized that maybe he was going to feed Angelo to Capone and Moran and I didn't like that one bit. It wasn't like the Boss, who always said the employees have to be happy. Happy, secure people work harder, he always said.

So I was worried for Angelo, even if he was still wearing that same white suit just as shiny clean as the first time. Why he couldn't wear dark blue like the Boss or black like me I do not know. But

Angelo went along smiling like always. Sometimes I wondered if he was funny in the head, him always smiling like that.

Anyway, we was waiting there at a quarter till when Angelo asked, "What are you going to do with the church wine?"

Now what kind of stupid question is that? But the Boss didn't look at him and said, "It's almost Christmas, right? So I'll give it to the Church. I'll give it to every church in Chicago and have them say prayers for me."

"How about having them pray for you on St. Valentine's Day, so you'll propose to Ginger?" Angelo asked.

No one ever had the nerve to say that. Ginger is a great gal but a little fuzzy, if you understand me. Definitely fuzzy, but pretty and she loved the Boss. And we all guessed the Boss loved her, too, when he gave her the fur coat. But he never asked her to marry him and no one would ever dare mention a delicate question like that. Excepting Angelo, who was a little funny like I said.

The Boss must have had a real great plan, because he said, "Sure. Sure, why not?" And then he laughed and patted Angelo on the back.

Then we was quiet because we heard them on the stairs. Capone and Moran wouldn't even sit in the same room together if the Boss wasn't there to sit between them. Which he did like always. I took my regular position, ready in case any of the other muscle should make a move and they was watching me likewise.

"Gentlemen," the Boss said, standing, "gentlemen, we have a problem. And I will tell you the problem and I will tell you my solution and we will all be happy. Because the recent shipment from Canada turned out not to be the fine quality gin we usually import, but something far inferior. Something that in good conscience I cannot sell you."

"So I'll buy someplace else, Mr. Valenti," Moran said.

"But you see," said the Boss, "the supplier has to be punished."

"Your muscle can't handle it?" Capone asked, nasty. Capone was always nasty, especially when Moran was around.

"No, no, gentlemen. It is far worse than that. Think on this. When you kill a man, what happens? He dies. He does not suffer.

And he dies knowing that his wife and children and his parents will be taken care of by his organization. Isn't that the case?''

They all agreed, grunted, and the Boss continued. "So how is that a punishment? No, I ask your help for something much more severe. We will cease to buy from him forever, all of us. I have another shipment coming in soon, from England. The quality is quite high and I would like you to consider this instead of the Canadian swill. What will happen to this weasel in Canada is simple. He will not die, no, he will suffer. He will suffer terribly because he will have no business. And he will starve. And he'll watch his babies starve and his wife will sell her coat and her wedding ring and take in washing. He will be humiliated because he cannot support his family. His old parents will not have the warm apartment he provides and they will be turned out on the street. His children will get polio and TB before his eyes and wither. And then, when he has watched his whole family sink into filth and degradation, then he will be punished.''

There were tears in the room. Even I was ready to cry.

"Boss," I said, "Boss, let me just go up and kill him. I can't stand to let his kids suffer." I was thinking of my niece Gloria who was four. "It ain't right."

He turned ugly on me, like I never seen before. "Frankie, you will do as I say. And I am in no mood to be merciful. I am in no mood to be kind. I am in no mood to give in one inch."

Moran looked on and he looked scared. "Well, Joey, it's your stiff, it's your game. And I like the idea of selling English drink, it has class."

"And a good bit of profit," the Boss added.

That was when Dolly brought up the tray, and I was always wondering how she knew just when to show. But I never seen the Boss in such a mean mood before. He didn't touch a thing, not one sandwich, not one drop, nothing.

"Come on, Frankie, Angelo," he said. "Ginger's waiting. I have given you my decision, gentlemen, and God help him who tries to mitigate my wrath."

I didn't know what that meant, but it sure sounded good.

Now the Boss had a reputation for being tough and mean, and I heard later, through the grapevine, that the story got out. I heard that we was actively starving the whole family, that we had guards around their place in Canada and shot every food delivery truck in the area. I heard the youngest boy was dead of malnutrition. Only I knew we didn't have no one in Canada. We didn't have no one to spare. Business was booming like usual and there was the Christmas rush on top of it.

Angelo didn't stop kidding the Boss about proposing to Ginger on Valentine's day, but I didn't listen. I like Ginger okay, only she ain't dignified. Like I seen the women Capone hired and they didn't chew gum and blow bubbles during important dinners or nothing. But Ginger had her good side and she'd have died for the Boss. She said so lots of times.

The Boss always said Ginger was lucky. If Ginger showed up for a little game, he always won, though he never played seriously. If she showed at the track when his horse was racing, his horse came in. Ginger was a luck charm and I think the Boss might have married her, only other things happened first.

The papers didn't make no mention of Ginger, which is right, I guess, because now she's a nun, Sister Mary Adelaide. But she still chews gum. I know because I bring three cases to the convent every year.

Anyway, I spent Christmas with my sister Maria and her husband and kids. I like those kids and I used to slip Maria money once in a while. I still do. Her husband is a good-for-nothing that worked in one of the Boss's casinos, a real nobody. The kids liked their presents and Maria made a really nice Christmas dinner. I was happy, like I hadn't been in a long time. How did I know what was going to happen?

Then it was New Year's and a great night for business. I drank in the new year with the Boss and Angelo in the Boss's private lounge. And he distributed one free drink to each employee to celebrate the year.

Only while we was busy getting ready to bring in more imports for the year, Moran and Capone was making plans to hit the mattresses. I guess I should have seen it before, and I know the Boss

. and Angelo did, but there was nothing we could do. The Boss tried to deal one side and then the other, but they was beyond deals by a long ways.

Angelo, funny like he was, started talking about praying for there not to be a war. I said, yeah, sure, cause it ain't good for business, but I didn't really care. If we could stay out of it, fine and great. Let them go at each other and we just stand back and mop up afterwards.

You know, sometimes I wondered about Angelo's loyalty to the Boss. I mean, after it was all over he didn't show up or nothing, not even to the funeral. The Monsignor asked about him because they were looking for him too. And I figure if the Vatican can't find him, he can't be found. But if you see some guy in a pure white suit without a spot on it, report it to the priest.

But anyway, the Boss was worried, too. He wasn't sure that we could stay neutral. I said who cared, whatever side we went with would win, but the Boss looked unhappy.

"Frankie, it's like this," he said. "Very simple. Okay, whoever we side with wins. But you think they could split Chicago two ways, either of them? They only don't worry about me because I stay low, they don't know the extent of our business or we'd be in trouble. Either one of them would turn on us as soon as he won, and I don't like that. I don't want Moran or Capone to run Chicago."

"But you could win, Boss," I said. "How about you running Chicago?"

But the Boss looked more worried than before. "That's the problem, Frankie," he said. "I think we need all three of us, Capone, Moran and me, all three of us, to keep New York out. And if there's one thing I don't want, it's for Chicago to become a slave of New York, run by some boss who doesn't even know the names of the streets here. And we need all three of us and our full organizations to keep New York out of it."

I was really surprised. I didn't think anyone in New York cared. They had their own problems. But then the Boss sat down and put his hands flat on the desk. "Frankie," he said, "I got a letter today. Big Nicky from New York is coming up. He's so happy about Capone and Moran he can't even say. He's offering me to run

Chicago for him. But I can't, I don't work for anyone but myself. And you've heard of him, you know what his organization is capable of.''

I said yeah real fast. Who hadn't heard of Big Nicky in New York? His own people were afraid of him.

"Well," said the Boss, "I invited him over to dinner one night while he's in town. I think he's got some deal in mind and I want to say no in person. I have met Big Nicky once before and I don't like him. He gives me the creeps.''

I never heard the Boss talk like that. But I hadn't met Big Nicky yet, so I didn't know. Creeps was too little a word.

There was a lot of gossip out in the street, and at Dolly's it was thicker than you could eat with a spoon. And some of it was true, but I kept my mouth shut like the Boss said. But I did like to listen.

Big Nicky was trying to muscle in on Chicago, and even knowing that gave me the chills. And there was stories about Big Nicky down in New York, how Big Nicky said the word once and two organizations was dead. How Big Nicky walked down to the dock and requisitioned a shipment of Scotch from Rothman and Rothman didn't do nothing. How Big Nicky had a different dame on his arm every night, and how he killed four hit men in the dark. I didn't believe half of those stories, but I knew that Big Nicky wanted Chicago and he wanted it bad. And he knew the Boss was the key to the city, so to speak.

I was depressed. Even Angelo had stopped smiling all the time. I had him over Maria's for dinner and Maria said that *Redbook* said February was a depressing month. Angelo tried to lighten things up by saying the Boss was going to propose to Ginger and Maria's face lit up. "And she's so nice," Maria said, "and so devoted to Joey."

I was very surprised. I didn't know my sister knew Ginger. Her husband was no good, but I still didn't want my sister being friends with a girl like Ginger who peroxides her hair and does things that aren't right for unmarried girls to do. Not with my sister! I knew I'd better talk to the Boss about that, but Angelo pulled me over when we was listening to the radio and said, "It's okay. Ginger is going to be a proper wife soon. And Maria's too good to have to worry."

Well, I knew Angelo was right, but I didn't like it any better. I mean, my sister is worth ten of Ginger, even if Ginger is a fine girl and all. Then, I mean. Now they're good friends but it don't bother me none, seeing as how she's Sister Mary Adelaide and all. Maria can be friends with all the nuns she wants.

It didn't hit me till later that Angelo said that. I mean, look at it. I never said nothing about it, about talking to the Boss either, but here comes Angelo just like he heard what was in my head. Did I tell you Angelo was a little funny? Well, I was a little scared of him then, like I never been before. I don't like it when somebody knows what's in your head, that's between you and yourself and God, if He happens to be listening, which I sincerely hope He is not most of the time.

Big Nicky set the date of the Dinner Meeting, as it came to be known. It was even reported in the newspapers in New York as well as Chicago, and somebody told me Boston, too, but I didn't believe that. He said February thirteen, and Angelo was real upset because the Boss was supposed to propose to Ginger the next night and make an honest woman out of her and a fit companion for my sister.

We was holding the meeting at the Boss's house. It was a fine big place on the lake, right up near Lakeshore Drive. The Boss liked to live right in the city, not like those New York dandies who commute from Scarsdale. The Boss was more vigilant than that.

Ginger was in the kitchen watching the three cooks work on the menu, mostly getting in the way and eating everything. Ginger is going to be one fat woman, only now she's not because she's stopped doing that. But I was supposed to keep her out of everyone's hair, which was more difficult than hitting one of Moran's people any day. Angelo was in the house, too, only the Boss was keeping him out of sight. He wasn't invited to eat, just to be available. After all, Big Nicky was coming with just one bodyguard, even if it was the famous Bugsy Dees, so the Boss had to match him exactly. Which meant I got to eat with them and all.

So I was in the kitchen trying to make Ginger stay put, like she was my niece Gloria or something, when Big Nicky came in. How it was him or how I knew he'd come I can't tell you. It was like something went ping in my stomach and I knew it was no good. I wanted to run to the bathroom or maybe out the window. There was a smell, too, now that I think about it, and maybe that was how I knew. It wasn't nice, like how a match smells, I don't know what it's called.

Now a funny thing about Big Nicky that somehow reminds me of Angelo, even if I shouldn't say the names in a single breath, is that no one knows anything about him. Like there's no one from any neighborhood who ever knew him as a kid. These are not things people think about, but in light of what the pope said I think it is now important to note these facts.

Ginger was trying to be a good hostess, all dressed up and wearing her fur even though it was about a hundred in the house.

Yeah, it was extra warm, I remember that part. At first I thought it was just the kitchen, but the whole house was too hot. I wanted to run, to get away to the outside with nice fresh air, that smell was making my head ache.

But then I thought of the Boss in the library alone with Big Nicky and his muscle, and I knew I could not leave him alone. It was not right. He needed me and I must be there, and I knew Big Nicky was dangerous. But I will admit that I was afraid.

I never seen nothing like it in my life. It, him, them. There was three of them, Big Nicky, his muscle and his dame. The muscle, Bugsy Dees, looked like two scoops of Genghis Khan with a little Attila the Hun for topping. I never seen anyone so big, so mean looking, in my life before or since.

The dame was beautiful, they all are, only this one had natural blond hair, not peroxide like Ginger. And she wore a necklace with the the biggest rubies I ever seen.

In any other room I would have looked at those two for a very long time, but next to Big Nicky they was nothing. Big Nicky was not a large man but he filled the room. I would not have noticed him special only he looked at me when I come in with Ginger, and I seen his eyes.

I only seen eyes like that one time before, when I took Gloria to the zoo. We was at the snake house for the feeding and I seen that same look on a cobra facing a live mouse. And I knew how that mouse must have felt because I never thought to see those eyes looking out of a human head.

"Well, everybody, dinner is ready. Shall we go in and eat?" Ginger said. She was trying real hard to be a good hostess.

"I think we can wait a while," Big Nicky said smoothly. He was smiling, or at least his mouth was turned up at the corners. "We have some business to discuss. Perhaps you would like to show Natasha your library."

Ginger didn't know her cue, so that Natasha creature spoke up. "You'll have to excuse me, gentlemen, but, Ginger, would you be so kind as to show me where I can powder my nose? I'm afraid it's a little shiny."

Ginger led her out and didn't say a word, and that's the first and last time I ever seen Ginger not able to talk.

"Joey," Big Nicky said, "I think we need to come to some sort of agreement. I want Chicago. And with Moran and Capone ready for war, you know what will happen. They'll destroy each other and then there's only you. And please don't think you can stand against me when I'm ready to make my move."

"And why do you do me the courtesy of telling me this now?" the Boss asked, almost as light as Big Nicky. I was ready to cry, to see the Boss face him so cool.

Big Nicky tried that smile again and lit his cigar. He didn't use no lighter and never struck no match, and he done it twice more that night and I never did catch the trick.

"Why," he said, "I have a lot of business in many places. I can't come up and run Chicago personally. I need someone I can trust, someone who will take care of things for me. In return, you'll get a generous share of the profits."

"I'm sorry," the Boss said smoothly, "but I've never worked for anyone before and I don't intend to start now.

"That's too bad," Big Nicky said. "Much too bad. You see, it's nine o'clock now. The thirteenth. In less than twelve hours, Capone will hit Moran like no one's ever been hit before. And he'll be ready to turn on you. What if I tell you that I have Capone in my pocket already?''

"Then why come to me at all?'' the Boss asked. I didn't like the way it was going at all, not at all. I didn't like Big Nicky's attitude. How did he know what was going to happen tomorrow? But when I looked at him, I believed him, and the Boss believed him too.

"Because,'' Big Nicky said, real careful, "I already have Capone. I can do what I like with him. I want you. I want you to handle Chicago my way. I have Capone, but I don't want to use him for this. But maybe I'll have no choice.''

Big Nicky looked at the Boss again and his eyes seemed red, like there was little fires where the pupils ought to be.

Then the Boss smiled, and even if I was scared, I trusted him. He's educated and he's always got a plan. "I don't think I can take the offer,'' he said slowly.

Big Nicky seemed to snarl like the dog in the cartoons, and he was quiet for a very long time. Then he said, real quiet-like, like he was in church, "There's a very old tradition, you know. We'll play for it. At midnight.''

"Exactly,'' the Boss said. "But let's agree on the terms now.''

I felt all caught. I didn't know what they was saying. Old tradition? With craps? The Boss hadn't rolled craps since he took over his first casino.

"If I win,'' Big Nicky said, "then you run Chicago my way. You'll be my man, body and soul.''

The Boss thought about that for a long time, and I didn't like the sound of it. Then the Boss said, "And if you lose, Moran and Capone come to terms. No war. And you, and the rest of New York, leaves Chicago alone forever.''

Big Nicky looked straight at the Boss with those cobra eyes and said, "I accept,'' silky as you please.

"Well, shall we join the ladies?'' the Boss said, like he was talking to his best friend. "I'm sure they have their powder done by now.''

It was Big Nicky's fault I didn't enjoy the dinner for which the Boss had paid three cooks, or the pool game afterwards neither. And mostly I love to play pool. But then it was midnight and the Boss said, "Frankie, get the dice. Big Nicky, I assume you will do me the honor of using my dice?"

Big Nicky looked amused. "I know you run a clean game, Valenti, a thing that will change when I win. But for now, yes, your dice are fine."

I was happy to be out of that room. When the door closed and I wasn't near Big Nicky anymore, I felt better, like I could do something. It wasn't that I was yellow, but he was different from anybody I'd ever met, and I didn't like how.

I went to the library for the Boss's personal dice, and there was Angelo. "He's rolling?" Angelo asked, worried.

I answered him, and then Angelo asked me something strange. So I told him just what Big Nicky said and then he repeated it. "Body and soul, he said? You're sure, Frankie?"

"I have a very good memory," I said. "Body and soul, just like that."

Angelo looked scared, and his white suit looked even brighter, like maybe he'd been dipped in Borax. I got the dice and Angelo came with me.

"Look, Frankie," he said, "You've got to stall them. I'm going to get Ginger."

I got his meaning. Ginger was always the Boss's luck. You know, I was starting to like Angelo. He seemed to care about the Boss almost as much as I did.

They had the pool table cleared by the time I brought the dice, and the Boss offered Big Nicky the first roll as guest. Big Nicky smiled and said something I didn't catch, a lucky word maybe, and he smelled of matches more than ever. Then he rolled the dice on the felt. No Angelo, no Ginger. I could barely look at the dice. If only it wasn't a natural we'd have some time for the Boss's luck, only I didn't think Big Nicky could lose.

Well, he didn't win, but he didn't lose neither, and my heart was going up and down like a pony on a carousel. A ten point. He had to match that point or crap out. I held my breath and began to gag. Big Nicky looked at me like I was the mouse in the snake's cage while the Boss got me some water. And then Angelo showed with Ginger on his arm.

"My lucky lady," the Boss said, pulling Ginger over to him.

Except Big Nicky was looking at Angelo and they both seemed to have changed. Big Nicky hissed, like a snake, and Angelo stood like a soldier in front of the White House.

Angelo never took his eyes off Big Nicky. "Don't you have another roll?" Angelo asked. It was a little thing, but I never seen anything like it and I never hope to. There was Angelo looking like an electric bulb, and even his hair was glowing. Big Nicky smelled stronger and the little red flames in his eyes got brighter, only it didn't look like one of them optical illusion things.

"Rafael," Big Nicky said. No, I thought, his name's Angelo. If he was Rafe we'd of called him Rafe.

"Roll," was all Angelo said.

Big Nicky took the dice and breathed on them. He rolled and I didn't want to look. Five. He hadn't made his point or crapped out. It was going to be a long game. Big Nicky looked shook by Angelo but I couldn't figure it. I mean, Angelo is harmless.

"Why don't I let Joey the Action try?" Big Nicky said. "And if he just rolls point, I get the dice back?"

The Boss took the dice from him but I was confused. I mean, that's not the rules. On point you roll till you make point or crap out. The Boss held Ginger and rubbed the dice on her. Then Angelo came over and put his hand on the Boss's, over the dice.

"You stay out of it," Big Nicky said to Angelo.

The Boss rolled. I did not open my eyes, not until Angelo put his hand on my shoulder, and then I was never so relieved to see an eleven, a natural, in all my life.

"Nice practice," Big Nicky said, "Now back to my point. It's been an interesting diversion, but you know the rules. . . ."

I started to pull my gun there and then. If they changed the rules that was one thing, but to welsh on a bet, that was another. We don't go for that at the Boss's games.

But Angelo shoved me aside and stood in front of Nicky. "I stand witness," Angelo said. "Satan, get thee gone!"

Then Angelo pointed a finger at Nicky, who seemed to get all smoky all of a sudden. I didn't know what Angelo was saying, only I told you he was a little funny in the head.

It were all big Nicky and Angelo then, only I was watching Bugsy Dees, too. I learned early in this game that you got to watch the muscle all the time. So I never seen the signal but I seen the motion.

"Boss! Ginger!" I yelled, and went for my gun, only like I said before I wasn't fast enough. They was too close together. I didn't see it. And there was the Boss dead on the floor, bleeding all over Ginger's pink dress and her crying.

And then I seen that Big Nicky and Dees and Angelo were gone, but I didn't see them go. I was too busy with the Boss, only it weren't any help. He was dead. And Ginger wasn't any help neither. She was just lying on the floor, her leg all out at a funny angle and bleeding. The Boss had fell on her when he was hit.

She did a funny thing then, Ginger did. She dragged herself over to the pool table and took the Boss's dice. "He did win, my Joey won," she said.

Only then she stood up and her leg was fine. I don't know what happened and I don't want to know. Only Ginger, or Sister Mary Adelaide knows and she ain't talking.

Well, you know the story from there and if you don't you can look it up in *Time*. Like that the dice have cured over sixty people already and the Church decided that the Boss was a saint. The Monsignor wasn't too interested in Chicago, though, or the truce between Moran and Capone or the rest of it. All they wanted was to put the dice on some altar somewhere.

Boss, I hope you and St. Dizzy are running a game up there, because I'm old enough to hope to join you soon and I'd like a piece of the action.

The Magi

Damien Broderick

Damien Broderick is an Australian writer whose fine novel,
The Dreaming Dragons, *was well received in this country in*
1981. His agent, Virginia Kidd, passed on to me the following
excerpt from a letter she received from Broderick: "My little
old globe-trotting Mother ran into the Pope the other day amid
a mass of pilgrims and, quite beside herself with delight, cried
out, 'Greetings from Australia, yore Holiness!' and bugger me
if the supreme pontiff did not breast through the crowd to offer
his mitt."

I feel confident that the pontiff, supreme or otherwise, is not
going to shove his way through any crowd to thank Broderick
for the dark and troubled view of the future Church presented
in "The Magi." But I think he should.

I

How art thou fallen from heaven
O day-star, son of the morning!
...And thou saidst in thy heart:
"I will ascend into heaven,
Above the stars of God
Will I exalt my throne;
...I will ascend above the heights of the clouds;
I will be like the Most High."
Yet thou shalt be brought down to the nether-world,
To the uttermost parts of the pit.

Isaiah 14: xii-xvi

The forsaken City is all one thing, and devastatingly lovely: a filigree of silver, shadow, light.

Looking across it, Silverman is near to tears, like a green boy flushed with early love, transfigured by a first kiss. His throat knots; for a lingering moment, a heady anesthesia rebukes his senses. At last joy takes the aging man like pain, compressed and burning beneath his ribs, an exalted melancholy. That bitter joy tells him: cherubim lived here.

It is a reflection scarcely detached and scientific, and there is about it as well more than a whiff of heresy. Yet he can find no safer response rich enough to bear scrutiny. Peace is instinct in the empty City. With absolute conviction he tells himself: It's waiting for them to come home.

Exile with all his Order from High Earth, professed in the Society of Jesus under four solemn vows and five simple, Father Raphael Silverman gazes down with misery. From the edge of the cyclopean cliff he can smell warm wind rising from an unpeopled world of rippled grasses, a breeze that washes through the selective membrane of his filter-skin like memories of boyhood. At the horizon stand blurred violet hills, falling in the distant east to an ocean's cerulean shore. In the crucible of his breast they mingle. They streak into a haze on the moist film of his eye's curve.

Regretfully, then, Silverman turns his back on the dove-grey lace coral of the City and works his way back to the skiff. A sizzle of interference is still the best he can raise from his telemetry systems. Cirrus feathers the sky; from the ground, the forces which shield the City are transparent to the visible spectrum. No doubt a signal impressed upon a maser beam would reach him, but it unlikely that he could return an answer.

His shadow goes ahead of him, stretched by the slant of the morning sun, gaunt anyway, climbing the hard stone which separates him from the Monastery skiff. Paradox, an internal wound, sends darts to every vital place. The routine trick of scientific analysis is already in play, shredding the City and its planet into notional constituents, worrying with a terrier's impertinence at the anomaly of a structure (A) deserted for eons which (not-A) bears no sign of decay. And this is the paradox: that from the deeper seat he cries out in pain. Where are they? Silverman demands. Where did they go? Their radiant and somber City speaks solely of beauty and sanctity. There is no hint of corruption, of vice, even of mere worldly utility. They had known God so well that their dwelling place is a tabernacle, a temple, the New Jerusalem raised three thousand light-years from those dismal hills of Palestine where His Son walked briefly before men slew Him.

The transponder in Silverman's belt sounds as he steps over a modest rise, and the hidden skiff's refraction field collapses. In the center of a flat clearing the vessel stands on its tail, curved titanium hull catching the planet's sun dazzlingly.

Silverman's joy returns, it has no bounds. The Master of the Universe has extended him a reconciliation. He is fifty-five years old, and has been lost in despair and oppression for the last ten. It seems to him that in this year of our Lord 2040, quincentenary of his Order's foundation under the Bull *Regimini militantis ecclesiae*, a reprieve has been proffered. Silverman will never purge the abomination of *Southern Cross,* that intolerable memory which crouches always at the shadowed fringes of his being, but now there is a kind of counterweight, and he feels the balance of his soul pivoting once more into light. For there is joy as well as grief in the lambent, empty City. In My Father's house, yes, there are many mansions. The Jesuit smiles gladly within himself.

Without guidance the computer systems of the skiff find their alignment with the Monastery's orbit. And Silverman is floating into the darkening bowl of the sky, balanced in a great arc with the natural forces of the planet. The stars come out, and the City's world is a shimmering crescent beneath him.

"We have reacquired your telemetry," an urgent voice tells him. Silverman knows that all his vital signs were instantly accessible to the Monastery's computers the moment he came out from behind the City's shield; they cannot fail to realize he is aboard the skiff, in perfect condition. Still, ancient habits place tension in the voice. "Father, we lost you as you went in. Are you all right?"

"Fine," he assures them. "Never been better. It's beautiful. Sorry if I alarmed you. It seemed sensible to take the opportunity to look around." He wonders if elation is apparent in his tone.

Above and beyond him, the vast light-jeweled Latin cruciform of the *St. Ignatius Loyola* looms like Constantine's pre-battle vision as the skiff falls up into docking orbit. The sight of the huge weightless icon enters Silverman's heart with the force of a shaft of illumination from the collective unconscious; he expels his breath. Indeed, only Jung among all the tawdry interpreters of mind might have responded with insight to the wisdom which informed the starship's builders. Crux and patibulum, stake and crosspiece, radiate in an archetypal mandala which tells at once of a Man hanged from a tree and a solstice sun reborn in seasonal resurrection. But the image causes a pang. It is too grand, lofty, austere; there is no authentic sense of home.

With lowly autonomic wisdom, the skiff takes itself into the shuttle niche. The *bidellus* is waiting behind the hermetic seal of his oversight cubicle as Silverman climbs from the lock. In his sleeveless gown, lacking the fabric wings which hang from the shoulders of the clerks-regular, the lay brother could be any stolid porter attending the gate of a Jesuit House on Earth prior to the suppression.

"*Laudetur Jesus Christus*," Silverman says in greeting.

"*Semper laudetur*," replies the porter. "The Father-General wishes to see you as soon as you've showered. If you're hungry I could have some lunch sent up."

"Thank you, Brother. I think I'll wait for dinner."

Only simple decontamination is required for the skiff. For Silverman, more stringent measures are obligatory. Alien infestations are not welcome. Patiently he suffers the irradiations and sluicings which beat down on his filter-skin. Satisfied at grudging length, the computers permit him to peel away the suit and pass into a second snug ceramic chamber where he may attend to his personal hygiene. As always, the ambiance is slightly chilly. He rubs his hairy arms and chest with alcohol, cleaning off the gummy residue where life-sign telltales have been cemented. A gush of tepid water rinses his skin, and blasts of warmer air dry him off. He manages these motions without attention, murmuring the prescribed prayers as he dresses.

Ship-time is late afternoon. He has advanced ten hours in the leap to orbit, and the queasiness of readjustment will have its toll. Silverman considers the elevator but shakes his head minimally with regret. Planar gravity-effect within the Monastery is kept to three-quarters Earth normal due to structural constraints, and a metabolism designed for Earth needs all the extra exercise it can find. At the entrance to the main corridor on this level there is a rack of small-wheeled bicycles. The Jesuit heaves one down from its hook and mounts the saddle, tucking up his cassock, his calves protesting in advance. Like a village *abbé* displaced a century and a half and trillions of kilometers, he pedals off along the corridor for the ramps which climb five levels to the Father-General's quarters.

The journey leaves him only slightly breathless; he has found a nice compromise between brisk exertion and that sedateness ordained in the Common Rule. Parking the bike, he uses his research-status prerogative to trigger the office door and goes straight in. Monsignor

Alvarez, the General's secretary, waves Silverman through with a cordial smile.

Niceto Cardinal Miguel Rodrigues de Madrazo y Lucientes, S. J., Father-General of the remnants of his Order, Prince of the Church, papal elector and councillor bound in duty and privilege to sit in consistory on High Earth yet barred from that assembly by secular ban, the pontiff's *legati a latere* aboard the exiled starship, sits hunched before a holofiche reader, his intent eyes darting across the screen. Silverman contains himself in patience. A band of wires crosses the red zucchetto perched on his superior's scalp, strobing alpha-frequency impulses to the cardinal's temporal lobes, enhancing and focusing his attention. There will be no rousing him until the fiche is digested.

Madrazo is an aristocratic son of Alcalá, the Andalusian town which gave St. Ignatius his first theologian, the fiery half-Jew Diego Laynez, second Father-General of the Order, and Silverman cherishes the remote link with his own ornate and bastard spiritual heritage. Now in his seventies, Madrazo retains an intellect certainly as fine as Silverman's and an equanimity unbroken by the tragedy which has diminished his charges from fifty thousand to less than a hundredth of that number, all five hundred of them confined within the hull of *Loyola*.

"Sit down," the General says abstractedly. "I shouldn't be a moment." Pale light from the screen dances in reflection from his cheeks, the blade of his nose, as words flicker frantically. Madrazo stabs with one finger and the light clears; the fiche pops up for replacement. Silverman blinks as dark eyes lift to seize him with electronically augmented force. "Father Silverman." The cardinal lifts the band away from his skullcap and settles back, but there is no perceptible dulling of his attention. He straightens his mozetta, the short cape which hangs from his shoulders over his scarlet cassock.

"We're all relieved that you came to no harm. Shall I wait for the digest, or is it worth a full personal report?"

"Your Eminence," Silverman says, and finds something choking his larynx. "There's a city down there."

"So." Madrazo props his chin on steepled fingers. His ring of office gleams like a living eye. The considerable shock he must feel elicits no more than a moue of interest. "I've just been studying the final sensor evaluations. They show a profusion of fauna and flora in stationary ecological equilibrium, but no evidence of intelligence. We surmise that the shielded anomaly is of extraplanetary origin."

"I don't think so. The design of the city is absolutely integral to the mood of the planet."

Acutely, Madrazo suggests, "The good stewards."

"Yes." Silverman hesitates. "It's totally deserted."

"You can see no reason to prevent our sending a team into the ruins?"

His heart stills for an instant close to syncope. It seems that banners of light stream above him. The wonder of the City is a swelling organ note.

"Eminence, there are no ruins. It is perfectly preserved." Without caution, his heart swollen with excitement, Silverman leans forward and presses his damp hands on the desk. "It looks as if it's . . . *waiting* for someone."

The City of the angels calls him, calls him home.

II

The synagogue is a brothel, a hiding place for wild animals. No Jew has ever prayed to God; they are all possessed by devils. Instead of greeting them, ye shall avoid them as a contagious disease and plague.

St. John Chrysostom, 349-407 C. E.

Silverman's earliest memory must be composite: layered and glazed from the complaints and resentments of those old enough for some density of accurate recall, a *sfumato* the reverse of Leonardo da Vinci's, shade aching into shade, glowing with bitter depths of light. Spitefully, the Soviet officials had waited for Shabbos. Harsh kliegs crusted the street, empty canvas-clad trucks growled and coughed, bodies pressed sweating in hallways and on stairs, the candles guttering, legal imprecations in Russian and Yiddish, a man in uniform pushing past the puzzled children to jerk bedclothing from the parents' mattress onto the floor, kicking it into a heap.

"We cannot pack tonight, it is forbidden," Raphael's father said, facing the man in a fury. "To save a life," the mother pleaded, pulling Rebbe Silverman's arm, in tears, scooping up their belongings. "Master of the Universe, they'll kill us all."

"You traitors sicken me," the policeman told them. Raphael wailed, clutching the mother's legs. "Haven't you been whining to leave for long enough? Hurry it up, there's rain on the way."

"We have been Russian for three hundred years, you Cossack bastard," the Rebbe said. His face was blotched. "There is a higher allegiance."

"Your names are on the manifest. Eh? Here? My job is to get you into the truck. Conscious or unconscious doesn't fuss me. Take as much junk as you can carry, but no animals."

"Why aren't we being sent to Israel?"

"I don't care where you go, Jew. But I don't suppose the Poles will want to keep you."

Rebecca protested as the mother bundled away two of her dolls, leaving her the shapeless rag creature she loved best. Raphael gazed about blindly, located his brother David, toddled to him and shrieked in sudden, absolute terror.

Too many people, too little space, the skies weeping fat drops onto the tarpaulin and then opening in earnest to drench the trucks, tires drumming, headlights streaked on the roads behind and ahead. "It is the Holocaust again," an old man said over and over. "Ribbono Shel Olom, why do You hate Your people?"

And that is all Silverman remembers. It was not the Holocaust again, not yet. Troop trains took them through Poland, through East Germany. At the border they waited for months while politicians and their masters diced. Finally the exiles crossed into West Germany, into the other half of the land of the beast which took them now grudgingly and gave them shelter while crowds bickered in the streets below their crowded apartments, with increasing boldness bore banners denouncing this imposition, and the Rebbe's family lived double-outcast among the Hassidim in whose de facto quarter they were billeted, grim-faced, bearded men in *shtreimel* and *bekesheh*, women like black ghosts with disapproving eyes, the pious excess of their holy-day dancing and singing coming from the midst of this sober contempt like a slap to the face. Raphael was just old enough to enter the primary grade of yeshiva when they were moved again, to Randers in Jutland where the blond Danes offered Lutheran tolerance and allowed the Rebbe's family to settle with the uprooted Hassidim while Israel made ready her tents for the millions who cried their dispossession at her gates.

Raphael remembers his first years in Denmark with a sweet longing. Most of all, though, he recalls a picnic in an ancient village outside Randers. The Protestant church in the village was old, older than any building he had ever seen, built in the golden age of Catholicism hundreds of years prior to the Reformation. Six years old, his exuberance quenched by some intimation of awe, Raphael stole into the church of the false moshiach. From a triumphal arch a faded painting shone in blues, cinnabar, lamp-black, rusted green. Two women stood beneath a lamb. To the left, her eyes hidden by a scarf, hair cascading to her green dress, one of the lovely women stabbed a spear into the lamb's vulnerable throat. Even as the helpless animal's lifeblood gushed from the wound, the woman to the right held out a cup to catch it; regal, her coat was crimson as the fluid she preserved. The painting was inexpressibly beautiful, tender and cruel, and Raphael gazed up at it in a state near to trance.

The Rebbe was livid. "An *ilui* you might be, but what good is cleverness without obedience to your father?"

Flabbergasted and confused, the child said: "The ladies were so pretty. Who are they?" And something secret within him crowed. Nobody before had ever told him he was a genius, even though he had learned to read long before starting at the yeshiva.

"Do not speak back to your father," the mother told him. A certain gentleness removed the sting, but he was frightened by what she said next. "It is a filthy thing, that picture. A child should be spared such sights. It is from the sitra achra."

The Other Side. The pitiless gulf of nothingness, of worse than nothingness, which rebuked the Master of the Universe. The matter was dropped: Raphael said his Krias Shema, head bowed, and the growing curls of his earlocks brushed his cheek like the soothing caress of the mother's fingers.

Years later, still in Denmark, the mashpia of his school mentioned the ancient painting to the boys who were preparing for bar mitzvah. "The goyim hate us," he explained, "because they are taught that our people—the chosen people of God!—murdered the false moshiach. In the picture, their messiah is shown as a lamb. A woman in green represents the people of Israel, the synagogue. The other woman is the Christian Church. That painting came from the hand of the Angel of Death."

It seemed as if that awful being had laid aside his palette and taken up the sword: on the following Easter, inflamed by the cruel anti-Israel embargoes of the Moslem petroleum nations, a mob of louts stormed the school erected by the Russian Jews and their bomb blew the Rebbe into bloody shreds. An old Hassid came to their house with the news. "We have had our differences," he told the weeping family, "but the Rebbe was a good man. Most of us," he said, taking Raphael against his knee, "must strive always against the lure of sin, for our souls are blind to the Mishnah and Gemara. Some few lead lives which are blameless in deed but whose thoughts remain snared by the world. Very rare is the tzaddik, who has mastered his own heart. Rebbe Silverman was of the tzaddikim."

The Silvermans departed almost immediately for Israel. It came as a surprise to Raphael to learn that the family could have taken up residence in the Homeland years earlier, but that his father had found a higher duty among the outcasts in northern Europe. But now the flood was in full torrent: nobody wanted Jews, not the Americans or the Europeans. Oil and gasoline were drying up as the Jihad intensified; madmen ruled the Arab states, godstruck or venal, it hardly mattered which. It was politic to export Jews, before inflamed citizens recreated on a world scale the horrors of Kristallnacht.

Aviation fuel was under jealous rationing. The four Silvermans, with hardly more possessions than they'd taken from Russia, wallowed across the Mediterranean from Genoa in a stinking refitted tanker crammed with their fellows. Ashdod harbor was temporarily closed while police and army units sought a bomb which terrorists had planted in one of the warehouses. The tanker turned and sailed north, and berthed at the sprawling foot of Mount Carmel. Raphael stared at the clutter of pale apartment complexes and the endless accumulation of ma'abarot pinned to every spare hectare of soil between them: tents and tin shacks, hastily erected accommodation for the millions of Jews fleeing from the brooding, pent hatred of two hemispheres. On a high spur he could make out the monastery of the Carmelite Christian monks, and on another the shrine to science, the Technion. A ferocious excitement grasped him, a sap rising full and strong in his maimed, severed roots: it was a homecoming.

Almost immediately, his brother David was inducted into the Israel Defense Army, deferring his rabbinical studies for two years. The mother, despite her burdens of grief, seemed somehow to blossom, organizing the neighboring immigrants, prettying their own rudimentary shack, allowing Raphael to run more freely on the leash—even gifting him, on his fourteenth birthday, with a compact Japanese calculator endowed with 10K memory. Raphael let his study of Talmud slip, devouring science texts, crouching in the night over the tiny green numerals, commanding them to dance for him, to sing, a chorale to the fecundity of the universe. His teachers were not slow to appreciate his precocity. On the day the family heard that David had been killed in combat on the border of the Islamic Theocracy, he was already deep into physics at the Technion.

A double blow sent his faith tottering. His brother's slaying was not senseless, but it was unconscionable. Raphael raged, tore the yarmulke from his head and trampled it under his feet. Already the grounds of his apostasy had been established. He had walked in the streets of Jerusalem, the new city and the old, among the cypresses of the Mount of Olives, and beneath the Dome of the Rock where Muhammad had leapt into Paradise on horseback, and beside the Wailing Wall, and a slow horror at the multiple unreason had crept into his breast like a growing sponge. He had barely escaped without a beating from his tourist visit to the mosque, and that conjoint savagery and breathtaking beauty poisoned his ease with his fellow humans in a way the vile painting in Denmark had not.

"How could the Torah have been given to Moses! I mean literally written down by God?" he asked Rebecca one night. She stared at him aghast. "Do you really believe that, that the Word of the Master of the Universe was dictated in seventy languages on Sinai?"

"Raphael, be quiet! You have been listening to the lies of the malshinim. This is apikorsishe blasphemy!"

It was unfair, she was a simple woman, but he railed at her. "Why call them slanderers? They use their brains, Becky, that's all. Would you recommend the gullible stupidity of the Neturei Karta, cowering behind their walls in the Mea Shearim?" He had never lost a measure of loathing for the Hassidim, barricading themselves into the past, rigid with bigotry. "They deny the State of Israel, and they justify it by Torah. They refuse to speak Hebrew because that is sacrilege. Should I grow my payos back and tug out my ritual fringes for all to see, and join them in their blind adherence to superstition? Or is Orthodox nonsense sufficient?"

She ran from the room in tears, and he turned angrily to his printouts, where the limitations were the bounds of imagination and logic, and the diagnostics told you without pity where your own stupidity lay.

For his mother's sake he retained the trappings of ritual, and found a kind of authentic comfort in its practice. If now the ceaseless argument and nuance of Talmud seemed arid to him, the eight-hundred-year-old nitpicking of Maimonides the Rambam and Nachmanides the Ramban, the clamor of Rashi and Ibn Ezra and Buber and Sforno, all the desperate ingenuity of brilliant minds dissecting the unreal, at least in the candle lighting of Hanukkah there was calm pride, especially in a land where you could see the lithe Maccabee runners pounding with the flame from Mode'in all the way to the kingly menorah, the Tabernacle candelabrum in Jerusalem, yes, there was comfort in the braying of the shofar, for it spoke of a unity of place and time which his heart desired more than truth.

On Pesach in the last year of the millennium of the Common Era, Raphael sat at Seder with his mother and his sister and voiced the

Four Questions. The meager Passover feast lay on the table before them. The curtains were drawn. David's empty seat was a rebuke. "How is this night different from all other nights?" Raphael asked. "On all other nights we eat leaven and unleavened bread, tonight only unleavened—" He could not hear the next word. Spacetime had blinked, for a moment. Had his heart stopped? In the dim room he closed his eyes and watched the hard afterimage bloom: the table, a silhouette of his mother and sister, the edge of a door frame. The chair fell with a grinding, splintering sound as his thigh muscles contracted, hurling him up and away from the table. "Cover your faces," he said, shouting into a place with no resonance. "Quick," and he seized his mother's limp arm, dragging her to the floor, pushing Rebecca with her beneath the table. He forced himself to time eternity, studying his watch. The tin roof drummed, and a vast flat surge of thunder went over them like the wing of the Angel of Death. There were screams, screams. A siren was bleating, and others joined it. Six minutes? "God in heaven," he said, "Jerusalem is gone." He ran to the television set. Snow hissed on the screen. Panic was beginning to lock his muscles. His mother lay underneath the table, her breath coming in stertorous grunts. Becky cradled her in her arms. He found a transistor radio. Through the static, a voice dehumanized by appalling self-control was saying: "—enhanced radiation device, triggered by laser, so there will be negligible fallout. The device was detonated, according to satellite information, at ground zero in the vicinity of Mount Zion. Most of the force was expended as prompt neutron radiation. I repeat, stay indoors and cover your windows. Prepare for evacuation. Arab invasion forces are massing on—"

A desolated voice, outside their shack, was chanting, chanting. The words tore Raphael to the soul: *"Sh'ma Yisroel, Adonai Elohenu, Adonai Echod. Sh'ma Yisroel—"*

Hear, O Israel, the Lord our God is one Lord.

III

To make sure of being right in all things, we ought always to hold by the principle that the white that I see I would believe to be black, if the hierarchical Church were so to rule it. . . .

St. Ignatius Loyola, *Spiritual Exercises*

The City burns in his mind like a shrine of illuminated flowers.

Silverman paces uneasily in the narrow confines of his cell. The habit of composure is sloughing from him, as if his soul had begun to shed some dried constricting husk. He discovers himself naked and defenseless without its protection.

Madrazo undoubtedly was taken aback by his outburst but had chosen not to press the matter. Nobody had expected Silverman to find anything as drastic and unsettling as the City. Orbital surveillance had registered the valley only as a mild magnetic and gravitational anomaly, tagging it for closer scrutiny, but redundancy photoscan failed to reveal anything remarkable. The small puzzle teased the physicist in Silverman sufficiently to send him to the surface. Artfully camouflaged, yet plainly uninhabited, the screened City confused his expectations. Still, to suggest that the City was waiting for the return of its builders, as if it were a sentient creature, was patently ridiculous. But Silverman balks at his own rationality. Something he cannot fail to see as vital has touched him, balm to his woes: something breathlessly expectant.

His uncertain steps halt finally at the prie-dieu angled from the foot of his bunk. Lowering himself to his knees before the crucifix, he gazes on the image of the hanging Man. The City's bright image superimposes itself, an affirmation. A flood of gratitude suffuses his being.

Once before he has known illumination. At his ordination in Rome, in St. Peter's cathedral, under the hands of the great Franciscan pontiff Sixtus VI, he stood at the boundary of transcendence. Pungent and near to sickening, incense had risen in his nostrils. The palpable intensity of thousands gathered in solemn common worship, the unspeakable antiquity of tradition and love and anguish, conspired with sentiment to lift him free, a newly made priest according to the order of Melchizedek, from the horror of the Second Holocaust, his family's pitiful and useless martyrdom, his guilt and doubt. Today in the City he has known it again.

A chill of fever afflicts him. It is not sickness. If anything, this roaring in his vital centers is a surfeit of life. He strives against it, battling for detached clarity, lest pride make this grace a most subtle temptation.

For all that he is a scientist and priest in this most militant of Orders, he has never renounced his sense of poetry. In a decade on the run from himself, he has dreaded the stars. Through the opaque hull they have seemed to stare in at him, a thousand brilliant haunted eyes plaguing him at the edge of sleep. His poetry has been bleak; it has addressed him from a universe cold and uncaring and baited with traps, where the purest soaring of theology has been perverted into mechanisms of murder, where the spasms of nature throw men heedlessly into existence and the corruption of nature sucks them dry at death and leaves them less than nothing.

More than once the sour words of the Talmud, memorized in childhood, have returned to jeer at him: "Akabaya Ben Mahalalel says, 'Whence thou art come?' From a putrid drop. This is *Pirke Abot*, the Wisdom of the Fathers. Rabbi Simeon ben Eleazar says, 'I shall tell thee a parable: to what might this be likened? To a king who built a large palace and decorated it, but a tannery pipe led through it and emptied at its doorway.' So too is man. If then, with a foul stream issuing from his bowels, he exalts himself over other creatures, how much the more would he exalt himself if a stream of precious oil, balsam or ointment issued from him!" Now the words take on new meaning for Silverman. He beholds the gnarled timber representation of his Lord's Corpse, recovered to glory in resurrection, and sees how profound his error has been. Nature is finally beneficent. Yes, as Loyola said, it is created for man's sake, to help him fulfill the end for which he was created. If it is unfathomable, that is precisely because it is the "letting be," the creative outpouring, of the Infinite.

Even this Monastery, a spangled cross hurled into the black sky, token of everything infertile and plastic and contrived, never truly home to the limping mendicant, finds its place in his assent. He clasps his fingers and lets his gaze drift to the arresting nondevotional print framed on the wall.

With surprise it occurs to him how premonitory the madman's drawing is, its embedded borders and obsessional hood-masked faces, its Edvard Munch-mouthed elongated ghosts or spectral otters or eyed slugs or spermatazoa slithering back to belly, interlocked but never crossing, the pallid green and yellow and orange and blue of the hospital's crayons, the unfrightened capital letters identifying its draughtsman and his century, ADOLF—1917, and the hard, anxious script which scrambles across the exploding water beneath the crowded ferry with its double smokestack and triple masts and its windows crammed like nightmare with half-seen faces asphyxiated in terror. Poor Adolf Wölfli, contacting some limb of the absolute in his psychosis, drawing on doors and cupboards and walls and any vagrant scrap of paper in the asylum, his fierce blurred eye of truth still open for want of a psychopharmacology accurate enough to calm his craziness and his fear.

The print was an ironic gift from a fellow Jesuit before they packed their scant belongings for exile: Father Thorne had got it from the University Psychiatric Clinic at Waldau, in Berne, where the original Wölfli collection is housed. Had Thorne meant quite so explicitly to tell him that they were embarking on the Ship of Fools? But neither of them had known, then. In any case, as Silverman sees now with an immense lifting of his burden, that analysis of their condition has always been trite. Even the doomed starship *Southern Cross* had been more than a ship of fools.

It is no accident that the *Loyola* resembles the plan of a cathedral. If the Monastery lacks ribbed vaults, pointed arch and flying buttress, masons' tricks hardly appropriate even in esthetic mimicry to a starship, still it glows with its own luminous flamboyance. Nave and transepts fling themselves out like exultant limbs, multicolored metallic glasses soar in a clerestory wall irradiated by strange suns. Here is a vindication of the proud genius of Pope Sixtus, who found in a shattered world, revolted by the Jihad's savagery, such a loathing for faith that he called all Christendom to a new raising of cathedrals, a moral equivalent of crusade, a sign in heaven. The world's first starship, fourteen years in the building, had flamed from the solar system in 2015; but *Southern Cross* was merely the final monument to an expired technology. This high cathedral is purely the creation of unitive physics, lilting between stars in the cryptic transition of dream.

And if Sixtus VI's own dream has soured, his monastic cathedral, outcast under prohibition by the godless owners of 21st century Earth, outcast with the remnants of his pledged soldiers and diplomats and (as those rulers believe) masters of insidious casuistry, why, a kind of blessing can be found here too, for the Word of Gospel is thus scattered into the skies like a memory of the black-garbed missionaries who strode without dread into unknown Asia and the Americas five hundred years before.

Silverman stirs, glancing at his watch. He is bone tired. There is no slightest sound: the Monastery is deep into the *maximum silentium*, the Great Silence. Before he sleeps, the Jesuit must say his daily Office. He reaches for his worn leather-bound breviary and turns to the litanies of the day, for the feast of St. Andrew Corsini, Bishop and Confessor.

When that is done, he kneels once more to make a full Examen of conscience. The City has convicted him of sin. And a cold memory comes to him, hard and clear: his first confession, close to four decades ago, in his bolthole in Rome. Did he truly believe? It seems to him now that that Jewish youth, fresh from the renewal and risk of baptism, had believed nothing. Nothing.

IV

The Spirit of the Lord moves on its course with relaxed reins, to illumine souls and to draw them closely to Himself. He has methods without number.

> Claudio Acquaviva, Fifth Father-General
> of the Society of Jesus

"Come in, Raphael. I imagined you'd be older. Have that chair. You took instruction from poor Father Hertz, didn't you?"

"Yes, Father."

"A tragedy. God forgive them, they're like animals. I suppose it was his name. Morris never struck me as looking like a . . . Well, anyway, Raphael, you're stuck with me. It really is a pleasure welcoming you into the family of Christ. Have you prepared your general confession? No need for all the gory details, the intention of repentance is sufficient."

"Thank you, I don't mind. Unless—"

"Bless you, son, take as long as you like. I don't have a golf date, if that crossed your mind."

"I never learned to play. Uh, I somehow expected you to be solemn and grim, sort of the Grand Inquisitor."

"How odd. In my neck of the woods Jesuits are regarded with some suspicion for their levity. You're thinking of the Dominicans. That's a shop joke. We've always maintained that the sacrament of reconciliation should be made as painless as possible, though with due regard to the gravity of sin. 'My yoke is sweet,' Our Lord said, 'and my burden light,' and I'm sure He meant it."

"Yes."

"Okay, away we go. In the name of the Father, and of the Son, and of the Holy Spirit. Amen. May God, Who has enlightened your heart, help you to know your sins and trust in His mercy."

"Amen."

" 'What proves that God loves us is that Christ died for us while we still sinned. Having died to make us righteous, is it likely that He would now fail to save us from God's anger?' That's a lovely text, Raphael, St. Paul to the Romans. Shoot."

"Uh, I confess to almighty God that before my baptism I sinned grievously against faith, for I denied His truth, and against hope, for I fell into despair when all my people were . . . I'm sorry—"

"That's all right, son, get it off your chest. I've never thought it unmanly to weep when grief truly touches us. Did your family die in Jerusalem?"

"No, Father, a little later, when the Jihad blitzed Israel. The mullahs blamed us! They actually blamed *us* for destroying their holy places."

"Tell me this, Raphael. How pure was your intention in renouncing Judaism? Was it to save your skin?"

"Wow. You don't believe in fighting clean, do you?"

"To answer my question honestly might be the most important thing you ever do in this life, Raphael. We would have given you sanctuary anyway, you know."

"Look, don't think I haven't put it to myself. Father Morris kept me dangling for six months before he'd baptize me. Obviously there's an element . . . I'll tell you how it was. Before they preempted Jerusalem, I'd lost my faith. My old faith. I was studying physics, and there didn't seem any room in quantum theory for the Yahveh of the Torah."

"Yet there is for the Blessed Trinity?"

"I can't pretend to explain it, but yes. I worked it out after the priests smuggled me here to Rome. No classic conversion number, no bolts of lightning into the brain—"

"Generally humbug. St. Paul's got a lot to answer for. Neurotics and hysterics dote on bolts of lightning."

"You're a refreshing man, Father. The thing of it is, I spent a lot of time so depressed they had to feed me with a spoon. Then I put in quite a deal of praying even when I didn't know Who to, and reading a couple of books a day about Judaism and Islam and Christianity, and I finally understood that we'd been punished."

"Really? The entire Jewish nation?"

"Like original sin. The whole human race shares in the sin of Adam. Well, the Jewish people rejected the Messiah when He came, and we've been punished, to open our eyes."

"I'm glad you added that last bit. The Jews were not responsible for Christ's murder. That's an error which has been formally condemned by Pope Sixtus as heretical."

"No, no, of course not. The beasts out there claim that when they're napalming us to death. But I read St. Paul, the same epistle you quoted before, I forget which chapter. There is no distinction between Jew and gentile, everyone who calls upon the name of the Lord shall be saved. But how are they to call upon Him until they've learned to believe in Him?"

"And how are they to believe in Him, unless they listen to Him? Yes. And that metaphor in the next chapter about the olive tree which is pruned and grafted with alien stock. You think the Second Holocaust was God's latest nudge to His chosen people? A rather harsh educational technique. Wouldn't it be better to place the blame where it really lies—in the wicked, scapegoating hearts of men?"

"I'm not the theologian, Father. But why else would the Master of the Universe permit the obliteration of my people?"

"Raphael, I imagine we'll be pondering that terrible question to the end of time."

"Have I answered *your* question, Father?"

"Our Lord clearly has given you a very special grace, Raphael. You must nurture His flame within you."

"Father, I have to be honest. I chose Catholicism because right now it seems to me to be valid. It's the sole branch of Christianity which can trace its roots directly to Jesus and the apostles. But I'm a scientist. To me, understanding is always provisional. I'm still tormented by doubts."

"Ten thousand difficulties do not make a single doubt, my son. A keen awareness of difficulties is the occupational hazard of Christian intellectuals. Sometimes I think how much easier it would have been to live in the 12th century, but then I remember their sewerage. Look, let's wrap this up with a general declaration, and we'll go up and have some coffee."

"Yes. Lord. I have offended against Your commandments, and I am truly sorry."

"For penance I'd like you to make a novena of Masses to Our Lady during the next nine days. Express your sorrow to God, now, and I'll give you absolution."

"Father, I have sinned against You and am not worthy to be called Your son. Be merciful to me, a sinner."

"God, the Father of mercies, through the death and resurrection of His Son, has sent the Holy Spirit among us for the forgiveness of sins; through the ministry of the Church may God give you pardon and peace, and I absolve you from your sins in the name of the Father, and of the Son, and of the Holy Spirit."

"Amen."

"Give thanks to the Lord, for He is good."

"His mercy endures forever."

"The Lord has freed you from your sins. Go in peace."

"Uh, Father, one final thing. I believe I have a vocation as a Jesuit."

"Hmmm. Let's take a rain check on that one."

V

I used in imagination to see the bridges collapse and sink, and the whole great city vanish like a morning mist. Its inhabitants began to seem like hallucinations, and I would wonder whether the world in which I thought I had lived was a mere product of my own febrile nightmares.

Bertrand Russell, *Autobiography*

Shriven, buoyant with the promise of the City, Father Raphael Silverman dons amice, alb, chasuble and stole, his vestments blood red in honor of St. Agatha, Virgin and Martyr, and says Mass in the Lady Chapel behind the great altar reserved for the Father-General. With so many priests aboard the Monastery, the listing of chapels is orchestrated in a timetable by the computers. Even so, Silverman concelebrates the Mystery with the two priests who will go down to the planet with him this afternoon. Brother Kohler, his team's electronics specialist, serves the Mass, burly in white surplice.

It is a cause of some irritation that Cardinal Madrazo has insisted on the inclusion of an Eclectic. Silverman cannot feel at ease in the presence of radically lateral insight. The Father-General discerns the private roots of his disquiet and resistance.

"Eclectics are a jumpy breed," Silverman has argued.

The Cardinal smiled. "Father Chan is made of sterner stuff. Raphael, you were a little skittish yourself yesterday. Tsung-Dao is a discreet fellow. Besides—if that thing down there is as peculiar as you suggest, you really ought to have a coordinating synthesist with you."

Silverman introduces Father Chan to the other Jesuits during descent. The Chinese priest knows their work, of course, and they have seen him at Mass this very day, but incredibly he has never spoken to them before. Even in the closed environment of the Monastery, Eclectics tend to relate to others chiefly through the cybersystem. It is a mark of "singularity," that vice most swiftly extirpated under the Common Rule, but their special gifts and training make it permissible.

Deliberately, Silverman gives them no warning of what they might expect. Coronal effect flares about their vessel. The survey boat, far better equipped with instruments than yesterday's skiff, plummets through the City's screen, trailed by a mild magneto-hydrodynamic storm. They bypass the scarp, falling to rest amid the wet green fields which spread on every side around the City.

Not one of them moves a muscle.

The tiers rise like the airy battlements of a castle of crystal, a tracery of translucent marble and quicksilver. Dew-wet grass is a carpet of gems, unmuted, glistening in the morning sunlight. The City humbles them. They simply sit.

If Silverman has half feared the penetrating insight of an Eclectic at this naked moment, that trepidation is gone. The sheer ontological impact of the City is scored in the small silent movements (a hand half-lifted, a foot drawn back), the pent breath, the trapped gaze of his colleagues.

Yet grandeur is not indefinitely paralyzing. Slowly the scientists come to themselves. In continued silence, they begin to gather their instruments for the trip across to the City. Henry Walson slides a cassette roll expertly into a camera. For a moment, after his hands have completed their automatic task, he stands helplessly before the viewpod. But the imposed discipline which has shaped them all is finally no less automatic. Bending his tonsured head over the camera, the xenologist shoots a rapid series of holograms.

Brother Kohler piles the gravity polarizer with field equipment. By the time Walson has finished his cassette, Kohler is looking to Silverman for permission to cycle open the hatch. Chan, unused to expeditions beyond the Monastery, is once more checking the seals on his filter-skin. The camera beeps and disgorges the first windows. Silverman plucks them from the slot. His face drains of blood. The world moves away from him.

"Wait," he says. His own voice resonates strangely within his head, like a cry heard underwater. The engineer lifts his stubby hand from the hatch control. Walson halts in the process of inserting a fresh cartridge of holotape.

"Let me have them, Father," comes Tsung-Dao Chan's cool voice. Like all of them, he speaks in Latin. From Silverman's numb grasp he takes the vivid colored prints. Surprised, the others peer over his shoulder, and their mouths loosen.

Each of the hologram windows is technically perfect. Grass sparkles lustrously, with here and there a clump of merry wildflowers, and the cloudless daybreak sky shines in true dimensional depth. And where the City itself lifts like a cantata outside the survey boat's clear viewpod, the windows show only three enormous pieces of statuary, dwarfed and foreshortened by distance, alien and powerful and each of the most blazing and absolute malevolence.

Silverman finds his mind cringing into stupidity and denial. He stares from one man to another, stares in repeated incredulous darts back to the curved transparency of the hullpod. A kilometer away at most, the City reaches up to the bowl of heaven. If it is not real, nothing is real. If the City is not as palpable as his trembling hand, as the titanium body of the spacecraft, as the soil and rock and magma of the planet they stand on, then all of that too is no more than whimsical illusion. Dr. Johnson kicks his stone. The City has gripped the minds and bowels of four men in a rapture of the ultimate truth it embodies. The holopics say it is not there. And the grotesque filthiness they put in its place is a paralyzing blow to Silverman's fragile, breaking sense of decency. He is plunged once more and without reprieve into the abstract and bestial madness of *Southern Cross*.

At a remove, he hears Kohler's challenge.

"Why didn't the sensors show us this from orbit?" The lay brother's voice has a thwarted, ugly note. That in itself is an appalling thing. Horst Kohler is the most hardheaded of empiricists. Yet some part of this moment's monstrous nausea has transmitted itself to his armored sensibilities.

Wearily, bile in his mouth, Father Silverman finds his seat. "The sensors were fooled by the City's shields, Brother. That's why the computers allowed me down here alone in the first place. The fact of it is, I was astonished to find anything this large and complex."

A rasping, perhaps laughter, works at his throat.

VI

Or to put it another way, they can become alienated from Being, although they have received their being from the letting-be of Being; and having become alienated from Being, they let themselves slip back from fuller being to less being, and toward nothing. This in turn frustrates the letting-be of Being, for the beings that Being has let be fail to fulfill their potentialities for being, and slip back from them.

Dr. John Macquarie,
Principles of Christian Theology

> *In meditation on invisible things . . .
> consider that my soul is imprisoned
> in this corruptible body, and my
> whole self in this vale of misery, as
> it were in exile among brute beasts;
> I say my whole self, that is, soul
> and body.*

Imprisoned in a quite literal sense in the closeted sanctuary of the Collegio di San Roberto Bellarmino on the Via de Seminario, launched on the fearsome thirty-day catenary of the Long Retreat which would conclude his novitiate, Thomas, born Raphael, composed his spirit to the mournful contemplation of the First of the Spiritual Exercises of St. Ignatius. If under the waters of baptism he had adopted the name Thomas, on that trembling day six years earlier, it had not been from any transparent impulse of pride. Father Morris Hertz had chided him mildly, surmising that Raphael was placing himself under the particular protection of St. Thomas Aquinas, that prodigious intellect known to his contemporaries as the Ox and to Mother Church as the Angelic Doctor. Raphael had smiled; his devotion was to Thomas the Apostle, the Doubter, the empiricist brought to faith in the risen Redeemer only by the gross insertion of his fingers into the Lord's palpable wounds.

Now that same obdurate hankering for proof, for logic, for a place to stand where his mind as well as soul might own its sense of integrity, that inevitable flaw faced a massive battering which would either anneal its lesions or shatter it. So the Retreat had been designed. Raphael knelt upright, a penitential exercitant embarking on a profound harrowing which had fetched men during nearly half a millennium abruptly up against the hard edge of mystery.

"You must call most strenuously upon every faculty," the Director of the Retreat had urged the novices. He was a stern Japanese, with a lined face. "St. Ignatius stresses the 'three powers of the soul.' The first is memory, which is the storehouse of truth: the life of our Lord and the teachings of the Church. The second is understanding, by which we bring that knowledge fully within heart and mind. And the third is will, our active compliance in that knowledge under the free grace of God.''

Each step presented an abyss, waiting for Raphael's stumbling feet. He forced himself to heed the advice of the author of the Exercises, though his mind revolted: It is not abundance of knowledge that fills and satisfies the soul, so much as the interior understanding and savoring of the truth.

> *Bring to mind the sin of the angels, how they were created in grace, yet, not willing to help themselves by the means of their liberty in the work of paying reverence and obedience to their Creator and Lord, falling into pride, they were changed from grace into malice, and hurled from Heaven to Hell. . . .*

"You may treat the angelic revolt as metaphor," the Director told them blandly. "Scholars tend today to view them as intrusions into the early Hebrew oral teachings, derived by assimilation from the messengers and demiurges of their pagan neighbors."

Instantly Raphael was in trouble. His three years of neo-scholastic philosophy still lay ahead, but he had read sufficient of his non-namesake Aquinas to grasp that, in the hierarchy of being, purely spiritual creatures were a logical order standing between God and humankind. Beyond logic, the indubitable fact of angels was attested by Scriptures common to Jewish and Christian faiths (and Islamic, for that matter). Nor was there anything in the idea of angels remotely offensive to a man with a doctorate in unitive physics. Now that the Jogesh Pati-Abdus Salam scholium was effectively proven, with all spacetime a skein of pre-quarks, or preons, it was plain that immaterial being was precisely as intelligible as the single dimensionless constant of the preonic Planck mass.

No, the difficulty looming like a lion was the nature of sin, the subject of this meditation. For the oldest opinion of the Fathers of the Church insisted that humanity's very genesis lay exactly in those fallen stars, plunging to damnation in the wake of their brilliant leader Lucifer. The doctrine lacked popularity these days, yet by tradition mankind was a kind of surrogate for those first demonic criminals; their places in Heaven—reserved, so to speak, on their behalf and now vacant—were to be made up in the numbers of the elect. Just as the original sin of our proto-parents had at once cursed us and occasioned the coming of God in human form for our salvation, the lapse of the fiends was the "happy fault" which first opened the way to our felicity. Myth, undoubtedly, but myth inspired at the Divine Source.

Raphael stirred minutely, keeping his eyes modestly lowered. Cramp twinged his left leg; he ignored it, seeking fiercely to crystallize his problem. It was this: angels, according to the most profound of metaphysics, were simple in nature, not divisible into parts, unmingled with matter, perceiving and understanding by intuition, seizing essences direct, without the limitations which oblige men to infer principles from sense data and consequences from principles. Their apprehension was nondeductive, free of hypothesis and test, free indeed of time itself. No emotion could blur their reason, nor was reason prey to logical error or inaccuracy.

How, then, could such sublime beings sin? It was madness. It defied precisely that rationality which angels possessed in superabundance. Loyola, in harmony with tradition, indicated pride as the source and nature of angelic revolt. Yet wasn't this ludicrous anthropomorphism?

Better to rule in Hell than serve in Heaven? For an earthly potentate, or an arrogant scientist, no motive was easier to comprehend. Yet the beatitude of Heaven lay centrally in the witness of God's unshielded Face, in subservience to the logic, as it were, of necessity: the triumph of will governed by reason. It was not merely a matter of self-interest, though it was certainly that also, at a crass level; the self-damnation of the fallen host was utterly at odds with their defining essence.

*The sin of Adam and Eve: bring
before the memory how, for that
sin, they did such long penance,
and how much corruption came upon
the human race, so many men being
put on the way to Hell.*

When the Director softly announced the second point of contemplation, Raphael was startled by the degree to which his cassock adhered to his chest and upper arms. He sniffed carefully: his own flesh stank with sweat. Now the novices stood with their arms crossed, while the Director redoubled his advice to treat the point as a praiseworthy metaphor, an archetypal figure which must not occasion scruples of conscience in those for whom original sin was an existential truth rather than a fundamentalist event in history.

Again, Raphael was plunged at once into his struggle with pythons. The Hassidim among whom his father had worked would have been scandalized to hear the words of Torah reinterpreted so unblushingly. Not that the notion of original sin as primal hereditary fault had any place in Raphael's Judaic heritage: it had been with some astonishment that he had found it at the core of his new faith. Of course, Orthodox and Reform rabbinical opinion had long understood that evolution left no role for an historical special creation of proto-parents for the race.

Pinning the problem down as well as he might, Raphael saw it as the relationship between creation, knowledge, will and sin. "Corruption came upon the human race." Yes, men were scarred by a proclivity to sin, to disobedience, to every kind of vice and corruption. It could hardly be due to the limitations inherent in their mode of creation, spirit and matter conjoined, for that would impute blame to the Master of the Universe. Origen Adamantius and other early Christian heretics had proclaimed creation itself evil, a doctrine so perverted that its principal proponent betrayed its source by hacking off his genitals. Still, creation was at root tragic. It groaned in travail.

Raphael was fetched back to the putative sin of the angels. It was the risk of God's creation that unbounded Being, the dynamic Triune force which the Apostle's Creed affirmed as Father, Son and Holy Spirit, would "let be" a prodigious universe teeming with particular beings. Risk, yes, since each of these contingent created beings would then view itself as center and goal, chafing under its dependence on the Source of Being, striving in the heart of its idolatrous consciousness to usurp the rightful position and power of God.

It was, in short, sin against the first of the Ten Commandments. An angel might intuit at some horizon of clarity the primordial Father, the expressive Son and the unitive Spirit as that transcendent dialectic which supported its own secondary existence, and still crave the apotheosis of its individuality. How much more so might human beings tumble into this trap, with each individual consciousness clamoring for supremacy within each skull?

And sustaining that lust for power, Raphael realized, were the multiple impulses printed in DNA, each creature inheriting four billion years of evolutionary strife: the yearning not only for individual survival but for corporate destiny, with its dire counterpart to altruism, a ruthless directive to obliterate all that stood in the path of the extended self.

Raphael blinked. Beads of perspiration crept stingingly from his forehead into the corners of his eyes. Even so, he felt dissociated, adrift. Perhaps he was succeeding with memory and understanding, but the application of this knowledge to an act of will seemed farther away than ever. His stubborn will cried out, in fury, that the arguments he had rehearsed were specious, a tangle of linguistic fallacies adorning a dung heap of savage superstitions, no whit better than the faith he had renounced. Desolation moved on him like the Angel of Death.

'Am ha' aretz,'' he groaned in Hebrew. Ignoramus. He sought the words of the Psalmist. Lord, who shall sojourn in Thy tabernacle? Who shall dwell upon Thy holy mountain? He that walketh uprightly, and worketh righteousness, and speaketh truth in his heart.

> *Consider the particular sin of some*
> *one person who for one mortal sin*
> *has gone to Hell; and many others*
> *without number have been condemned*
> *for fewer sins than I have committed.*

The gravity and malice of a single man's sin. Abruptly, all the opaque walls of abstraction segmenting Raphael's spirit collapsed into dust. An image plunged into his mind and gibbered there: the caricatured hook nose, the grasping outstretched hand, the treacherous kiss. . . .

"No!" he cried, involuntarily, aloud. With a sharp look the Director warned him to control himself. An equally involuntary snigger came from one of the other novices, strained to breaking point by his own fearsome efforts. Raphael hardly noticed them. The image was vile, poisonous, unjust, and frozen into his brain.

Raphael looked at the traitor Judas, the Jew, and saw Reb Silverman, his father.

VII

> *We are driven to conclude that the greatest mistake in human*
> *history was the discovery of truth. It has not made us free,*
> *except from delusions that comforted us, and restraints that*
> *preserved us; it has not made us happy, for truth is not*
> *beautiful, and did not deserve to be so passionately chased. As*
> *we look upon it now we wonder why we hurried so to find it.*
> *For it appears to have taken from us every reason for existing. . . .*
>
> Will Durant

It is as if his life's aspiration has been befouled for the final time, as if now the dream toward which he has striven so long has been plucked away by cruel daylight.

God has departed from the shrine of the City. The veil of the Temple is rent. Silverman is left vacant and drained. That secret core of a man, the emotional nexus half a billion years more ancient than the cortex, tells him that in an instant the universe has changed. No, worse than that: once again, he finds its chimera shattered.

Slumped in his padded seat, he looks at the desecrated shrine and sees a lie.

"Well," Silverman says at last, as if another man speaks through his lips, "we might as well go out and take a look at it. Even if it isn't there."

They conspire in a compact of shocked silence. Kohler quickly slaps a button, shoves the polarizer with its load of delicate instruments through the opening hatch, steps out after it. Onto the springy grass after him go Chan and Walson. Before he follows, Silverman reaches to the panel and sets the refraction field, a habit of caution inlaid on planets more strenuous with hostile life than this one. As the lock hatch hisses shut behind him the field effectuates: the boat vanishes. How comforting, Silverman thinks ironically, testing his bitterness. The real things are invisible and what we are shown does not exist.

But which is it that does not exist? The diabolical statuary, or the numinous City? There is no faintest doubt of the answer.

Without speaking they trudge across the grass, and even in his despair Silverman cannot deny the physical invigoration of the cool fresh breath of morning, sweet through his filter-skin. It is an exquisite world. If and when High Earth repeals its in-turned prohibition on starflight, it is a world which will fill quickly with the voices of men and women and their fearless children.

Behind the Jesuits, a dark swath extends as the pure droplets of dew are brushed away by their protective clothing.

Above them is the City, majestic, buoyant as helium. Gravity drags at their limbs, more forceful than the Monastery's, and their breathing begins to rasp. No doubt remains that this place has been a dwelling for men, or beings like men. The tiers of aching light had their purpose, and their function was their beauty. It is a more clarified purpose than any human technology has ever contrived, outside the intoxicated fantasies of light-drunk moviemakers at the close of the last century's Big Spree.

And in the depths and salt reaches of Silverman's emotional sources, the City's sham is toxin to the very spirit it purports to nourish.

He halts the party near the outskirts of the nearest section. Despite its complexity, the entire edifice seems an integral entity. Silverman turns, indecision in his face.

To Horst Kohler he suggests: "Perhaps you might set up your instruments here. Let's see what we can salvage from this." His indiscretion makes him grit his teeth. He turns to Walson. "Try a few holograms from here and we'll figure out exactly where those disgusting things are." Chan he ignores.

The Chinese priest has been staring with unemotional curiosity at the towers. As though addressed, he swings back and shakes his head.

"Raphael, you're off center." Universal thinkers are blunt and faltering by turn; they have no instinct for the amenities. He cocks his head to one side in a quick, nervous gesture. "This is all alien. We have no grounds for projecting our own values on it. Those statues might have no greater significance than, oh, the hygiene systems in the *Loyola*. Maybe that's what they are—a kind of psychic purgative. The worm in the heart of the rose. Unless," he adds with the faintest touch of sarcasm, "you think it's all a cosmic practical joke."

Silverman shakes his head. That is exactly how he reads it. The City is a napalm grenade wrought by the naked hand of that dark angel in whose literal existence he can no longer believe. It is a lie uttered from the foul mouth of the Father of Lies.

The xenologist makes a series of swift forays through the drying grass to calculated stations, fetching back holograms from each position. He hands Silverman a bundle of windows. In varying perspective they show the same three horrifying objects.

Silverman twists the windows from side to side. They afford only a limited parallax, but he discerns that the statues are set at the vertices of an equilateral triangle. The nearest is perhaps six hundred meters from where they stand; it coexists with a lofty tower soaring above the opalescent curve of the greater portion of the City. He passes back the windows.

"Ride the polarizer up a few hundred meters and develop a full perspective. No instruments."

Father Walson nods keenly. At forty he is culpably boyish, for all the brilliance of his accomplishments. It is evident that to him the City is already merely one more enigma he means to crack.

The gravity cart lifts into the sky, and in its wake a zephyr blows cool past Silverman's cheek.

Kohler is grumbling almost inaudibly at his machines. He glances up, mouth taut with frustration. "It's crazy."

Silverman studies the offending instruments. Kohler points to a bank of log-scaled readouts. "It says here the power output is only marginally higher than background. There isn't enough kick in there to lift a grasshopper off the dirt, and no neutrino flux." He flicks on the integrating display of the field detector. "There's your city." Against the dull red screen, in white depth histograms, the City is as real and measurable as the geophysical reference points. "And here," growls the lay brother, heavy shoulders thrust forward, left hand menacing a third set of meters, "we're informed that there's no mass in the vicinity except us and whatever's at those major loci. Even if the city's nothing but a vast preon field—and how you'd sculpt a thing like that I can't imagine—it should still activate the detectors as mass equivalence."

"Heads it's there," Silverman ventures. "Tails it's not."

"Right." In disgust, the German glowers at his treacherous, fallible instruments.

Silverman shoves both hands into the side pockets of his filter-skin, staring upward in impotent rage. Hatred boils in his belly for the heedless godlings who have left this thing for men to impale themselves on.

The gravity cart drops like a stone, to hover centimeters above the tufted grass. Father Walson, grinning, clambers off it, presses half a dozen crisp line drawings into Silverman's hand. If the Rule did not forbid bodily contact, undoubtedly he would clutch his superior by the arm.

"Father, this is marvelous." The younger priest is flushed, overwhelmed by the elegance of his discovery. "It reminds me of the trophic mounds we found on Rho Ophiuchi II. Those were insects, of course, but I'll show you what I mean. Start here, or right over here, say, and independent horological vectors torque you to *there*." He points to a projection on one of his drawings. "When that's gridded against the windows, it's right at the centroid of the triangle formed by the three statues."

Silverman glances at the drawings in silence, hands them back. Walson cannot disguise his disappointment and hurt at the lack of enthusiasm.

"Go and show this to Father Chan," Silverman grunts. The man's thoughtless ebullience dismays him. "An Eclectic can probably do more with it than I can." He strains for some bone of kindness to throw. "Thank you, Henry. I'm most impressed."

Profoundly troubled, Silverman turns his back on the City and walks away into the rustling grass. At a distance from his companions, he crouches on his haunches and peers through slit lids across the meadow to the long bluff where he'd stood shaken by joy twenty-four hours earlier. The sky above the scarp is a cloudless blue transparency, the cirrus gone, unpolluted, unpeopled by shrieking aircraft.

Slowly he regains his feet. Pain twinges in swollen veins. It is not only the unaccustomed gravity. I'm getting old, he tells himself, and does not smile. I'd thought the time was past for making decisions about the ontology of the universe.

So the City is designed to lead an unwary sophont into its throat. For what purpose? To complete the destruction it began when a man first discovered the blasphemy it embodies? The Jesuit glances toward the others. They are busy about their work. Is he, then, the only one genuinely afflicted by the City's message of annihilation? He puts a cold hand to his face, to the puckered flesh sagging at his jaw. It comes to him that Chan might be correct after all, that he is reading into an alien technology some phantasm conceivable only in a mortally diseased mind.

Calm in the despondency of that thought, he walks back to them.

"It's time someone went in," he announces. "It'd be best if I go in alone. If I'm away more than three hours, I don't want anyone

following me. Take the boat out beyond the screen and report to
Loyola. They'll probably want to send down an extra boat.''

Some part of his chill is communicated to them. In silence they
nod, though Kohler's eye is sour at the idea of a man going
unprotected into the enigma which has baffled his instruments. The
synthesist opens his mouth. At once his brash nerve fails. He drops
his eyes and lets his mouth close again.

"Tell me, Tsung-Dao."

"Uh, well, Father Silverman, I have a first approximation. But
it's a radical analysis, and I'll have to run it four ways through the
full cybersystem before I could say with any precision—"

"Let's hear it."

"Okay." Chad gives him a grateful glance. It means nothing to
Silverman. Habit makes him listen, makes him act when action is
called for. The City's jaws are waiting for him, waiting to devour
him. "Briefly, the culture which constructed this complex was quite
similar to us. I didn't think so at first, but that was an emotional
reaction to those repulsive things in there. Even if the statues are
completely realistic—portraiture, say, instead of gargoyles of the
Hindu variety—the City's builders were orthogenetically not unlike
human beings. But their culture *was* different, in one key technical
respect." Chan hesitates. "That one difference has spectacular
implications. You see, they developed their field theory along a
branching path from ours prior to the invention of tensors."

Kohler makes a vulgar sound. "Speculative poppycock!"

"Please, Horst!" Silverman chides. "What are those implications, Father?"

"Naturally," Chan says, "I can't possibly extrapolate the full
range of technical advances their Weltanschauung might have made
feasible . . . but that structure over there is one of them. On this first
approximation, though, I can tell you one technology they could *not*
have developed, any more than Aristotelean physics could have done
so—and that's faster-than-light preonics. So where are they?"

"Like *Southern Cross,*" Silverman whispers.

"Pardon?"

"Satan," he murmurs, "has no need of that."

"I'm sorry?"

"No matter," Silverman says, unutterably weary.

He looks at the three Jesuits for a moment, and then turns abruptly and walks toward the waiting City.

VIII

The radical remedy lies in the mortification of the four great natural passions: joy, hope, fear and grief. You must seek to deprive these of every satisfaction and leave them as it were in darkness and the void.

St. John of the Cross

In darkness and the void, Father Raphael Silverman drifted weightless on his preonic sled toward the moribund hulk of humanity's first starship.

At his back glared the distant lights of the *Loyola*, but by now they added scarcely more illumination than the massively "starbarreled" firmament. The universe, to his eyes, was shrunken to half size. Two terrible chunks had gone from it. Ahead, he seemed to be moving into a perfectly lightless void sixty degrees in expanse. He took care now, after one appalling moment of vertigo, not to glance behind. There, the cone of pure blackness was a ghastly 120 degrees in extent.

Relative to the galaxy, both immense craft hurtled at the constellation Centaurus with a velocity nearly half that of light, time slowed by rather more than ten percent, the spectrum of those stars which were still visible shifted blue-white forward and reddened aft.

Detector relays from the Monastery shimmered on Silverman's console, still reporting what he had known for days. The fusion power system on *Southern Cross* was functioning, though at a greatly reduced level. Vented gas fractions affirmed a large biomass aboard, easily the equivalent of crew and colonists asleep and awake. The vast magnets, which once constrained a hundred thousand tons of frozen hydrogen fuel, both matter and anti-matter, were slagged into ruin. And that single male voice, with its hair-stirring, melancholy, unintelligible lament, remained all that the starship beamcast on its Earth-aimed maser.

Despite every rational foreboding, joy glowed in Silverman's heart. A presence bold and kingly remained with the defunct craft, a presence which was quite simply the force of human heroism. He had not yet been ordained a priest when *Southern Cross* flared at the moon's orbit like a new star, taking the rekindled hopes of a reprieved world into the oceans of eternity. She had begun as an industrial habitat in a 2:1 resonant Earth orbit, a way station for the manufacture of power satellites during the Oil Wars. With the coming of preon physics, her role was obsoleted. Bursting quarks into preons was suddenly inexpensive, and segregating their recombined products into magnetic repositories of matter and anti-matter reasonably uncomplicated as a problem in engineering.

Something had to be done with the billion-dollar habitat. So she became a starship, driven by the absolute annihilation of mass into radiant energy.

Commissioning the *Southern Cross* had been a conspicuous act of faith by the United Nations, a stunning gesture of optimism aimed at the hearts of the whole world. These are our emissaries: they bear with them all the best the human species has attained, the finest that is in us in our prospects of renewed destiny. Silverman had cheered as full-throatedly as any when that brilliant point of light seared the sky, dropping toward the horizon and the spangled glory of the southern heavens.

"Main core lock is opening," a voice from the Monastery told him. "980 meters to docking."

The lock had refused to respond to their initial robot probes. Someone is watching me, Silverman told himself, feeling cool sweat prickled beneath his EVA suitskin. There was an absence somewhere—

"The man has stopped beamcasting, Father."

"Yes. I still can't see. . . . Lights have come on in the lock. It's still cycling open." Either the craft's processors had been specifically reprogrammed to deal with an approaching and identifiable human figure or an operator on board had adopted manual control. Silverman peered ahead, every instinct and faculty primed. His sled's own guidance systems, of course, were autonomous, informing its passenger of its trajectory and intentions without distracting him with any need for routine executive intervention.

Deepest gray on black, the enormous arc of *Southern Cross* moved steadily to blot out the more dreadful blot of the dopplered cosmos. The priest felt his sinews relax, and smiled. In whatever attitude, the *Cross* didn't look like a cross. Nothing could have been topographically more remote from the cruciform than the squat, lumpy cask whose structure remained that of an O'Neill ''Crystal Palace'' habitat. With her redundant orbital shielding stripped away, and with it several million tons of inertial mass, and her monstrous acceleration bracing, her designer might not have recognized his 20th-century brainchild. To the literal-minded, Silverman thought, it might be more fitting if the two starships had their names transposed. On the other hand, it might escape the pedantic that *Southern Cross* resembled a bust of the Founder wrought by, say, the sardonic hand of a Marcel Duchamp. His smile broadened.

Seeing the bright rectangle of the open lock had revived his spirits. He permitted hope to touch him. A disaster of the first magnitude had smitten the vessel, there was no denying that. Yet intelligence remained alive inside the crippled ship. The multiple star system which had been her goal now hung more than four light-years astern, lost in the deep infrared. We are as far from the Centauri suns as that barren triumvirate is from our sun, the priest told himself. But they have not abandoned themselves totally to despair.

His sled's vector altered marginally, and his velocity vanished back into the fabric of spacetime. With the faintest clink, magnetic docking rods joined their counterparts jutting from the rim of the lock.

''I've arrived. Nobody in sight. Do you want me to wait?''

''There's been no further word from the crew, Father.'' Only once had the eerie dirge from the ship given way to sense, and that had been to insist that only one visitor would be permitted to enter the *Cross*. The Monastery was hardly equipped to mount a boarding party against the will of the incumbents. Silverman heard the clear Latin of Cardinal Madrazo come into his channel. "I doubt that anything will be gained by lingering at this point, Father Silverman. Go with God."

"*Deo gratias,*" said Silverman, releasing his webbing.

As planned, the craft had been rotated two light-years from Earth so that its engines faced the direction of flight. The axial shaft was a cylinder 700 meters long. Its huge docking station was not pressurized, nor was the shaft itself, with its twin maglev buckets capable of zooming like bullets from the dock to the drive engineering sections. This airlock, though, gave directly into a curved corridor leading radially to the first of the twenty contiguous inflated toroids, the tire-shaped habitats which made up the outer shell of the starship.

Silver placed one of several radio repeaters on the inner wall of the airlock. The instruments would maintain his direct link with the *Loyola* despite the massive shielding which otherwise would block his broadcast. Invisibly, the repeater began diffusing its multiplex threads of conducting crystal through the hull. The lock cycled shut. Silverman waited for his radio to come back on line.

Air hissed into the compartment. He declined to shed his suitskin. The absence of rotation on the habitat was alarming, perhaps even more so than the crew's silence. During the one g acceleration which had brought the *Cross* to half the velocity of light no spin was needed: ceilings became temporary floors. But burn had terminated in the first year of flight. Now, in free fall, pseudo-gravity was essential to both physical and mental health. Perhaps spin had been taken off to effect repairs, but that dismal attempt must have been made a decade previously. Who would live in free fall by choice?

A frantic voice told him: "Maintain your suit integrity! Don't go ambient, there's something wrong with the air."

"Okay, I'm fine, still sealed. My gross readouts show normative on pressure, constituents and ionization. What do you have?"

"Protein decomposition products. Something's rotting, Father. It can't be the algae beds."

"Toxicity?"

"We're waiting for the micro-organisms. But even if the air's not poisonous, the stench'd have you puking your guts out." There was a pause. The same voice, thin with self-reproach, added: "Sorry, Father."

Fear spurted in Silverman's blood. Not only are they all dead, he thought numbly, but they have perished within sight of rescue. How long? Days? A week? The coincidence crushed his spirit. Flexing his legs against the slight resistance of the suitskin, the priest launched himself into the narrow corridor and ascended, in a space with only a single polarity of direction, toward the corpses of mankind's first stellar dream.

"They must have been dead for years," a voice rebuked him. "Our analysis suggests that hibernation failed when the crew died, but that one or more individuals survived. Temperature was run down throughout the ship to arrest decay. Our arrival triggered the resuscitation of the man who warned us off. With the *Cross* back to operational status, the remains have begun to putrefy. The shock has almost certainly unhinged him, Father Silverman. We advise caution in your approach."

The first five habitat rings were unbreached but vacant to quick inspection. Silverman passed from one to the next through locks designed to seal rigidly if a ring were ruptured. The sixth torus was not empty. Gigantic translucent jellyfish hung in the air, globes of dead, pale tissue like masses of frog spawn. He battered his way through the extraordinary bubbles of decaying organic matter. At the touch of his hand a globe would tremble, shatter, spill into spherical fragments and glistening streamers. There were no corpses, but his sensors told him that death was everywhere. His mind closed in on itself, awash with dread.

In the next ring, and the one after that, the slimy organic substance was confined by surface tension to vast plastic sheets arrayed on stanchions in labyrinthine three-dimensional tunnels like an Escher paradox. Bulkheads of polyurethane foam had been torn out, equipment unbolted where possible and shoved aside to make room for this surreal handiwork.

It could not have been done in days, or months. The Monastery's analysis was wrong. Clearly, someone had labored for years to construct the maze. Tubes strung across and between the sheets leaked a colorless liquid onto the living culture. It was a kind of hydroponic nurturing apparatus, built in a hurry with no concern for aesthetics or rational planning beyond some incomprehensible urge to get the maximum amount of biotic material into production.

Near the lock giving onto the ninth ring, a hairless man floated upside down. With fantastic agility, he righted himself as Silverman pushed into the new labyrinth. He wore an old-fashioned hard suit with its own oxygen supply. "I know, messy I agree, it's getting a bit beyond me," he said apologetically to the priest, his voice going out through the beamcast to interception by the Monastery's remote sensors and coming back through the repeaters. "It's a good thing someone's here finally to help me. I recycle the tissue every few months, but it does pile up. You're just in time, actually." The tone of lament was quite gone. He stopped speaking and regarded Silverman suspiciously. "You're not a Muslim, are you?"

Sickened with pity, the priest told him: "No. My name is Raphael Silverman. What happ—"

The man's toes touched the deck for an instant and propelled him away like an aerial fish. "A perfidious Jew! Ah, now I see it. Lucifer has his minions. But these little ones are God's."

"I'm not going to hurt you," Silverman said. His tongue and mouth were dry. The Monastery whispered to him: "We have voice-print identification. He's Dr. Martin Herbert Baldwin, one of the four reproduction engineers. Stress Evaluator indicates acute paranoia. His records list Dr. Baldwin as a practicing Catholic, which might facilitate matters."

"Martin, I'm a priest." He put authority into his tone. "A Jesuit. I'm also a physicist. There's nothing to fear."

Baldwin's body convulsed. Before he could tumble, he stilled the motion with one lightning touch to a stanchion. "That's impossible. I'm hallucinating. Say something in Latin."

Horror was building in Silverman. *"Gloria Patri,"* he said, making a slow sign of the cross, *"et Filio, et Spiritu Sancto."*

"Amen," said the biologist, voice trembling. He lifted up his eyes and clasped his gloved hands. "O Lord, thank Thee for this miracle. May Thy work always be done. Now we can get through it in half the time," he explained sunnily to Silverman.

The priest asked, gently: "Is anyone else alive?"

Baldwin laughed uproariously. "I am large, I contain multitudes." With a lurch of mood, he snapped: "Are you blind, your Holiness? These are the generations of Moab. Was it Moab? They're all dead, your Grace. Even the frozen ones. God spared me alone, you see, in His great and bitter mercy. I was working in the shielded stock room when the magnets went. He has placed His miter upon my head for the completion of the universe. The number of the elect shall be one hundred and forty four thousand. I can assure you, we've passed that tally by a long chalk. How terrible was that fall, when one third of the hosts of heaven went unto perdition. And it is left to us to replace their number. Frail mortals, doomed by Adam's curse to damnation unless we are reborn of water and the spirit. If I am to be damned to Hell everlasting for the work of purification I count it a fair exchange, to have brought so many to His glory. Romans 9: iii. Now you must help me with this batch. You know the words, of course. I'll start the water running. We must use a general rite, the bare matter and form, you'd need a bloody microscope and a thousand years to do it on an individual basis."

The madman darted to a jumble of hastily welded taps and altered the flow. Turning his back on Silverman, he faced the glistening sheets of organic culture and raised his right hand in a blessing. *"Ego te baptizo in nomine Patris, et Filii—"*

A frenzy of revulsion and grief swept through Silverman as at last he understood what abomination the engineer had contrived. With a frigid, will-less clarity, he grasped that *Southern Cross* had become the vastest slaughterhouse ever imagined by the human mind. When his paralysis had passed, he moved with clumsy force, tears pouring unchecked, to hold down the demented biologist.

"They're human zygotes. Aren't they?" Silverman wept. "Master of the Universe, why have You permitted this atrocity?"

Baldwin offered no resistance. The two men spun, locked together. One heavy boot swung inadvertently in the restricted space to catch and rip a sagging plastic sheet. Jelly peeled slowly from it in an obscene pale flap.

"Blastulas," the man agreed with some pride. "A hundred billion of them to the square meter. I cloned them from the frozen embryos. Trillions of separate human souls conceived each week and dispatched to the heavenly ranks in a state of grace. They never know sin, poor little things—"

"Shut up!" Silverman shrieked.

Grief and horror possessed him utterly. How long had this holocaust persisted? Years? It was inconceivable. It was diabolical, literally. His hand rebounded from a sheet coated with microscopic cloned human embryos, and he drew it back in a paroxysm of distress.

If a single abortion was the murder of a defenseless infant, how much more unspeakably appalling was this manufacture and destruction of numberless human lives? And the ghastly rationality of it stopped his throat, came near to stopping his heart.

For Baldwin's rite of baptism was theologically sound, efficacious, capable according to doctrine and dogma of ushering these teeming trillions of souls into God's grace and salvation. Human volition had been stolen from them, but they were spared the torments of temptation and mortal sin. When Baldwin sluiced them away, his monstrous murder would dispatch more souls into the Kingdom of Heaven than the instantaneous extermination of all life on Earth.

If the insignia of sanctity was the number of souls one fetched to God during one's span, he thought with a terrible comedy close to insanity, then Dr. Baldwin was overdue for canonization as the premier saint of Mother Church.

It can't be true, Silverman cried within his soul. That cannot be the meaning of it. I repudiate You. If You exist, if You have allowed this, that must be its meaning, and You are indeed from the sitra achra. From the Other Side it is Your Face I see leering. No. This meat is no more than the simulacrum of human flesh. It has never been quickened with spirit. Doctrine and dogma are mistaken. Your universe is a cesspool. You are the Master of Lies, the Father of Dung.

Damned in his own apostasy, Raphael Silverman, S. J., permitted his last hold on consciousness to slip free.

IX

Atta vechartanu mikol ha'amim
Thou hast chosen us from all peoples

Hebrew holy-day prayer

Silverman walks steadily into the City.

Like a compulsive tropism acting at the level of his cells, the imperative tug of its architecture draws him in toward its center.

It is a maze of sensuous delights. If, earlier, its design has seemed monumental, integral, now his perspective discovers fine detail endlessly ornamented, an intoxicating contrast to the barren confines of steel and glass which extend without longing into the grey skies of High Earth. Chan is correct: this is a place meant to be lived in, by beings not utterly different from humanity. Silverman passes through gay forums open to the breeze and galleries spiny as the skeletons of abyssal fish, through alleys crooked and charming as any in a medieval town, crowded with what can only be tiny shops and inns, and bowers meant to be choked with blooms; arcades and cloisters he finds on every side; shadowed snuggeries which tempt him to enter for refreshment; gabled porches and piazzas decorated as lavishly as St.-Maclou in Rouen, drapes of electric flame which do not burn, like autumn leaves burnished by the sun, filigrees of brass and iron and silver and gold and platinum, tenements which stand soothingly apart in their own breathing space, and towers which might contain opera halls or automated factories or power stations or themselves simply be works of civic art; minarets that rise in dappled courtyards and shafts shot with delicate veins like translucent marble.

Silverman comes into the heart of the City.

The loveliness of the place has overwhelmed him. He weeps like a child. Light cascades: it is a vision of the City of God.

And he finds that he is motionless. Here the City has permitted wild grass to grow and blow unhindered. He waits in despair.

The City speaks. It is like joyous thunder, yet it enters his mind with the fragile clarity of a single silver bell. Silverman knows that he is listening to the ones who have left the City behind them.

"Brother: welcome!" says the voice of the City, and in a blinding moment of understanding the Jesuit realizes for the first time in his life, in its assuaging, the height and depth of his arid loneliness. Light enfolds him.

"There was a star," the City says.

—and the poignance of that simplicity has the sweet melancholy of a lover's cry in the room of his absent beloved.

"Look upon our City," the cherubim instruct him. "We have put into its making everything of ourselves, for it was our home and the expression of our being. It is the sun's bright warmth, and sweet air, and food shared amid laughter with friends. It is the glory of discovery always renewed. It is everything we have worshipped: grace and joy and virtue. For this was how we saw ourselves, and the universe which gave us birth.

"But look again, for this also is the City—"

For an instant the campaniles stand brighter against the sky. And then they are gone. All the City is expunged.

Silverman jerks his lids closed against a reeling world. Vertigo brings bile to his throat. Slowly he opens his eyes again, and the malevolent statues glare down on him like demons.

Against the orange slash of the distant bluff, the other Jesuits are small figurines frozen in convulsive astonishment. The priest forces himself to regard the statues, to engage their depravity.

Tsung-Dao Chan has compared the creatures to gargoyles, but that is wide of the mark: there is nothing innately distorted or grotesque in the lean torsos. The builders of the City had been tailless pumas endowed with passion and intelligence: sleek, dark as night, bipedal, powerfully clawed, dexterous and able.

The first effigy depicts callous, brutal murder.

That it shows cats instead of human beings detracts not one atom from its force. Head thrown back on his iron-sinewed neck, the killer crouches over his small defenseless victim, excited to a pitch of cruel pleasure. In one taloned fist his serrated blade seems almost redundant; it sings toward the fallen cub's throat, pent in mid-stroke only by the artisan's eye, lusting without pity for the blood of the innocent. Silverman retches from the nightmare of *Southern Cross*, for the murderer's victim is plainly a child. The statue is an archetypal slaughter of the innocent, the sin above all against Charity, against love.

The Jesuit wrenches his gaze away. The second work strikes equally to his heart. From a clumsy scaffold jerks a gagging, swollen-eyed being, savage claws kicking uselessly for the support he has kicked away, his neck fractured and painfully twisted, the breath choking in his constricted breast. The creature has rejected Hope; he hurtles into oblivion and damnation by his own hand.

The last statue is the most appalling. This third alien commits no immediate crime against his brother, or his own flesh, yet his absolute ruin is scored in the tension of every muscle, the mask of his feline face, the upraised brandished fists. In his overweening arrogance the creature rails against dependence, against limitation, against his creator. His fanatical eyes burn with his own glory. There is no nobility to him: he is Lucifer standing against God, doomed and laughing, sick with a pride which would eat and vomit back the universe.

Silverman hunches into himself, stricken. Unbidden, the Krias Shema prayer from his childhood comes to his lips: "May Michael be at my right hand; Gabriel at my left; before me, Uriel; behind me, Raphael; and above my head the divine presence of God."

If the holograms had been desolating, this direct impact is entirely devastating. And yet the builders of the City had known and faced the sin which lay within their species, the sin of Satan and Adam repeated without end on world after world, Silverman guesses now, wasting the promise and freedom of creation. If they have surmounted the outward and compulsive expression of that primal crime, their partial victory has not allowed them to conceal that central corruption from themselves.

Abruptly, the Jesuit understands the source of his bitter pain. Between the horror of the sculpture and the grandeur of their temporal dwelling, there is no hint of immanent transcendence. Where is the Redeemer in this City? They hunger for salvation in every tormented guilty line of their art, as Silverman's own butchered people had cried for the coming of the moshiach, and He has left them comfortless, stumbling in the wilderness.

"This is our self-portrait," the City tells Silverman, compassionately closing away the vile things in lucent banners. "And the Star was manifest to us in the sky, showing the path we must follow."

Bowed in humility, Silverman listens to the assent of the pagan Magi. For him there is no return to rapture: he is beyond all the emotions of joy. He listens, and he accepts. Finally, like his baptismal namesake, Thomas, shown a sign, he accepts.

"So we are leaving our world," the voice says. "We are embarked on a pilgrimage which perhaps only our farthest descendants will see completed. But we are going, for He has shown us His truth, and directed us to the world of His incarnation. We leave our City in gift to you, brother wayfarer, in memory of our youth, as a compass to any who have not yet received the gift of His envoy."

Even without the star-drive they have gone, Silverman tells himself again and again. They have cast themselves trustingly into an Exodus two thousand years in the going and hardly begun. His eyes burn with tears. He looks at the sky, at the stars beyond the bright sky, to the boundless dark desert where a race of men follow the Star of Bethlehem to their journey's end.

"It is our glory," whispers the City, "that He has chosen us to follow His Sign—for we are the least of His children."

Raphael Silverman is oblivious to the City's splendor. He sees in imagination only the dust-pitted ships, and the beings who will come like great pumas to High Earth, or its successor, to find their God murdered and risen from the impotent clutch of the sitra achra, the Other Side.

"We will be waiting for you," Silverman cries aloud, to the City, the stars, to his alien kin. It is a promise he makes them. "We will be waiting."

Lest Levitation
Come Upon Us

Suzette Haden Elgin

Suzette Haden Elgin's reputation is based on a relatively small body of work, published since 1969, most notably her Coyote Jones series and the more recent Ozark Trilogy. She has also won a strong following among feminists, not for any shrill polemics in her work but for the best and most substantial of reasons: her female characters in particular are presented as strong and memorable people.

One of those characters, a lady named Valeria Carterhasty Cantrell, lives in the story that follows. You might know her—and as the title suggests, if you're not careful, you might be her.

If it had been only her own circumstances, her own convenience, only her own *self* to be considered, Valeria thought she might in fact have been able to manage. There would have been adjustments and accommodations, but she was a woman; and, accustomed as all women are to adjustments and accommodations, she would have coped somehow. If nothing else, she could have let a tale be leaked, one bit of trivia at a time . . . little note cards in a spidery hand with weak excuses on them, and the word going round of a chronic disease. Nothing fatal, and nothing ugly; but something that would have made coming by to see her a chore to avoid, while at the same time explaining why she was never seen in public anymore. And pretty soon she would have been forgotten, one of those enigmatic and eccentric Southern ladies with a decomposing corpse to protect in the cupboard . . . the teenager who delivered her paper, and the elderly man who could still be hired to deliver groceries if the order was kept to just a bag or two, they would have set things down on her front porch and made hasty tracks. For fear of what they might see behind Valeria Elizabeth Carterhasty's spotless white curtains.

But it was *not* like that, as she was no longer a Carterhasty, nor could she consider her own self. She was much-married, mother of three, wife to Julian B. Cantrell, up-and-coming attorney-at-law, and consideration of self was far down the list of her priorities, somewhere below keeping the flea collars up to date on the requisite dog and pair of Siamese cats. Clearly, she was going to have to think of some way to deal with this inexplicable affliction an unknown deity had seen fit to visit upon her.

That Julian had been furious the first time it happened seemed to her entirely reasonable; after all, a lawyer does not maintain a practice at $100,000 a year and support a family without maintaining a certain image. The elegant home, with the redwood deck. The pleasant wife with the knack for noncontroversial conversation. The matched set of well-groomed and well-behaved children, each with a hobby that might in time become a profession. Daryl, with his microscope and his white mice. Philip, with the ranks of labeled shoeboxes each containing an electronic something-or-other, and the lust for a personal computer—even without a printer—that Julian sternly refused to satisfy. "When you have earned and saved half the money for it, I'll match that with the other half, young man." That was Julian's way. And Charlotte. With Charlotte it was ballet. Charlotte had not really wanted to take up ballet . . . had wanted to go into baton-twirling, actually . . . but when it was explained to her that there would be a problem making that fit into Daddy's image, she had sighed, and exchanged glances with her mother, and gone dutifully into the ballet classes as requested. Whether she ever took out the wooden baton with the gold dust and the red tassel and the cheap silver cord, won at a carnival and put away in her closet, Valeria did not know and was careful not to ask.

They had been at the Far Corner, she and Julian and a Mr. and Mrs. Tabbitt from Memphis, right between the cocktails and the trip to the salad bar, and Valeria had known Julian was satisfied by the way things were going. He'd leaned back a little in his chair, and the tension in his hands that came from trying to quit smoking had relaxed a bit. The light was dim enough to make everyone look attractive, but not so dark you couldn't see what you were eating, and the Muzak was doing "Rhapsody in Blue," when it happened. Mr. Tabbitt . . . Wayne? . . . she thought he had been a Wayne . . . had leaned forward and peered at her, his eyebrows a little vee of intense interest, and remarked that however she achieved the effect it was surely very becoming. And when she'd asked what effect, he had said that he was talking about the way she glowed.

"Glow? Do I?" Valeria had turned to Julian and pointed out how nice it was of Mr. Tabbitt to pay her the compliment, and found him staring at her too, and all the relaxation replaced by the kind of tight-strung attention he paid to juries he wasn't sure of yet.

"It must be the light in here," he'd said slowly.

"Must be," agreed the Tabbitts, especially Mrs. Tabbitt, whose name Valeria could no longer remember.

"It would have to be," Julian added. "I wonder how they do it? They should make a fortune at it."

Valeria sat there, fiddling with her glass, wondering; and the murmurs from behind their table began to work their way through to her conscious attention. And about that time the rose petals started falling, and that was really the last straw. Julian was a patient man ordinarily, for the stress that he was under, but he took her out of there as fast as if she'd thrown up on the table, and the Tabbitts not only didn't give him their malpractice suit to handle, they were practically at a full run by the time they reached the parking lot.

Julian's main concern, after the loss of the Tabbitts, had been for the publicity.

"How the hell are we going to keep it out of the papers?" he had demanded, handing her brusquely into their Mercedes in a way that made her elbow ache and coming very close to slamming the door on her white silk skirt. She only just managed to snatch it free in the nick of time.

"Keep what out of the papers, Julian?"

"Oh, come *on*, Valeria!"

"Sweetheart, if you don't look at the road once in a while I don't see how you can drive—it can't be a good idea."

"Well, damn it, Valeria, just look at yourself! Go on—*look* at you!"

She had held her arms out in front of her, obediently, and sure enough, she did glow. Not just the rosy glow of health, or the metaphorical glow that came from the right sort of cosmetics and a good hairdresser. You could have read a newspaper by her.

"My goodness," she said. "How embarrassing for you . . . I'm sorry, Julian."

"Yeah." Julian swerved viciously around a dog that wasn't bothering anybody. "Your goodness. What the bloody hell is going on with you, anyway?"

Well, she didn't know, so far as that went. What it reminded her of more than anything else was one of those white plastic statues of

Gentle Jesus, Meek and Mild, that came for $6.98 from a radio station that broadcast all night long from the very depths of Texas. The statue, according to the preacher hawking it, not only glowed in the dark with the light of *Truth* and the light of Sal*vat*ion and the ever*last*ing light—provided you put the batteries in, presumably—it also could be made to revolve slowly on its stand. Valeria was grateful that she was not revolving, either slowly or in any other manner. But the glow was really in very bad taste. It was not soft, it was *bright,* and it was the same shade of gold as the stuff glued to the top of her daughter's carnival baton. And it spread out from her skin to a distance of a good two inches or so.

Tacky, thought Valeria, and brushed off a rose petal that Julian had missed while he was hustling her out of the restaurant.

"My dear," she said, genuinely concerned because she could see that he was, "you don't need to worry about the papers. Really."

"I don't, eh? I suppose you think people are *used* to going out for a quiet dinner in an expensive restaurant and seeing the woman at the next table light up like a damned Christmas tree, not to mention having rose petals rain down on her from the ceiling. For God's *sake,* Valeria . . . I mean, the people who go to the Far Corner are reasonably sophisticated, but they won't have seen *that* number before."

"Julian."

"What, Valeria? What?"

"It won't be in the papers," she said.

"The hell it won't."

"It *won't,*" she insisted.

"One reason why not, Valeria—just one!"

"Because, when people see something like that, they won't admit it. Not to each other, not to themselves . . . not to the papers. By the time they've all finished eating they'll be convinced they didn't see anything at all, or they'll think it was a stunt for my birthday with the waiters throwing roses at me or something. I assure you."

"You think so?"

"Julian, if any of those people were to suddenly look up and see an angel, twenty feet tall and with a wingspread like a 747, you know what they'd say? 'Biggest damned bird I ever saw,' that's what they'd say. And then they'd order another strawberry daiquiri.''

"You really think—"

"I really do, dear heart. There's absolutely nothing for you to worry about. Even the Whatsits—"

"Tabbitts. They were a damned good *case*, Valeria."

"Even the Tabbitts . . . they won't be three blocks away before they've convinced themselves they didn't see anything either."

She saw the tightness go out of his shoulders. She patted his hand, and waited.

When they pulled into the driveway he finally asked her, tentatively, if she could—maybe—explain it.

"No, Julian," she said calmly, "I'm afraid I can't. But I'm sure it won't happen again."

"Like those stories you read about it raining frogs."

"Something like that."

Valeria was quite wrong. It happened over and over again. The children didn't appreciate rose petals in their breakfast pancakes when it happened while she was cooking. Julian set out for her logically the reasons why, since he differed from almost every other American husband by not snoring, it was unfair and unreasonable for her to keep him awake by glowing at him in the dark. Her protests that she had no control over it at all, and no warning either, didn't help matters, and Julian suggested to her that she stay home as much as possible until they could work something out.

She *was* at home when the cookies thing occurred. It was Charlotte's turn to have Camp Fire Girls, and Maryann Whipple's mother was supposed to have sent the refreshments; but, Mrs. Whipple being the sort of woman she was (not Maryann's fault, and a nicer child you couldn't have asked for), there weren't nearly enough cookies to go around. There Valeria was with a plate of cookies—store-bought, too, and not a bakery, either—with only one dozen cookies on it. And seventeen Camp Fire Girls holding glasses of Kool-Aid and looking at her expectantly.

She had just opened her mouth to excuse herself, meaning to go to the kitchen and see what she had in *her* cooky jar, when she heard Charlotte make a funny little strangled noise and cover it with a cough.

"Oh, how nice of your Mama!" the child said—she was one quick thinker, was Charlotte—and before Valeria could say anything to confuse the issue, Charlotte had whisked the plate out of her hands and was passing it around just as bland as you please. If any of the girls had seen the one dozen nondescript lemon supermarket cookies on that plate suddenly become a pyramid of dainty little cakes, each one with its own icing and its own trim of chopped nuts or candied cherries or silver sprinkles, that girl hadn't mentioned it. So far as Valeria knew, it was just herself and Charlotte who had seen it happen, and Mrs. Whipple would never remember that she'd sent a plain white plate and gotten back good china with a narrow rim of gold, and that made two things to be thankful for.

"*Really*, Mother!" Charlotte had said, when the door closed behind the last of the Camp Fire Girls. "*Really!*"

"You handled it very well, dear, I must say," said Valeria. "I was impressed."

"Thank you, Mother," said Charlotte, tight-lipped and fuming, her arms folded over her chest just exactly like Julian.

"Charlotte," Valeria chided, "that's not attractive."

"I don't care if it's attractive or *not!*" wailed Charlotte. "*Really*, Mother—what are you going to do *next? ? ?*"

"Ah," said Valeria solemnly, "if I knew that, I would be much more comfortable about this whole thing. I could plan ahead, you see, if I knew that."

"And you think *that* is attractive?"

Valeria raised her eyebrows, thinking that Charlotte had more than a touch of the Cantrell temper from her father's father's side, and that puberty was going to be a storm-tossed sea for the child, but she said nothing. She only looked, until the girl's eyes dropped and a high flush spread over her cheeks.

"I'm sorry, Mother," said Charlotte. "That was sassing, and it was uncalled for. I know you don't do it on purpose."

"I surely don't," Valeria answered.

"Can you stop, do you think? I mean, that's not sass, Mama, it's just that I want to know. Do you think you can?"

Valeria sighed.

"I think it will stop of itself," she said slowly. "The way everybody around a town sees UFO's or hears mysterious thumps or something for a week or two . . . and then it just stops. Provided you don't pay a lot of attention to it."

"And if it doesn't stop?"

"Well! If it doesn't stop, then I will have to get some sort of help, naturally. We must wait and see."

She stayed home more and more that summer, and Julian went so far as to let the word get out that the doctor thought she might be just a touch anemic and ought to stay in bed a good deal. But there were times when she really did have to go out, and no way to avoid it. When your next-door neighbor is in labor, and there's not a single soul around to take her to the hospital, and her husband's away in Atlanta on business and her parents clear off in California . . . might as well be on the moon as be in California . . . ! Well. Valeria had yet to see the day when she would send a woman off to the maternity ward in a taxi, always supposing they could have gotten a taxi, which was not anything you could have counted on. Before it was over she was to wish fervently that she had called an ambulance, or delivered the baby herself (which would have been no great shucks, though the mere suggestion had nearly sent the mother into hysterics); but at the time, her duty had been as clear to her as the freckles over the bridge of her nose. And she had bundled up Carol Sue and the suitcase and headed straight for Skyway Memorial without giving it one more minute's thought—as would any other woman, under similar circumstances.

That time it did get in the papers. Never mind what people might have thought they did or didn't see. The traffic helicopter that was doing the feature for the six o'clock news about the tangled mess at the intersection by the defense plant got pictures that had nothing to do with subjective impressions. There was the Mercedes, on the six o'clock news, and her, Valeria Carterhasty Cantrell, at the wheel, rising into the air every time there was a little bit of a knot in the traffic and just wafting right over it to the next empty space before settling sedately back into the row of cars and their flabbergasted drivers.

It got them to the hospital in record time, and the inconvenient glow got them past the Admitting Office without one word about insurance *or* money, which had to be a first, but if it didn't mark the baby it would be a miracle. And nobody was speaking to Valeria. Not her husband, not her children, not Carol Sue, not Carol Sue's husband (back from Atlanta) . . . Carol Sue's parents, flying in in great haste from California, had been threatening to sue until they learned that Julian was an attorney.

Julian once more had a good deal to say about last straws. Not divorce, of course; Cantrells did not divorce. Divorce, furthermore, would do nothing for his carefully made plans to move one day into the Governor's Mansion. It could be added that he was truly fond of Valeria, and aware that she could not be easily replaced.

Valeria, who appreciated both his concern for her and his concern about her, came to the rueful conclusion that it was not going to just go away of itself as she had hoped, like a spree of UFO sightings. She would, she told Julian, do something about the problem.

"The problem."

She did not like the way he was looking at her; it had overtones of *naming* the problem, perhaps *defining* the problem. Valeria did not think that would be in Julian's best interests.

"This afternoon," she said quickly. "I'll see to it."

"How? What?"

"But right now, Julian, you are late for the Jaycees Luncheon. That Municipal Center thing."

"God, I forgot all about it!"

"Well, you'd better go, dear, hadn't you?"

"I'm not sure I have the guts."

"I beg your pardon, Julian?"

"I am going to hear one hell of a lot about what they saw on the six o'clock news, Valeria. And the ten o'clock news. *This* time, it's

a horse of a different color. Television cameras do not imagine they
see . . . what they saw.''

''Mmmmm.''

''Valeria?''

''Julian,'' she said, tapping her lower lip with her finger, ''I
suggest that if they bring it up—which would be extraordinarily rude
of them, I must say—you tell them that we are bringing suit against
Mercedes for one million dollars. And another couple of million on
behalf of Carol Sue and her baby.''

Julian stared at her, and she could have sworn there was a flash of
admiration in his eyes.

''I never would have thought of that, darling,'' he said, grabbing
his briefcase.

He wouldn't have, either. Valeria had explained to Charlotte, on
the single occasion when the child insisted on knowing what was the
matter with men, anyway, that they lacked motherwit; and that this
was an inherent deficiency that could not be held against them.

''I don't see why not,'' Charlotte fretted. ''They could learn . . . they
learn law stuff and medical stuff and how to blow up the whole
world, don't they?''

''Not the same thing at all.''

''What's motherwit?''

''Motherwit is what makes you notice the messes men get themselves into, Charlotte Rose. And what gives you sense enough not to
let on you notice.''

''And to clean up the messes after them.''

''Precisely. And we will never mention this again.''

''Can I tell Judette McElroad? We've been best friends going on
three years this March.''

''No.''

''Not even Judette? Mama!''

''Not even Judette. It's up to Judette's mother to tell her.''

''Like the Curse.''

''We do not say 'the Curse,' Charlotte. It's tacky.''

As was this situation.

*   *   *

"Can you just give me a simple description of your problem?" the priest had asked her, no doubt wondering what a nice Methodist lady like herself was doing in a place like his, crucifixes on the wall and candles flickering in niches, and him with his long black gown.

She had tried, beginning with the disastrous dinner that had lost Julian the Tabbitts case and going straight on to the end, with the trip to the hospital and the Mercedes.

He looked at her, when she paused, in precisely the way she had expected him to look, and she knew he had not watched the news. He looked at her dubiously, for which she could in no way blame him. And then the look in his eyes changed abruptly, and his fingers flickered through the sign of the cross, mutter-mutter-mutter, and she assumed she must have begun doing something convincing. Glowing. Rotating. Levitating. Whatever.

"—and the Holy Spirit. Amen," said the priest. Adding, "Oh dear. Oh dear me."

"Why, Father?" asked Valeria, as reasonably as she could after the dreary recital of her humiliations, and feeling as if she had a bit part in one of those Italian movies about devout peasants with flocks of goats. "It seems to me that *I* am the one who should be saying 'oh dear.'"

The priest, to her astonishment, lowered his head to his hands and gripped it fiercely, all ten fingers buried deep in the thick black curls of his hair, and he moaned. Moaned!

"Father?"

Valeria waited, and then tried again.

"Father!"

From the depths of his hands came a muffled "Please allow me to compose myself" and some mumbling about not having believed it even if the call *did* come from the Bishop, but now he'd seen it with his own eyes, and "Please forgive me," and then he was at last looking at her. Or perhaps through her. Beads of sweat on his upper lip and forehead, and a bit shocky-looking, but no longer in a state of collapse.

He cleared his throat twice, and folded his hands, and said, "Mrs. Cantrell, I fear I am in over my head."

"As if I needed an ophthalmologist and you were an oculist."

"An excellent analogy, dear lady."

"Nevertheless," said Valeria, "we could *discuss* this. It is, in some sense of the word, your field . . . and you are the expert, isn't that right?"

"A most inadequate expert, I'm afraid."

"That's twice now you've said you were afraid. You have nothing to be afraid of."

He shook his head vehemently—he did have beautiful curls!—and crossed himself again.

"Oh my, oh my," he said. "You're wrong there, Mrs. Cantrell."

"In what way?"

"Either you are a visitation of the Dear Lord, in which case I have good reason to be afraid—I was never in the presence of a living saint before, you see, and I don't have the remotest idea how to behave. Or you are a visitation of the Evil One, in which case I have good reason to be terrified right out of my cassock, if you'll pardon a feeble joke."

"Is that possible?"

"Is what possible?"

"That all this might be the Devil's doing," said Valeria. "It never occurred to me, but it would surely simplify things."

His jaw dropped, and then he shut his mouth in a way that made his teeth click.

"I don't see it, I'm afraid . . . there, I've said it again. But I *am* afraid. And I don't know why you would prefer the workings of the Devil to the workings of the Almighty."

"Because," Valeria pointed out, "if I am bewitched, or possessed, or whatever the label is, there's a cure for that. You just haul out your exorcism kit and fix me up, and I can go home to my family and tell them life is normal once again. I would much prefer that, Father, to the other thing."

"Tell me again," he said flatly.

"All of it?"

"All of it. This time I will be able to listen more carefully, since I know what's coming. Please don't leave out anything, not the smallest detail."

She told him again, feeling bored and hopeless, while he steepled his fingers and peered at her over them and, every now and again, made a soft noise like a half dozen bees.

"Mrs. Cantrell," he asked when she got to the end of it again, "have you always been a devout woman?"

"Never," she said promptly.

"Never!"

"Never. I'm a Methodist. I went to Sunday School when I was a child because my parents made me go, and I go to church now because my husband's law practice would suffer if I didn't—and I make my children go for the same reason. I suppose my mother made *me* go for the sake of my father's medical practice, come to think of it."

"Do you pray?"

"Of my own accord, you mean?"

"Yes."

"Father Genora—if there is a God, a matter on which I'm no authority—I would certainly have better taste and better manners than to think that He or She was interested in the kind of things I have to pray about. Can you imagine a God that would be interested in my profound hope that my daughter won't have to wear braces on her teeth? Can you imagine a God that would be concerned about that rash I get when Julian tries a different aftershave lotion. . . . Father, I don't think for one moment that God doesn't respect my ability to manage my own affairs. And I have an equivalent respect for God's ability to run the celestial mechanics, so to speak."

"You don't want to be any trouble to Him," said the priest gently.

"Or Her. As the case may be."

The priest winced visibly, but Valeria did not apologize.

"My dear child," said the priest, "there really isn't any question about it. I don't think there has been any question, from the beginning. I don't *understand* it—but then I don't understand Job, either, or Judas, or Biafra. My Bishop would have my head on a platter if he heard me say this, but I would be a coward if I didn't—my dear child, you are . . . for some utterly unfathomable divine reason . . . a saint. Not a *certified* saint; for that you have to be dead. But a saint all the same.''

"Father Genora, couldn't you be mistaken? I think the Devil version is far more likely, now you've brought it up. The Devil's not nearly so choosy, as I understand it.''

"If you were possessed,'' said the priest firmly, ''you could not look me in the eye and talk of . . . the Almighty the way you have. You wear the armor of holy innocence, and I can only say that in this situation I wish *I* did.''

Valeria drew a long breath, and asked: "And do you have something in your procedures manual for that? You can cast out devils in the name of God—can you cast out angels, or whatever it is I've caught?''

He shook his head, and his fingers seemed to be searching in his cassock for someplace to hide.

"You must try to understand,'' he told her. "The Church cannot even imagine such a thing as wishing to be . . . unsainted.''

"Well, that's absurd. It's a terrible nuisance.''

"I imagine it must be. The masses have always loved the saints, and their families have always hated them. Nobody wants to *live* with one . . . some of them have done the most repulsive, stomach-turning, not to mention outright demented things. But if God picks you to be a saint, my child, the Church is assuredly not going to presume to question His choice. Do you see what I mean?''

Valeria was thinking hard. Here she was, with her marriage falling apart, and her children turning against her, and Julian's entire future on the line, and all this holy man could do was make excuses.

"Father Genora, what if you were to say the exorcism service backwards? Do you suppose . . . oh dear. Father, I apologize. I did *not* realize it would upset you so much—it's an entirely empirical question, you know. Put a car in forward, it goes forward; put it in reverse, it goes backward. Do an exorcism, you undevil the bedeviled; do an *anti*-exorcism, you might unsaint the besainted. But I can see that you wouldn't care to try that, so I'll have to manage on my own, won't I?''

The priest was pale and shuddering, but he managed to ask her how she intended to proceed. Valeria thought it best to be gentle with him.

"Father," she said, "you'll be far better off if you don't know."

"Mrs. *Cantrell!* How do you suppose that I am to live with my conscience, if I let you just walk out of here like this? A saint comes to me, to *me*, for spiritual counsel; and all I can do is mumble and sweat. You must give me an opportunity to discuss this, to see if there is not some solution, to. . . ."

She did not really like to cut him off in mid-stream, having learned long ago that a man frustrated in that way would tend to take it out on somebody else at the first opportunity, but she was tired. Tired, and disgusted; after all, she had not asked for this. She had *not* gone about doing good, trying to entice the birds and the squirrels and the butterflies to light upon her person, healing the sick and the maimed, praying and preaching. She had been going about her business, *minding* her own business, and not bothering anybody, and then to have this happen—it was a bit much. And this priest, this holy tinkerer who appeared not to know one end of a religious question from another, was a great disappointment to her. It just went to show how limited her experience had been.

"Father," she said carefully, "sainthood is something you get into by not sinning enough. I intend to go home and *sin* until I have become too wicked to be a saint. If you want to help me, you might save me some time by explaining to me what the *worst* sin is—that one against the Holy Ghost. I could start with that and skip some of the minor infringements."

There he went again. Oh dearing. Oh dear me-ing. It was more than she could bear, and to avoid beginning her career as a sinner by the wanton murder of a man of God, she simply left him nattering and went home. She was late in any case, and Julian did not like for her to be late.

*   *   *

Valeria believed in *system*. Flounder about, doing things at random, and you got nowhere. She began, therefore, with the Ten Commandments, although she was not quite willing to go through them in order.

The one about having no other gods was easy enough. Valeria went down to an import shop where she was accustomed to getting those paper lanterns you put in the garden to help people wander around outside at parties without breaking their necks. She bought a Buddha, a Kwan-Yin, an Indian deity with far more arms than any god ought to need, a very badly done Venus, and something the clerk swore was a statue of Isis—if she was mistaken it didn't really matter, it was sure to be some minor god or other. That made *five* forbidden gods, all of them graven images (or cast images, which ought to be equally wicked, given the Almighty's own knowledge of how things had changed since Moses and that calf), and she set them all up in her sewing room, locked the door, and bowed down to each and every one of the five in turn. While she was at it, getting two commandments with one stone, so to speak, she took the Lord's name in vain repeatedly, feeling that the Lord had it coming anyway.

Sunday, instead of going to church with the rest of the family, she hemmed a whole set of curtains, carting them into the sewing room where she could sit surrounded by her heathen images and getting up every now and then to bow to each one of them. And on the off chance that the sabbath day mentioned in Exodus was Saturday instead of Sunday, she spent a Saturday in there, too, taking the hems out and putting them back in again despite the fact that they'd been done perfectly in the first place. When she found that she'd spotted one of the panels with blood, sticking her finger with a pin, she turned her face up to the heavens and said aloud: "God damn it. God damn it all the way to hell and back."

When Charlotte knocked on the door to find out if she was ever coming out to fix lunch, Valeria took a deep breath and said "Fix it yourself, God damn it!"

"Mother!"

"You heard me," said Valeria. "Now, God damn it, do what I told you. I'm very, very busy."

Next came dishonoring . . . no, failing to honor was all that was required, thank goodness . . . failing to honor her father and her mother. She took care of that and worked false witness into it at the same time, telling Julian's mother on the telephone that he wasn't home when he was standing right behind her. Valeria had never lied to Mother Cantrell before, and didn't enjoy doing it now, but putting things off wasn't going to help.

"No, Mother Cantrell," she went on, "I don't know when he'll be back. He didn't say. You know how Julian is, he does as he pleases, goes where he pleases, and shows up when the spirit moves him. God damn it."

Lies, all of it. Julian wouldn't have gone around the block without giving Valeria an exact schedule, and if he'd turned any one of that block's four corners later than promised, he would have stopped to call her and let her know.

Moving right along, she tried coveting. She coveted everything she could get at. She put her back into it and coveted an awful phony waterfall in Carol Sue's yard, along with the phony boulders that made its basin, and she hoped she was making a good impression.

Stealing was a nuisance, but she did it; she stole a girdle from Macy's, ostentatiously parading it through the store inside her blouse, and throwing it into a Salvation Army pickup box on the way home when nobody so much as questioned her about it. Killing was easier; she got an assortment of spray cans and killed everything that crawled or flew within the reach of her narrow stream of noxious chemical death. She stepped viciously on spiders she would ordinarily have carried carefully out to the rosebushes. And she reminded herself that each and every time she showered, each and every time she brushed her teeth, she slaughtered tens of millions of innocent bacteria and assorted bystanders. In the long run, it must count up.

Thinking that *combined* sins were more efficient, she went to see her father and his new wife, lied to the wife about her father's age, stole a crystal vase of her mother's, stunned both father and bride with her incessant string of "God damns," and resolutely flushed down the toilet a tropical fish that any fool except her father could have seen was swimming at that bizarre angle because it was sick and in pain. As the fish gurgled out of sight, Valeria said, "Thank you, holy Isis."

By the end of her first week as a dedicated sinner, Valeria felt fouled from the gut out and wondered how the habitual sinner stood it, not to mention all the *time* it took. But it wasn't working. It seemed to her that the more she sinned, the more brightly she glowed and the worse the rose petals falling about her stank, and when Julian moved to the bed in the guest room she did not blame him one bit. In his place, she would have moved even sooner.

Somehow, Valeria had thought she would surely be excused from the last of the proscribed activities, but it clearly was not to be. Like Job, or Aristotle, or somebody, she was going to have to drink her nasty potion to its last dregs. And that meant adultery. It was not an interesting sin, but she could not think of anything wickeder, and the complicated arrangements it involved made it possible to drag in a number of associated sins in the false witness line along with it. She did it twice, with two separate willing strangers; and then to top it off she did it with a few of the husbands in the neighborhood. Afterward, she understood why so many of the women she knew were so cross and so vicious, and she treated them with special tenderness. She had had no idea what they had been putting up with, or how lucky she was to have Julian competently sharing her bed—or at least visiting it.

And that didn't work, either. She'd run through the whole list, much of it dozens of times, and things were no better. Putting in tulip bulbs, and trying to keep her mind on doing that properly, Valeria fretted and wept and impatiently brushed away a herd of butterflies that insisted on settling around her, and swore terrible oaths.

"I will be *damned*," she cried desperately in the general direction of the heavenly parapets, waving her trowel, "I will be damned if I will murder a human being just for Your satisfaction! I warn You, You will go too far, do You hear me? You hear me down here? I am *blas*pheming, damn it! Praise Isis! Praise Zeus! Praise Satan, for that matter!"

And when the pure white dove came out of the puffy cloud above her and flew down to circle over her head, Valeria lay down in the ditch she had dug for her flowers, heedless of the carefully worked-in manure, and wept in desperate earnest. And the burden of her complaint was: "My God, my God—what will it take to get You to forsake me?"

It was Maryann Whipple's mother, of all unlikely people, who finally solved her problem. Nobody would call Ruby Whipple a saint, that was for sure and for certain. A trollop, perhaps, a liar and a thief and an awesomely poor excuse for a mother *or* a daughter— but never a saint. Valeria, forsaken by everyone she loved and tormented by a god whose attentions she had never sought but could not now get rid of, went to Ruby Whipple and told her the whole story. Valeria was long past caring if Ruby believed her or not and Ruby, monumentally fortified with straight Scotch at ten o'clock of a Tuesday morning, was in no condition to doubt anything.

"Shoot, honey," said Ruby, leaning back on the pillows her couch was piled with and knocking half a dozen onto the floor, "you haven't been sinning at all."

"I have!" Valeria was furious. "I have been sinning *so* hard—"

"Yeah, yeah," scoffed Ruby. "Sure you have. Honey, I am a Baptist minister's daughter, and I know whereof I speak, and I am here to tell you that you can't sin for *shit*."

"Nonsense!"

"Nonsense, my rosy butt," Ruby said. "You tell me *why* you're racing around like a chicken with its head cut off, lying and stealing and cussing and hopping in and out of bed with anything that can get it up and plenty that can't! Not to mention bowing to Isis and Kwan-Yin and hemming drapes on both Saturdays and Sundays!"

Ruby lay back and laughed fit to burst, spilling Scotch down her front, and Valeria's heart ached for Maryann Whipple.

"Every one of those things," she said firmly, "every last one that you find so funny, is supposed to be a sin. Every single one has a special commandment all its own forbidding it. You *can't* say I haven't sinned."

"Valeria . . . tell me *why*. You haven't been doing it because it was fun, have you?"

"Fun?" Valeria moaned as the priest had moaned. "I have never in my life done anything so tiresome and so boring as all these sins. Fun!"

"Then why?"

"Because Julian and the children are entitled to a normal wife and mother and a normal ordinary wholesome life, that's why, and I am determined that they shall have them!"

"Uh-huh," said Ruby emphatically. "That's the problem, sweet thing. You sin for the sake of those you love, you lay down your soul for your friend. Valeria, that doesn't *count*. You've been wasting your time, child."

"It's not fair!"

"No, it's not," agreed Ruby Whipple, "but then, nothing is." And she passed out cold on the couch.

Well, even a saint has limits to her patience, and Valeria came to the end of hers that day. She could see what Ruby meant, and was fervently grateful that she'd listened to Ruby before she took the next step she had been contemplating. True, old Mr. Hackwood would have been released from his misery, lying there with all those tubes and monitors and lights and buzzers in a strange place he hated, with nothing but his agony for company. True, his poor wife, not really well herself, would have been released from the seemingly endless burden of watching him die by fractions of inches and hearing him plead for release around the clock; Adam Hackwood no longer knew that the woman who'd shared his life for over fifty years was in the room, but he hadn't stopped believing that there was a Jesus somewhere who would step in and set things to rights if you only asked Him often enough and nicely enough. True, the nurses on the floor where Mr. Hackwood was would have had more time to spend with other patients who were *not* dying, and would have had to spend less time comforting the ones in the rooms nearby his who had a tendency to weep at what they heard from their "terminal" colleague. True, if the Bible were to be believed, Adam

Hackwood would have traded a hard bed, with a stiff rubber sheet and every invention of misery a fecund modern medical science could provide, for residence in Paradise and nothing more uncomfortable to do but learn to tolerate the brightness of the Almighty's shining face and the duty of praising Him everlastingly. All true.

Well, let it be true. All of it. She, Valeria, was *not going to do it*. Let them all suffer, let them writhe and bleed and wail; she was going to grit her teeth and let it pass her by, because nothing she had done so far had helped one bit and nothing she had in mind along the same lines impressed her as having any greater potential for releasing her from *her* misery.

She hadn't the heart to go back and torment the priest further, but she knew what she needed now, and she thought she could manage. She needed a way to work within the system, instead of against it. She needed to break a rule that the High-and-Mighty would have no choice but to pay attention to. No more Mrs. Nice Lady, no sir . . . not *this* saint! Valeria set her teeth and headed for the theology section of the University library. And it turned out that the books on fornication and adultery and murder and all their repulsive ilk weren't even *in* the theology section; if you wanted to read those, you had to go to the social science shelves, or Family Studies. No doubt Ruby Whipple could have told her that.

She learned a lot in the theology stacks. She learned that women were the gateway to Hell. She learned that despite claiming that what they had seen and experienced could not possibly be expressed in words, the mystics went right on and expressed it at extraordinary length. She learned that the Vatican had curious problems, and that it was possible to commit a crime called "fishing in Papal waters." She learned vast amounts about things that not only did not interest her but clearly had not interested those who wrote about them, and it became obvious to her that if all theology were written in Latin it would be no great loss. Her frustration grew, but she did not let that distract her from her task, and would have been ashamed to do so; she was literate, and she had been a Carterhasty, and nobody was going to tell her that she couldn't get to the bottom of this.

And there came the day when she found what she was looking for.

Lying and murder and other-gods-before-me and stealing and working your tail off on the sabbath...those, she discovered to her amazement , were piddly little sinlets hardly worth mentioning. Those were such everyday common garden variety in the way of sinning that it was no wonder Ruby Whipple had laughed, and Valeria flushed along the delicate ridge of her cheekbones, remembering. The place to find out about sins was not in the Bible, it was in the books that mortal men had written *about* the Bible, and it was there that Valeria learned the name of the sin that would get you smacked no matter how well you might be doing otherwise.

"Hallelujah!" she said, right out loud and no reverence intended.

Who would have ever guessed that the Sin of Sins would not be something interesting like infant cannibalism, but simply *pride?* She shook her head, overwhelmed.

Pride. Pride! That was the one that wouldn't be tolerated and, from what Valeria read, it was a source of real difficulty for anybody fool enough to go out for sainthood, since the more good and pure and holy you were, the more likely you were to tumble into the pit of being proud of your own goodness. People might watch Valeria lie and cheat and fornicate (horrible prospect!) and learn nothing at all from that; the Almighty could afford to ignore that, what with everybody and his housecat doing it right and left all the day and all the night long. But pride, now! If Valeria were allowed to get away with pride—even to *seem* to get away with pride, especially now that they were trying to get her to go on television talk shows—that would set a precedent the Almighty wouldn't dare overlook.

Valeria slammed the book shut, chuckling to herself, and went straight home to call up the television pests and say she'd be delighted to appear on their fool show. Julian roared and swore she'd ruin him, and the children all threatened to run away, but Valeria was not to be budged.

"You just wait and see," she told them. "I know what I'm doing."

"You do not!" snapped Charlotte. "You absolutely do not."

"This time I do," said Valeria.

"Valeria, if you go on that television show and millions of people all over the country get a long look at your little bag of tricks—"

"Julian Cantrell," she said, thin-lipped and sounding almost snappish, "I said I know what I'm doing, and I do. Now, I don't want to hear any more about it, not one word. You just go on about your business, and I'll go on about mine. Daryl, I'm going to need your help."

"My help?" Daryl was bewildered.

"I need you to go shopping with me," she told him.

"Mother—"

"Valeria—"

"*Mother*—" That was Charlotte.

"Daryl will know where we should go," Valeria insisted, "he's the right age." And Julian threw up his arms in despair and went off to work.

"All right, Mother," sighed Daryl. "I don't understand, but then I haven't understood any of this yet. Sure, I'll go with you . . . what are we going after?"

"Bumper stickers," she said. "And those little round buttons with the pins on the back that make a hole in your clothes when you wear them. And maybe a T-shirt, though I'd rather not."

"Oh, I see," said Daryl.

"Well, I don't," Philip muttered, and Charlotte declared that her mother had gone over the hill at last and should be restrained instead of taken shopping, which obliged Valeria to explain the difference between joking and Taking Liberties.

"You *will* see," she said comfortingly. "I promise."

She knew she had gotten it right when she appeared on the talk show and nothing happened. They were very nice about it, considering; they explained that they were always getting people who could bend spoons just by staring at them hard at home and in their friendly neighborhood bars but then couldn't do it on television.

"It's the lights," they said. "And the stress. You're not used to all this confusion around you, you know." And they assured her that they firmly and truly did believe that when she wasn't on television she had showers of rose petals falling around her and doves flying over her head and that she glowed not only in the dark but even in daylight.

But they didn't. It was obvious that they didn't. They just felt sorry for her because she'd sat there in front of all those people and nothing had happened. Valeria was encouraged, and she tugged at the button on her lapel to be sure everybody noticed it, and she threw a couple of handfuls of buttons into the audience, and left a stack of her bumper stickers in the studio for anybody who wanted them.

"I'm of the opinion," she said happily, "that it's over. I really think it's all been just . . . an oversight."

And she was right. Valeria Carterhasty Cantrell is a saint no longer. The masses don't even know she exists. She is a mere codicil to a footnote in the obscure histories of religious phenomena. But her *family* adores her.

Daryl has a scholarship to Cornell, and will be going into law as his father hoped he would; he has given his microscope and his white mice to the Boys Club. Philip has just become an Eagle Scout, and he is only thirteen dollars short of the money needed to pay for his half of the computer. Charlotte is dancing in everything she can get permission to dance in and saving every penny to set up a school of baton twirling in Tulsa, Oklahoma, the minute she turns eighteen. All three children refer to Valeria's little episode as, "when Mother was so nervous," and are especially gentle and tender with her lest it happen again.

For their anniversary, Julian gave Valeria a mink jacket and a pair of diamond earrings and promised never to change shaving lotions again; for Christmas he is giving her a small vacation cottage on an island off the coast of Maine. He worships her; their marriage is the envy of every couple who knows them; he has not slept anywhere but in her arms (except on business trips) for two years. And last year he made $350,000 *after* taxes.

Valeria, for her part, no longer feels obliged to wear the lapel button, and never was forced to buy the T-shirt or go on to the sky-writing that she had saved as a backup if her first plan failed her. But she keeps the bumper sticker, and when it gets faded she has a new one made to replace it. Valeria does not intend to take any chances.

She doesn't drive the Mercedes anymore; she drives her own car. (After all, putting the bumper sticker on Julian's Mercedes would have been a bit much to ask of him.) It's the bright red sports car—with the shiny wheels and the ooga-horn and the fur upholstery and the quad sound system—that costs more than an average person earns in a year or so.

It's the car you see on the freeway with Valeria at the wheel, driving along flat on the ground like everybody else, tangled up in the traffic jams like any other sinner.

It's the car with the bumper sticker that reads, in giant Gothic letters:

HELLO THERE! I AM A HOLY BLESSED SAINT! FOLLOW ME!

The Rose of Knock

Alan Ryan

Visitations and visions, stigmata and conversions are all part of the popular notion of what the religious experience is or can lead to. But visitations are not limited to angels or saints, and visions do not always give us an insight into heaven; nor are stigmata necessarily holy, or conversions limited to one accepting a holy doctrine. Popular belief aside, the lyrical is very often attuned to the dark, and few romantics care to remember that Hawthorne's perfect rose was growing outside a prison.

Alan Ryan temporarily shifts gears here to the short story, of which he has published over two dozen in the major magazines and anthologies of the sf and dark fantasy fields. He is also the author of the well-received thriller, Panther!, *and brings his admirable skills to the upcoming dark fantasy novels,* The Kill, *and* The Dead of Winter.

My job be keeping the dirt.

I've done it for years now, and my father done it afore me and his father afore him and so on and so on. It's good work, keeping the dirt, healthy and clean, you know, and outdoors. There's much to be said for outdoors work. Much indeed.

And good dirt it is too, and never mind what some be saying. They be making jokes about Mayo—"Mayo, God help us!" they be saying and laughing fit to burst—but Mayo is fine country, the best, God's own country, and the dirt be the finest in all Ireland. And it be my job to be keeping it. And so I does.

The best Mayo land of all, for my money, is the land hereabouts, all the lovely rolling hills round about the shrine at Knock. Oh, it's fine, it truly is, this land of ours. And well it might be, as if Our Lady and her suffering Son had planned it all that way from the beginning, as no doubt, come to think, they did. Me, I'd take it for a fact. No better place could Our Blessed Mother have come by for a visit than the hills of Knock, County Mayo, and the shrine sits today in the very place she touched.

And the flowers. I keeps the flowers too, of course, the roses, oh, the roses, and every other kind of flower a soul could be wanting. But the roses is best, full and strong, scented enough to make you dizzy, they are, and the color as rich as a strong man's blood. The thorns, of course, is wicked, and that's only as it should be. A thing as lovely and sacred as the roses has the right to be protecting itself, no argument about that. There's some that say it's the thorns as does it, pricking at prying, thieving fingers and drawing blood from them and so feeding the blood to the flowers and that's where they get their color. But, me, I'm keeping my own counsel on that one for now. All I does is keep the dirt, and my lips is sealed for the rest of it.

*   *   *

Well, the story I'm telling you is about the shrine itself, the shrine of Our Lady, and it starts at the time the Pope himself come for a visit. It was a grand time, it was, that time, what with the crowds and the holidays and himself up there on that big altar built special for the occasion. A fine Mass it was, and a fine talk he give, and everyone there said they'd never seen a finer. Of course, the ground took something of a beating and a wearing down, thousands of feet tramping all over the hills, but it was a fine time and it's not every day in the year that the Pope himself comes by for to say the Mass. When it was all said and done, and the Pope gone on from here to America, I got the dirt back into shape very smart, and there was no lack of willing hands to help with the work.

So the Pope says his Mass and moves on. But before he goes, he tells the local bigwigs and the priests at the shrine how much he loves the people of Ireland. And he gives over a token for all to remember him by and, don't you know, it's a rose, this lovely rose, full the size of our own here at Knock, and it's gold, or gold-covered or whatever the term they use. A golden rose, same as our own right here, right down to the wicked thorns and all. And so of course they be telling him how they'll treasure it and all of us in Knock and Mayo and how we'll be making a special place for to be showing it off proper the way it deserves. And so they done it, built this special little shrine sort-of thing, with a special glass case inside for the rose and hours posted when you could come inside to see it and the tour buses with the Americans is coming thick and fast ever since, I can tell you that for sure.

And the rose sits there, all shiny and grand behind the glass in its case, and a few years go by, the way they will, day in, day out, nothing much changing. And then along comes some thieving good-for-nothings and steals it, steals it right out of the shrine.

It hardly needs saying that the first thought everyone had was that it was the dirty Protestants from the north that done it. They'll steal anything, was the general thought, spoil anything, kill anything, and you'd best be locking your doors of a night and not be answering to strangers. Why, the rose'd be the perfect target, don't you see, for them to be stealing, who do they hate more than the Pope, and wasn't it the Pope himself that give us the rose! Many's the argument and the anger that foamed higher than the froth on a good-sized pint in the locals for weeks after the affair.

But it wasn't the Protestants that done it, though, truth to tell, I wouldn't put it past them. Oh, no. It weren't them at all.

I know.

I know who done it.

I seen them with my own two eyes when they first come to the shrine. I seen them when they was hanging about, looking things over, so to say, and planning out how they'd do it. And I seen them when they done it and, God knows, I seen them after.

They were two young fellows, nothing special to notice about them at all, and they come driving into the village one afternoon as easy as you please. There I am, working the dirt, as usual, by the side of the road just on the way into Knock, and they bring the car over beside me and come to a stop. It's an old car, nothing much to be remembering about it, but I see that they've come onto the grass by the road, and the ground being still soft and wet from the morning's rain, them tires is going to be leaving terrible deep tracks in the dirt. But they're strangers and maybe don't know any better, so I says nothing and the two of them get out and come walking towards me.

They're pleasant-looking fellows, I'll give them that, and they're clean-shaven and dressed a cut above the average. They could be university fellows, I says to myself, not thinking much of anything. So I straighten up from the dirt where I'm working and lay the tools down and push back my cap and straighten my jacket and the two of them come on walking towards me.

"Morning," says the one.

By which I knew they weren't country boys and had been sleeping in late half the day.

"Afternoon," I says.

The two of them smiled, as nice as you please.

"Is this the road for Knock?" says the one that spoke before.

"You're in it," says I.

"Well, then," says the one that does the talking, only now he doesn't know what to be saying. The other one hangs back a little and keeps looking off across the field.

"Well, then," the talker says again. "Could you recommend a decent place for us to be staying the night? We've been driving all day and we're looking to rest now."

Which I knew already was not the truth, but of course I says nothing. So I told them to look in on Mrs. Boyle, in Church Street, who has rooms to let for bed-and-breakfast, nothing fancy but it's clean and quiet, and right across the way from her was Billy O'Mara's Greentree where they could get a pint and a bite to eat if they were minded. So they said they'd do it and thanked me very polite and still smiling and then turned and went back to the car and in a minute were on their way. I could see in the dirt where the tires had left tracks as deep as your hand and no hope of mending it.

There's roses all around the shrine, great bushes and trellises and the stone walls covered with them, and more flowers lining the pathways and usually, when the weather's fine, I end the day by tending to them. So there I am, coming on to dinner time, looking over the roses and improving them where they'd let a hand get at them through the thorns, and here's these same two fellows strolling in with the last few stragglers of the day to visit the shrine and see the golden rose from the Pope.

They never seen none of me that time for I didn't like the look of them, putting on airs with their clothes and their smiles, and sleeping half the day and speaking other than the truth, so I stayed hid behind the bushes and just watched them going in. They kept with the bunch they went in with, tourists and all, never separating nor drawing attention to themselves, and then come out the other door with the same group. Me, I'm still hid in the bushes, because now my curiosity's aroused.

Well, the two come out and start walking along the path back to the car park, but then they begin to drop back a little behind the others, who of course are the last ones, and me following along on the other side of the bushes where the roses keep me safe but I can see the two of them plain as day.

They're talking quiet to each other and laughing. Then the one I called the talker says something very clever and reaches out to the bushes to pluck at a rose. He gets the rose all right, because he went at it pretty bold, but the rose got him too. That is to say, the thorns stuck him hard and made a good job of it.

"Christ!" he says and snatches his hand back quick, and if I was inclined to smile at the likes of them, I would have.

But the other is laughing his head off. The talker, he just keeps shaking his hand to kill the pain and then he sees the blood welling up from the fingers where the thorns went into him and he starts in to swearing all over again, which of course only made the other one laugh all the harder. They went on like that for a minute, then the talker flings the rose away on the ground and the two of them goes off, and the last I hear or see of them, the talker is saying, "Ah, stuff it, will ya?" and the other be laughing still.

Once they're gone, I come out from the bushes through a little space known to none but me and stand in the path. The two of them are gone and good riddance to them. The only sign of their coming is the rose torn from the bush and lying now in the path.

I picked it up and held it for a minute, thinking about the work of idle hands that destroy the good things of God's earth. But it was dinner time already and I could feel the rumblings, so I went off quick and done what I had to do.

If anyone was watching, which no one was, they might have thought the thorns would get me too. But the plain fact is, the thorns have never touched me. Nor did they ever touch my father afore me. That's the way of it with the roses.

I took this one, which had a couple of branches still attached and a couple of buds that would never see the light of day now they were picked, and went around to the place I use behind the shrine. I dug a little shallow pit with my bare hands, never using tools when I have to do this so as to keep the dirt and roses pure, and lay the rose in it and covered it up and smoothed the place good. Burying the dead roses returns them quicker to the dirt. My father taught me that.

I always bury the roses.

And the thorns have never touched me.

I seen them later at the Greentree and Billy O'Mara himself putting their dinner in front of them. I kept to myself, just talking to the regulars, at the other end of the place, but sort of keeping an eye on the two of them. Still, there was nothing to see, of course, excepting the way the talker kept looking hard at Billy's girl, Noreen, who was bringing out food for some of the others. Now, it's a known fact that Billy's Noreen is not above flinging an eye at a stranger, but it's all in good fun, so to say, and no one really thinks nothing ill of it. But there was Billy himself carrying the food instead of her and I figured he must have sensed something irregular about these two or else he would have let Noreen do the carrying same as always. But they just eat their dinner, nothing fancy, and paid and left a few coins on the bar for Billy and went on their way.

Mostly I give it no thought after that for the rest of the evening, except of course to think about the rose.

Two days went by and I sees nor hide nor hair of them. It happened then that a little errand brought me round to Mrs. Boyle's and I stopped, as a body would, just to pay my respects and take a cup of tea and a slice of bread, and it turns out that the two stayed but the one night and paid up fair and square and went on their way in the morning after breakfast and not a bit of the silverware missing.

It was a week later when they come back.

This time, though, it's not by daylight they come, but in the dark of night. It was only the purest happenstance that I was there to see them at it, as if it were the will of God, though of course it made no difference, me not being one to take on two young fellows by myself, not being as dumb as all that. But it did happen that I'd left a pair of gloves outside, near the roses, when I was working at the end of the day, and then forgot them when a call of nature summoned me off. Later, in the Greentree, I remembered them and, since it was a fine clear night, with the moon shining bright on the hills, I thought to take a stroll, easy like and peaceful, back out to the shrine and retrieve the gloves or they'd be spoiled with the damp from the night. And the long and the short is, I'm making my way along the row of rosebushes towards the rear of the holy shrine itself, and there right ahead of me I hear the voices whispering in the night and of course I know it's them and of course I know what they're after.

Well, I creep up very quiet as close as I can get, with only the roses betwixt me and them, and of course they're planning what I thought. Tools they have, I see, but so cocksure are they of getting away with it easy that they haven't even bothered themselves with masks. It's them, the same two, no mistaking it, and not a bit surprised I am, neither.

Then the next thing I know, they're working on the lock of the door. They must have already disconnected the alarms before I got there, because nary a sound is there to hear except a little scraping of metal and tools at the lock and the rustling of the roses before me. So upset I was, I could have sworn I heard the thorns almost rubbing and clicking together with anguish.

And then they're inside, the thieves, and the door closed tight behind them.

So I wait, crouching behind the rosebushes and listening to the queer little sounds of the night and the shifting of the branches and the leaves. There was nothing for it. If they were set on stealing the Pope's golden rose, then steal it they would and be damned. So I waited right there, feeling the dampness seeping into my bones but waiting it out till the end.

And finally they come out and I see the one, the talker, smiling in the moonlight and the other, looking more solemn and serious, following close behind on his heels, like he was wanting to start running but hadn't got up the nerve in front of his friend. The talker has the rose in his hand, so they must have broken or cut the glass of the case to get it out and now they're on their way, just as easy as you please. Almost on their way, that is, for they haven't got off yet with their little prize. I can see it, shining in the moonlight, that golden rose come all the way from Rome, Italy, and the Pope's own gift to Knock. There it is, shining and glowing like a thing alive, looking almost to tremble with anger in the thieving hand that held it. And of course, it wasn't enough to be stealing it, no, they has to stand there in the moonlight and be gloating over it, proud-like and pleased with themselves and holding the thing up and looking at it all around. Even the nervous one was getting into the spirit of the thing and starting in to smile just a bit around the edges, like now he thought maybe they had actually pulled it off and were getting away with it after all.

But it almost hardly needs saying, that was not to be.

So finally they're done looking at the rose and congratulating themselves with their wit and cleverness. The talker, the one that's holding it, goes to stick it inside his coat and the thorns on the thing cut into him and he yelps like a dog with its tail trod on and drops it in the path. He stands there cursing and nursing at his hand and sucking at the blood on his finger and the other one, the jumpy one, is looking every which way up and down and not knowing what to do. It takes them a minute or two to sort themselves out, with the rose lying there on the ground between them and the both of them leary to touch it. Then the talker bends over and picks it up by the bottom of the stem, very gingerly like, and holds it just with the tips of his fingers, and they start off.

But they're spooked now, see, and eager to be off the pathways, which is, for one thing, lighted up bright by the moon and for another walled in by the rosebushes.

"Here," says the second one all of a sudden and heads towards where I'm crouching, for he thinks he sees an opening, which indeed he does, through the bushes to the other side, desperation being good for the eyesight.

It'll come as no surprise that, the very instant he puts out a cautious arm to widen the opening just enough to slip through, he stumbles on a branch or a root or maybe just on his own fear and worry and lurches backwards and tumbles right into the other fellow, who swears all over again as the rose he's carrying catches at his hand and draws blood anew and then he stumbles forward into the other fellow and it's a pure circus to see the two of them thrashing and crashing about in the rosebushes with the thorns snatching and tearing at their clothes and their faces and hands. It could have played on any music hall stage in the civilized world and brought down the house every time.

Me, I never said nary a word, just waited till it was over, and over I knew it soon would be.

You'd scarce think it could happen, but I've seen it once or twice before this, and my father and grandfather seen it too in their times and I know it myself for a fact. There was the two of them, lying still at last, and the branches of the rosebushes wrapped tight around them, all about their arms which was pinned to their sides and about their throats which was dark with blood and about their faces which was darker. Them thorns was sticking right into them, like they was meaning to burrow inside if they could, buried deep as a sturdy nail in a slab of wood.

I let them lie there for a bit, all tangled in the bushes, giving them time to let the thorns drink deep, as you might say, and slake the thirst that was on them. They don't drink often but they drink full deep when they do. And the dirt, of course, my own precious dirt, was getting its own too, just sopping up what was spilled.

When I thought it was near enough time, and it's a thing to be patient about too, I went off to the place behind the shrine and started in digging. It was a hard job I had of it, what with using my bare hands to get a hole big enough, and it took the wind out of me, I can say that. But it wasn't as hard as you might think, neither, for the earth, rich and thick as it is, come away fair easy for all that. Eager and willing, you might almost say.

When I had the hole dug deep enough, back I went to the bushes and began extricating the two fellows from where they lay tangled. They might have wished for the same ease with the bushes as I had, for the flowers brushed soft against my hands and the scent was rich and sweet in my nose and the thorns, not a one of them, ever touched my skin, no more than they might have touched my father's. All in all, I made a fast job of it and had them out of there quick and dragged them in, the earth not being particular about gracefulness and all such under the circumstances, and scooping the dirt back on top of them, which likewise went real easy and natural and lay flat like it had been to start with.

And of course the rose of Knock lay with them, buried in the earth to return all the quicker to the dirt. It's where it belongs, seeing as how it was picked, so to put it, at least for a while, until it renews itself and grows again and is ready to return, like the other roses of Knock and hereabouts.

That's the way of it. What's taken from the earth goes back to the earth, at least for a time. The roses have their way and their rights and likewise too the dirt itself, and even the thorns, and wasn't it thorns, remember, that drew the blood of Christ Himself. They protect their own, they do, keep themselves whole and safe and in the end they come back even stronger.

One day, when enough time has gone by, I'll dig around among the bones of those thieving fellows and take out the golden rose and put it back in the shrine, and I have no doubt it'll be taken for a miracle. That's none of my concern, though. It's just God's simple work I be doing here and not for me to question: tending the roses, feeding the thorns, keeping the dirt.

Confess the Seasons

Charles L. Grant

Charles L. Grant has been called by Stephen King, "one of the premier fantasists· of our time." He began his writing career in the science fiction area of speculative fiction, appearing in everything from Orbit *to* Analog, *and winning two Nebula Awards along the way. Most of his recent work has been in the realm of dark fantasy and horror, and in that field he has won or been nominated for an armload of World Fantasy Awards. If he never wrote another word—unlikely, since he writes as constantly as other people breathe—his reputation would be secure, for his editorship of the* Shadows *series of horror anthologies, for his Arkham House collection of stories,* Tales from the Nightside, *and for his recent best-selling novel,* The Nestling.*

Not least of his achievements is the creation, in a long series of novels and stories, of the small Connecticut town of Oxrun Station, a town where almost anything can happen. "Confess the Seasons" is set there . . . which means it could happen on your street, too.

So why didn't you tell me?—*a universal form of self-absolution, the refusal to accept unquestionable blame, thus accepting instead lesser guilt with ill grace. Understanding the ploy, however, seldom alters the plea. It is far too easy, as I've discovered far too late, to ignore the signs and the signals and fall back on instinct. And to plead there were only brief moments in my lifetime which allowed me opportunities to know, perhaps to win—had I known what the moments were, and had I believed them—doesn't stay the nightmares, doesn't mitigate the fear.*

But damn, *it isn't fair when you don't know the rules!*

I

"Confess the seasons, Alex," was the somewhat puzzling advice my grandfather gave me each time he left the house on King Street for his daily walk. In striped shirt with white cuffs rolled neatly to the elbow, worn suspenders and narrow brown belt, trousers not quite baggy and shoes not quite scuffed, he would use the porch railing to ease himself down to the flagstone walk, use the air thereafter with fluttering fingers at his sides to keep his balance as he headed for the park, almost like a child using the pavement as a tightrope.

At the time I didn't think I understood what he meant. He certainly wasn't quoting Irish or English poets because he was too toughly Scots to admit Culloden wasn't Armageddon, and I was positive he wasn't commending me to conversations with God because he was not, in those days and in any sense of the word, a churchgoer. That latter observation came much later, however; when I was in grade school, that's precisely what I did believe—that I had to wait until the end of the year and, in a speech good enough to cause envy in Daniel Webster, serve as advocate for the previous twelve months:

Well, Lord, spring screwed up again. You remember that wicked storm we had right after Easter? Well, it flooded out the Cock's Crow and nearly drowned Gail Hancock. And summer wasn't so great either, what with the heat wave lasting most of July, and lightning hitting that hundred-foot hickory behind the Toal mansion, making the tree fall and tearing out half the house's back wall. Autumn was okay, I guess, but the leaves turned too early, and winter was so cold that Chief Stockton told everyone in town he was going to retire after all. So, Lord, what do you say, huh? A few Hail Mary's and fifty-two pretty good Sundays in a row?

It didn't make any difference that I didn't know what a Hail Mary was. I'd only heard it in the movies and from some of my friends, but it sounded right—a punishment not too horrible, not too easy. A pain in the ass as effective as a spanking. When I told Gramp about it, though, he only laughed and kissed my cheek and told me not to worry, he had everything in hand.

Bittersweet days, when I was ten: my father died on the way home from work, of a heart attack that turned the commuter train from New York to Oxrun Station into a personal cortege that had most of the town out to meet it when the stationmaster in Greenwich wired the news ahead. Dad was Gramp's favorite person, and my mother was his favorite daughter; when she seemed unable to handle the blow, when she threatened a slow, painful retreat from the world, Gramp suddenly seemed overburdened. Physically, he was no different: stocky, rounded shoulders, a few inches under six feet, his hair dark grey and thin, and his face not quite full enough to sag into jowls and pouches; but after the funeral, something wasn't the same. I didn't know what it was then; I was too busy trying to understand dying. And by the time I thought I had it pinned down, eight years had gone by.

Gramp turned sixty-five the summer bridging my high school graduation and my leaving for college, and one night we walked through the streets after a late supper. We stayed within the village proper, away from the small estates that spread into the valley beyond the park; even so, the well-kept and large Victorians and Colonials, salt boxes and Cape Cods, were sufficient to give any visitor to this western Connecticut community the correct impression that this was rather more than a middle-class town, and that the money here was generally comfortable and old.

I never questioned it; I'd lived here all my life. Oxrun Station was, simply, Oxrun Station.

So we walked the extra-long blocks, not only because it was pleasant and reassuring, but also because Gramp never drove within the Station's limits. To him, automobiles were for long distances, nothing more, a method of getting from right here to way over there only because there was no better way of doing it.

But that night I didn't mind. I'd just received my diploma, Mom was more like her old self, and I considered myself officially an adult. The air was cool, the foliage emerald rich, and the evening's songbirds were determined to outlast the kids playing in the yards. I was telling him about my plans, how I was going to study my butt off not just to keep my scholarship, but also to unlock every secret in the universe there ever was or ever would be. I would become a famous professor and writer and inspire my students to even greater standards than mine. I would publish fantastic books and be on the Jack Paar show; I would give Mom all the dresses she ever wanted, and Gramp could have a new pair of suspenders.

And it would be fun, all of it, just the way Dad said it was supposed to be.

Gramp didn't laugh. He nodded thoughtfully, flicking a blunt finger at my arm now and then to show he was listening, keeping his left hand in his pocket to jingle the change kept there for emergencies. And when I was done—my tongue worn out and my cheeks cracking from all the grinning—I put an arm around his shoulders and impulsively I hugged him. I'd never done that before. I think it startled him. He blinked slowly and pulled at his nose, scratched at the stray feathers of hair poking around his ears. I don't know what he was thinking, but I know that I, for the longest moment, felt like crying, I was so explosively joyous.

It occurred to me suddenly that I'd be leaving him at summer's end.

It occurred to me less quickly that I didn't want to do it.

"You know," he said as we walked on, the moment passed, his voice deep and slightly rough, "you'll do it, Alexander."

"Yeah," I said, grinning again, while our shadows born of streetlamps skittered away from our heels. "Yeah."

He shook his head. "No, not that, lad. Oh, I think you'll do all right in that place, too. What I mean is . . ." He paused, looked sideways at me, and I caught an expression I'd seen off and on for years—a probing, a measuring, a vague misapprehension.

He never finished. An ambulance howled by, and he turned sharply to watch it, anxiously rubbing the back of his neck. Behind it was a dull red Packard, trailing so closely it nearly touched the ambulance's bumper. He sighed as if something had jolted the air from his lungs, his shoulders sagged, the coins stopped jingling.

"Damn," he whispered. "Damn, I thought they'd wait."

"Gramp?" I reached for his arm. "Hey, Gramp?"

He walked away from me, not hurrying but purposefully, back toward our house, across the street from the hospital. I followed him silently for a while, then began pestering him, practically dancing like a kid at his side to find out what it was I'd learn when I got older. And finally he had enough. He shut me up with a brusque wave, pointed at the house when we reached it, and crossed over to the hospital. When I complained to Mom, she said it was probably another one of his friends stricken, and quoted me Ogden Nash, that "the old men know when an old man dies."

It sounded like sentimental nonsense to me then, but I was forced to acknowledge the possibility of truth when, over the next three weeks, three more of his closest friends passed away. And each time it happened he seemed a little more hunched, as if trying to huddle against a wind only he could feel. He took to muttering to himself, and he grew more solemn, less likely to laugh at what was on TV or at my mother's small jokes; he would peer through the windows before going out, checking the back of the house as well as the front;

and he had dreams, raucous dreams that screeched through the house like a nail down a blackboard. Then he began studying the Bible, Shakespeare, Locke, Hume, and names I'd never heard of. He still didn't go to church, but his walks took him past rectories where he'd talk for hours at a time with any cleric who'd listen, returning home grumbling and ill-tempered, refusing even a quick game of cribbage to pass the time until dinner.

It frightened me even as I grew increasingly excited and nervous about going off to college, because Gramp had always had a hold on the world that appeared unshakeable to me, and now he was losing it.

One afternoon in the middle of August I returned home from the store, brown bags in my arms and my face drenched with perspiration. All I wanted to do was unload the groceries, get a bottle of soda, and head back to my friends. A few steps inside the front door, however, I stopped, hearing voices in the kitchen—Gramp, Mom, and they were arguing. I stood in the living room frowning in nervous disbelief, unable to move, as if the vines in the floral carpet had taken hold of my ankles.

"I don't care," Mom said. "I'll not have you filling his head with such bloody damned nonsense."

A muttering: my grandfather answering.

"You'll *what?*" She was yelling now. I never, but never heard her yell before, and certainly not at her own father. "Like hell you will!"

Another brief answer.

"Because they're old, that's why," she said angrily, close to bitterly. "Old, for god's sake. You can tell yourself anything you want to, but they're old and there's no other reason for their dying. And so help me, if you try to tell Alex anything else, if you tell him this nonsense about talking to God, I'll . . . dammit, if you tell him what you told me. . . ."

She started crying, and I didn't know what to do so I stayed where I was for what seemed like hours, then goaded myself into racing for the kitchen, dumping the bags onto the counter and racing out again. I didn't look at either of them. They said nothing to me at all. And I walked for a long time that night, wondering what in hell was happening to my summer.

The incident was nearly forgotten, however, by the end of the month. I started packing, worrying about grades I hadn't even begun to earn, and generally made a nuisance of myself until, I think, Mom was just as eager as I to see me go. Then, the day before I left, Gramp asked if he could talk with me for a minute. I wasn't in the mood. Jenny Michaelson was waiting for me at the park, and I couldn't see standing her up for some sage advice from an old man who was beginning to define for me the meaning of senility. A look from my mother, however, was all it took to change my mind. So I followed him upstairs to his attic apartment, the place where he'd been staying since the day my grandmother died.

It was a long room and spare, heavy with the scent that belonged only to him—talc and witch hazel, old clothes and old flesh. I sat on the edge of his bed and squirmed impatiently while he shuffled to the curtainless window overlooking the back yard.

"Happens," he said, running a finger around the back of his left ear. I wanted to see his face, but he wouldn't turn around; I wanted him suddenly to tell me he really was Gramp, not some unpleasant gnome who'd taken over his skin.

"Not always this close, not always in the same family, but I suppose it happens." He sighed, a sound like pebbles rattling down sheet metal. "Had a call a few minutes back, Alex. Duncan Michaelson died an hour ago."

I blinked stupidly. Jenny's grandfather, dead? That old man, Gramp's dearest friend, was like an oak tree that spat sap at the weather, ignored thunderbolts and hurricanes, turned up its crown at earthquakes. Nothing but the Second Coming itself could ever finish him off.

I didn't know what to say.

Gramp cleared his throat. "He was standing on his back porch at the time. He saw them, I expect, but he couldn't get to me straightaway. He died. We were supposed to be together, all of us, but. . . ." He shrugged. "One by one. It's not fair sometimes, Alex. They don't play fair, coming at us one by one like that."

"Gramp, listen. . . ."

He turned, and the bright glare behind him shaded his face to black. "I was your age, y'know, lad, when I got the letter. It was a long time traveling to me, from London. M'father, he was *bodach* then, a very old man. Name was *Seóras*, same as me. We was living on *Eilean Sgitheanach* in those days and—"

"Gramp." My hand was out, and trembling. The last time he'd lapsed into Highland Gaelic was the night Gram died and he thought he was back on Skye. "Gramp, the letter?"

A pause, while his hand slipped into his pocket and the change there sounded once, sounded twice. "Yes," he said. "Yes. My dad thought it was a joke, but the man came up to see us, to see *me*, and I never forgot it because I thought him crazy and I still have the letter, and it wasn't until I saw . . . saw them out on the street right here in town that I knew the truth of it, Alex. And I never thought I'd see it in the family. I thought. . . ." He shrugged. "I don't know what I thought. A name would come to me, or a face, and I would know that if I didn't do it, then it would pass to him."

He stepped away from the window, and his face lost its dark shadow. "It happens, though, I suppose. It happens."

"What, Gramp?" I wanted to get out, to get to Jenny. He was frightening me, and eighteen-year-old men are not supposed to be frightened.

His other hand went into his pocket and he straightened his arms, pulling down the trousers and stretching his suspenders. "You'll be a natural leader, laddie, and that's a fact. They'll come round you and you won't know, but you'll be their leader. A general. Like me and the other lads." He puffed one cheek, released the air in spurts of soft sighs. "They didn't believe me at the end, though, except for Duncan, and now he's gone and I'm the only one, you see."

"Gramp," I said, spreading my hands to show him my confusion. "Gramp, honest to god, I don't know what's going on."

He smiled sadly. "Just so you know, laddie. Just so you know."

"For god's sake, know what?"

A long stare, then his gaze darted from ceiling to floor to my own troubled face. "You don't know. You haven't guessed."

I rose, crossed the room and put a hand on his shoulder, a gesture Dad had used on me a hundred times to mark tolerance for incoherence. "Gramp, I'm supposed to be at a picnic ten minutes ago. The guys, we're having a farewell party, y'know? I don't know if I'll ever see these guys again, and today's the last day."

His eyes were blue-pale and watery, and I couldn't look at him for very long.

"I had a chance once, Alexander, and I didn't do it. I didn't give the order. You know your Shakespeare, laddie? 'Bid the soldiers shoot.' I didn't do it. Now Duncan is dead."

"Gramp," I said as he walked over to his dresser, "you're talking crazy, you know that? Shoot who? Who did Mr. Michaelson see today? Who are those guys you said were around?"

He pulled open the top drawer, turned around and showed me the gun. A dark thing, with a dark handle, and I backed away so quickly I nearly tripped myself. He turned it over in his palm, nodding, and while I watched he laid it back inside the drawer, covered it with a handkerchief and closed the drawer again.

"I should have," he said. "I should have, but I wasn't sure."

"Jesus, Gramp!"

He turned to me abruptly and, for a moment, it was the old Gramp, the George Barton who played soft-hearted monopoly with me and my father, who gave me his change when I went to the movies, who on Sunday afternoons before he moved in would show up on the porch with a cake from the bakery, hand it to my mother, wink at me, and leave. It was the old Gramp, the one who wasn't crazy.

"You don't forget me now when you go, laddie. Remember that Gramp did his best."

There was nothing I could say. I wanted to shake him, hug him, instead shook his hand somberly as if I knew exactly what he wanted.

He waited until I reached the door: "Alexander?"

"Yes, Gramp?"

"Confess the seasons."

II

It was maddening. But I was eighteen, and what was I to make of events years apart when there was my life to live? College took most of my time. I wasn't that fine a natural student, and had to work like hell just to hang onto my scholarship. Weekends, then, I studied, returning home only on holidays like Thanksgiving and Christmas. And each time, Gramp would meet me at the door, examine me intently, and disappear into his room. Mom was worried, but I put it off to old age—the callow assessment of a non-thinker who'd left first-year philosophy with a crisis of faith that ended in my having no faith. It was fashionable, besides. And I grew so used to it that in time I never missed God at all.

Two months after graduation I married a woman I thought I loved; by the same token, she thought me more ambitious than I was. She was also disappointed when, three weeks after the ceremony, I was drafted and didn't elect to hightail it to Canada. Twenty-two months in Vietnam, and when I returned I was single again.

It didn't matter.

I didn't want to be living with anyone then, anyway. I'd seen a lot, had seen too much, and all I asked was to be left alone with myself.

And I was: a week after I'd taken a teaching position at Oxrun's Hawksted College, Mom died in her sleep.

Then, in October, I was in the front yard raking and cursing the first fall of leaves when I heard a voice calling. I looked up and over the privet hedge and saw Gramp standing in front of the hospital. He had that damned gun in his hand, and he was shouting, beckoning me frantically with one hand, pointing up the street with the revolver. I threw the rake aside, had taken no more than five or six steps toward the curb when suddenly he screamed. It wasn't the theatrical gurgling of a doddering old fool, but the full-throated bellowing of a man terrorized, a man dying. He jabbed at the air again and, just as I broke into a run, fell face first into the gutter.

Even now I can recall little of the next few days. There was Gramp's head in my lap, interns and nurses trying to crowd me to one side, a few passersby, two men standing in front of our house, a policeman demanding to know what the hell was going on. Then Gramp filled his lungs with air and I thought he was going to scream again. A hand on my shoulder, gently urging me away. Gramp's chest slowly, slowly collapsing. Blue lips parting: "Alex."

"Yes, Gramp, yes, I'm here."

A muttering: "The soldiers, Alexander, the seasons," and nothing more. Nothing more. The suspenders sagged to either side of his ribs; his trousers were suddenly five sizes too large; only his face remained taut, almost trembling.

I took the gun from his hand and slipped it into my shirt; when I rose, my knee brushed against him and the change in his pocket jingled.

A viewing, a wake, a funeral, some friends; alone, completely alone this time, in less than six months all family gone.

I did what most sane men would have done—I buried myself in my work. I wrote articles, gave lectures, started a book on Keats, cleaned the house twice from attic to cellar, spent Christmas and Easter vacations in England, the summer in the Rockies. Alone. Always alone, save for those I met along the way.

Years later, on my thirty-eighth birthday, I received a caller. She was my height, green-eyed, with thick auburn hair, and a soft chin that would probably recede before she was sixty. I was on the porch with some champagne and two friends, Greg Willoughby and Ed Maken. Greg was an Oxrun native like me, returned to practice medicine because he claimed larger towns made him too nervous to sleep; now he was on the porch swing, a stethoscope draped over the crossbeam. He was using it for a punching bag while he recalled with quiet fondness our high school legislator, one of those "men with a future" who'd once seemed destined to move his family to Washington and now was somewhat bewildered that he hadn't found the ambition.

It was twilight, and it was cool, the first bottle already lying empty on its side, the second in Ed's shovel-hands refusing to release its cork. We'd all noticed the woman as she made her way slowly up the block, peering at the houses, a shiny purse held close to her stomach. None of us were really prepared, however, when she suddenly strode right up to the porch and asked for Alex Munro.

I was in the rocker, wearing cut-off jeans and a baggy sweatshirt; my hair was uncombed and curly, my beard eight days old and struggling. Her gaze quite naturally drifted to Ed, who was leaning against the porch post by the top step, and I was grateful for her momentary distraction. It gave me an opportunity to clear some of the fuzziness the wine had nestled around my brain, and to wonder if she was a reporter or free-lancer hunting an interview without calling ahead. Though I hadn't toppled the academic world with any theories I'd devised, I had managed to develop what one newsmagazine coined LitPop, a foul designation I'd not in six years been able to disavow. Neither did I believe the ensuing acclaim all that richly deserved. All I'd done was fumble through my courses until I'd developed a primary and secondary school curriculum whose sole purpose was to avoid killing literature before students reached college, or the age of illiterate consent. Those who used it swore by it, and admittedly it was successful. What followed were guest lectures, tours, a small book, a few TV spots on morning programs, and people like this woman who came up unannounced to unearth my secret, which was simple in the extreme—I loved reading.

"Mr. Munro, my name is Jennifer Crane." She glanced from Ed to Greg, and finally to me when I acknowledged her introduction with a smile and a nod. "I'd like to talk to you for a moment, if you don't mind."

"What paper are you with?" Ed said, straightening, preening.

"None," she said, as if it should have been obvious.

"Ah, an independent."

"No, nothing like that at all."

"Ah."

Greg unfolded himself from the swing, took a last swipe at his stethoscope, and grandly offered Miss Crane his place. "It's time I was heading back to work anyway," he said, taking off his dark-rimmed glasses and cleaning them on a shirttail. "They can't live without me, you know." He saluted us and sprinted across the street.

There was an awkward pause until Ed grunted softly and smoothed his knit tie down over his paunch. Two years younger than I, he was totally bald—by choice, not genetics. He believed what they said about women and bald men.

"Alex, once again, felicitations."

With a flourish he opened the second bottle, pocketed the cork and left the champagne at my side. Then he marched down the steps, down the walk, down the street. He was always marching, and I'd yet to understand why.

"I'm sorry," Jennifer said, hesitating before taking the swing, gesturing vaguely toward the bottle. "I didn't realize—"

I held the wine up in offering and she shook her head. "A birthday," I told her. "I normally ignore these things, but those two enjoy rubbing it in." I grinned. "I'm their laboratory rat, you see. Alex, how does one react to turning thirty-five, thirty-six, thirty-seven? This year it's thirty-eight. They're hoping for some inside information on the magic forty."

She was unmoved by my babbling. "Mr. Munro, my grandfather was Duncan Michaelson."

I gaped in disbelief. Jennifer Crane, née Michaelson, biology wizard, cheerleader, the last I heard working for the Peace Corps in one part of the world after another. I had been hoping to lose my virginity to her my last summer before college.

"You remember." She was smiling shyly now.

"Yes. My god, yes." An elaborate display of the tulip glasses, the bottle, and she was holding champagne before she could demur again. "To reunions, Jenny. Welcome back."

The porch light wasn't quite strong enough to reach the swing's shadows, but I could see her take a sip and touch a finger to her chin as if she'd left a drop there. Then she set the glass on the floor and pulled an envelope out of her purse. When she thrust it toward me I hesitated, took it, still somewhat off balance at seeing her again.

She spoke as I opened it: "My grandfather died twenty years ago. He was a friend of George Barton." I glanced up; her tone seemed suddenly too formal. "Five men in less than two months died that summer. They were all friends of your grandfather." I stiffened, the paper crackling in my hand as I fumbled it out of its envelope. "I didn't know that before. I just knew Poppa shouldn't have died, he had no reason to. It bothered me for a long time, a hell of a long time, but there was nothing I could do about it. Then I sort of forgot until I came back last week to go through my mother's effects. I found that." She pointed at the letter. "Now I'm more confused than ever. I didn't know . . . I didn't know he was crazy. He adored your grandfather, Alex, and I. . . ."

She pushed back in the swing, and the boards creaked, the iron pins complained. I could see she was bothered still, perhaps worse than when it happened. But the accusation I perceived made me sound defensive.

"I take it you want me to read this."

"Please."

A chain of cars sped past, horns blaring, headlamps flashing, flowers on the roofs, streamers rippling back from the hoods. I watched them until the evening swallowed them, leaving behind only the echoes of their noise, their celebration.

I tapped the letter. "Now?"

"I'm leaving tonight. My brother is driving me back to Hartford."

I swallowed an ill-timed question about her marital status—I could see no rings on her fingers—and instead looked pointedly toward the hospital. "My grandfather died right over there," I said. "A massive coronary that dropped him in the gutter. I was holding him when he died."

It was the first time I'd actively thought of that day since it happened. And immediately I did, it all came back, all of it, for no reason at all—from his meaningless advice to the rambling farewell that August before college, from the argument with my mother to his mental disintegration. With all the time between suddenly squeezed out, I was disturbingly aware there was a connection to be found. I didn't like the feeling. I didn't like the way cold crept into my June.

*   *   *

I read Michaelson's letter:

George says we got to do it, and George always knows what he's doing, but I'm not so sure this time. It makes sense, a very bad kind of sense. And I thought he was off his rocker in the beginning because there ain't been a man since Moses, I think, who's seen God close enough to touch. But George says it's true, and when he talks about it I can't help believing him. He's never gone to church all the years I've known him, so when a man starts talking about God that way you have to figure he's on to something, or he's too damned old and he's afraid of dying. I've known George since we was on Skye, and he's never been afraid of anything in his life. Sam thought he was losing his marbles, and Tyrone didn't say anything because he'd follow George into the mouth of Hell blindfolded if George asked him. But Sam is gone now and so is Tyrone, and Willy, and Rob.

I don't know. I believe there's a God out there, like most everyone else, but I'm afraid to believe what George says is going on. And if what he says is true—and they're all dead, every one of them—then we have to kill the right guy before there's more trouble. Or, like George says, before the guy finds out about us and gets us first—like Sam, and Rob, and Tyrone, and Will. That's the way of it, George says. The guy comes around to check up, him and his partner, and there's trouble, and as soon as a few people catch on there's more trouble and the people are gone and the two guys just disappear.

George showed me the letter today, the one he got from the cobbler in London. And the cobbler says he got a letter from a man who'd seen them at Victoria's coronation and knew about them right away. If this is right, and George says it has to be, then there's been people like us all the way back.

And George says we have to shoot him and I don't know why.

I don't know. And George says it has to be soon, real soon, and I don't have anyone to talk to and I don't think I want to do it because it sounds wrong. George says that's the way they want us to think, so we'll be off guard. But it is wrong. It has to be. I can't do it. George, I'm sorry but I can't do it, you'll have to do it alone. I saw them yesterday and they saw me and they knew me. George, I know you're right, but I can't do it.

I can't.

Oh Christ, George, they're standing in the back yard.

The bottom of the last page was torn away.

As I refolded the letter I was aware of the cicada in the elms flanking the porch, the distant insect buzz of a streetlamp, something prowling on the pavement side of the hedge. But the chill had not faded; the letter had underscored Gramp's own madness, had answered a few of those questions I'd thought I'd forgotten.

God. The old man thought he was being stalked by God.

I looked to Jenny (no longer Jennifer, though I couldn't have said why) and I frowned. "Why did you want me to read this? Why are you here?"

Bewilderment shimmered the foundations of her composure. "I loved that old man," she said, "and I was never able to convince myself he was meant to die just then. When I found that letter—"

"You found someone to blame. My grandfather."

She nodded without hesitation, without apology. Then she rose, took the envelope from my hand and gathered the purse to her waist. "I'm sorry, Alex. It was dumb. This was dumb. But when I read it tonight I was so damned angry; and it made me, I don't know, cold. I'm sorry."

She started down the steps, almost stumbling on the last one.

"Jenny?"

She looked over her shoulder.

"Do you really have to go?"

"My brother. . . ."

I pushed out of the rocker. "Can you at least tell me where you'll be?"

She was beyond the reach of the light now, as vague on the walk as she'd been in my memory. I couldn't tell if she was frowning or not. "Why?" she said, "Do you know something? Do you have any idea what he was talking about?"

"No. I don't know. That sounds so much like Gramp before he

died, it's rather frightening almost. Just like you, I hadn't thought about it in a hell of a long time." She seemed unconvinced, and as she hesitated something not quite a chill stroked the back of my neck. "I think I know what the last thing was your grandfather said to you, though."

The voice was disdainful. "Really. I've seen you on TV, you know, but I didn't know part of your act was being a psychic."

I inhaled slowly. "He said, 'Confess the seasons.' "

And even in the shadows I could see her face pale.

III

It happens: an awkward meeting, a flurry of subliminal insights, an equally awkward separation. At the time there is nothing momentous about the occasion, but something lingers tiny and burrlike, a residue of the flashquick emotional confluence you hadn't known was there.

I went inside immediately, puzzling over the snatches of my past wrenched into images I couldn't get hold of long enough to examine. By the time the kettle was boiling, however, and the water poured over the tea, my unease at Duncan Michaelson's last letter had shaded rapidly into unease about Jennifer Crane. Dormant instincts and unfamiliar emotions were sluggish, weak, and I distrusted them instantly; as I sat at the table staring at the wall, pale-skinned daydreams writhed away from the sun. I felt like an idiot for not asking her address, and felt like a fool for even thinking about asking.

I pushed the cup away and went into my study alongside the kitchen. I stared at my desk—a rolltop found in someone's garage sale—and shuffled the papers there, pages of the manuscript for a book I didn't want to write, but probably would have to if I wanted to keep what little fame I'd garnered. None of it, that night, interested me in the least.

I remembered the champagne, fetched it from the porch and sang "Happy Birthday" to myself as I poured it down the drain. I considered calling Greg at the hospital, but he'd only prescribe roses, boxes of candy, poetry, walks in the park, rides in the country. Ed, on the other hand, would have a campaign mapped out before I'd finished speaking. I was inclined to forget the whole thing—the same road inclinations had taken me from the time of my divorce—but several times over the next forty-eight hours I found myself returning to Duncan and Gramp. Even so, I made no progress (if progress was to be made) because Jenny was there too. As she was two weeks later, on the telephone and talking with me for over an hour about everything on earth except the letter, and the madness.

I drove to Hartford and took her to dinner. We spent most of the time in silence, nervous and staring.

A month later, without telling me a thing, she'd taken an apartment on Devon Street and had found a position with a real estate firm, one that handled only the larger homes out beyond the park. It seemed less than the blink of an eye before she was settled in as if she'd never left.

I continued to lecture, to teach, to travel, to write, but whenever I looked up Jenny was there, in person or not. I chided myself often for being too much like Greg, and finally admitted it was beginning to unnerve me. I said as much to Greg late one afternoon at the Chancellor Inn. We were at the bar—he'd just finished his rounds, I'd just finished the book—and I wondered aloud about an impasse I'd reached, a feeling over the past eight or nine months that something was straining to get off its mark, and it was driving me crazy because I couldn't give it a label.

"Jenny," Greg said with a shrug that told me it should have been self-evident. He raised loose fists boxer style before his face and thumbed the side of his nose. "She's got you on the ropes, pal. My prediction is you'll never make it to the end of this round."

"You're nuts, you know that, don't you. I'm too busy for that." I looked away and squinted. "You're nuts."

"So are you, Alex, if you let her go."

He returned to his drink just long enough for me to wonder, then poked my arm and grinned. "Hey, you and Jen want to come over tonight? Alma says you're the worst pinochle player in the world, and she needs a few bucks to send the kids to camp next summer.''

"I'll see," I said stiffly, rather abruptly annoyed at the idea Jenny and I were considered inseparable. "I'll give you a call later."

"Suit yourself, prof."

My turn to shrug, then stare at the bar mirror. Sound faded, sensation died, and I grabbed the bar rail tightly to keep from slipping off the high-backed stool. At the front of the room, near the entrance, two men were just leaving. I only caught them in profile, but I nearly called out to them, and would have done so if I'd only known their names. As I spun around, Greg grabbed my arm.

"Alex, you okay?"

"Yeah, yeah."

He stared at the front door. "What?" The two men stepped outside, the door closed behind them. He scanned the room. "What, Alex?"

He hadn't seen them. They were right there, and he hadn't seen them. "Nothing," I muttered, fishing in my pocket to pay the tab. "Just some guys I thought I knew, that's all."

"What guys?"

"It's all right. They just surprised me."

He relaxed, but not enough to take off his frown. "Oh yeah, that happens to me all the time. You see a zillion people in the hospital, all those sickies walking around with all their relatives, and before you know it you'd swear you were seeing them in Paris or Tokyo, or some four-horse town in Nebraska. Alma says it's because I need glasses."

I smiled absently, excused myself and left. Outside, on Chancellor Avenue, I searched for them through a rising wind filled with dead leaves and cold dust. I trotted to the nearest corner and peered up the side street, ran a few steps with one hand closing my suit jacket over my chest. It was dusk, and the street was empty, the parking lot filled with nothing more than cars. I ran back to Chancellor and up to the next corner. The wind gusted, nearly tripped me, blinded me with my own hair until I realized what I was doing and headed straight for home.

Greg, of course, was right. It had happened to me, too, on a number of occasions. With all the people I'd met in my travels I was bound to run into similar types somewhere, to be bothered with the idea I should know who they are but couldn't bring their names to mind. But I'd never reacted this strongly before.

Or thought I hadn't until I'd turned on all the lights in the living room, and found on the end table beside Gramp's chair (now my chair) a scratch pad with names scribbled on it. I'd been toying with the idea of writing a novel, and the night before had wondered what I would call my characters if I did. The last two on the list were Duncan and George. I picked up the pad and stared at it. Threw it on the chair and stalked over to the fireplace in the back wall. Stared at the fresh logs placed so neatly on the andirons, looked up to the pictures of my parents and Gramp silver-framed on the mantel.

I stepped off the hearth as if I'd been scorched, and coldly informed myself that I was working far too hard, that I was attempting to cling too tightly to my brief moment in the limelight, that I should not be seduced by either glamour or fame or the monies that supported me far better than ever; I should, I lectured myself, forget about the novel, about the tours, and stick to what I enjoyed most—facing my classes and watching them turn from skeptics and despisers to, at the very least, appreciators of what was printed on a page; I should *not* permit fancies to overrule reason.

It was almost nine when I knew it wouldn't work.

It was almost nine-thirty when it entered my head that I was meant to see those men, that nothing was an accident where they were concerned. And that wasn't possible. There was no such order in the world, in my life; I'd long since discarded that notion, could in fact mark the day of its demise from the moment in college I'd decided Browning was wrong, God's not in his heaven, he's not anywhere at all.

Then for no reason at all I recalled the August afternoon I'd overheard Mom ordering Gramp not to tell me he'd been talking with God.

Working too hard, fool; you're working too damned hard!

By ten I was too nervous to stay in the house alone, and too frightened to go outside. Frightened not of those men, but by what I was thinking. I reached for the phone; it was Jenny I called. She came right over, took one look at my face and eased me down onto the couch. Businesslike, then, she brewed us some tea, keeping me silent with a glare and a wave. When she was ready she stood in the middle of the room and looked around critically.

"It's too warm in here."

Before I knew it she'd taken sweaters from the closet and had tossed me one. A moment later we were on the porch swing, the wind vanished, a harvest moon casting shadows where no shadows should have been. She was patient; I was hesitant, and confused, unable to sort through all the images I faced. Especially because I'd decided I wanted to marry her, and I didn't want her thinking I was as crazy as Gramp.

"It was in the army," I said, not looking at her face. "I was in what passed for a small city over there, and I'd just gotten out of the hospital."

"You never told me you were in the hospital."

I shrugged. "It never came up."

"Why?"

I paused. "I'd been shot."

She squeezed my hand for a very long time.

"I was back on night patrol, see, working with some new kid who thought being an MP there was just like working at home. I was trying to tell him we didn't go into alleys, didn't drive beyond the town limits, didn't talk to anyone who wouldn't come into the light. Then we get a call that there's activity at the Circle. See, the streets of this place come together in the center, around this little park. When we got there so had other patrols, and the new kid was out before I'd even stopped the jeep.

"They had what you'd call a tradition or something. There'd been a firefight outside town that night—we could hear it while we were riding around, could see the tracers and stuff once in a while—and the Koreans had brought in three dead Viet Cong, had dumped them in the middle of the park for the Vietnamese to see the next day. It was a way of telling them the Koreans were on the job, and a warning to the Cong to stay the hell out. It never worked, by the way, but they kept doing it just the same.

"Anyway, there were three of them. Two boys and a girl. Young. Very young. In blue pajamas, and you couldn't see where they'd been shot, or stabbed. A bunch of the other MPs were standing around them, joking, poking the bodies, explaining things to the new kids. Then these two sergeants come up with a Polaroid. They started taking pictures. Someone put a cigarette in the girl's mouth, and they stood there with their rifles up and their feet on her chest like they were big game hunters or something. The guys who were taking the pictures, they only took four. One would take one, and then the other. They never smiled. I wouldn't get out of the jeep. Then the sergeants took off, and I was the only one who asked who the hell those jokers were because I knew they didn't belong to my company.

"Nobody knew. Nobody cared. Sometime between then and dawn the dogs who lived in the streets ate most of the girl's face."

I looked to Jenny then, and tried a smile. "I'd seen them before, Jen. This afternoon, when I saw them in the bar, I knew I'd seen them before. It came back, and I knew."

A warm palm caressed my cheek. "Alex—"

"They were the same guys." And I knew it was true. For the first time. I knew it was true. "I'd swear to it, Jenny. They were the same guys. And they were there the day Gramp died in the gutter. And I'll bet they were in the back yard when your grandfather died, too."

"Alex, please."

I wanted to hold her, but I couldn't; I wanted to tell her to tell me how marvelous my memory was, my perception, my presence of mind in the face of losing it, but she didn't; and I wanted to believe that I was, in fact, over-reacting to a simple, commonplace phenomenon I'd experienced before, just as Greg had. But I couldn't.

They were the same two men. Nondescript in every imaginable way, bland and unassuming and the more I thought about it the more terrified I became. Jenny spoke to me, but I had no idea what she was saying, only reaching for the sound of her voice and panicking when, at one point, she stroked my hair and left me, returned years later to speak again until Greg came racing up the steps, Ed lumbering right behind. I was trembling violently, reeling from alternate washes of intense heat and December chills. Ed, who was forever saving me from the rocks of Greg's romanticism, knelt in front of me and soon replaced Jenny's velvet caresses with no-nonsense preachments of his own. He smelled of cigar ash and cologne, not like Gramp at all.

It took an hour, I think, perhaps more, before I could lean back and close my eyes, before the perspiration stopped icing my chest and back, before I could lick my lips and taste moisture there again.

"God!" I said, explosive in my relief. "Jesus, I'm cracking up."

Ed was softly derisive, Greg cheerful, Jenny silent.

"Greg, listen," I said. "Those two guys I saw at the Inn this afternoon, remember?"

Greg lifted a helpless hand. "I didn't see them, Alex."

"You must have!"

He winced. "I didn't, honest."

My hands were clasped tightly in my lap, and I could feel the skin taut over my knuckles. A few more ounces of pressure, I thought, and I could rip through to the bone. My knees trembled, my jaw ached, and a faint mocking ringing began in my right ear until I cut it off with a harsh slap to my temple.

"Alex, you've got to calm down," Ed told me. I know he grabbed my wrists, but I didn't feel a thing.

Like peeling flesh from a raw wound I opened my eyes, and as I looked from one to the other—sitting, kneeling, crouching there in the dark—the terror deepened.

Ed, who had never quite made it up through the political ranks, and who professed not to care because his current position enabled him to remain near his friends, near me; Greg, who had never read Keats and who brought roses home to Alma every Friday just to celebrate the weekend, and who called me nearly every day just to see how I was even if we had talked only a couple of hours before;

and Jennifer, whose brother had brought her to Oxrun Station so she could show me a letter and find blame and absolution for an old man's death.

They didn't belong here, any of them, and here they were. With me.

Just like Gramp said.

There was no air for me to breathe, nothing solid for me to touch.

And there, over there, was Gramp as a young man, reading a letter he didn't understand, and I didn't believe for a minute until decades afterward when he discovered he had shadows who waited until he *knew* before they took form; and Gramp as an old man, believing now and wondering how much like him I was, trying to get me to understand too soon, my god too soon, and dying trying to rectify his error.

True. Not true. I didn't know, couldn't know because it didn't slip over me but came at me, too much at once, and my head began to ache. But to tell them . . . to tell my friends as Gramp had told Duncan and Sam and Tyrone and the others . . . if they believed too. . . .

I chased them away that night, and every night for the next three weeks. I paced through the house, dusting off memories, old photographs, old scars; I walked the streets staring at church steeples, standing on the depot platform and watching the trains retreat into midnight; I scoured the park, the alleys, the cemetery, the woodland; I ate little and I slept less and kept the phone off the hook and never answered the door.

I found that letter of Gramp's, and it was almost the same as Michaelson's: there were two men, and they walked among us like spies behind the lines, and they studied and altered and sometimes created chaos, and there were those among us who would recognize them when we could.

I still didn't know why, and I still didn't know the rules, but it seemed I was expected to shoot the one Gramp called God.

IV

After the first week I lay in bed weeping for my sanity, and my life.

After the second I decided to use what reason I had remaining and deny the possibility.

After the third I wept again, because I had failed—out of a dead man's madness my crisis of faith had been resolved.

I went up to Gramp's room, and I destroyed it. I used a carving knife on his bed, I splintered the dresser and the chest of drawers; I shattered the window and I dragged all his clothes from the closet and burned them in the yard. I hunted through the family albums and tore out his pictures. I cursed my mother for creating in me my grandfather's madness, and I damned my father for leaving me so soon. I didn't eat for four days; I didn't wash or shave or change any of my clothes.

On the fifth day I found myself straining, gasping in the house's musty air and I stumbled out onto the porch, and saw the two men watching.

They were on the pavement, dressed in lightweight business suits; their hair perhaps brown, their eyes perhaps brown, everything a perhaps, nothing definite about them. They watched as I grabbed hold of the post to keep myself on my feet, and in the daylight that obscured them I almost screamed. I was right; it was them. Across the street when Gramp died, in Qui Nhon, in other places I had been in my life. They had been there, wondering, I suppose, if I'd finally come around as they went about their business. They were there, in front of the house, and from the expressions on their faces they knew that afternoon that I knew who they were.

They smiled, and walked away, and I was too weak to chase them.

I fell back inside, kicked the door shut and virtually crawled up the stairs to the bathroom, where I vomited. Then showered. Then shaved. Then dressed and prepared to call my friends. Stood before a mirror and rehearsed my little speech:

"Assume—and I grant you a large assumption here—but let's assume I'm not crazy. Indulge me a moment while I work all this out. And assume for the moment too that I'm neither the first, nor the last. If you can do that for me, then follow this—that the Jews will never have their Messiah nor the Christians their Second Coming nor the others any of their higher planes of existence. They won't, because that Intelligence—which, for want of a better word, I'll call God, and *only* for want of a better word—that Intelligence has never left us at all. He's not up there, nor over there, nor out there; he's here, around us, not insubstantial but very substantial indeed. He walks among us like a goddamned tourist and sparks little armageddons, little miracles, little trials for our faith, though I'm not at all sure he cares about our faith, or even about us. But the worse part is, he's not alone, he's with his partner, a partner I've seen and he doesn't have horns or a tail or a silly red suit. Twins, almost, because there's a balance in the world.

"No one pays them any attention. They're not invisible, they're just not seen. Unless they want to be. Unless they pick on people to see them, and to know. People like me. People like me, who somehow come to understand that there's . . . there's a game to be played. A game that has to be played out whether I keep the ball or not.

"Why me? How the hell should I know? It's a game, one that began at a place we'll call Start, and there have to be players and tag, and right now I'm it. Someone tagged someone who tagged someone who tagged Gramp who tagged me. And I have this horrid, foul feeling I know how to win it and I can't find the words so I can tell you how it's done."

And when I made my little speech, my hands quivering and my stomach jumping and my knees trembling, Ed laughed and Greg wept without tears and Jenny took my hand and didn't say a word. Until I took Gramp's gun from my pocket; then she sobbed.

Ed rose slowly from the couch and jammed his thumbs into his waistcoat pockets, glaring from under that overhanging brow as if I were a political opponent. "So you're right, let's say—and for god's sake, Alex, I'm definitely not saying you are—what are you going to do? You going to walk right up to this, uh, god-fella and plug him in the heart? Is that going to kill him, huh? Or is it going to kill the other guy, the devil?" He stopped and cocked his head, scowled, and his hands became fists that pressed the sides of his neck. "Jesus Christ, will you listen to me? God, Satan. . . ." He stomped over to the sideboard and poured himself a drink.

"Alex," Greg said, a tic in his cheek like the tears he was holding back, "I—don't get me wrong, okay?—but I want you to check in tomorrow, all right? I want to look you over. Christ, with that book and all that work, those trips. . . ." He fell silent and stared at the floor.

I stared at Jenny for her turn and just as quickly turned away. I could see it in the set of her lips, the steady gaze, the even breathing—Jesus, she believed me. She believed me, and I hated her for it. Hated her so much for not trying to save me that I thrust her hands out of mine and walked over to Ed.

"Do me a favor," I said to his back. "You go into your office tomorrow and you look through those publicity files of yours, okay? You check out the crowds, the meetings, and you find the two guys standing off to one side, maybe in the corner, maybe across the street or in the back of the plane. You look, Ed. You look good and hard."

Ed emptied his glass. "You're not going to drag me into this, Alex."

I thought of Duncan Michaelson. "Ed, I'm sorry, but I don't think you have a choice. If you see them, you've no choice at all."

Then I sat beside Greg, grabbed his jaw and wrenched his face around to mine. "The next time you're in the O.R., you look up into the observation seats, at the interns or the visitors in the top row, the ones near the door, the two guys whispering in the corner. The next time there's an accident, check the crowd, near the back."

"Your office, too," I said when he yanked out of my grip. "Look at the photographs in those old magazines on the table."

"Alex—"

"Don't!" I snapped. Then I rose and walked into the hallway, turned at the foot of the stairs and glared back. "You look, and then you call me and tell me you can't find them, goddamnit!"

I went upstairs, closed the door to my room and slumped on the edge of the mattress. I was panting, and perspiration dripped from my chin into my lap. I had no idea where all those words had come from, but I suspected Gramp would know because he'd spoken them himself, maybe even had a little scene just like this one with his own friends—after he'd decided he was crazy after all.

There was a noise, a soft one, and it was a moment before I realized it was me. And realized further that I finally believed.

It was well past midnight when I went downstairs again and saw that I was alone; it was well past dawn when I went outside and began walking the streets, looking, listening, every so often dropping in at a rectory to see a cleric acquaintance of mine, leaving disgruntled after being quoted reams of scripture and philosophical chapter and verse. The verdict was as simple as it was predictable: preposterous, even blasphemous, since all I implied reduced everything to a game. There are no rabbis in the Station, but the one I visited in Harley suggested I'd do better living in Germany in the Thirties.

And the more I was rebuffed, the more righteous I grew, then more sullen, more suspicious of smiles and how-are-you's. But nowhere, not in Shakespeare or Locke or Hume or the Bible or the Koran could I find a clue as to how the game was played.

Jenny did.

The first thing she said when she came back was, "I love you, Alexander Munro, don't ever forget that," and we spent too short a time in an embrace that seemed created just for us and our need. Then she pushed me gently down onto the couch, curled into my side and rested her head on my shoulder.

"You said it was a kind of game, and I think it is," she whispered after several false starts, a few deep breaths to provide her with an anchor. "I don't know the rules, either, but I wonder if it didn't begin with a form of liberation."

"Liberation? Whose, God's?" I was skeptical without thinking about it, as if I were Ed and appalled at the prospect of having to humor a loved one's madness.

"Yes," she said. "Yes. It's a part of it, don't you see? The deliberate exposure of a target, a taunting that's just as much physical as it is intellectual. It's a vile test of faith; if you believe, you have to shoot, and the game—or one phase of it—is over."

"That makes a hell of a long game."

"He has a hell of a long time."

I didn't quite understand; yet by the same token, if I did, I'd know more than I could possibly deal with. But I thought about everything Gramp had told me, and had *tried* to tell me all those years. And it may well fit, though the sense of it seemed overwhelming to obscurity.

Jenny watched me, excited now, unable to keep still. She unfolded her legs and paced across the room, turned so abruptly her skirt kept moving, swishing, hissing, rocking as she stared. "Think of it, Alex. You're someone chosen to do this thing; not everyone can. God—this Intelligence we're talking about—God has your life in his hands, and you have his in yours."

"That's ridiculous. God can't die or he wouldn't be God, right?"

"Of course he can't, but he can move on. He can change. He's not static, you know. And this thing is a way of making the inevitability of change more . . . more—"

"Fun?" I shook my head. Then I laughed, loudly and long, and it was an ugly sound there in the room, in the house, in the village where I was born. When Jenny took a step toward me, uncertain, a little nervous, I stopped her with a grin. "Jen, listen to what you're saying, huh? Listen! Hey, Lord, whose turn is it, huh? Who's got the dice? Do I take a card? Jesus. . . ."

And I knew then what a fool I'd made of myself, what an ass I'd become to be ridden until I'd regained my sanity. Jenny had done it. In her way she'd known what it would take that I didn't know myself, what she'd have to do to jar me back to the world. Suddenly, as if shown a whole picture of which I'd only seen a small segment before I understood—my life until now had been one of gratification, and loneliness. When my marriage collapsed I retreated into my head; when Mom and Gramp died so close together, I went even further. I had been walking through my days as an observer, not a participant. I made love mechanically, I spouted romance by rote, and developed an acting ability that fooled everyone but my three closest friends. I was, in sum, less a human being than an automaton, a self-made man in almost the literal sense.

My mania, and my fear, were gone.

"Alex?" She put a hand to her chin. "Alex?"

"It's all right," I said at the end of a sigh. "It's fine." And when I told her what I had just seen, down there on the moors that passed for my brain, she closed her eyes slowly. I smiled because I thought she was pleased, but the smile became little more than a parting of my lips; when her eyes opened again, she picked up her sweater and left the house without a word. Like an idiot, I didn't go after her. I was too astounded. And I was bewildered. My god, I thought; after all that, and after a release that illuminated corners of my soul I didn't know I had, she left me. Just like that.

But I didn't let it bother me—for the moment, at least. I had things to do. I had new lectures to write for the fall term, new slants on old subjects. I would be what I'd promised Gramp I would strive for, and I would lead, not in his sense but my own. I could feel it in every joint and every pore, and it was exciting; and when Ed called me a week later I laughed his name as if we were brothers too long parted.

"I looked," was all he said.

"What?" So cured was I, I'd nearly forgotten the disease.

"Those pictures."

"Oh, that." I laughed again.

A pause. "Alex, are you all right?"

"I am so fine you wouldn't believe it, Ed." I grinned at the receiver, at the wall, at my shoes. "So?"

"So you were right. You're a bastard, Alex. God *damn* you." And he rang off.

I wasn't right. Of course not. I'd planted a suggestion, and out of hundreds of photos his publicist kept for him, Ed had discovered a few that conveniently suited the hypothesis. If I'd said look for a one-legged man with red hair and blue eyes, he would have found him. But I didn't call back because Ed needed the time to find his mistake.

An hour later, Greg called and I asked him to dinner.

"No, Alex, I can't."

"Why not? For crying out loud, I haven't even told you when."

"I can't, that's all. I . . . I did what you asked me to."

I lowered my hand and stared at the mouthpiece, the earpiece, and rang off while he was still talking through tears born of superstitious fear. I laughed nervously at myself, reminded myself of the resolutions made and the progress visible even in the length of my stride. "God," I whispered, "does not play games."

I dialed Jenny's number, and there was no answer. I tried all night, and the following morning, after too little sleep and without turning off the lights, I hurried up to her Centre Street office; it was locked. I walked over to her house; it was empty. I went to the hospital, and an intern told me Greg hadn't shown up for his rounds, nor did his office receptionist know where he was. I didn't talk to Alma because she'd never liked the way he came when I called. Ed's law firm was next—gone, all gone.

I struggled with confusion for several moments before starting for home, my left hand jingling the change in my pocket. I adamantly refused to believe I'd been wrong a second time. It just doesn't happen. There is a way to the world, we all try to guess at it, to order it, or at least pretend that we do. We have too short a time, dammit, to be playing at games.

I stopped at the corner, staring absently down King Street toward the hospital. There was an ambulance parked in front, and when I paid attention to what I was seeing I noticed Greg standing beside a stretcher. As I moved toward him hurriedly, someone touched his arm, and he glanced up. His face was florid, his lips taut, and he marched inside before I could reach him. The stretcher followed at once, but not before I saw Ed's face.

"Weird," said one of the ambulance attendants when I stopped him and asked. "They were taking pictures over there at the *Herald*, and all of a sudden he pushes everyone out of the way and starts to run. He gets about four steps and falls. Dead as a—oh, hey, sorry, Mr. Munro.''

For Jenny's sake more than mine, I went over to see the editor, Marc Clayton, and he showed me the photos they'd taken at the session. They were there, the two of them, back by the curb. Marc couldn't spot them.

I was falling without moving; I was drowning out of water.

I walked to the cemetery and found Gramp's place, to the right of my mother's. ''I don't want to play,'' I whispered while I cried, and while my teeth chattered as if it were winter.

Jenny didn't answer her phone, didn't open her office, didn't come to her door.

That evening, for the first time in over twenty years, the train jumped the tracks where it crossed Williamston Pike. Alma was driving the station wagon. Greg was beside her. Their three children were in the back.

''No, Gramp,'' I said when I heard the news.

Bid the soldiers shoot, he'd told me; a good general uses his men for the real action while the general makes all the plans for the fighting. But what the hell kind of plans can you make when you don't even know what the hell kind of war is going on in your goddamned yard?

I knelt at the foot of the grave and began pulling at grass, throwing clumps in the air, dusting dirt on my trousers. The sun was low, the night breeze already stirring. It was the end of August, and the summer already dying.

''Please tell me I'm crazy, Gramp, okay?'' But his gun had somehow found its way to my hip pocket, under my jacket. ''Gramp, it's so goddamned lonely out here. Now I've got Jenny and I know what need is. I know now how you felt about Gram, how Dad felt about Mom. I know now. And it's so goddamned lonely, Gramp, and I don't want to do it. Dammit, he's forcing me to play, and I just want to go home.

''Goddamnit, Gramp, what the hell were you trying to tell me?

''Damnit, I can't do it!''

It took me over three hours to get back to King Street. The sun was gone, the streets' whisper quiet. There were no lights on in the house, and it wasn't until I had the key in the front door that I realized someone was sitting on the swing. I turned slowly, licking my lips, reaching for the gun. And stopped.

"Jenny?"

I was beside her before I knew I'd moved, my arm around her shoulder, my free hand cupping her chin. She was cold, unresponsive, the flutter of her pulse an abandoned bird in its nest.

I knew it, then: she'd seen them.

Footsteps on the porch steps turned me around, and there were shadows there, watching. Then they stepped into the light, and I held Jenny closer.

"Alex," a voice said, a perfectly ordinary voice that constricted my throat and harrowed me with the sound. "Alex, it's your turn."

Confess the seasons: *Gramp, now I know. It was the game, wasn't it. The game I played was right, and you only patted my head and told me not to worry because you didn't know I'd stumbled on the rules. It was right. I take the year and I play the advocate and I find a damned good reason why it should all go on. And if I make the right speech, say the right words, make the proper supplications, that's the other way, Gramp, to start the game on its next phase. But you didn't know the words, and neither do I. I know the rules now, but I don't know the words.*

So I've got to shoot, Gramp, or Jenny's going to die.

They're standing in front of me, right here in front of me, and it's my turn and I've got to shoot. God or his partner.

I'm scared, Gramp.

I miss you, and I'm scared.

Oh Jesus, how can I shoot him when I can't tell which is which?

A Private Whale

Brian Aldiss

For almost thirty years British author Brian Aldiss's reputation has been secure throughout the world as one of the finest writers the field of speculative fiction has ever had. He is the author of such distinguished, and widely varied, novels as, The Long Afternoon of Earth, Barefoot in the Head, Frankenstein Unbound, The Malacia Tapestry, *and, most recently,* Helliconia Spring. *Besides that, he is a fine anthologist and an important critic in the field.*

In the same letter I quoted in the Introduction to Perpetual Light, *Aldiss wrote: "I'm not religious myself, but have to admit to being full of a religious sense of life." I think you'll find that the same is true of his novelette, "A Private Whale."*

This was how Feng Xi escaped from his bedroom at night, and ran to where the whales flew.

He waited till his two younger brothers were asleep and then, very quietly, he edged the window open, leaned out, and set his foot on the wooden ledge of the glass lean-to below. Easing his weight over the sill, he got himself outside and breathed warm air into his lungs. The trick was not to try to climb down here—that way, you were certain to break a pane of glass and wake the parents. No, you worked along to the left, tiptoeing along the wooden ledge, with your body brushing against the rough stucco of the wall of the house, still warm from the day's sun, until your outstretched fingers grasped the rainwater guttering where the roof came sweeping down from the gable. Two more steps, and you could heave yourself up with all your strength and climb onto the roof. There you had to be careful in case you dislodged a tile. It was then a matter of scrambling over the ridge of the roof, with all the stars and all the planets of the zodiac blazing above you, and sliding down until you could slip onto the roof of the outhouse. From there, it was a simple matter to jump down to the ground beyond the fence. Then you were in the lane to which the row of houses turned their blind backs, and it was a matter of running to freedom, over the road, across the wild heathland, to the cliffs themselves, and down the precipitous path—a path so familiar that Feng Xi could negotiate it even in the darkness—until there you stood by the rocks on the edge of the estuary itself, with the salt air thick in your throat and the swift-rushing roar of the waters in your ears.

By night, the estuary was like a great animal, by turns sighing, frolicking, wallowing, snoring, fuming, rolling, galloping, dreaming, escaping, charging, burrowing, billowing, bellowing, bolting, blasting, bubbling, beckoning in its bed.

By night, it was the boy's estuary, his own creature, his foundling, his very bloodstream. He lay by it, dangling himself in it, embracing its moistened rocks, its stones.

The men were gone. They worked by day, the whale-fishers. Rowing their aluminium hulls out into the sea itself, until they were lost in the day-dazzle the ocean threw up, they would be gone into the unknown, to reappear unexpectedly, rowing, rowing for glory, veins standing out over downward-turned faces and shoulders and arms, rowing, driving the whales before them. Great tails, great backs, lips as big as God's lips, rose from the water and fell back again as the whales crowded into narrower water, snorting as they snuffed the muddier streams of estuarine current.

Feng Xi's mother stood with her child on the cliff, watching, watching the great weekly spectacle of race and carnage, clutching Feng Xi to her breast or, as he grew, as his brothers arrived out of the mystery of unbeing into the living world, clutching his hand, watching, watching, glimpsing through the driving spray her man— he always number one in the boat, always with his knotted torso bare to the elements, to the plunging animals. In her clutch rested fear, manifest as sweat. Men died. But Feng Xi from infancy watched not the men but those leviathans with lips like God, from their first buoyant appearance with the aligned demons tiny behind them, when they plunged merely sportively, believing in their invulnerability, in the sure power of some mighty whale-god who had granted them eternal ocean, eternal life, to their last failing thrash as, in the midst of waters their own blood had incarnadined, they submitted to the harpoons dragging them down to the black beach of unknowing, where all gods ceased and offal reigned.

Now Feng Xi was too old to stand meekly by his mother's side. He congregated instead with older boys and yipped and yelled with them as the killing race drove in; and, when the tide was at slack, went out with them, number eight, in the long, leaky boat, driving his oar into the indecisive water, urging, willing, the hull forward, humping it bodily and by spiritual force over the eddies to the far stony bank and back again.

In the fugitive night, from among the crannies in the rocks, Feng Xi dragged his secret possession, his one thing, his one toy, his second life, his dream that made him part of the great estuary as it flowed through God's veins: his boat. The hull was plastic, and a plastic oilskin came up to tie about his neck as, almost horizontal, he thrust off his paddle from the rock and launched himself into the flood. In the immense confines of the dark, the shore was lost almost at once.

As the current took hold, it swung the hull over its broad back and carried it away like a leaf. Feng Xi breathed the breath of the animal.

So carried—only when dawn greyed the waters would he attempt ordinarily to return to the dry land and again become a boy mammal—Feng Xi let his thoughts drift with the motions of his craft, of the monster that guided the craft. Sometimes he imagined he was the estuary, sometimes he was the hunters, bold in their boats, sometimes he was the whales, and sometimes, where the craft became the lip of God, he was a wisdom tooth in the divine smile itself.

Overhead, when he cared to notice, gleamed more wisdom teeth, spreading their sparkle down like a falling rain, to be saturated in the seawaters. It was an intense part of Feng Xi's belief that the whales could swim beyond the waste of horizon-waters into the waste of western stars, rising, rising smiling into the heavens, their great rudders steering them beyond the polestar to places where the universe was oceans deep, and the oceans deeper than whole universes.

So it was no surprise to him when, upon this certain midnight, with water and universe turning in their mysterious precision, Feng Xi saw a great whale sailing down out of the western sky, leaving a trail like a snail among the stars and planets of the zodiac. He idled his paddle, so that water chased itself up the blade to his hand, while he watched as the mighty animal sailed straight toward him. He floated on wonder and gratitude. A glimpse of the infinite was open to him.

The whale seemed hardly to move: yet equally it came at a great rate. Above its enormous head, the tip of its tail showed. Its prow as it breasted sparkling space was black, its edges glowed, dull, mighty, infernal, as if it plunged through fire to reach the boy.

In awe he opened his mouth. Why not? God's jaw was open, spilling out wonders—why not his? Now the celestial whale was blotting out a whole area of starry sky. Already in his mind's eye he saw the fountains and floods of its descent. Jubilation cast out fear.

This was his whale, heaven-born, heaven-sent.

The offices of Fabrican, Inc. were embedded in the urbstak of Expectation II, high in a syncline of one of the satellite's two petals. They filled a low-rental area behind the Euthenics Department, away from direct sunlight. The points of sunshine blazing across Saito Warner's office ceiling were conducted there by glass fibres.

Though penned in the entrails of the planetoid, Saito Warner strove to be a free spirit. He had exercised his spirit in the gymnasia of belief and disbelief for over thirty years, and was still undaunted. He still showed a brave front to the world and sang in his shower every morning; yet world-weariness was creeping upon him, and never more so than now, when he was confronted by a new challenge and an old bureaucrat.

Hunching his shoulders, Warner was arguing—more precisely, grunting and arguing—over the flattie to an official on a distant zeepee, *Jefferson IX*. The nine zodiacal planets of the Jefferson group clustered at a Lagrangian point, were mainly administrative; in token of this honour, their male and female inhabitants wore their heads shaven, except for a patch of hair above the left ear, the home of monitive wisdom.

The old bureaucrat was talking at length, thus implementing Warner's world-weariness factor considerably. He felt his will to be happy vacating him, and broke in upon the discourse.

Bleakly regarding the ganoid skull of his superior, Warner said, "Please, you need not brief me on the early history of *Clytemnestra*. I realise there has always been a curse on it. Send me the details through the terminal, and I'll process all the documentation on my way there, if I must go."

"You must go. It is urgent." Thus the voice of *Jefferson IX*.

"What Go status am I allowed?"

"We can authorise an A for Travel priority and a Double D for Payload."

They were despatching him into trouble bound hand and foot by red tape.

Warner tickled his keyboard and regarded the results of his computation without cheer. "Double D? That's meagre, isn't it, if the job is so important? By the time I get my equipment aboard the shuttle, a D payload will allow me just one assistant—and a thin, not to say spindly, assistant at that."

The distant official sighed, expressing his sense of martyrdom at having to deal with human beings.

"You know full well, Warner, that fuel is rationed among the zeepees while we have an export drive to Earth. You will require only one assistant on *Clytemnestra*. You alone will have to solve the problems you find there. Double D it has to be." On the flattie, no change in the official's expression. "Your tickets and trajectory are being punched through to you contemporaneously. When your astrologer clears you, leave for *Clytemnestra* at once."

Saito Warner began a fresh grumble, rolling it over his lips, but the distant official cut him off. "Whatever my astrologer says, it's a dangerous mission—"

"One further thing. There's an art historian called Ernst Krawstadt living alone on *Clytemnestra*. Bring him back with you. I have orders to make sure he is safe."

"How can I bring him back, with a Double D rating?"

"Leave your assistant behind to use one of *Clytemnestra*'s lifeboats. Return with Krawstadt in his place. You will receive a plan with lifeboat stations indicated. Understand? That carries a bonus."

"State amount of bonus." He was embarrassed to find himself using their idiot terminology.

"Five thousand five hundred."

"I'll see." But he was impressed, and mollified by the size of the figure. As he switched the screen off, the bald official dwindled in the flattie, sizzling to light-minute distance in a flash, and was gone beyond call. His personal ziggie spangled there for a nano, to be scanned by the Fabrican comp: then electronic night reigned.

Glancing at his watch, Saito Warner crossed his office and walked across to the relaxer room, which was empty at this time of day. A Smics predestimeter stood against one wall. Warner smiled at it encouragingly and put the palms of his hands to its plastic palms.

The machine analysed what it found there, wheezed, and presented him with a read-out which predicted how his next twenty-four hours would be.

It seemed as if an exotic day lurked among the predestimeter's ambivalent phrases:

** Doubt brings usual trouble on the side

A new companion may lead to a journey

   Don't let argumentation deflect your purpose

Your work will present rewarding challenges

Water is forecast. Rise above it

Any falling off may be dangerous

   But greater trouble springs from human error

Your vision may be clouded but you will see it through

   When in doubt, avoid any obvious openings

   Unsleeping vigil is necessary for safety

   You may experience a grave come-down

   You will find what you seek

Options: Crucial   Hence: only 62 rating

Warner read the card carefully twice, scratched a buttock with a thumb, and looked about vaguely. A sixty-two percent likelihood of the predicted events happening meant little; all could be fulfilled if he took the right (crucial) options—or so the makers of the predestimeter claimed. Scepticism was ever present. Existence was not yet an exact science. Nevertheless, the card represented one of the most hopeful of the many new sciences springing up among the zeepees; being forewarned on a day-to-day basis was worth something. Alarming though it sounded, taken phrase by phrase.

He looked at the card once again, then pocketed it, grinning to conceal his agitation from himself.

"What *am* I seeking?" he asked himself. "Women? Money? God? Excitement? Return to Earth?" At least it sounded as if there should be a break in dull routine, despite the deliberate fuzziness of the language.

It was with good humour that he phoned his personal astrologer.

His astrologer was Jewish-Japanese, and equipped with an untidy beard to stroke as he read off Warner's coordinates on his horoscope. "Well, personally you are okay, Saito," he admitted grudgingly, "and travel could bring profit, financial and spiritual. But *Expectation II* is in a curious astral position, with Uranus boxed against Titan in the fifth declension and a subjective higgle over the fourth house. With Earth in opposition against Taurus—*Expectation's* launch-sign—you could encounter an unexpected collapse of your project."

Warner was always impatient with zeepeescopes, which had recently become fashionable among the *Expectations* and neighbouring groups.

"I'll settle for personal clarity," he said, smiling, signing off with his ziggie. "Thanks for the warning."

Saito Warner was a compact man with good musculature and a genial expression on his face which screened the frequently solemn thoughts within. He was of Japanese-American descent, and had come to the zeepees six years previously, working his way up until he was senior zee-systems engineer in Fabrican. Success tied him to his desk increasingly, and depressed him. The thought of action made him smile now, as he walked down the office-trak to Person-

nel and enquired about an assistant for the job on *Clytemnestra*.
He asked for Jazz Mallard, the best man in the business.

Mallard rang through, looking forlorn. "Daren't leave home this morning, chief. A two star ruck-up on my card for today, with high prob quotient. Sorry. I'm a slave to the stars."

"I thought you were still a Christian God believer, Jazz."

"So I am, but God doesn't always show up, not in the face of high ruck-up quotients." He put his head to one side, as if sympathising with God in the circumstances.

"And you up here in His free-energy zone—what more do you want?" Warner smiled to conceal his impatience. People should believe what they believed and forget either-or-ness; living in the confined areas of the planetoids was bad for decision.

"God didn't invent the concept of a free-energy zone, Saito. Man did."

"Who invented man?"

The melancholy face on the flattie said, "Belief in God should never be infinite, to my mind. That's why I consult astrologers as well as priests. Infinite belief in God leads to miracles and similar countermanding of the physical laws of the universe, which nobody needs. Or it leads to absurd philosophical positions, like the 19th-century guy who believed that God put fossils in the rocks to test mankind's religious faith. . . . Hey, Saito, you okay?"

The call was prompted by Warner's sudden rictus of pain. He clutched his left side and doubled up, so that he was no longer visible in Jazz Mallard's flattie.

Gasping, he straightened slowly, alert for another spasm. He managed a smile in Mallard's direction.

"I'm fine . . . An old wound—or God striking. Does God strike suddenly like that?"

"It happened on the way to Damascus." Mallard was still looking concerned.

"Well, I'm on my way to *Clytemnestra*," Warner said, not feeling up to more badinage, and cut the connection. He stood for a moment, testing his rib cage.

Doubt brings usual trouble on the side

The pain was psychosomatic, prompted by something in Mallard's remarks, and based on a physical event some two years old. Two years previously, Saito had reported to hospital, prompted by dull pains in his left side. Acupuncture anesthsia had been administered when his signs were propitious, and surgeons had cut from behind his ribs a cyst the size of a tennis ball. Warner was told that the cyst had been growing slowly since the day of his birth. It was a blob of misplaced matter, forming an incongruence within his system. The surgeons cracked the cyst before his eyes, like an egg.

A whiff of fire and brimstone escaped into the ward. Inside the anatomical tektite, hair and teeth were growing. The two halves opened up to him like scabrous mouths which would in time have devoured his being.

Leaning against the wall, he recalled his emotions of sin and shame on that occasion; now he perceived that the sin had been the sin of the surgeons, who should never have permitted such a revelation at such a time.

Preoccupied by gloomy thoughts, he allowed Personnel to order up the first stand-by assistant they could contact. When they told Warner that the assistant would meet him at the shuttle, he merely nodded grimly and went to pack his bag and order up equipment from the stores.

He had a vacuum of unbelief; perhaps God was growing inside him like a cyst. What he really needed was a miracle. But the predestimeter had said nothing on that score.

The assistant was a doleful, stooped man of middle age and of Scandinavian extraction, by name Sven Kevins. Warner had worked with the man before, and recalled his habit of whistling under his breath. Still, Kevins was an effective engineer. Warner smiled and shook his hand.

They met in Expectport, where a post-rococo madness had seized the designers. Fake columns burst all over the vaulted ceiling in showers of grotesque flowers and petals. One approached one's launch-gate through a herbaceous parody of the nature left behind on Earth.

Their craft awaited them. Since they were travelling within the zeepees, they used the local port, and escaped the attentions of Customs, Medical, and Expatriation. Only Ecology detained them, giving them a quick vacuum-dust to remove grosser biological organisms before they climbed into the shuttle.

A new companion may lead to a journey Low accuracy!

The moguls of *Jefferson IX* had already programmed the shuttle's trajectory. Once the two men were belted in, and the local Clearance signal came through, the spacecraft began to thrust. It would find its own complex way to malfunctioning *Clytemnestra*. The great lips of the hangar opened before them, and they were moving into a shimmer of light.

Expectation became not a world but a mathematical construct based on the structural imperatives of a tulip. As it dwindled, the screen opaked to cut down sunglare. The other *Expectations* sailed into view, dinghies with a perpetual flood of energy to voyage on, forever tacking about their libration point.

Warner got down to reading his print-out work schemes. Kevins whistled to himself. Beyond their heads, the plane of the zodiacal planets glittered about Earth like an upmarket version of Saturn's rings. The shuttle lifted itself on a pre-programmed course out of the plane, until in the distance Ceres could be sighted emerging from Earth's shadow: the asteroid had been captured and used as outer shepherd to anchor the flotillas of zeepees into position. As for those poker chips themselves, so largely were they the gambles and gambols of engineering theory that an expert eye could distinguish them by shape rather than beacon identification. Every year, the theories had changed; obedient computers had elongated central axes or contorted conic sections to toric or dodecahedral configurations. The hulls of the worldlets formed geological strata of fashion in satellitic knowhow.

Among the bizarre shapeoids, craft moved. The outlines of the craft also bore more the stamp of the mutable thinking of mankind than of immutable universal laws. They dipped like moths in and out of the zeepee buzz saw.

"Good example of situology," Kevins said, gesturing towards the glittering panorama outside.

"Uh-huh," agreed Warner, without looking up from his script. *Clytemnestra's* malfunctions were of long standing.

"You know, situology—the science of situation-preparedness created by organisms before the situation exists."

"Mmm." The closed environment of the zeepees had spawned as many new sciences as religions. Warner continued to read his work scheme. *Clytemnestra* certainly had its share of problems; it had been finally evacuated two years ago.

"A challenge to Darwinism, situology is," said Kevins, clearing his throat and looking sideways at Warner, whose eyes remained fixedly on his reading material.

"Situology studies the way manmade environments have become increasingly complex over the years. The common view used to be that mankind was no longer in command of his environment, that the complexities overwhelmed him. Situology shows the reverse to be true. Prehistoric man had a craving for a more complex environment; he determined the pattern of our world. We fulfill *his* desire for complexity, while scheming for our own higher levels. And, for instance, we invent computers to control present complexity, and the computers then multiply that complexity. But experimental evidence shows that we could tolerate situations of over a hundred times greater complexity. Unlimited time travel would be the human ideal."

"Mmm. So?"

"I'm taking an evening course in situology at present, as it happens."

Abandoning the script, Warner looked up. "It happens I have instructions to leave you behind on *Clytemnestra* in exchange for some art historian who is there illegally. Annoying for you, for me. But that's government instructions. They merely had to allow us more fuel, and programme in an extra payload body, and my life would be simpler. *Clytemnestra* is a leaky old crate, where no one would wish to be. Would situology say that I inwardly desired such complexities to my life?"

"Uh—I think situology would say that the complexities of governments are actually pattern-normal, as we say. You should not make the common mistake of seeing your dealings with government as an Us-Them situation. They are also Us, conforming to our own complexity norms, and we would behave as they do in their situation. Character is infinitely mutable. But I certainly don't want to be left on *Clytemnestra*, thanks. I understand it is a disaster—almost full of water and drifting out of orbit.''

"I was going to talk to you about that.''

They were back in the plane of the ecliptic. The palace-like facades of the *Ingratitudes* drifted by, barred with corinthian shadow.

"We're deputed to get *Clytemnestra* in working order again.''

The man lapsed into silence. Kevins started to whistle under his breath.

"What about the fossils in terrestrial rocks?'' Warner said. "Someone told me that a guy in the 19th century claimed they were put there by God to test mankind's faith. There they lay, waiting for people to dig them up and solve the situation.''

"The existence of God, or otherwise, is not important, since there's no possible proof that would satisfy everyone, one way or another. What situology would say is that the fossils were always there and often stumbled on throughout the ages—but could only be recognised for what they were when civilization reached a certain level of complexity. Suppose some entirely new fossils were discovered now, in an entirely unexpected rock—say, in recent rocks, post-cenozoic. Then we would have a new, worked-for, level of complexity to occupy us.''

"Our entire world-picture would be changed by such a find.'' Warner thought again of the yellow teeth, jostling in rows among pebble gums and coarse black hair. Another kind of fossil. He was slowly realising how the cyst had changed his world picture.

"We should adjust very quickly,'' Kevins said, rubbing his hands together.

The gesture annoyed Warner. "Situology—the meddling of the ape to justify his meddling,'' he said.

Don't let argumentation deflect your purpose

Kevins started to whistle under his breath.

*   *   *

Clytemnestra was a cigar shape with a dent in one end. Very functional. It was revolving about its long axis. Its main dock was situated at the apex of the dent. Their spacecraft matched velocities with the zeepee and spiralled in towards the opening that began to gape at the apex.

Most of the zeepees had been constructed by private enterprise, under pressure from the power crisis. Power eternal was here, blasting from the sun; yet even here it was not free, but must be worked for. Lives had to be shaped, as the zeepees themselves were shaped, to gain maximum advantage.

Clytemnestra had been designed as an agricultural station, when the oversimple theory of mono-productive zeepees had prevailed. It proclaimed its age in the stains and pitting which disfigured its hull.

The shuttle sank with mathematical resignation into the dock. The outer hull sealed as the craft settled on an inertial way. Atmosphere was pumped back into the bay with a series of spasmodic hisses which recalled the sound of Kevins whistling under his breath.

Saito Warner climbed out and stood on the deck. He listened.

Drip. Drip.

He walked over to where a small puddle was already gathering. The drops of moisture came winging down from the plastic plates in the ceiling high above, curving away from the line of *Clytemnestra's* progression as they fell. Beyond them was another noise, its source less easy to define. It sounded like an ocean in a tank.

"Come on, then, Sven," Warner called. "Let's get to work."

Kevins looked out of the ship's hatch.

"I'm not getting out of here just to be left behind."

"We'll discuss that issue when and if we meet up with this guy Krawstadt."

"And when's that going to be?"

"First, we have a job of work to do. This zeepee is becoming unstable. It's a danger to the system. If you refuse to work, you lose your job, and situology will not be much help to you then. Out, man, fast."

Kevins climbed out and tested the deck below his feet by springing on it: not a very effective procedure in the light gravity. He pulled a face, and then obediently unlatched side lockers and watched as equipment piled itself onto an electric dolly. Meanwhile, Warner opened the inner lock doors. Breezes stirred, bringing the sound of slopping liquid in a hollow stomach.

Warner moved forward, leafing over the plans of the zeepee which had come with his print-out directions and peering about into the increasing darkness. He smiled to demonstrate cheerfulness.

Clytemnestra had been functional for four decades. It proclaimed its obsolescence. Built before monomolecular metals were freely available, its internal bracing system was succumbing to stress, as was apparent once the two men left the port area. The corridors took on dangerous downward slopes never intended by their designers.

Your work will present rewarding challenges Check. Smile.

Dramas of half-finished or abandoned zeepees were the common stuff of scatter programmes. Here was one in real life. The artificial excitements of the scatters were replaced by melancholy, and a sense of danger. The $1/20g$, centrifugally induced gravity contributed to a sense of unreality.

Sitting on the equipment dolly, the men steered forward slowly. Warner switched on the headlights. He checked the gas indicator at intervals. The air was oxygen-rich. It smelt of acids, bone marrow, and fungi.

"Did anything amusing ever happen to you, Sven?" Warner asked.

"My mother died one summer when I was eight years old, back in Sweden. And do you know my father would not permit the burial until the first foggy day, which was two months later. Isn't that funny? I was just thinking about it."

"Why did he do that?"

"Oh, he thought fog added to the mystery of passing away, I guess."

They halted when they saw water in the corridor ahead. To either side were shops, their windows smashed or cracked, their contents looted. Dust lay over them. Rubbish blew about indecisively. Warner saw from his plan that the agricultural hall and fly terminus lay ahead, with the old farms beyond. The floodwater would be deeper there.

Without speaking, Kevins looked at the map Warner showed him. Without speaking, Warner indicated the way they had to go. The operations room was most easily reached by elevators ascending from the fly terminus. They needed to get to the operations room.

"Break out the boat," he told Kevins.

"This zeepee is beyond saving," Kevins said. "Everyone knows that. So let's not do anything heroic."

"There's nothing heroic about going to the operations room. The report from *Jefferson* states that *Clytemnestra* is shifting out of orbit. She's a menace to other traffic, and Fabrican's orders are to get rid of the danger one way or another."

"Meaning what, exactly? It sounds heroic to me."

"Sven, just break out the boat, will you?"

As soon as the boat came out of the dolly and the umbilical was tugged, it began to inflate. The men attached its outboard engine as it did so. When Warner had settled a case of tools aboard, they launched the boat and climbed in. Sven whistled under his breath.

The headlight had puny illuminating power in the echoing hall. They were sailing into the throat of a giant whale, the water growing ever deeper under their hull. Waves parted slowly and piled up to a dreamlike height as they flowed away behind. Oily snakelike movements above them threw back the light, as they moved into a cylinder of water. The water overhead cast back sound as well as light.

Some distance on, the flood was divided by an arch, which dipped low and lopsidedly. It had once signified the division between the agricultural hall and the recreation area of the fly terminus. As they passed under it, the temperature dropped noticeably, and a veritable gale slashed rain at their faces.

Not only was the visibility growing worse; they found themselves enclosed in a tube of water. The rain was sucked in from the far end of the tube. It exhaled itself on to their eyes and mouths.

All kinds of flotsam drifted on the flood, beside them and overhead. Much of it congregated round the central elevators, whose row of glasplex tubes cut through the storm. After a while, they nosed alongside the tubes and secured the boat.

What was now mid-flood had been mid-air in normal times. But aerobatics had been a favourite sport in the fly terminal. Consequently, the shafts had entrances halfway up, as well as at top and bottom. Warner wrenched open a door just above the waterline and shone his torch up the shaft. It had remained watertight.

He hefted the tool kit under one arm. "Come on," he said.

"I don't like it," Kevins said, following. "It's too heroic for me."

"This is one of your complex situations, laid on for the benefit of students of situology."

Water is forecast. Rise above it   That was what he intended to do.

He kicked off up the tube, travelling slowly, correcting his flight with taps of the heel of his free hand and his toecaps against the sides of the tube. The tube seemed to seesaw, first to a horizontal position and then to invert, as he landed lightly, turning head-over-heels in the cushioned exit bulb.

They had three exits to chose from. Two were underwater. They took the third, to emerge in a travel trak which took them to the operations room.

Overhead lights still functioned in the operations room. Kevins went over and depaked a curving window. Sunlight flared in from space, making the whites and cerises of carpeting and upholstery blossom. The blossoms were killed instantly as the sunlight died again—to return a moment later. One of the nearby zeepees had transited the sun.

"That was pretty close," Kevins said, and went to stare cautiously through a pakeport. The operations room was perched in the forehead of *Clytemnestra*, commanding a view of the crowded solways— the solways earlier generations of mankind had known only as space. Because he knew they were there, Kevins could almost see the torrents of radiation and particles through which the zeepees moved.

Warner did not give the outside world a glance. Setting down the tool kit, he went over to the banks of controls and began to pass his hand over them. In most cases, he got readings. As long as a zeepee—even a deserted one—rode an orbit, its energy panels ensured that there was power for the technology to function.

When he began to feed figures into his own computer, Kevins came over and watched.

"What was the storm we passed through down below?" he asked. "Did we hit a runaway swimpool?"

"Worse than that. *Clytemnestra* is a sinking ship. Literally. It's taking water aboard."

Kevins laughed disbelievingly. "Pull the other leg. A *Titanic* of the spaceways. . . ."

'*And* we have some fragile icebergs all round," Warner said, frowning, studying a graph that blinked up before him on the screen. "Will you please check out orbital deviation."

Kevins went over to work the orbit recorder, playing back the traces of past years when the zeepee had remained unvisited, except perhaps by sky pirates or the odd hermit. As he worked at the keyboard, he whistled tunelessly to himself. When he had results, he regarded Warner, who was busy. Another zeepee transited and cast a brief shadow over the long room.

Shrugging, Kevins crossed to the seried monitors which gave visual access to the entire zeepee. Most of them were still on automatic working; the TV cameras, designed to function in vacuum, operated even when submerged in water. There were screens dimmed by flood, screens dark where light circuits had failed, screens showing haphazard prospects of corridor, private quarters, offices, machinery, stores—all deserted: Drizzle was falling in cabins and closets. Kevins walked along the racks, bringing every screen into life, summoning from nothing a complex prospect of emptiness more forlorn than the remotest wilderness on Earth. All it needed was fog.

He switched on the intercom.

"Hello, hello. Fabrican here. Everyone on *Clytemnestra* is warned to prepare to evacuate. Show yourself to a screen, please. Ernst Krawstadt, if you are aboard, show yourself, please. We want you to proceed to the departure bay at once."

His gaze scanned the rows of monitors. Nowhere did anything

move, except the litanies of water. Emptiness, rubbish, corridors, corners, rain, decay. . . .

Warner climbed onto the instrument board, reached up, and peeled off a section of the flock ceiling cover. A plastic panel was revealed, set in the shell of the room's structure. When Warner flipped back the four securing lugs, the panel fell away. In the opening, a section of a further shell could be seen. Thrusting himself up, Warner stuck his head through into the space and listened.

He could hear water running.

Above his head was a further panel, better secured, with a warning notice on it.

He looked down. Kevins had come to stand beneath him.

"As I thought, it's raining," he said. "How do you like that?"

Kevins rubbed his nose. "I thought that zeepee storms were an invention of scatter drama. The contrasting temperatures in the hall and the terminal would account for the winds we met, but. . . ."

"Correct. The engineers of early zeepees like this one went for large open areas and high roofs, to prevent claustrophobia. What they got was built-in freak weather. They were, after all, playing God, and creating their own mini-worlds. They got mini-weather thrown in for free. It has always been extremely difficult to control the circulation of air. Nowadays, we go for lower ceilings and higher gravitation to combat the problem."

He turned his attention back to the panel with the warning above his head. It was set in the outer lining of the zeepee, a plastic shell that was some feet thick in places; beyond it lay the metal outer skin of the planetoid.

The seal on the panel turned under his spanner. As it opened, the panel eased and Warner lifted it away. Water fell slowly into his face. He grunted with satisfaction.

He climbed down and stood beside Kevins, tucking his spanner away. Water drops floated into the operations room, spreading gradually on the carpet.

"That's the whole problem here," Warner said. "The hull lets in water. The *Clytemnestra* is a *Titanic*, as you say. It's sinking."

"Yes, but I was speaking sarcastically."

Warner shone his torch upwards so that a small square of the outer hull could be seen through the opening he had created. The hull here was constructed of small lozenge-shaped sections, each lozenge with a teat at its middle. Each teat dripped water.

"See those lozenges? They're hydrolytic tiles. *Clytemnestra* was designed as an agricultural factory. Its job was to grow and export food to other zeepees. It was always going to have a water-deficiency, since vegetables are over ninety percent water. The gods in charge of construction laid on a supply of free water, inventive fellows. They built several sections of hydrolitic tiles into the hull—that's one section up there above us. The tiles scoop up hydrogen and oxygen molecules from the solways, while their power is supplied by heat differentials between different constituent layers in each tile. The result is precipitation of H_2O on the inner surface of the tile, drawn down into reservoirs through tubes attached to those central teats. The tubes have perished, but the pennies from heaven continue, and leak into the ecosystem somewhere."

"So all we have to do is switch off the tiles?"

Shaking his head, Warner said, "They're automatic. The tiles are rather like the famous dinosaur fossils in the rocks; they are fossils of a way of thought. The engineers thought the future was going to go on unchanged forever, even when they had had the contrary demonstrated to them. Directly other zeepees diversified, the monoculture here was in trouble, and directly food exports slumped, there was a water surplus, an unstoppable one. No one had thought of that. We're stuck in a washing machine filling up from the pipe with no faucet. And zero drainage."

"Not exactly stuck. Unstuck." Kevins's melancholy face grew even longer as he said, "Come and look at the orbit-recorder. The extra water mass is slowing *Clytemnestra* appreciably."

They confronted the evidence. Graphics showed how their position had fallen from their prescribed orbit by four degrees. The divergence was increasing exponentially.

Any falling off may be dangerous

Without comment, Warner hit keys to get an extrapolation of course. He received the same reading as Kevins had done earlier.

Inside twenty hours, Clytemnestra would collide tangentially with an unmanned vagra (Variable Automated Geometry Radio Antenna) several miles long.

"I see what *Jefferson* meant," Kevins said, shifting uneasily.

"If *Clytemnestra* hits that vagra, the debris will spill out and the whole zeepee system will be put in jeopardy." He clutched his side.

"What does *Jefferson* suggest?"

"They suggest what they have suggested before. Only now that the problem has reached emergency proportions, they have had the guts to turn the suggestion into an order. We have to expel *Clytemnestra's* water in space."

He turned to see what had caught Kevins's attention. In a group of the far screens, movement showed. A man was moving furtively through the depths of the urbstak.

Different monitors showed the stranger from various angles, in close-up and long-shot. When Kevins switched on a hologrammic of the zeepee, the man's location was pinpointed by a moving light dot. Avoiding the flooded areas, he was traversing a residential district in the direction of the agricultural hall. He went from light to shadow, then back to where illumination was still functioning.

The man was in his mid-thirties, below medium height. His face was sharp and alert. He carried a suitcase. He looked about constantly.

A door panel slid open. He entered an area of darkness—and disappeared from view. The screens continued as before to show an uninhabited world. Disgustedly, Kevins indicated the screens that were blank.

"He's somewhere where a circuit has failed. The trace has also stopped. We should pick him up again in a minute. It must be your man Krawstadt. Shall we speak to him when he shows again?"

"I'll speak to him." Warner went over to the address system and said, "Are you hearing me, Krawstadt? Will you reply, please? This is Fabrican. We are evacuating the zeepee. Your life is in danger. Reply, please."

His own voice came back to him over the monitoring system, distortedly echoing from the resonator of the empty urbstak.

No reply.

They waited, made uneasy by the furtive appearance and disappearance of the stranger. Then the monitors caught him again. He was on an upper level, scurrying through a wrecked shopping area. The scan in the hologrammic showed him beyond the agricultural hall. He was making for the main dock.

Warner and Kevins realised the truth of the matter simultaneously. They shouted at Krawstadt, but the fugitive did not pause.

"We've got to stop him taking our ship," Kevins said.

"There should be lifeboats in the hangars we can use, fore and aft," Warner said. But he followed Kevins at a trot. Leaving the tools behind, they swarmed up the elevator-tube to where their boat was moored. The rainstorm seemed to have intensified. They pointed the bow about and headed down the turbulent cylinder of flood-water. Waves curved like the ridges of a corkscrew before them under the Coriolis effect, as if trying to screw them into the neck of an infinite bottle. Neither man spoke. Warner stood, legs braced, his chunky body rigid against the rain.

As the boat bored through into the agricultural hall, the storm lessened abruptly. They reached shallower water and cut the power. As they gained the point where their dolly stood, the rain died. It was appreciably warmer. They beached their craft on the deck.

Together, they ran back the way they had come at first.

The double doors of the bay were closed, the sirens wailing, the warning lights flashing. They caught the howl and the fast yellow dazzle reflected in broken windows before they rounded the corner into the reception lounge. Krawstadt was preparing to take off in their machine beyond the airlock doors. They were a little too late.

But greater trouble springs from human error The predestimeter knew what it was talking about.

They stood by the doors, listening to the sound of acceleration within. A nearby flattie, cracked but still functioning, showed them a high-angle view of their Fabrican craft lifting as the hull slid open before it. Warner clutched his side in sudden pain. It was his human error.

Next moment, a slamming noise assailed them. The zeepee shook, reverberations fading away into the distant shadows. Kevins lost his balance and fell.

"What . . . ?"

"The fool used manual over-ride in his hurry to get away," Warner said. "He struck the outer doors as he went through."

They watched the flattie as the fumes cleared in the bay beyond. The ship had got away—with what damage to itself could only be guessed. The hull doors were buckled and wedged open like a drunkenly laughing mouth. The warning sirens and lights continued to operate, the inner doors remained locked.

Warner punched the doors with his fist.

"We're not going to get into the dock now. The lifeboats are through there. We're stuck now, on a sinking ship."

"You planned to leave me here anyway."

"Not in these circumstances." Warner clasped his forehead. "Listen. There's the cargo dock at the opposite end of *Clytemnestra's* main axis. According to the plans, there are two lifeboats housed in the dock. We'll use one and escape that way."

Kevins's melancholy face registered fear and anger. "This ship has been looted, Saito, as any fool can see. What makes you think that there are any lifeboats down there? In any case, I'm not going back through that storm. We'll drown. I'm staying here."

Warner hesitated.

"That's your decision. If you're staying, make yourself useful. Above here is the auxiliary control room, with the automatic beacon. Go and radio Fabrican and *Jefferson*. Report the situation. Stress the urgency. I'll check on the lifeboat situation as soon as I can."

"You'll drown down there."

"I'm going to put on a suit."

Spacesuits still hung in the glass cupboards in the walls of the reception lounge, with signs saying BREAK IN AN EMERGENCY. Some of the glass had been smashed, but Warner found an intact suit and checked it out. The oxygen cylinders had not been molested, and all was as it should be. He climbed in, made a farewell gesture to Kevins, and set off back down the corridor in the direction of his inflatable boat, carrying the helmet. Once he looked back. Pride stopped him pleading with Kevins to accompany him.

As the boat carried him towards the stern of the *Clytemnestra*, the storm grew more intense, the wind colder. Damp enfolded him. He clamped the helmet into place before his suit filled with water. Waves lapped over the sides of the boat, and he listened with relief as an automatic pump woke and began to chug-chug.

He passed the bunch of elevator tubes. Mist closed in, lying in wafer-thin cylindrical strata above the water, teased by the wind.

Driving slowly forward, Warner saw that the floods were growing deeper all the while. He steered under a low arch, finding himself in a farther hall, where the wind was yet more shrill. The cylinder of turbulent air through which he travelled grew narrower. If he stood, his helmet would touch the higher waves overhead. So he crouched, while the boat laboured to deliver him into a tightening sleeve of water. It was like plunging head-first into a whirlpool.

Your vision may be clouded but you will see it through

At the end of the sleeve was a confusion of air and water. Warner struggled out of the boat, fighting to stay upright, feeling as if he were in a giant mixer. The boat was snatched away. Every so often, it returned on a wave, and he had to evade a side-swipe from it.

A metal wall gave him some shelter. He clung against it, working his way along. It was one of a pair of sliding doors. He had reached the cargo dock. Through these doors, the agricultural products of *Clytemnestra* had once been despatched, exported to other zeepees.

The struggle with the elements was beginning to tell on him. He just wanted to rest. Bewildered, he tried to recall what his destiny card had warned was in store next. Something about avoiding any obvious openings—but at present nothing was obvious, except his exhaustion.

Little could be seen for frothing water. He knew there was hand apparatus somewhere nearby, for getting the doors to work in an emergency. In the end, he almost fell over it.

Sliding up a plastic guard, he felt a compterminal under his hand. By putting his faceplate close to it and shining the torch, he saw how the device worked. He pressed the keys.

As soon as the dock doors started to move, he knew something was wrong. The water about him went mad. An invisible force seized him and shook him. Unable to understand what was happening, he clung to the nearest post, terrified.

Terrible thunders blasted over his body.

The doors slid wider. The tide of water sank. He wiped his faceplate with one hand, and breathed deep. As the flood died to a trickle, he could see what the trouble was.

Someone had burned their way into the dock from outside. They had caused considerable damage, stripping away much of the metal deck cladding. It could have been the work of pirate wrecker gangs. The inner air-lock had also been stripped. Warner had opened doors leading direct on to space; since the warning system had been stripped away, there was no way he could have known of the danger. In a calmer minute, he saw how the zero chill of space against the doors had created a permanent low pressure area in the ecosystem of the zeepee, resulting in the miniature storm he had come through.

He fought to close the doors again, but they had fouled some wreckage, and would neither open nor shut. Through a gap some six feet wide, the last of all the water and air of *Clytemnestra* was thundering.

When in doubt, avoid any obvious openings

Warner fell to one knee, letting the monster roar past his legs. He could do nothing but fight against being drawn out into the solways, perhaps to be encased like a fossil in a boulder of escaping ice. Survive, he told himself, clinging to his post. It felt as if his blood were being drawn over his head and into the void.

The roaring thinned to a scream and was gone. The stream rippling past his feet dwindled. All of a sudden, it froze, ridge-backed, solid. The sheet shattered under its own tension and scattered noiselessly about. The pieces of ice were not sucked towards the hatch. *Clytemnestra* was emptied of atmosphere.

He stood up, trembling violently inside his suit. For the first time, he thought not of his own survival but of Kevins, and fought down an impulse to weep.

A wedge of sunlight burned into the ruined hatch. Gigantic

shadows like mechanical clouds rolled across it. To divert himself, he plodded across the ruined deck and stood on the lip of the hatch, a small figure peering into the firmament.

The traffic of the zeepee belt was above him. Prominent in the ever-chaging panorama was the filigreed arm and dish of a vagra, almost directly overhead.

Such was Warner's emotional state that it took awhile for the significance of this positioning to dawn on him. He looked down and saw only stars, distant in frozen time. The sudden ejection of the flood of water and air had altered *Clytemnestra*'s course. The zeepee had dipped far off its orbit.

To one side was the cool eye of Earth.

He regarded it with foreboding. The zeepee was on its way down. "Well," he thought wryly, "perhaps it was a mistake in the first place to name the satellite after such an ill-fated lady as Clytemnestra."

Sven Kevins had died in the auxiliary control room. His body was wedged behind a desk which had jammed against the entrance. Not an heroic posture. Warner looked down, shaking his head, sorrow overtaking him. The business of life and death was a poor arrangement—final, yet not final enough in a sense, for he would be burdened from henceforth with the memory of Sven lying here, to add to his share of world-weariness. Aging, he thought, was more than anything an attrition of joy. God, if He existed, almost certainly had rat's teeth.

So why then did he want God so badly? He had been praying involuntarily at the cargo hatch doors, when the storm broke over him. When all else fails, you believe that there's someone coming to bale you out.

He caught his own thoughts, was aghast at them, and said aloud, "You're just thinking about yourself, not about Sven Kevins. Or you're thinking about God, Who must be the biggest self-indulgence ever invented. . . . When I think about God, I'm just thinking about how *I feel*. And all the time Sven lies like a mummy at my feet, his life gone.

"He was a good enough guy. Was I good enough to him? What

did he say about his mother?... At least I told him straight out that *Jefferson* wanted me to leave him here. That was honest. ... But I had no real feeling for him. That's proved by the way the predestimeter, reading my chemistries, could not foretell his death, made no mention of him. I wish I had a son to care for, not just a cyst. ... The zeepees are short of children. ... People are too wrapped up in dreams and sciences—they've lost the art of blood relationships. ..."

Some of this he said to himself, some came out loud and strange inside his helmet.. Then he recollected that he was, after all, a zee-systems engineer, and had a job of work on hand.

As he was crossing to the radio, it blinked, and the flattie over the radio desk lit up. A pale face, sober beneath a gleaming skull patched with hair over one ear, looked out and mouthed at him.

He sat down and plugged himself in to the sound.

"I was about to call you."

"What's gone wrong, Warner?"

Warner explained, wearily, as the frown from *Jefferson IX* deepened.

"According to our calculations," said *Jefferson*, when Warner had finished, *"Clytemnestra"* is headed for destruction, and may break up as it hits Earth's atmosphere in a few hours' time. Have you any idea of the estimated value of *Clytemnestra*, Warner?"

"Why was Krawstadt so valuable to you? He did the damage."

"The tax authorities want him in connection with non-payment of tax on his last publication."

Warner started to laugh. All that he had endured seemed to gather in his diaphragm and demand to be expelled in laughter. He rolled about helplessly, and was unable to control himself for several minutes. All the while, the official from *Jefferson* stared frostily out of the flattie.

"Now I feel better," Warner said at last. "Now tell me you have a rescue ship on the way to pick me up before this derelict comes apart,"

"That matter is being discussed," said the official, and signed off. His personal ziggie spangled briefly and then was gone into whatever limbo is resolved for dead electronics.

"Thank you, mankind, and good-bye," Warner said, feeling lonely and exhilarated by his loneliness. Fear had left him, expelled by the laughing fit. It would take time before the zeepee entered Earth's atmosphere; meanwhile, the administrative sector would have to send out a rescue ship. Whatever they might feel about him personally, they would ensure his safety; their reputation depended on it. Understanding the tight communications network which existed among the zodiacal planets, Warner knew that his predicament would be news already. The media would have a fix on him, and every scatter from here to Jupiter would be carrying bulletins on *Clytemnestra's* descent into death.

"What I need now is a miracle on the way to Damascus," he told himself.

He drifted slowly back through the dead shell, back to the cargo dock, placid now under vacuum conditions. Vanity made him stroll to the edge of the hatch and look out. He had to restrain himself from waving, knowing that cameras would be trained on him from a distance.

It startled him to see how far below the ring the zeepee had moved in a short time. A crescent Earth beamed to one side. He could see cities glittering on the nightside. A cloudless midnight for most of North America.

The notion came to him that he would be even more of a hero if he rescued himself. He went to investigate the situation regarding the lifeboats hangared nearby.

The pirates who had wrecked the dock had left one boat. That they had managed to jam in its exit tube. It was intact but immobile. Warner climbed into it with relief and secured the lock behind him. He was then able to remove his spacesuit and take a shower—which he did rather circumspectly, in case, by some cunning new development of technology of which he was unaware, the shower head held a Systemwide camera, and his toilet was being scattered to a grateful humanity.

He dried in the airbeam, put on a toweling robe, and sat with his feet up in the snug cabin, to drink coffee and eat self-heated turkey and hash browns. Pretty soon, he fell asleep, his head on the table.

When he woke, *Clytemnestra* was breaking up.

* * *

Deep organlike groans sounded. When he touched the wall, he felt an irregular vibration. The lifeboat made uneasy movements.

He groaned. *Unsleeping vigil is necessary for safety*

Thoroughly alarmed, Warner climbed into his spacesuit as quickly as possible, left the lifeboat, and went back into the cargo dock.

Clytemnestra was bucking and bumping under him.

A despairing voice spoke in his earphones.

"Where are you?"

"Warner? This is Emergency Service. We've been trying to contact you for the past six hours, damn you. Where have you been?"

"I've been asleep. . . . Where I was, I must have been shielded from your signal. And I forgot to switch the radio on. . . . Are you going to pick me up? Something seems to be wrong."

"You're entering the fringes of Earth's atmosphere. You're about ninety miles out. You've left it too late to be picked up. We can't rescue you now. Our calculations indicate that your zeepee may turn turtle at any moment."

"What am I supposed to do?"

"Hang on tight."

"Hang on! Thanks a lot. . . ."

"According to our computer, you'll be okay if you hang on. Descent will be swift and you should come down in the North Atlantic—a relatively soft landing. You may not break up. Good luck."

It was not the best conversation he had ever had. As the signal faded, the deck below Warner's feet began to tilt. He grasped the rungs of a ladder leading to an upper walkway, in danger of being pitched right out of the vessel through the open hatch. *Clytemnestra* began to turn over like a twirled cigar.

The Earth rolled into view, bright and near. He recognised the alligator tail of South America, twitching angrily at the white pudding of the Antarctic, then sheets of vapour streamed across the view. With thunderous complaint, everything rolled upside down. *Clytemnestra* was not an aerodynamic shape.

A forklift truck fell from overhead, smashed against what had been a roof, and slid here and there before finally breaking through the inner airlock doors and disappearing. Warner clung to the ladder, praying.

When things stabilised slightly, he climbed down, collected a length of rope, and returned to the ladder, where he tied himself loosely.

He shouted over the radio, but got no answer. The zeepee was into atmosphere and screened from the world of words by a radio blackout.

The glide became smooth, but was only biding its time. A tremendous jolt almost dislocated his shoulder.

In the wall behind the ladder, a crack showed. It widened. He looked away.

Bad things elsewhere. Flaming gobbets were catapulted into the hatch, like blazing cinders from a volcano. The hull was starting to burn up. The hatch opening looked like the mouth of hell.

He began to laugh wildly.

You may experience a grave come-down Oh, yes indeed. . . .

The wall behind him opened. The plastic was thick, feet thick, red in colour. It peeled away as if it were soft rubber.

Or was he looking at molten rock? For inside the wall were fossils of an older time. He saw the fossilized remains of earlier strata of technological beings—the body of a Cadillac, a V2 rocket, a steam locomotive, and—deeper still as the wall continued to peel apart—a crystal radio, a penny-farthing, a fixed-type press, an axe, a few arrowheads. They fell away, dissolving before his gaze. In the final impact, he lost consciousness entirely.

The whale came from the stars with its belly aglow. It blotted out the suns behind it and left a trail of glory in the night sky.

Feng Xi crouched in his boat with his mouth open, drifting on the waters of the estuary as he watched the monster approach. Though it seemed to him that he had been watching it for hours, it was close before he knew it.

There in the dark, it sailed down from the ebony rivers of the western sky and smote the waters of the estuary. Mists and fountains rose. The entire estuary went into a convulsion. Wave after wave bore down on the boy's boat, bringing the news of the miracle.

He was already in action, sailing his vessel up and down the waves. This was the biggest whale in the history of the world, and he certainly was not going to let it escape.

The monster shape loomed above him. Steam and mist hissed below it. Under the friendly starlight, dull eyes gleamed in the head.

Feng Xi aimed his harpoon gun and shot it right through one eye. He pulled the line taut.

He had it secure. It did not struggle.

Swinging his boat about, he began to head for the distant shore, towing the great beast behind him. God had excelled Himself—no whale-hunter had ever made such a catch as Feng Xi's.

In the stern of the great metal beast, a man stood and breathed the night air. At first, he merely breathed, drawing the air—which smelt of leaves, grass, ponies, fogs, fish, pastrami sandwiches, old jeans, barns, autumns, and mating jellyfish—mightily into every last cranny of his lungs. Then his elation would out. He started to caper. He ran about on the hissing deck. He waved his arms. He bellowed and sang.

He believed in God. And technology. And miracles.

He believed in everything.

You will find what you seek

IN OUTER SPACE!

__SHADOWLINE
by Glen Cook   *(E30-578, $2.95)*
The first book in The Starfishers Trilogy starts with the ven-
detta in space. They were the greatest fighting fleet in the
universe—battling betrayal and revenge, and the terrible
fate that awaited them on the edge of SHADOWLINE.

__STARFISHERS
by Glen Cook   *(E30-155, $2.95)*
The second volume in this trilogy, *Starfishers* is science
fiction the way you like it. They were creatures of fusion
energy, ancient, huge, intelligent, drifting in herds on the
edge of the galaxy, producing their ambergris, the substance, precious to man and the man-like Sangaree alike.

__STARS' END
by Glen Cook   *(E30-156, $2.95)*
The final book: The fortress on the edge of the galaxy was
called Stars' End, a planet built for death—but by whom?
It lay on the outermost arm of the Milky Way, silent,
cloaked in mystery, self-contained and controlled...until
...a sinister enemy approaches from the depths of the galaxy, in hordes as large as a solar system. And its mission is
only to kill...

TO THRILL YOU TO THE BONE!

___**POLTERGEIST**
a novel by James Kahn, based on a story by Steven Spielberg   *(B30-222, $2.95)*
This is a horrific drama of suburban man beset by supernatural menace. Like "Close Encounters of the Third Kind," it begins in awe and wonder. Like "Jaws," it develops with a mounting sense of dread. And like "Raiders of the Lost Ark," it climaxes in one of the most electrifying scenes ever recorded on film. A horror story that could happen to you!

___**ALIEN**
by Alan Dean Foster   *(E30-577, $3.25)*
Astronauts encounter an awesome galactic horror on a distant planet. But it's only when they take off again that the real horror begins. For the alien is now within the ship, within the crew itself. And a classic deathtrap suspense game begins.

___**THE AMITYVILLE HORROR II**
by John G. Jones   *(B30-029, $3.50)*
The terror continues...When the Lutz family left the house in Amityville, New York, the terror did not end. Through the next four years wherever they went, the inescapable Evil followed them. Now the victims of the most publicized house-haunting of the century have agreed to reveal the harrowing details of their continuing ordeal.

A MIND-BENDING FORAY INTO ADVENTURE AND DANGER!

__OUTLAND
by Alan Dean Foster   *(E95-829, $2.75)*
Even in space, the ultimate enemy is man. In orbit out from
Jupiter in view of its malignant red eye is OUTLAND. Here
on Io—moon of Jupiter, hell is space—men mine ore to
satisfy the needs of Earth. They are hard men, loners for
whom the Company provides the necessities: beds, food,
drink and women for hire. Now, in apparent suicide or in
frenzied madness, the men are dying...

__STRANGE WINE
by Harlan Ellison   *(E91-946, $2.50)*
Fifteen new stories from the nightside of the world by one
of the most original and entertaining short-story writers in
America today. Discover among these previously uncol-
lected tales the spirits of executed Nazi war criminals,
gremlins, a murderess escaped from hell, and other chill-
ing, thought provoking tales.

__2150 A.D.
by Thea Alexander   *(E33-056, $2.95)*
The brilliant, futuristic novel that explains a new way to
live—macro-philosophy. It's a mind-expanding exodus
from the imperfect today into a better tomorrow. Discover
the beauty and the emotional demands such a journey can
bring. This is a novel you can't put down, and a philosophy
that can change your life.

TO BE REISSUED
IN DECEMBER